GLASS THORNS

BOOK FOUR
WINDOW WALL

GLASS THORNS

BOOK FOUR
WINDOW WALL

MELANIE RAWN

TITAN BOOKS

WINDOW WALL
Print edition ISBN: 9781781166666
E-book edition ISBN: 9781781166673

Published by Titan Books
A division of Titan Publishing Group Ltd
144 Southwark Street, London SE1 0UP

First edition: April 2015
2 4 6 8 10 9 7 5 3 1

This is a work of fiction. Names, characters, places, and incidents either are the product of the author's imagination or are used fictitiously, and any resemblance to actual persons, living or dead, business establishments, events, or locales is entirely coincidental. The publisher does not have any control over and does not assume any responsibility for author or third-party websites or their content.

A CIP catalogue record for this title is available from the British Library.

Printed and bound by CPI Group (UK) Ltd, Croydon, CR0 4YY

Did you enjoy this book? We love to hear from our readers.
Please email us at readerfeedback@titanemail.com or write to us at
Reader Feedback at the above address.

To receive advance information, news, competitions, and exclusive offers online, please sign up for the Titan newsletter on our website:
WWW.TITANBOOKS.COM

In memory of
Marian C. Kelly

1

Real Mieka Windthistle arrived at the kitchen door of Number Eight, Redpebble Square, with a frown on his face. It was not an expression that suited him. Yet with the exception of the hours he spent onstage, these days it seemed all his face could do was frown.

He conjured up a smile for Mistress Mirdley and for Derien Silversun, but the frown returned when the Trollwife, busily slicing carrot bread, told him why a huge basket was being filled with baked goods.

"Tea. It's his Namingday. He won't come here, so Derien's taking it to him."

Cayden's Namingday. Thoroughly ashamed of himself, Mieka didn't bother to pretend that he hadn't forgotten. Dery, seeing the expression on his face, only shrugged and said, "I don't think he wants to remember, himself. Which is stupid, of course. It's not as if he's turning fifty or sixty—he's only twenty-four. But I'm sure he has nothing planned."

Mieka slouched on a stool by the worktable and felt his frown grow even deeper as he regarded his tregetour's little brother—who admittedly wasn't so little anymore. Not that Mieka had been around to notice. Redpebble Square hadn't seen much of him these last two years. He was no longer welcome when Lady Jaspiela was at home; indeed, she hadn't spoken to him or even acknowledged his continuing existence since he'd attempted a bit of softening magic on her. How she'd been able to sense it, what with the Hindering put on her long ago, he'd no idea. But sense it she had.

Today Mieka had arrived just after lunching, confident that he wouldn't be running into Lady Jaspiela. This was her day, every fortnight, for visiting the Archduchess whenever the latter was in Gallantrybanks. Mieka made it his day for visiting his brother and sister-in-law at the glassworks. Sometimes—well, rarely—he called in at the kitchen door of Redpebble Square, where Mistress Mirdley provided tea and Derien provided conversation. Cade no longer lived there. He had taken his own flat just after Touchstone's third Royal Circuit. And even though Mieka saw him every single day when they were traveling and at least twice a week for performances in Gallantrybanks during winter, he had to go to other people to find out what Cade was thinking.

Not that either Mistress Mirdley or Derien knew. That was made clear when the boy slumped down in a chair beside Mieka and said, "He hasn't been round to see us in almost a month. And it's not that long until Trials, and then he'll be gone on the Royal again, and—and I miss him."

So do I, Mieka thought glumly.

"There's an item about him in the latest *Nayword*—did you see it?" Dery made a long arm to snag the broadsheet from a pile by the kitchen fire. "Not that he talked to Tobalt Fluter, either."

Mieka had read the piece, just a few lines about how Cade would doubtless have new and startling plays to be performed in Gallantrybanks and at Trials. The tone of it had been just slightly sardonic, as if Tobalt was annoyed that he could no longer get an interview from the eminently quotable Cayden Silversun.

Mistress Mirdley had finished wrapping the carrot bread.

"Here, and take some of this honeycomb along with you. He always liked it when he was a little boy."

Mieka was appalled to see sudden fierce tears in her eyes. He leaped to his feet and threw his arms around her. "I'll bring him back here soon, I promise I will—and with three pages of apologies in rhymed couplets set to music for being so horrid to you!"

She shook her head and extricated herself from his hug. "He'll come round when he comes round. And it's a few dozen more turnings he'll be doing before that happens. Is that basket full? Tuck a cloth in, then, and get along with you."

"Did you put in something for Rumble?" Dery asked.

"Of course. A nice bit of fish. Go!"

Cayden's only companion in his flat—well, his only steady companion; there were plenty of girls, all of them transitory—was a ginger-striped cat named Rumble, inexplicably brought home as a kitten by Blye's cat, Bompstable. It was as if, Jedris had remarked, Bompstable knew Cade required some sort of company, and went out to find a suitable candidate.

In the hire-hack, with a hamper of food between them, Mieka looked at Dery and asked, "Could we stop off someplace maybe? I really ought to bring a gift."

"Well . . . can you make it quick? Mistress Mirdley will be furious if I'm out after dark. And I want to spend some time with my brother," he finished in a voice much too grim for someone not quite twelve years old.

Mieka directed the driver to take them through a convenient shopping district. For a full quarter of an hour, he turned from side to side in the hack, peering through the windows, desperate for a shop that caught his imagination.

"You're giving me a neck ache," Dery complained. "He won't mind if you don't bring him anything. I'm sure he'd rather nobody remembered at all."

Especially after what happened last year, hung unspoken between them.

When Cayden turned nineteen, Dery had given him a silver hawk pin and Mieka had taken him to see the Shadowshapers at the Kiral Kellari. On his twentieth Namingday, he'd been at Fairwalk Manor, giving Mieka no opportunity to celebrate. To make up for that, Mieka had thrown a lavish party at Hilldrop Crescent for Cade's twenty-first. His twenty-second had been another Shadowshapers show—the one where Princess Miriuzca had shown up with Lady Megueris Mindrising, both of them dressed as young men. And a grand lark that had been; an exploit Mieka wasn't sure he'd ever be able to surpass . . . though Cade had once had an Elsewhen about his forty-fifth, something about bubbly wine and a surprise party and a diamond in Mieka's ear. Forty-five; Mieka couldn't imagine it. But Cade had seen it, and by his scant telling, it had been a wonderful evening.

Last year they'd all gathered at Blye's glassworks, ostensibly to watch her make their new withies but in reality to present Cade with the complete table service for eight she had spent weeks making. She had forbidden them to transport the plates, bowls, cups, goblets, and platters to Cade's flat that evening, relenting only when Mieka promised a doubling and tripling of the cushioning spell his mother had taught him. Problem was, he'd had quite a lot to drink—although so had everyone else, raising the new wine goblets again and again, then deciding that the brandy snifters also deserved a try-out, and of course there were those bottles of Auntie Brishen's whiskey that needed sampling in the cut-crystal glasses, and . . . the conclusion being that Blye had had to spend another week replacing the broken items. Mieka still winced with the memory of the crashing and splintering of two inadequately cushioned crates down four flights of stairs. And one couldn't mend glass with an Affinity spell, not and have it hold water ever again.

There were plenty of things that needed mending after these last two years. Nothing that was permanently broken, or at least so Mieka told himself with grim resolve—well, except in Alaen Blackpath's case. The loss of his cousin Briuly two years ago this Midsummer dawn had shattered him. A month later, he'd shown up at Sakary Grainer's house in Gallantrybanks with a glass thorn in one hand and a little gold velvet pouch of dragon tears in the other, and announced to Chirene, Sakary's wife, that if she didn't run away with him that very night, he'd begin using and wouldn't stop until she was his or he was dead. Romuald Needler, the Shadowshapers' manager, had succeeded in hushing up most of the scandal. But the fact remained that Chirene had taken her children and gone to live with Chattim Czillag's wife, Deshenanda, until the Shadowshapers returned that autumn from the Royal Circuit. Alaen wasn't dead. Yet.

"Here, stop," Mieka said suddenly, and hopped out of the hire-hack before it had come to a full stop. "Won't be a tick-tock!" he called over his shoulder to Derien, and hurried inside.

The shop featured all manner of decorative collectibles. Mirrors, figurines, clocks, imagings, paintings, exotic flowers from faraway lands preserved under glass or with magic. But Mieka knew exactly what he wanted, having seen it displayed in the window, and a few moments later emerged with a wrapped package almost as tall as Derien.

"What is it?" the boy wanted to know as the hack started up again.

"Not *it*," Mieka said. "*Them*." He teased a corner of the paper wrapping to show a glint of iridescent blue.

"Peacock feathers?"

"A round dozen of 'em."

"But, Mieka, aren't they horrid bad luck for theater folk?" An instant later, he understood. "Whistling past the urn-plot?"

"Exactly. Because if what we've been having is good luck in

the theater, I'll risk it. Me Mum calls it *un*sympathetic magic."

"Do the opposite of what you really want to happen? That's a little crazy, y'know."

"My specialty."

Not that anything truly awful had happened onstage—unless one counted Cade's last new play. That had been over a year ago now, and the reactions had been . . . regrettable. Nobody, including the rest of Touchstone, really understood what he'd meant to do. Mieka's analysis was that whereas theater patrons didn't mind thinking a bit, both during and after a play, they didn't much enjoy thinking as a grim hour-long slog through far too many ideas.

"Turn Aback" was in Cade's hands an exercise in stupefying boredom. Boy and girl in love. Girl dies in tragic accident. Boy tries to broker a deal with the Lady to go get her; Lady is moved by True True Love and says fine, but on your way out, you mustn't look back. Boy girds himself to travel into whichever Hell girl inhabits (though why she deserves any of them is left unclear), journeys through various unsavory provinces of punishment, increasingly nasty but not gruesome or bloody or even scary. At least Mieka could have had some good old gory fun with that sort of thing, been creative with the dragons that feasted on flesh that healed in an hour, or that poor stupid pillicock forever putting sand into a leaky hourglass, or the one about somebody standing lip-deep in a lake of shit.

Cade's Hells were all intellectual (which didn't surprise Mieka one bit, but made for a colossally dull play). Boy is distracted from search for girl by philosophical conversations with the tenants of each Hell, blither blather blether. Boy finally remembers what he's there for, finds girl, fingers burned and bleeding as she spins molten gold into straw. Boy leads girl back to the entrance gates. She trips on a rock (silly cow). He looks back to make sure she's all right, and just as their Eyes Meet with Longing and then with Sudden Horror, she vanishes. The End.

Tobalt had tried to put an interesting interpretation on it—something about how Cayden Silversun had woven scholarly moral speculation into a heartbreaking love story—but even he knew it was a bad play. Touchstone had performed it exactly three times. Then Mieka, Rafe, and Jeska all rebelled, and the script was mercifully scrapped.

But the fact remained: Cayden Silversun had failed.

He hadn't liked it much.

Derien subsided into a corner of the hack, and Mieka read *The Nayword* during the rest of the drive to Cade's place. The broadsheet had grown in recent years from one very large page folded in half to three very large pages folded in quarters—more the size of a book, really, than the standard broadsheet. It wasn't the same old *Nayword* anymore, as its front page trumpeted.

THE NAYWORD
WHAT TO READ—WHAT TO SEE—WHAT TO WEAR— WHAT TO AVOID!

In this issue:
Special reports from our correspondents at Court,
throughout the Kingdom, and on the Continent
PRINCE ASHGAR and PRINCESS MIRIUZCA
welcome a daughter
Exclusive interview with VERED GOLDBRAIDER
Complete coverage of this year's Trials hopefuls
Student unrest at Stiddolfe after a rise in fees

With: ideas and advice from our regular columnists on all the latest in theater, books, dress, food, wine, gardening, and interior design

Mieka felt rather smug about the theater and fashion

sections, considering that Touchstone (with the Shadowshapers) constantly innovated in the former and were known (with the Shadowshapers) as exemplars of the latter. He was even more smug about the gardening, because one of the regular columnists was his sister Cilka. Just fourteen, still in school, and already an authority (under a pseudonym, of course) in her field. Their mother, Mishia, wasn't terribly surprised; her own sister Brishen had started up a little herb shop at the age of fifteen. The Greenseed Elfen line obviously dominated in them both. Cilka and Petrinka were already doing a brisk business in sculpted hedges, as prompted by Mieka's description of such at Princess Miriuzca's home castle on the Continent, and would someday take over Grandfather Staindrop's gardening business.

As for "design"—for certes, Cade never paid any attention to advice columns about interior design, or exterior either. Rather than the grand town house Mieka had once envisioned for him, he had taken a corner room on the top floor of a building near the Keymarker, one of the old abandoned manufactories refitted as blocks of flats. The view was spectacular—from his windows one could see the Keeps in one direction and the Plume in the other, with the rooftops of Gallantrybanks spreading between, though these rather blocked any sight of the Gally River—but the hike up four flights kept most people from visiting very often. Mieka knew that was precisely why Cade had chosen it.

The staircase was stone to the second floor, then wood—nice and sturdy, according to Jed and Jez, who had insisted on examining the place before Cade signed the lease. Originally the top floor had been fitted out as a dormitory for the workers. Mieka shuddered, as he did every time he visited, at the idea of waking before dawn, working all day, and trudging back upstairs for food and sleep without ever once having breathed fresh air or seen the sun. A great many manufactories had moved out of the main sections of Gallantrybanks as the city expanded and the demand for urban housing increased, and there was no reason to believe that conditions were any better for workers even if the places were now in the countryside.

A knock on Cade's door elicited an annoyed, "What?" Derien grimaced, tried the handle, found it unlocked, and traded scowls with Mieka.

"On the other hand," the boy murmured as he opened the door, "except for the books, what's he got worth stealing?"

"I heard that," Cade said from the depths of his big, soft, overstuffed chair. "The brass is bespelled to recognize you. I've forgotten her name, but she was rather good at useful little tricks."

Mieka resisted the urge to roll his eyes. There were lots of girls whose names Cade had forgotten. That there wasn't one at the moment was obvious; the place was a mess. Clothes, glassware, paper, books, broadsheets, spent candles, towels, pillows, empty bags that must have contained food at some point because there was nowhere to cook—all manner of clutter was spread about the room.

Jez had built Cade a platform bed that was seven feet long, four feet wide, and six feet off the floor. The little cavern beneath was where he huddled at a desk to write. In the winter there was a firepocket to keep his feet warm, and in summer all the windows were left open to cooling breezes, but it was dark under there when the lamps weren't lighted and there was nothing to look at but bricks and the bed's wooden scaffolding. The other features of the flat were Cade's big black upholstered chair, some uncushioned wooden chairs that did not encourage visitors to linger, a huge standing wardrobe to hold Cade's vast collection of clothes (nearly as impressive as Mieka's), a massive carpet given him by Lord Kearney Fairwalk, a small table that seated four, a cabinet for the glass dinner service made for him by Blye, another cabinet behind a latticework willow screen for the piss-pot, and bookshelves—also built by Jez—almost to the twelve-foot ceiling.

Of decoration there was very little. No placards advertising Touchstone, no tapestries, no paintings, no imagings. His Trials medals—two Winterly, three Royal—were in glass boxes on the bookshelves, and Mieka had the feeling whenever he saw them that the only reason they weren't stashed in a drawer somewhere was that Blye had made the boxes. The counterpane made by Mieka's wife and mother-in-law was crumpled at the foot of the bed. The only color in the room was the rug, its greens and blues like a forest pond in the middle of the city. The peacock feathers, fanning out in a jar or vase, would be an improvement.

Derien ignored Cade's mood, putting on a smile and wishing his brother a happy Namingday. Cade expressed his gratitude indifferently. Mieka busied himself clearing off the table and setting out Mistress Mirdley's tea. The search for a kettle took some time, and he kept his expression carefully neutral as Dery tried to engage Cade in conversation. Mieka went out to the landing where the spigot was, and encountered Rumble coming up the stairs.

"Anything to report?" he asked the cat, who curled around his ankles a few times before stepping lightly into the flat. "Big help you are," he muttered, and hoped that Dery could coax Cade into some semblance of good manners.

No such luck.

When he got back, Dery was reading bits from *The Nayword*. "There's something in here about Briuly, too." Before Cade could say he didn't care, Dery read out, "'Still no word on the whereabouts of Master Lutenist Briuly Blackpath. His family is initiating legal proceedings to have him declared dead so that his estate can be sold to pay his debts.'"

"You'd think," Cade mused, one finger scratching idly at his pathetic excuse for a beard, "that Lord Oakapple, his esteemed cousin or whatever he is, would pay up Briuly's debts just to keep the family out of the law courts. But I never did get exactly how they were related, so perhaps it doesn't signify." He turned to

Mieka. "How was Lilyleaf?"

"Fine. Croodle sends her best."

Nodding to the new silver bracelet on Mieka's wrist, he said, "Very nice. What did you give your lovely lady?"

"She saw a pink pearl in a shop. I had it made into a pendant." It had cost a bloody fortune, too, but that was a small price for peace in his household.

Derien was the one who conjured up Wizardfire to heat the water. There was an iron ring for the kettle above a small iron cauldron, and the glances the boy gave his brother told Mieka that this was a new skill. Cade didn't comment on it at all. In fact, nobody said anything while the water had boiled and the tea was brewed. The three of them sat there like polite strangers who have exhausted every topic of conversation and could find no reason to keep up any pretense of being interested in one other. As Cayden bestirred himself to pour out, Mieka considered various methods of shocking a reaction out of him—any reaction at all. But he'd been trying that, hadn't he, for going on two years now, and with what results? Rarely, a response of the *Do that again, and I'll feed you your own balls marinated in plum sauce* variety. Mostly, a look of mild contempt for his childishness. It was infuriating.

"Uncle Dennet died."

Cade looked up from pouring out. "I hadn't realized he was still alive."

"Well, he was," Derien went on. "And now he's not. First we learned of it was when the Shelter sent his ashes to Redpebble."

Mieka searched his knowledge of Cade's family tree, and came up with Dennet Silversun, elder brother of Cade's father Zekien, mad as a sack of snakes.

"Wasn't he the one wounded in the war?" Mieka asked.

"What a refined way of phrasing it," Cade observed. "He was seventeen and got in the path of somebody's spell. He's been in a puzzle house ever since."

"Almost forty years," Derien added. "It's called the Shelter and it's supposed to be very nice, very clean and kindly—"

"—as insane asylums go," Cade interrupted. Then, with a nasty little smile, he said, "That's our fate in the theater, Mieka. Forty years surrounded by madmen."

Mieka eyed him thoughtfully. "Y'know," he said at last, "you're being a right pain in the ass. You've *been* being a right pain in the ass for a long time, and everybody's tired of it. Write yourself some new lines, why don't you?"

Cade's smile spread fractionally. "I prefer to improvise."

Mieka paid no heed to the pleading look on Derien's face. He'd had enough. Long ago, he'd had enough. Setting down his cup, he snatched up a slice of carrot bread and made for the door. "Rehearsal tomorrow at the Kiral Kellari," he said by way of farewell, and took the stairs three at a time.

Emerging into the thin spring sunshine, he found himself in luck at last: a hire-hack was just pulling up at the building's front door, which meant he wouldn't have to go searching. He signaled the driver with a raised hand, but the man shook his head.

"Hired to return," he said, just as a boy of about ten jumped out and, on seeing Mieka, demanded, "Cayden Silversun?"

"Top floor. What's the worry?"

"There's been an accident. Mistress Windthistle sent me to fetch him at once." He yanked open the front door.

"Wait—*which* Mistress Windthistle?"

But the boy had vanished.

Mieka's mother, his sisters, his wife, Blye—all of them and plenty of others besides were Mistress Windthistle. He dithered in place for a moment, then asked the hack driver, "Where'd you come from?"

"Originally? Ambage Road. In this case, Lord Piercehand's new gallery."

"The woman who hired you—was she little and blond?"

"That she was. Bit of the Goblin about her, mayhap, but nothing to notice outright."

Blye. Something had happened to Jed or Jez. "Cayden!" he shouted. *"Cayden!"*

It took forever before he and Cade and Dery were in the hire-hack driving towards the river. The traffic leading to the bridge was maddening. Even if a gallop had been legal, carts and riders and other hacks were so thick that only a walk was possible—and even so, their progress was in fits and starts. The boy Blye had sent was up top with the driver, yelling, "Make way! Make way!" every so often, which had no effect except to infuriate everyone else, all of them going nowhere in a hurry.

The interior of the hack was silent with the tension of ignorance. Cade had explained tersely that on the walk downstairs he questioned the lad, who knew nothing except that there had been an accident and Mistress Windthistle had sent him with orders to bring Master Silversun.

Finally, with the Gally River in sight, Mieka could stand no more. "Get out," he ordered Cade and Dery. "We'll hire a boat. It can't help but be faster."

Scrambling down the embankment, they ran for a dock. Mieka dug in his pockets for coin, cursing himself for spending so much on those damned peacock feathers, coming up with enough to hire a craft that looked more or less able to hold the three of them plus the boatman. He forestalled the man's attempt to haggle the price by saying, "Double when we get there. Just hurry!"

"Double? Easy enough to say, young sir!" Then he took a closer look at tall, Wizardly Cade and short, Elfen Mieka. "I know your faces from someplace, don't I?"

"They're half of Touchstone," Dery put in. "They're famous

and they're rich—please, I promise we'll pay you double if you just get us there quickly!"

"Touchstone." After further scrutiny, during which Mieka strove to look as much like their placards as possible (though, truth be told, there was never any mistaking Cade's nose), the man gestured them into the boat.

Mieka hated boats. By the time they reached the site—a nice plot of land beside the river, nothing but the finest for Lord Rolon Piercehand—he had chewed his lower lip almost raw. Dery leaned forward in the prow, the way a rider leaned into his horse's neck to urge speed. Cade squeezed in beside the boatman, took one of the oars, and rowed white-knuckled. By the time they reached the site, Cade's hair and shirt were damp with the sweat of effort.

A gift to the Kingdom of Albeyn, it was, this new gallery to display a selection of Piercehand's foreign plunder. Castle Eyot wasn't big enough to hold the jumble of wonders and oddities and some genuinely beautiful things collected by His Lordship. On progress a year ago, Princess Miriuzca had professed herself enchanted with the place and very prettily persuaded him to share his haul with the public. The Palace would be lending certain of the Royals' own hoard of paintings and statuary. Whether or not the Princess had also managed to steer some of the contracts for building the place to Windthistle Brothers was a matter of conjecture, but it remained that Jedris and Jezael were doing the wooden parts of the building and Blye would eventually be making the windows.

The foundation and exterior stones were golden yellow, with two curving grand staircases leading up from the street to the main entrance. Scaffolding laced the stone shell together: a few walls, unfinished interior columns, steel support beams. Arches and balconies abounded, some completed and most not. But the most notable feature was a tower, tall and spindly, made of stone and rising two hundred feet into the air. Word had it that when the gallery was finished, the tower would be topped with a solid gold statue brought back from some remote land by one of Piercehand's many ships.

Currently the only decorations were clouds of dust.

"Right," said the boatman. "So where's my double the fare?"

Mieka and Cade scrambled up a few stone steps to the embankment as Dery snapped, "What you already have is all you get! My brother did half the work!"

Mieka blinked; for just an instant, the boy sounded like Lady Jaspiela. In the best possible way, of course.

"Rich!" the boatman sneered. "Famous! Rich and famous coggers is what you are! Come back here and honor your word!"

They left the boatman cursing unoriginally behind them. The crowd was all streetside: a mass of craned necks, like astonished cats peering out a window. Mieka got a good grip on Cade's elbow and an even better one on Dery's, and forced a route through the tangle. As he pushed and shoved, Mieka heard snatches of conversation, none of it pleasant. Speculation about how the scaffolding collapsed; contention that the scaffolding was intact but the stonework had crumbled; assurances that both wood and stone were to blame; estimates of how many had died. He wished he had Cade's height, because then he might have seen the two red heads that were his only concern.

Suddenly they were at the Human barrier that kept the crowd from pressing forward. Not constables, but Lord Piercehand's own liveried guards, dozens of them linking arms and looking grim. Mieka confronted the one directly in his path.

"I'm Mieka Windthistle—"

"Good for you."

"But my brothers are—"

"Nobody gets in. Not until the physickers arrive."

"They're not here yet?" Cade demanded. "All these people, and not a single—?"

"Some ugly old Trollwife is tending the injured, that's all. Stand back."

"Cayden!"

It was Blye, dusty and frantic, running through the maze of stacked stone and cut boards. Cade tried to push through. The guardsman snarled. Cade snarled right back. A brief tussle ensued, during which Derien ducked down and darted between guards. Mieka tried to follow, and got a knee in the ribs. As he doubled over, Cade's snarl turned to a roar.

"Stop it!" Blye shouted. "I'm Mistress Windthistle and these are my brothers! Let them by! Damn it, let them by!"

In the end, it was not a raised voice or angry words that got them through. It was Hadden Windthistle, in a calm, soft tone, saying, "Gentlemen, would you allow these young men through? Much beholden to you."

A sliver of space was made. They slipped through. Mieka looked in wonderment at his father and asked, "How'd you do that?"

Hadden only shook his head. But as they jogged towards the building, Cade leaned down and whispered, "Didn't you see that guard's face? Your father magicked him!"

2

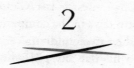

All told, in later years Cayden Silversun would remember very little about his life from Midsummer on that second Royal Circuit until the day he finally realized how trite his life had become. For quite a long time he subscribed to that most unoriginal of ideas: that if he didn't feel, he couldn't be hurt.

Strangely enough, his work didn't suffer. But his work was all he had. On it he lavished every emotion he refused to experience personally. Audiences applauded (with one mortifying exception). Accolades accumulated (with one mortifying exception). And during it all he gave a very good impersonation of an ordinary man with all the conventional and expected feelings.

Everyone was fooled. Even him. Especially him.

He laughed with his friends when something funny was said. He rejoiced with Rafe and Crisiant at the birth of their healthy baby boy. He was eloquent in his expressions of sympathy when misfortune occurred: the collapse into the river of Mieka's little tower at Wistly Hall, injuring a boatman unlucky enough to have been passing below it; the ugly divorce of Vered Goldbraider that deprived him by law of the right to see his sons and daughter, because his former wife's new husband was an influential justiciar and his own new wife had no interest in raising another woman's children. Cade frowned worriedly when it seemed warranted and smiled in all the right places. He attended the performances of his friends and of any new groups that looked promising. He went to dinner at Wistly Hall and was always welcome at the Threadchaser bakery. He attended charmingly on Princess Miriuzca whenever she requested the honor of his company at lunching or tea, and had guested last Wintering at Eastkeeping Hold for many pleasant days in the company of Lord Kelinn and Lady Vrennerie and their two children.

He took back to his flat any girl who happened to strike his fancy. They never refused him; he was Cayden Silversun of Touchstone. If those girls had names, he never recalled them.

He went over to Redpebble Square as seldom as was decently possible. It wasn't his mother he was avoiding, for she had always done most of the avoiding for him. No, it was Mistress Mirdley's sharp and all-too-knowing gaze he dreaded. He never went to Hilldrop Crescent at all.

The sole exception to his removal from emotional life was his brother. Derien grew tall, good-looking, self-assured, a favorite everywhere he went for his sunny smiles and gentle manners. Not that the streak of mischief had been blotted out, not by any means. He participated in, and quite often personally organized, enough trouble at the King's College to embarrass Lady Jaspiela and reassure Cade that Dery hadn't turned into a prig. He was the only person always welcome at Cade's flat. His was the only hand other than Cade's that would trigger the unlocking of the door.

As for that other young life, the one Cade had sworn he would protect . . . Jindra Windthistle was not his concern. She had no claim on him. She wasn't his. She was her parents' responsibility. Whatever might happen to her was not his to influence. Whatever might happen to her was not his fault.

Whatever happened, to anyone or anything, it was not his fault. How could it be? The Elsewhens had stopped.

Nobody knew. He'd never been particularly forthcoming about his foreseeings, anyway, and things were going rather well for Touchstone professionally and personally, so why worry about it? He refused to worry about it. None of it was his responsibility; none of it was his fault.

He still dreamed. He knew he did, because he remembered them when he woke up. Anxious dreams, bewildering dreams that scared him with their bizarre juxtapositions of scenes or people or events or conversations. A trifle awkward, for instance, when people who were dead showed up—it would be terribly rude to point out to them that they couldn't possibly be walking around alive. A few times he had wings and could fly, and woke sweating and shaking in the middle of a hideous fall. In one horrible heart-pounding nightmare he was being chased through the waters of the Flood by shrieking yellow *vodabeists*.

He might not have the sort of dreams other people had, but he had nightmares just like everyone else.

There were no more Elsewhen dreams, and neither were there any daytime turns. No glimpses of futures. Nothing.

He was just like everyone else.

Whether or not an Elsewhen could have warned him about the disaster of "Turn Aback," he had no idea. He didn't care to speculate. The fact remained, however, that the play had been a total failure. He'd worked so hard on it, muscling it past the doubts expressed by Jeska and Rafe and Mieka—which, truth be told, weren't all that emphatic. His partners trusted him. Rafe asked the day after the inaugural performance whether he hadn't seen it coming. Mieka had most conveniently spared his having to explain by coming robustly to his defense.

"He did his best—if he saw anything at all like this, I'm sure he worked to prevent it. I mean, who'd want to be him, standing there last night after we finished the thing? It's just that you can't ever tell with audiences. Isn't that right, Cade?"

Mieka hardly ever called him *Quill* anymore. He felt a twinge every time he realized it, and then deliberately pushed the sensation aside, much as he pushed aside the Elsewhens when they threatened him. And they didn't threaten all that often anymore.

But today, his twenty-fourth Namingday, he couldn't push aside the assault of this chaos of men slumped on heaps of stone or sprawled on the ground with other men kneeling beside them, holding rags to their wounds. The dust of collapse mingled with the smell of blood. The forecourt was a welter of planks and saws and overturned buckets of nails, fallen scaffolding, and the snarled ropes of rigs for lifting stone.

"Jed!" Mieka flung his arms around his brother, standing tall and unhurt and with one hand firmly gripping Derien's shoulder. "Where's Jez?"

"Don't know."

"You stay put," Hadden said. "Cade, keep Dery back. It's not safe."

Cade took over restraining his little brother, getting a good hold on the boy's elbow, and told him what Hadden was too kind to tell him: "You'd only get in the way. Where's Mistress Mirdley?"

Jed pointed towards the street. "Helping with the wounded, of course. Mieka, go see if you can give her a hand. Fa and I have to get back."

"I'll go with," Mieka said. "I can use that hover spell Mum taught me—"

"No," his brother told him. "Save your magic for Cayden's plays."

Cade saw how hurt Mieka was by Jed's words—as if Mieka were of no use for anything except what he could do onstage. Considering how dodgy that particular spell was in Mieka's hands, Cade understood why Jed forbade it.

Blye hurried up to give her husband a cupful of water,

looking at him as if memorizing his face anew down to each individual eyelash. He drank, handed back the cup, leaned down to kiss her, and strode off with his father through the billowing dust into the building's interior.

"What happened?" Cade asked Blye.

"Do I look like a construction engineer to you?" she snapped. "I was here to measure for the windows. Things fell down."

"Obviously," Cade couldn't help but say, earning himself a murderous glare. "How many injured?"

"Lots. Five were up on the scaffolding and fell thirty feet. Cuts and bruises on a dozen more. Two men had their legs crushed—they might walk again, and they might not. And three are still missing."

"Jez?" Mieka asked. When she nodded and bit her lips together, he went on bracingly, "Jed will find him. When we were little and playing seeky-findy, they always knew where the other one was. Mum says identical twins are like that. She—"

"Mieka," Blye said, nervous hands twisting the cup over and over, "shut up."

Cade had seen the plans for the gallery over at Blye's glassworks one afternoon this winter, and though he had made a conscious effort to forget entirely about the Elsewhens, there was nothing wrong with his memory. Two staircases led from street level to the first of three upper floors. Between those staircases was a pair of fluted columns. The ground floor would be filled with heavier exhibits—statuary and the like—with a tearoom at the back overlooking the river. Up one flight of stairs to a pair of long galleries and a series of smaller chambers; up one more flight, and at one side was a library and reading room, the opposite side a maze of glass cases for small and insanely expensive things; up yet another flight was a series of offices and meeting rooms. Windows let in natural light from dawn until dusk. Cayden squinted at the confusion of stone and timber, and guessed that something had gone wrong on the gallery floor. But it couldn't have been Jed and Jez's fault—they were always scrupulously careful about scaffolding and support beams.

He wondered all at once why he'd been sent for. What use could he possibly be?

He became aware that Derien was yanking urgently at his shirtsleeve. Cade very nearly bent into a crouch, as he used to when Dery was little, but realized all at once that doing so now would have him looking up at his brother. He wondered if he'd be glad or galled when they could both stand straight and look one another in the eyes.

"There's somebody over there," the boy whispered, and pointed to a tangle of wood and stone. "Under the rubble."

"How far under?"

"I can't tell." He spoke even more softly. "But I know someone's there."

"Is it Jezael?"

"I don't know. It's just a feeling."

Cade hesitated, searching the boy's limpid brown eyes. He whispered back, "Like Grandfather Isshak?"

It took Derien a moment to understand and consider. Then he shook his head. "No. I can't see through the stone like they say he could. I just *know.*"

Not for an instant did Cayden scoff. He knew this tone of voice. He had spoken with the same certainty when, at just about Dery's age, he'd told Mistress Mirdley about an Elsewhen. Derien had just discovered a portion of his magic. How that magic might ripen could—indeed, must—wait. The problem right now was how to use what Derien knew without revealing how he knew it. Cade was painfully familiar with that sort of thing.

"Right," he said briskly. "On me, then." And before Dery could say another word, Cade straightened up, drew in a deep breath, adjusted the muscles of his face, and turned to Blye. In a deliberately raspy voice he asked, "Have they looked over that way? Has that section been cleared?"

"Yes." She peered up at him, frowning. "Did you just—?"

He didn't want to lie to her, so he merely said, "They ought to dig deeper."

Her brown eyes widened, and then she strode off. Whatever she told the workmen, however she explained it, mattered not at all to Cade. He took Dery aside and asked quietly, "Anyone else?"

The boy half-closed his eyes, turning his head slowly from left to right. He hesitated about a third of the way, his face directed at the stately half-finished steps of an interior stone staircase. Cade knew better than to interrupt him. But he did brace his brother with an arm around his shoulders as Dery trembled.

"Behind the left-hand stairs."

"Blye!"

Again he arranged his face in the so-familiar expression that immediately followed an Elsewhen; again he gave instructions. This time there were no questions. Blye snagged another pair of workmen and sent them hurrying to investigate.

"It's not you," murmured Mieka's voice at his shoulder. "I know what it looks like on you. It's Dery, isn't it?"

Without looking at him, Cade said, "Drunk, sober, or thornlost, tell anyone and I'll kill you."

Whatever the Elf might have replied was lost in a new commotion. Lord Rolon Piercehand had just arrived in an open carriage and in a frenzy of shouts and gestures, accompanied by—of all people—Princess Iamina. His Lordship was standing up even before the horse had come to a halt. He sprang over the half door of the carriage and bellowed for someone called Needstraw. One of the workmen dashed over and said something that stopped Piercehand in his tracks with a look of horror on his face.

Princess Iamina hadn't worn well. Cade remembered what she'd looked like that year he served at Wintering, when he wasn't quite twelve years old. She hadn't aged gracefully. She had just aged. At long last admitting defeat in her self-imposed competition with Miriuzca, she had taken to wearing gowns as plain as the robes of a Good Sister. Rumor had it she had become ostentatiously pious as well. She sat primly in the open carriage, hands folded, watching through narrowed eyes as Piercehand stalked about, giving orders and behaving as if he knew what he was doing. Iamina's gaze snagged on Cade, then shifted to Mieka; she recognized them both, he was sure of it, from Touchstone's "secret" performances for the ladies at Seekhaven. Considering some of the magic they had deliberately sent in her direction during those performances, it would have been bizarre if she hadn't recognized them. Her upper lip lifted and her head jerked back, as if someone had waved a dog turd under her chin.

Cade wasted a moment wondering why she was here, then turned his attention back to his brother. "There are three people missing. You've sensed two of them."

"I've been trying," Dery whispered. "But it's—it's confusing."

"What's the feeling like? Is it heartbeats or breathing, or—?"

The boy thought about it, then said, "It's hard. Not like skin. This is cold and hard. Metallic."

He might be sensing gold or silver jewelry; it might be the steel supports of the building. There would be testings and evaluations, but later. And in strictest privacy, because if Derien was indeed sensitive to precious metals, that would make him an extremely valuable young man. Almost as valuable as Cade. Or, rather, as valuable as Cade had been before he started refusing the Elsewhens.

Physickers had arrived and were sorting out the wounded. Suddenly a jubilant cry went up from behind the stone staircase, and soon a man was being carried to safety. Cade saw a thin glisten of gold at his left wrist as he reached up, fingers scrabbling mindlessly at rubble that no longer entrapped him. He was either married or bespoken, with a wife or sweetheart to take care of him as he mended. *If* he mended, for Cade saw with a sick lurch of his stomach that his right arm ended above the elbow in a snarl of skin, bone, sinew, and blood. Cade had just turned away from the sight when another man, supported by two others but limping along under his own power, came into view, and Piercehand sprinted towards him, yelling, "Needstraw!" Cade was numbly unsurprised to see an array of gold buttons on the man's torn and dirty jacket.

"Does Jez wear any gold jewelry?" Derien asked in a tense whisper.

So the boy had figured it out for himself. Cade gave a helpless shrug, thinking most irrelevantly that had this occurred after the exhibits were installed, there would be a hopeless confusion of gold in the rubble. Clocks and little statues and trimmings on boxes and settings for gemstones, all the oddments Piercehand's ships brought home from all over the world, currently on display at Castle Eyot—

"Cade," Dery said. "It's Jez. Look."

Hadden and Jed were carrying him. His left leg was wrapped in a bloodied bandage made from Jed's shirt. Cade heard a soft moan of anguish beside him, and then Mieka was running to help.

"That's all three of the missing, then," someone said. "Broken heads and broken bones, but nobody dead, praise be to the Lord and the Lady. His Lordship won't have the keeping of any widows or orphans."

"No, that'd be the builders' charge," another man said. "And as it is, they'll be compensating the one for the loss of a hand—or mayhap the wife, for her husband being able to squeeze but one breast at a time!"

"You're a one, ain't you?"

Undaunted, the second man went on, "And that other one, he was too tall anyway—and now, if they can't save that leg, he's likely to be the shorter by a foot!" He chortled at his own wit.

Cade turned slowly. The pair behind him, Lord Piercehand's

guards by their livery, were his own height but half again his heft. Very cordially, very coldly, he asked, "How would your own wife feel if you came home lighter by the weight of your balls?"

"Wife?" Derien snorted. "What girl in her right mind would marry a brains-in-his-buttocks naffter like him?"

It was madness, of course, to confront the man; armed with a lethal-looking cudgel and plenty of muscle, the guard could have snapped Cade in two with one hand while smashing Dery's skull to splinters with the other.

Happily, his companion was of a mind to calm things down. "Here, now," he said, "there's been enough ruckus for one day, I'm thinkin'. Apologies all round, and—"

"Apology accepted," Derien said quickly, and dragged Cade away by the elbow. The boy was stronger than he looked; Cade stumbled a bit, flinging a glare over his shoulder. "It's not as if they'd recognize your face, or even your name, being *barely* literate if at all, you know," he said, "and you have shows coming up next week—and besides *that,* it's your Namingday and you don't want to spend the rest of it and the next month besides with a broken jaw, do you?"

Fine thing it was, when his little brother got him out of trouble.

His little brother, who could sense the presence of gold.

"Dery," he said, low-voiced, "don't mention a word to anybody about what you just did. Not even to Mistress Mirdley. Not until we figure out exactly what it is you can do, and what you have to do in order to do it."

Dark eyes glinted up at him. "And you call yourself a writer!"

"Derien, I mean it," he insisted.

"I know. I'll keep quiet."

Along with the physickers had come carts for transporting the injured. Jez, Cade saw with profound gratitude, was in the capable care of Mistress Mirdley, who snapped over her shoulder at a physicker unwise enough to express his opinion.

"Forgive me for mentioning it," he said with an exaggerated courtesy that was worse than any open contempt for the elderly Trollwife, "but my credentials are from Stiddolfe and Shollop both. With respect, Mistress, I think I know quite a lot more about—"

"It's not what you do know as what you don't," she growled, working swiftly to staunch the bleeding and cleanse the wound. "He's Elf and Wizard and Piksey as well as the Human that gives him his looks. A thornful of dragon tears could send him into spasms."

He brushed that aside and shook out the dusty folds of his green gown, conspicuously decorated at the left breast with two embroidered badges: Stiddolfe University's lion and Shollop University's dragonfly. "That's as may be. But I really don't think—"

Hadden, who sat just behind his son, supporting him with both arms around his chest, looked up. "I quite agree. You don't."

Mieka was holding both of Jezael's hands. "Go polish your credentials and leave the work to those who understand it!"

The physicker took himself off in a huff. Cade stood there feeling useless until it occurred to him that Jez had to be conveyed home somehow to Wistly Hall. *Convenient* was not a word ever associated with Princess Iamina, but she—or, more to the point, her carriage—was excellently convenient right now.

When Cade set his mind to it, he could be almost as glibly garrulous as Mieka. In fact, he started talking even before he unlatched the little half-door of the carriage. "Your Royal Highness, I hope you haven't been too shocked and upset. It's so good of you to bring along your carriage to fetch the wounded back home—I'm sure it won't take above an hour or so, and I will be more than happy to escort you back to your own house. You'll know me, of course, as the tregetour of Touchstone."

The Princess scooted back into the far corner of the leather seat, scowling horribly. "I have no idea who you are, and I cannot say that I care! And to imply that a decent woman would know the first thing about anything to do with theater—I have never in my life seen a play! Sinful enough when men attend such performances, but ladies in an audience—though one could scarce term them *ladies*—is a scandal, utterly depraved."

Cade put a look of shock onto his face as he took the long step up into the carriage. "But—forgive me, but some dreadful impertinent woman has made a mockery of Your Royal Highness!" When she sat up straight and sucked in air, he went on, "Touchstone, you see, has performed for the ladies of the Court at Seekhaven—all very secret, of course, and I understand perfectly that Your Royal Highness's delicacy of mind would never permit attendance there—because of course it couldn't have been you, it was some disrespectful woman wearing a copy of Your Royal Highness's famous yellow flower jewel."

Derien obliged him by unfolding the steps. Cade took firm possession of Iamina's left elbow, tugging her adamantly from her corner. She was the sort of person whose indignation was boundless, but bound by one indignity at a time. Cade had given her four atrocities in quick succession. Commandeering her carriage competed with the implication that she had actually seen a play, but could not rival the outrage of being "impersonated," which faded to insignificance in the immediate affront of having her Royal Person touched. The claims of all these on her powers of speech resulted in paralysis.

Cade congratulated himself and delivered his final blow. "Your Royal Highness may rest assured that if I ever see that fake jewel again, I will tear the insolent woman limb from limb—" He paused and leaned in to whisper for her ears alone. "—much like that Woodwose many years ago at a private Wintering celebration. Tell me, can you still taste his blood?"

She reared back like a horse eyeing a snake. This put her off balance enough so that Cade could extract her from her carriage and set her on the pavement.

"So very kind of Your Royal Highness!" He rapped his knuckles on the side of the carriage. "Driver, follow my brother over that way. You may return for the Princess across the street at the Minster." Turning again to Iamina, he finished, "I feel sure Your Royal Highness's well-known piety will do much good for these poor people with your prayers. Here, you—" He waved at one of Piercehand's guards. "Escort Her Royal Highness to the Minster!"

He bowed to Iamina before hurrying to catch up to the carriage. The driver didn't look happy. Cade met him stare for stare and eventually the man shrugged.

There was room on the butter-soft upholstery for Jez, Mistress Mirdley, Blye, and Hadden. Mieka leaped up to sit beside the driver. Jedris stayed behind to make sure the rest of the wounded were taken care of and got home all right. Lord Rolon Piercehand was distributing handfuls of coin to every worker who filed past him. Cade noticed that some were going round twice.

"Can I stay with you tonight?"

He looked down at Derien. "What? No. Mother—"

"She's at Threne with the Archduchess for a week."

"She's *where*? She never goes anywhere to stay."

"I know. But that's where she is. Mistress Mirdley will want to keep an eye on Jez and it'd be just me at Redpebble. The footmen have the week free as well."

It was thus demonstrated to him how little he knew about his own family these days. "Well . . . all right. But be sure you wake in time for school tomorrow."

Lord Piercehand, still bestowing silver coins, called out to Cade—called him by name, in fact. For all that each group on each circuit spent several days of each tour on holiday at Piercehand's Castle Eyot, Cade hadn't known that the man had ever seen Touchstone perform. He was always off on some voyage or other, collecting. He was very charming, very rich, and very dissipated. Part Wizard and part Elf, with plenty of Human noble titles in his bloodlines and to spare, in his youth he had been all the craze at Court, where his good looks and merry wit made him the darling of Queen Roshien and her ladies. But that had been twenty years ago. He bore all the signs nowadays of indulgence in every diversion wealth could buy. The advancing ruin of a handsome face and fine body was something Cade had seen before, but he couldn't quite recall where. An Elsewhen, mayhap.

"Master Silversun! Yes, yes, over here, if you please!"

Cade dutifully approached. "Your Lordship?"

A monologue ensued, one voice meant for Cade and the other voice for the workmen queued up for commiseration in the form of silver coin—as if he were the masquer in a play that called for asides to the audience.

"A good thing it was that you did with the carriage, Master Silversun." With a quick, warm smile at a workman as he pressed a coin into his hand: "Here, my good fellow, glad to see you're unhurt. I don't know why she insisted on coming here, never any telling what that woman will do. Spend some of this on your wife, eh? Buy her something pretty. Invited her to my town house, gave her tea, asked if she'd part with a few of her better bits and bobs for my Gallery—yes, come back to work tomorrow, have to clear all this up, eh? On gracious loan from the collection of, and all that sort of thing. Then the runner came with word of this—" He waved his free hand aimlessly. "—and damn me if she didn't offer her own carriage and stepped right in ahead of me. Let's hope there's not too much blood on the upholstery. Bright and early tomorrow, my lad! We've an opening to make ready for, eh? Where'd she take herself off to, then?"

"The Minster across the way."

"Good place for her," said Piercehand. "Devout these days—admirable, I'm sure, but a trifle tedious, eh? Not at all the way she was in her young day, I can tell you! Damn, but I'm afraid I've run out of coin! Well, lads, there'll be more tomorrow. Tremendous apologies, and drink to your own good fortune tonight! This is *costing* me a bloody fortune," he muttered as the line dispersed with grumbles—most of them hypocritical, for most of these men had gone through at least twice, rightly trusting to the usual inability of noblemen to distinguish one member of the working class from another. "But it might have cost me Needstraw, and that would be beyond tragedy! My curator, don't you know— brilliant man, can't do without him to keep my trinkets sorted. They say you're the one who found him?"

Cade thought fast. "No, my lord, actually not. I only asked if that section had been explored, and nobody was sure, so they looked again."

"Well, he owes his life to you and make no mistake. I've emptied my purse for today, but there'll be a reward for you."

"That's very gracious but entirely unnecessary—"

"Of course it's necessary! And I'll hear no more about it. Now, let's find you a hack to take you home, eh?" As he smiled, Cade saw the remnants of the young man he had been, a gleaming past glimpsed behind tarnished decay.

"I am beholden to Your Lordship," Cade responded.

Someone was sent to find a hire-hack. After once again expressing gratitude to Lord Piercehand, Cade climbed in after his brother and frowned as he heard Derien say to the driver, "Wistly Hall, Waterknot Street."

"I thought you were staying with me tonight."

"It's closer to school. And there's always a place to sleep at Wistly."

They rode in silence for a time. Then, just as the hack was turning onto Waterknot Street, Cade snorted a laugh. When Dery arched an inquiring brow, he said, "And once again my Namingday turns out memorable. I think I'll stop having them. Twenty-four is quite old enough, isn't it?"

"I'll let you know when I get there."

3

Getting Jezael home to Wistly was a nightmare. Mieka was torn between a desire to shout the horse into a gallop and the equal and opposite desire to go as gently as possible. What Princess Iamina's driver achieved was an uncomfortable in-between: not fast enough to get them home as quickly as Mieka wanted, but not slow enough to prevent cobblestoned bumps and lurches from wringing strangled groans from Jez's throat—in spite of whatever Mistress Mirdley had given him for the pain. Every sound his brother made sent a spasm of sick panic through Mieka's body. He locked his fingers around the wooden side rail of the driver's bench and scanned the road up ahead, futilely trying to find the smoothest path.

Someone had had brains enough to send word to Mishia Windthistle about the accident; she and Jinsie were waiting at the front door with a makeshift litter. As they moved Jez slowly, safely out of the carriage, Jinsie climbed in the other side for the return journey, telling Blye she'd collar Jedris and get him home before dark.

Blye nodded gratefully. "He'll want to know how the accident happened, but it can wait until tomorrow, when he can actually see something."

Mieka helped carry his brother upstairs, and then was shooed out by his mother and Mistress Mirdley. Descending to the hall, he sat on the bottom step of the grand staircase and gnawed on a thumbnail and felt helpless. He didn't like feeling helpless. Rarely did he get himself into situations where he did feel helpless; he was an expert at strategic departures. The last time he'd felt like this was almost two years ago, that night just before Midsummer when Cade had been thornlost in his Elsewhens, and seen Briuly and Alaen Blackpath finding The Rights of the Fae. Mieka hadn't been alone in his helplessness; there was nothing anyone could have done. All the rest of that night and on into the next day, nobody had said much of anything, each of them imagining the sunrise scene at Nackerty Close—and, being players, they were exceptionally imaginative.

Only once had Rafe attempted to talk about it, saying that it was Briuly who had reasoned out that the sun would hit the hiding place of The Rights at Midsummer dawn as well as Midwinter sunset, so Cade really wasn't to blame for what happened. Mieka had the sense not to open his mouth and remind everyone that Cade had wanted the cousins to go after the treasure. Jeska had accused him more than once of pestering them about finding it so that everybody would know that it wasn't just a story made into a play, that it was real, and applaud Cade for his cleverness in working it all out.

Looking back, it seemed to Mieka that Briuly's death, which everyone else thought was merely a strange "disappearance," generally attributed to the vagaries of artistic temperament, was the last thing that Cade had really cared about, the last time he'd openly felt anything. There had been no change in the intensity of magic Cade put into the withies for a performance. Love, hate, fear, joy, contempt, anxiety, tenderness, indignation, grief, rage, pride—all the emotions that Touchstone used onstage were reliably there in the glass twigs. The feel of them had changed some, though Mieka stubbornly chose to attribute the difference to maturity and even to increased mastery of the magic. Cade primed the withies expertly, giving Mieka everything he needed for a performance.

Yet in his personal life, Cade seemed only to be going through the motions. He'd looked and acted grim enough this afternoon, but to Mieka's knowing eye it was . . . not *faked*, not exactly, but . . . *muted*. Rather like what that unknown fettler had done to them several times on that first Royal Circuit, only Cade was muting his own emotions, not onstage magic. It was as if he'd set up a barrier between him and any event that might cause him to feel too much . . . or feel at all. Like the barrier Lady Megs had raised to protect a sensitive little girl one night at the Keymarker.

And there, Mieka told himself, was another sore point. The noble Lady Megueris Mindrising was everything Cade could want—nice looking, smart, spirited, educated, adept at magic, and insanely rich besides—yet he behaved as if she existed only when he was looking at her. Mieka knew very well what it was like to want a woman, to be so hopelessly in love that every waking thought and every night's dreamings were about her. Any man with half a grain of sense would have been out of his mind in love with Lady Megs. Cade gave no signs of it that Mieka could recognize.

They'd met her quite a few times in the last couple of years: during Trials at Seekhaven, private performances at one or another of Lord Mindrising's many residences throughout Albeyn, at lunching or tea with Princess Miriuzca, at the races. Cade responded not at all to being teased about Megs. He neither flushed red with embarrassment nor snarled that it was nobody's business but his, nor laughed, nor threatened serious physical mayhem if they didn't shut up. He simply didn't react. The lady, of course, could not be similarly teased; Mieka did have some notion of manners. Though she was pleasant enough around Cade, she showed no particular partiality for his company.

Granted, it simply wasn't done: no self-respecting girl, wellborn or not, would be caught actively pursuing a man. But Megs wasn't the typical twitchy little titled ladyship, nor simpering simple-minded shopgirl. And, facts be faced, she was getting to be of an age when people sniggered behind their hands at unwed females. Cade wasn't the best catch in terms of the Court, but Megs had buckets of money and a name ancient enough for both of them. Mieka couldn't see why anyone would object to Cade. True, he was no beauty, and he'd talk the hind leg off a wyvern, and his sulks were the most infuriatingly boring thing in the world, but he had pretty manners and could talk interestingly when he felt like it, and he was famous and even had a few noble ancestors, and why was Mieka chittering inside his own head about Cade's love life when his brother lay upstairs—?

"How is he?"

Cade and Derien stood in the hallway. Mieka hadn't even noticed their arrival. Getting to his feet, he said, "We took him upstairs. Nobody's said anything to me since." And then, seizing on something to talk about that would distract him from thinking about Jez, he asked, "Why did you pretend it was you, Cade?"

Derien glanced briefly up at his brother—but not for permission to speak, and *that* told Mieka more than anything else could that Derien was not a little boy anymore. "You're right, it was me," he said to Mieka. "But Blye would believe it from Cade, so we said it was him."

"Yes, I believed it," said Blye from the top of the stairs. She continued wearily down to them, wiping her hands on a red-stained towel. "But not for long. Jez is resting. Mistress Mirdley says the wounds are—well, let's just say that she cleaned them out and stitched him up. Mieka, she wants a bottle of sweet wine to hide the taste of the medicine. He has to get some sleep."

"Pantry," he said, and led the way.

In common with the other grand houses on Waterknot

Street, which had all been built around the same time, Wistly Hall possessed a wine cellar. All these wine cellars leaked, no matter how thick the stone walls, the Gally River's underground tributaries stubbornly finding any crack or seam to seep through. The door to Wistly's cellar was kept locked. Finances in the Windthistle family had been tight for the last thirty-five years and more, so nobody knew how deep the water might be these days. There was no money for drainage and repair. So all the bottles and kegs were crowded into a pantry along with flour and spices and loaves of sugar. Mieka threaded past boxes and barrels and shelving to the back wall, where the paltry remnant of the once-extensive Windthistle wine collection was stored. Behind him in the kitchen, he could hear Blye confronting Cade.

"I believed you for a minute or two—but you only see things that you have the ability to change. So it has to have been Dery."

"I didn't tell you, because I don't want anyone to know before we figure out exactly what it is he can do."

"But you already know what it is."

"More or less," Cade admitted. "Why did you send for me, anyway? It's not as if I could've been any help."

"When Mistress Mirdley got there, she said Mieka and Dery were at your flat."

"So it's Mieka you were wanting? Even though he was no more useful than me?"

Mieka found a venerable bottle of mead and dusted it off. Honey-wine ought to be sweet enough to disguise any nasty medicinal taste, unless it had been stored too long and gone sour.

"Mieka needed to be where his brothers were!" she snapped. "You're right, you weren't necessary, and you've made it clear that nobody's necessary to you except when you're onstage. So why did you bother to come?"

Mieka winced. He was fairly certain he knew what Blye would say next.

Sure enough: "Tell me, Cade, have you figured out a way yet to present your plays without Jeska and Rafe and Mieka?"

He also knew what Cade would say. He found a corkscrew, opened the bottle, and took a swig. Not his usual tipple, but still good and perfectly suited to the purpose. As Cade answered Blye's question, Mieka took another swallow, wishing it were something stronger. There was no comfort in being right.

"Not quite yet. But I'm working on it."

Derien, with desperation in his voice, broke in. "It was the gold. That one man had a gold bracelet, and the other had gold buttons. But Jez doesn't wear any gold jewelry. His wedding necklet is silver."

"Now you know why it has to be kept quiet," Cade said.

Mieka wiped the cloying sweetness of the wine from his lips and returned to the kitchen. "Derien, old son, now that you're of an age for it, you'd best come up with some other sort of magic to tell people about, because telling anybody about *this* would be as much as your life's worth." When Cade scowled horribly at him, he merely shrugged. "He's not stupid. He knows what this could mean. I think we'd all rather he stayed put in Albeyn, not get himself hauled off on somebody-or-other's ship to the back of the bleedin' beyond, just so other people can get rich on the gold he can find for them."

Cade and Blye both looked shocked—not by what he'd said, because they had to have been thinking the same thing, but by the fact that he'd said it to the boy. Well, it was time they stopped treating Dery like a child. If twelve (or almost) was old enough to come into his magic, it was old enough to be told the truth.

"Here," Mieka said, handing the bottle of mead to Blye. "This should suit." To Cade: "You'll be staying here tonight, yeh? Let's find some blankets and things."

"You'd do better to find us all something to eat," Blye said. "Bread and cheese and beer will do."

It would have to, because what Mieka, Cade, and Derien amongst them didn't know about cooking would sink one of Lord Piercehand's ships. Mieka wasn't sure who else was living at Wistly these days, and was grateful that none of them showed up to complain about dinner or the lack of it.

At ten by the nearby Minster chimes everyone had been fed and put into order. Jez was asleep under his mother's watchful eye. Hadden and Blye took the younger children up to bed. Blye came back down to inform them that Mistress Mirdley had settled in a chair for a nap and would take over watching Jez in a few hours so Mishia could get a little sleep.

"Jed should be back by now," she fretted as Mieka poured her a tot of whiskey.

"Sit down," Cade said, "and tell us what happened."

"I don't know any more about that than I did the first time you asked."

"My brothers," Mieka stated, "are too careful and too good at their work for it to've been a structural failure."

"Much beholden for the endorsement," came Jed's voice from the drawing room doorway. "How's Jez?"

"Sleeping." Blye was at his side instantly. "No, don't sit here, come into the kitchen and eat." She pulled him out into the hall. Though she was a foot and a half shorter than he, her determination overwhelmed his exhaustion.

Jinsie crossed to where Mieka was sitting, appropriated the glass right out of his hand, and took a long swallow of whiskey. "You'll appreciate this," she said, and dropped a piece of something glittering into his hand.

"What is it?" Derien demanded.

"Glass," he said. "It's—" He thought better of what he'd been about to say, and tucked the shard into his shirt pocket. "It's just a bit of glass."

Jinsie gave him back his whiskey and looked narrowly into

his eyes. He met his twin's gaze levelly. "Probably bottle glass," she said, taking his meaning, for she knew as well as he did what it was. "No windows in the place yet for an accident to shatter."

If she put the slightest emphasis on the word *accident,* only Mieka heard it. "I'll ask Blye tomorrow. She'll know what sort it is. It might even be a chunk from one of those rings she makes for neck-cloths. And that remembers me—she owes me my percentage from sales of the things. They were my idea, after all."

Jinsie wrinkled her nose at him. "Money, money—it's all you think about. Me, all I can think of right now is sleep."

"Hint taken," Cade said, and looked pointedly at his brother.

"I won't be able to sleep," Derien warned. "Will you?"

"You've school tomorrow," Cade reminded him.

"And we have a rehearsal." Mieka finished off the scant swallow of whiskey Jinsie had left him, and set down his glass. "You take my room, Dery." He'd long since switched bedchambers with Jinsie, not wanting to spend any more nights in the place where he'd struck his wife for the first—and, he swore, last and only—time. When they were upstairs and Mieka turned left down the hall instead of right, a glance at Cayden showed him that the change had been noted. He was briefly shocked that Cade hadn't been to Wistly for an overnight in such a long time that he didn't know.

Despite his protests, Derien was yawning before his head hit the pillow. Cade collected the boy's discarded clothes while Mieka doused the candles, and once the door was shut said, "I ought to wash these for tomorrow."

Mieka hadn't a clue where the laundry was done. The only good-sized sink he knew of was in the kitchen. So to the kitchen they went. Jed was gulping hot tea; on the worktable before him was a plate emptied of all but bread crumbs and cheese rind.

"—possibly be your fault," Blye was saying as Mieka and Cade entered.

"But it happened, and I have to know why. Everything was just as we always do it. All the braces, the struts, the pulleys, the ladders—and all the workers are experienced men. It just doesn't make any sense." He finished his tea. "I have to be up early tomorrow. I want to go look everything over in the daylight. I s'pose it's no good looking in on Jez?"

"He's sleeping. Tomorrow, love." Blye linked her arm with his. "Come to bed."

Good-nights were said. Cade went to the sink and began rinsing out Dery's clothes. Mieka searched a few drawers and found some cord to string up as a drying line. The practical magic of household chores wasn't something either of them had ever taken the trouble to learn. Finally he broke the silence, twisting the loose end of the cord in his hands.

"Not a glimmering, I take it?" Mieka asked softly. "Not a hint of an Elsewhen about any of this?"

Not turning from the sink, Cade shook his head. "Blye's right—how could I possibly affect what happened this afternoon?"

There was something else, though. Something Mieka sensed but couldn't quite identify. Waiting Cade out was occasionally effective, and much the kindest method of finding out what he wanted to hide; bullying him into telling wasn't very nice, but prevented a great deal of frustrating boredom.

"Nothing at all?" Mieka pressed.

"No." Cade wrung out his brother's trousers and put them on the draining board, then reached for the undershirt. "Not anymore."

"What does *that* mean?"

A shrug of thin shoulders. "I don't anymore."

"You don't what?" He couldn't possibly be saying what Mieka was suddenly, sickeningly sure he was saying.

"The Elsewhens. They were a bit of a bore. So I stopped having them."

A *bore*? Visions of disasters that, forewarned, he could seek to avoid? What about the one where Thierin Knottinger of Black fucking Lightning had given Mieka some sort of horrid thorn that destroyed an important performance? What if he hadn't seen that in advance? And The Rights of the Fae—there'd have been no triumph with Touchstone's version of "Treasure" if he hadn't seen—

—and if he *hadn't* seen, Briuly would still be alive.

Thinking he understood, Mieka said, "They don't all have to hurt, y'know."

At last Cade turned to face him. "Who said anything about 'hurt'?" His voice was casual enough, but his eyes—Mieka always knew when Cade was lying. Those large, fine gray eyes always gave him away.

"Your Namingday," Mieka said desperately. "When you'll be forty-five. That was a good one, wasn't it?"

Cade only shrugged once more.

"But why? Did they just stop?"

"Did I outgrow them, like you outgrew your yearly head cold? No. I decided I didn't like them. So I don't have them anymore."

"Not even when you're asleep?"

Long fingers twisted the undershirt viciously. "You don't understand. You could never understand. I'm afraid to sleep. Not because of the dreams, the Elsewhen dreams. I don't have those anymore. I have nightmares instead. The kind other people have. Distortions, and running in place and never getting anywhere, and endless falling, and yelling but no one can hear me, and being helpless—but even if there weren't any nightmares, I'd be afraid to sleep because after I sleep I have to wake up, and there's another Gods-be-damned day to be faced and dealt with and slogged through somehow, and—even if I've pricked blockweed the night before, and have no dreams or nightmares at all, I still have to wake up. And sometimes the waking day is worse than the sleeping nightmare."

Mieka watched in mute dismay as Cade draped the undershirt on the makeshift clothesline. He'd never heard Cade's voice like this: quick, brittle, with an undercurrent of vicious mockery.

"And besides *that*," Cade went on, "I've got rid of all the Elsewhens I had before. I don't remember them. They're gone. You say there was a good one—I'll have to take your word for it, because I don't remember them anymore. I don't want them. I want to live the way normal people live. Without knowing what's coming."

"But—but—" Mieka was so shocked, he could hardly get the words out. "You can't do that, Quill!"

"Can't I? People think things, do things, decide things, without knowing what will come of them—"

"But we're just fumbling about in the dark. *You* know for certain sure!"

"I know what *might* happen. Used to, anyways. It's been interesting, actually. Not having all that lot rattling round in my head, confusing me all the time. Liberating."

"Blind," Mieka said softly. "You're blind, just like everyone else."

"What I saw, or thought I saw, it's all gone. I won't see anything else. Not waking nor sleeping. I won't do it." He hesitated, then said, "I just want . . . to be normal, I guess."

Mieka had gone to Redpebble Square this afternoon— Gods, had it only been this afternoon?—thinking to ask Mistress Mirdley if she felt the same changes in Cade that he did. He'd been unable to define just why Cade was different. He didn't have the words. The work was as good as ever (with that one mortifying exception), and he gave Mieka everything he needed inside the withies for each performance, but the magic had felt different for quite some time. The sense of *Cade*-ness that had always been in the withies along with Cade's magic had changed.

Now he knew why.

"Why didn't you tell me? We could've talked about it."

"And what would you have said? That at the very least I have advance warning of what might happen? Precious pile of good that did for Briuly and Alaen!" He wrung out his brother's shirt as if he had his hands round someone's neck. "You know what the funny part of it is? You didn't even notice. Not you nor Jeska nor Rafe—we all but live in each other's pockets for months at a time, and none of you noticed."

Mieka opened his mouth to protest, and shut it again. Cade was right. Gods in glory, did the man never tire of being *right*? Although Mieka had noticed and worried about differences in Cade, he hadn't asked.

"It never occurred to you that I'd started telling you about the Elsewhens, and then just stopped?" Cade shot him a sardonic glance. "Did you just assume that there wasn't anything horrid, so I kept them to myself?"

Mieka gave a helpless, shamed little nod. "You should've told me what you'd done, all the same."

"Oh, and of course you would've believed me. Just like you would've believed me if I'd told you the Elsewhens about your wife."

Mieka took an involuntary step back from the sneer. "But it—it's like *murder*. All those memories—"

"They weren't memories."

"They were part of you!"

"Not anymore. And you're forgetting something. The Archduke knows." Cade gave him a thin smile. "Credit where it's due, Mieka. He *knows*."

He felt his cheeks heat up, but he had no time for awkwardness and apologies. Because once more he thought that he understood. It took no foreseeing to know that eventually the Archduke would come round, wanting Cade to see the futures for him. "If the Elsewhens are gone, you're no longer valuable to him."

"That's the idea."

"You actually think he'll believe you when you say it doesn't happen anymore?"

A spiteful grin spread across the thin face. "I know—I'll make something up! Let's find paper and pen and get started on prophecies—you're good at jokes and pranks, you can help. I'll have to have a dozen or so ready for him—"

"Stop it, Cade!"

"As you wish." He turned back to the sink and started in on Derien's stockings.

Mieka was just as glad of it. He hated it when he and Cayden fought, though he considered that he ought to be grateful that Cade had at least shown some honest emotion for a change. He watched the long bony fingers rub soap into the stockings—sea green, to match the piping on the white shirts worn by students at the King's College. The full rig included brown trousers and jacket; as a boy progressed in school, the plain horn buttons were replaced, one by one, with silver. With discovery of part of his magic, Dery would be receiving another silver button, and instead of classes in magical theory, he would start attending classes in practical magic.

And then it hit Mieka, all at once: that in finding his magic, Derien had saved two lives, but in rejecting his magic, Cade had killed part of who he was.

But there was something worse. Never mind all that drivel about not seeing what he could have no hand in influencing; Mieka knew for a fact that Cade had seen things where that connection was so obscure that nobody could have figured it out.

"You might have seen this," he heard himself say. "You might have, and changed it. My brother's likely crippled, all because you think your Elsewhens are a *bore*."

Cade swung around in a fury. "It's not my fault. I won't have it be my fault!"

Mieka fled the kitchen and didn't stop until he was at what

used to be the entrance to his little tower lair. The doorway was boarded up now, the tower having at long last crashed down into the river below. It had taken with it, among other things, one of the three candle-flats that had been his eighteenth Namingday present (he'd given Jinsie one, and the other was at his house in Hilldrop), all the various blankets and pillows he'd nested there, his collection of Touchstone's placards, and his spare thorn-roll.

Now that Touchstone was on the Royal Circuit, Mieka had taken to dividing his time during the winter between Wistly Hall and the house where his wife, daughter, and mother-in-law lived. But Wistly wasn't home anymore, not really, and for all that he'd owned the place for several years now, Hilldrop wasn't home, either. In both places he always felt one step away from being a stranger. The Mieka who had grown up here didn't exist any longer, and he hadn't quite grown into being a Mieka who, between Royal Circuits, could be content with a quiet life in the country being a husband and father. The only time he felt truly real—alive, and happy, and *right*, and exactly where he'd been meant to be—was onstage. Yet even that feeling sometimes eluded him. Now he knew why.

Cade's fault. Deny it as he might, this was all Cade's fault. A flickering of humor curled his mouth in a bitter little smile, for hadn't Cade always felt guiltily responsible over his Elsewhens, and hadn't Mieka tried to persuade him that he couldn't be held to account for what other people decided to do? Now there were no Elsewhens to feel guilty about, but Cade was absolutely responsible not only for rejecting sight of things he might have changed for the better, but also for killing parts of himself that Mieka needed.

No wonder the withies had felt different.

He turned from the boarded-up doorway to seek a bed— there must be an unoccupied one somewhere in this house—and his fingers sought the little bit of glass in his shirt pocket. He wouldn't have to ask Blye what kind of glass it was. He knew very well, as Jinsie had known very well, that it was the crimped end of a withie. And the hallmark on it—a thing forbidden to Blye—was that of Master Splithook, who made withies for, among others, Black Lightning.

4

It so happened that Trials would be held early at Seekhaven this year, for King Meredan and Queen Roshien were going on progress throughout Albeyn to celebrate the twenty-fifth year of their reign. It would take them all summer to visit the most important cities, towns, castles, and country houses on a schedule almost as brutal as any of the circuits. Prince Ashgar was set to join them here and there; Princess Miriuzca, having just been delivered of a daughter, would stay at Seekhaven with her children until early autumn, when grand celebrations would be held in Gallantrybanks.

Thus it wasn't even a week after the accident at Lord Piercehand's Gallery that Touchstone set off in their wagon for Seekhaven. They wouldn't be returning to the capital until autumn, for the circuit schedules had been moved up as well, and the Royal would begin the day after Trials was over. The King wanted all the best groups in Gallantrybanks for the official festivities. And since the King paid room and board, transportation, and performance fees, all the best groups would do as they were told.

Three days before Touchstone's departure for Seekhaven, their wagon rolled in from its off-duty home at Hilldrop. Yazz, their driver, occupied the coachman's bench, but the reins were in the hands of Mieka's daughter, Jindra, perched on the half Giant's massive knee. She took her job very seriously. Mieka bit both lips together in the effort not to laugh as she pulled on the reins to stop the horses just outside Wistly Hall, her face screwed up with the effort. Yazz grinned down at Mieka, who scrambled up to lift Jindra down.

"Well done, sweeting! When Yazz gets tired of us, we'll hire you to be our driver!"

She giggled and wrapped her arms around his neck. At almost three and a half years old, she was adorably Elfen, with Mieka's changeable eyes (and thick eyebrows, poor darling), Mieka's elegantly pointed ears, Mieka's hands (the ring and smallest fingers of almost the same length), and Mieka's black hair. Only the full, soft, sweet curve of her mouth was her mother's.

Her mother emerged from the wagon's back door, wilting in the unseasonable heat and looking rather greenish; riding in an enclosed vehicle made her queasy. She smiled wanly at Mieka and accepted Petrinka's escort upstairs to sleep off the drive from Hilldrop.

Back when Wistly Hall was built, and the Windthistles had been able to afford their own coaches, carriages, and horses, a splendid mews had graced the mansion's western side. That time was long past, and these days the mews served mostly as storage and a home for the cats that kept the mouse population in check. The stalls had been cleared and cleaned, and Yazz occupied himself in unhitching and stabling the horses while Mieka stood with Jindra on one hip, listening to her prattle on about her friends, the birds she'd saved from her mother's pet fox, and the present she'd helped make for Uncle Jez.

"And what would that be, Jinnie?"

"Pillow. Down, Dadda!"

When he set her on the cobbles, she ran for the wagon and clambered up the steps. Yazz had finished with the horses, and came to Mieka's side to impart his own news.

"Fanna will be brothered by Wintering," he said with shy satisfaction.

"Good work!" Mieka clapped him on the elbow. "How's Robel?"

"Glad she'll be to have me home for the birthing. Not like last time."

"How d'you know it's a boy?"

Yazz looked pityingly down at him. "How did we know Fanna to be a girl? We just know."

The ways and knowings of Giants were as impenetrable to the other races as the ways of the Old Gods. Two months into her first pregnancy, Robel had announced she would have a girl; now she was certain she'd have a boy.

"Takes all the surprise out of it, if you ask me."

Yazz peered around the mews, frowning. "Who asked?"

Mieka laughed with him, and caught Jindra up in his arms again as she raced towards him holding a package half as big as she was. "And what's this, then?"

"I *said,* Dadda," she reminded him. "Pillow. I helped sew!"

"Yes, you did tell me. Sorry I didn't pay attention. Let's go see Jez, shall we?"

The pillow proved to be a beautifully worked creation of dark green silk embroidered in the center with a pale green thistle and scented with cinnamon and sage. Grandmother and aunts exclaimed over how pretty it was, and Jezael gave her a bow rendered no less elegant for his being propped up in bed. Jindra fussed over the placement of his injured leg on the pillow.

"Beholden, Jinnie. It feels much better already!"

She insisted on staying in his room that night, sharing a cot with Mishia, and when Mieka came in the next morning, he found her curled up beside Jez like a drowsing puppy.

His mother, who sat at the window sorting Mistress Mirdley's doses of medicine, smiled. "I keep wondering," she said softly, so as not to wake them, "how you ever managed to produce anything so sweet as that child."

"Mum! I was just as adorable at her age!"

"Actually," she mused, "you were. What in all Hells happened?"

He grinned and betook himself downstairs, intending to take breakfast up to his wife. They'd spent the night in separate rooms so she could recover from the drive. Only two more nights with her, he reminded himself, before several long months of separation. And this time, he thought with a wince, he really would have to behave himself. Month after month of celibacy . . . it didn't bear thinking about.

The spring sojourn in Lilyleaf came about because Mieka had been a very, very, *very* bad boy. From last year's Royal Circuit he had brought home toys for Jindra, a beautiful fur capelet for his mother-in-law, and, among other things, a case of the pox for his wife. Auntie Brishen had been applied to when his own affliction manifested itself most unpleasantly during Touchstone's giggings at Castle Biding. The cure had come by special courier (with a hefty bill and an admonition to keep his pants buttoned), and he'd thought he was over it by the time he got home. That he wasn't had become clear that autumn in ways equally unpleasant for his wife. Again Auntie Brishen was consulted, and again she had provided (for an even heftier fee, and with her solemn promise to tell his mother if it ever happened again).

Having broken one of his own rules—that it mattered for naught what a man did when he was away from his wife so long as he didn't bring home anything nasty—he made up for it the only way he knew how. They'd never had a real wedding trip, so in early spring when the roads were passable, he borrowed Lord Kearney Fairwalk's second-best carriage (complete with groom to drive and look after the horses) and took his wife to Lilyleaf for a month of pampering. He did whatever she wanted and bought her anything she fancied. He accompanied her to shops and escorted her to public balls—and private ones, too, for once it was known that the most outrageous member of Touchstone was taking a holiday in Lilyleaf, the rich or titled or both were eager for the now-legendary diversions of Mieka's presence. That he had a beautiful wife was almost consolation for the fact that he behaved himself perfectly. On mild days he took her for long drives in the countryside or partnered her at bowls on a green with only a few really muddy patches. He found something harmless and boring to do while she went to the baths. He didn't drink more than a single ale or glass of wine each day. He left his thorn-roll at home. They stayed at Croodle's inn, and every so often he caught a sardonic glint in her black eyes for the impeccable picture of sober husbandly virtue he presented. He had the feeling she knew the reason for it.

Mieka was able to take a whole month on holiday because of four things.

First, Rafe had declared that he was staying home in Gallantrybanks with Crisiant and their new little son. The occasional engagement at the Kiral Kellari or the Downstreet or the Keymarker would be fine, but no travel to the country houses of the nobility. None. Crisiant and Bram were his priorities, and nobody could blame him.

Second, Jeska agreed wholeheartedly with Rafe about staying strictly in Gallantrybanks, for he and Kazie had been married only a few months and he wanted as much time with her as possible before Touchstone left for Trials and the Royal.

Third, Cade had gone into yet another of his sulks and nobody wanted to be around him anyways.

Lastly, Fairwalk, far from despairing at the decrease in Touchstone's income, had decided that to deprive the city and the nobility of performances for a while would only increase the demand later this year.

"And besides that—do forgive me for mentioning it—but there's just the slightest hint of your getting stale. Not that you're not as good as ever, but—"

Before Cade or Mieka or Jeska could protest, Rafe nodded agreement with Fairwalk. "I'm sick of feeling that it's naught but a job of work," he said. "Like a being bricklayer or a hack driver. Good at the craft, no mistakes and no accidents—but nothing to point to with pride anymore."

Cade scowled and muttered, "You're just browned off because I haven't done up your children's play yet."

"You'll get to it when you get to it," Rafe replied. "Bram's not old enough yet to enjoy it, anyways. But Kearney's right, and we all of us know it. We've gone flat. It's habit, like we were back in littleschool reciting the multiplication tables. The only challenge we've had in the last year was that play of yours, Cayden, and—"

"Don't you fucking *dare* say it's my fault!"

"Of course it wasn't," Lord Fairwalk soothed. "People just weren't prepared for it, don't you see. One day they will be, and it will be a triumph."

"So we'll be taking a break, then?" Jeska asked. "From each other, as well as the work?"

"Suits me down to the ground," Cade snapped. "Leaves me in peace and quiet to write."

Thus Mieka had left his daughter in his own mother's care at Wistly, given his mother-in-law enough money to go and do whatever she liked for a month, and taken his wife to Lilyleaf. He'd originally thought she might like to spend the time at Frimham. Jinsie had disabused him of this notion the instant he mentioned it.

"Amongst all the people who knew her when she was scrabbling for a living? Once again, brother darling, you provide living proof that there ought to be laws against staggering stupidity."

"I thought she might want to see her old friends."

"And swan about with you on her arm, saying, 'Look at my adorable famous rich husband!' without actually having to say it out loud? Mayhap. But she'd also know they'd be sneering and gossiping behind her back. You're a *theater* player, remember!"

He was just as glad she took the sting out of it with a grin. "Oh, all right, then. Lilyleaf, I suppose."

Jinsie nodded her approval. "Nobody knows her there, and she can play the Great Lady to her heart's content."

No denying the spite tingeing his sister's voice—and no grin this time—but he had to admit she was right. So to Lilyleaf they went, and Mieka's reward for a month of tedium was a wonderful peace in his household. Well, tedium punctuated almost every night and quite a few mornings and afternoons with spectacular bed-sport. He had the distinct impression that Croodle knew all about that, too.

The renewal of their commitment to each other had been his wife's idea. One night she arranged with Croodle to give them an intimate supper upstairs in their sitting room, with flowers and candles and a new silk-and-lace bedrobe that matched her iris-blue eyes, and she'd given him the heavy silver bracelet.

"When we were married," she'd said shyly, "I couldn't afford to give you anything but that thin little chain. This is more manly, don't you think?"

The next day she'd seen the pearl, and he'd bought it for her.

"We must have someone bespell the clasps, just as the Good Brother did at our wedding," she'd said when he fastened the silver chain round her slender neck. "Mayhap Cayden would do it for us this time."

"That would be nice," he'd replied in as neutral a voice as he could manage, privately vowing that Cayden was absolutely the last person he would ask to perform the service, and not just because Cayden was the very last person who would want to.

As he waited in the kitchen of Wistly Hall for water to boil in the kettle, he thought over Cade's revelation of a few days ago. No Elsewhens. No dreams. No turns where he glimpsed a tantalizing hint of a possible future. Mieka had become so used to this odd Fae-bequeathed magic of Cade's that knowing it was gone set him off balance. And that was ludicrous, because he hadn't even noticed. How could he—how could any of them—have been so utterly unaware of what Cade had done? They were taking each other for granted. All the talent and skill and inspiration and sheer delight in playing that was Touchstone had become routine. Rafe had had the right of it, and no mistake. Not just their performances but their friendship had gone stale, too.

He ought to have known that something peculiar had happened to the Elsewhens. It said shameful things about him that he had not noticed. He could argue to himself all he liked that after that horrible night when Cade had seen Briuly and Alaen find The Rights of the Fae, talking about any Elsewhen was the very last thing he ought to do. He supposed it had become habit, this not talking; for the rest of that Royal Circuit, and on into the winter, and then through the spring, and then—good Gods, it really had been almost two years. Was it the compassion and consideration of a friend that had kept him silent, or the total self-absorption of an essentially selfish man?

The difference in the magic Cade used for the withies ought to have been a clue. But how could Mieka have explained it? *"It just doesn't feel like you anymore"*? Cade would have mocked his vagueness, denying that anything was different at all.

And then there was the *clever and mad* that Blye had prescribed years ago. Cade didn't laugh the way he'd used to at Mieka's jokes. Those first years had been such marvelous fun— oh, they all snarked and sniped at each other, to be sure, and pranked each other unmercifully—and here he winced, recalling what had happened when he finally got back at Rafe for the vanishing-clothes trick at the Lilyleaf baths.

Almost a year after the incident, everyone else seemed to have given up trying to scheme any retaliation. Mieka was simply biding his time, working out the best method of revenge. At last, one morning while Rafe was sleeping off a colossal drunk, which Mieka had occasioned through the simple expedient of paying for two rounds out of every three, the luxuriant black beard of which the fettler was so proud had undergone a radical transformation. Armed with a pair of nail scissors, which he reasoned was the only instrument delicate enough for such precise work, Mieka trimmed Rafe's beard as if it were a decorative hedge.

Rafe woke to find that both cheeks now sported stripes, his chin had been snipped almost clean, and his mustache had all but vanished except for two little tufts at the corners of his mouth.

There were no roars of outrage. There was no physical retaliation, nor even a threat of it; not a word about taking Mieka apart and putting him back together sideways. All Rafe did was examine himself very closely in a looking glass, arch his brows at Mieka—who stood there with Cade and Jeska, all of them holding their breath—and ask to borrow a razor so he could scrape his beard off altogether.

"It'll grow back," was all he said.

His lack of response, and the shock on Cade's and Jeska's faces, had been worse for Mieka than having his lungs ripped out through his nostrils. And he at last understood that he'd simply gone too far.

By way of apology, he'd behaved himself meticulously through the rest of that Royal Circuit. Eventually Rafe's beard regained its accustomed splendor. But having to think twice and even thrice about any larks he might dream up cramped Mieka's style. Truth be told, he hadn't pranked anyone in a very long time. Life, he found, was exceedingly dull when he had to rein in his sense of humor. And now here was another summer to be spent in the wagon with all his wilder impulses in check—and celibate besides. Something would have to be done.

Tea and toast, butter and apricot jam—Mieka surveyed the breakfast tray and wished he had a flower to decorate it with. If there'd been a primed withie handy, he could have worked a pretty little nosegay. A real shame it was, that it took someone else's magic added to his own to produce even the smallest effect. Like that joke he'd pulled at Lilyleaf, visiting the offices of the local broadsheet in a skirt and blouse created by one of Cade's withies that retained some magic from the night before. Oh, that had been a triumph, that had—he grinned to himself for a moment on his walk upstairs, then sighed and scowled, for Cade had absolutely forbidden him to do the like ever again with magic. That hadn't prevented him from one of the best stunts of all: showing up at one of their giggings dressed as a woman, and the comical patter between him and Cade that had set the audience to howling with laughter. It had been so much *fun*— and he resolved on the instant to work that trick again, for the benefit of an audience and to take that horrid half-dead weariness from Cade's gray eyes.

He woke his wife gently. She blinked a few times, stretched smooth white arms, and smiled up at him from the pillow. Gods and Angels and everything holy, she was beautiful. The most beautiful thing he'd ever seen. Any man lucky enough to be married to this much perfection who voluntarily left it for months at a time was nothing more than a damned fool. And there it was, the central dilemma of his life: He missed her desperately when he was away from her, but when he was with her, he missed his other life just as much. He was tempted to do what Vered Goldbraider had done on the last Royal: send his new wife, Bexan, to various of their stops on the circuit so she'd be there waiting for him and they could have a few nights together while the Shadowshapers performed. But Vered and Bexan had no children as yet, and whereas Jindra would be perfectly happy to spend the whole summer at Wistly—and Mishia would be thrilled to take care of her—he was sure his wife would pine for their little girl. Besides, traveling at an easy pace to Lilyleaf and back in one of Lord Kearney Fairwalk's carriages was one thing; day after day on the public coach was quite another. It wasn't as if she could come along in the wagon and snuggle beside him in his hammock each night.

"All better today?" he asked, setting the breakfast tray on the bed.

"Oh, yes. I don't know why riding in the wagon always makes me feel so dreadful."

And there was another reason he couldn't bring her along. The *real* reason, of course, was that none of his partners would stand for it. Lord and Lady forfend that they'd have to watch their language, leave alone abandon sleeping naked on hot summer nights.

"'Twas a thoughtful thing you did, giving Jez that pillow."

"All Jindra's idea. She helped with the stitching, and only pricked her finger twice, imagine! Is he better?"

"Mum says so. Mistress Mirdley's of the opinion he'll walk with a limp the rest of his life, but then she doesn't know how stubborn he is."

She munched a bite of toast, sipped tea, and sighed. "I think he'd look terribly stylish with one of those carved canes coming into fashion at Court. What are they calling them? Swagger sticks?"

"With a gold dragon's head for a handle," he agreed. "I'll mention it to Fa. He ought to have enough wood around his workshop to put something together."

"Does anybody know how it all happened?"

Mieka deliberately didn't think about the crimped end of a hallmarked withie he was keeping in a wad of wool inside his trouser pocket. "There'll be some sort of investigation. But they won't find that Jed or Jez did anything wrong, or were careless, or anything of the sort."

"Of course not," she stated indignantly. "I'm sure they'll find that it was naught but a dreadful accident."

"Mm." The lacy little sleeve of her nightdress had slipped down one shoulder and it took him a few moments to register what she said next.

"I thought—I mean, I was hoping that mayhap I didn't feel well . . . for a different reason."

Mieka saw the blush on her cheeks, and the sweep of heavy lashes as she lowered her gaze. His hands were shaking slightly as he moved the tray to the floor. "Mayhap," he said, hearing how thick his own voice sounded, "mayhap I could make you feel *much* better right now."

The blush deepened, and as she looked up at him with her wonderful iris-blue eyes, his last coherent thought was what a fool he was ever to leave her bed at all.

Touchstone departed for Seekhaven a few days later. Rather than drive the wagon through the maze of Gallantrybanks streets to collect everyone, they all spent the night before at Wistly. Jeska and Kazie arrived shortly before tea. Rafe and Crisiant were there by nightfall with their little boy, Bram. (It had become fashionable to give a child the mother's maiden name; the boy was lucky that Crisiant had been born Bramblecotte and not Rosecresting or Sweetwood). Cade showed up later that evening with Derien, Mistress Mirdley, Jed, and Blye. It was quite the extended family gathered the next morning to bid them farewell, Mieka reflected, remembering that first time when it was just the four of them yawning their way onto the King's coach.

Jezael insisted on being helped downstairs to join in seeing them off. Mieka noted with puzzlement the exchange of a furtive, significant glance between Cade and Mistress Mirdley when Derien commented on the pillow cushioning Jez's leg and Jindra told him who had made it. When Jez assured the little girl that he felt much better because of it, another glance went back and forth. But Mieka forgot about asking its cause when his mother began the unrewarding task of getting everyone into the wagon who should be there, and keeping everyone who shouldn't (Tavier, in particular) out. Mieka kissed his wife and daughter, promised Jinsie that he'd remember to look up her friends at the University in Shollop and his mother that he'd remember to send more letters this time, was admonished by each of them not to tell any more lies than were strictly necessary, and turned to climb the steps into the wagon.

He hadn't even put his foot on the second step when a hire-hack pulled up just in front of the wagon and decanted two frowning gentlemen in severe brown suits with the sea green collars and cuffs signifying a Royal office of some sort. To be fair, the short one probably couldn't help his expression; he was quite obviously of Gnomish descent, with the heavy scowling brow that sometimes went with that bloodline. The other, just as obviously Human to his toenails, simply looked sour and disapproving.

"Wistly Hall? Residence of Jezael Windthistle?" he demanded of Mieka's father.

"Yes. And you might be . . . ?"

"Royal Inquisitors."

Mieka was abruptly reminded of the glass shard still in his pocket, and cursed himself. He'd meant to give it to Blye earlier on, and forgot.

Calm as always, Hadden replied, "If you've any questions or suchlike for my son, it will have to wait. He's still recovering from the accident."

"Accident," muttered the Gnome.

Cade pushed past Mieka out of the wagon and descended to the cobbles. "What's the difficulty here?" he asked, drawing himself up to his full six-foot-four.

"Inquisitors Office?" Mishia said suddenly. "Why would the Inquisitors Office be interested in—?"

"Purely a formality, I'd wager," Hadden contributed.

"If you're not here for any of the members of Touchstone," said Mishia, "then would you please move your hack so they can get started for Seekhaven? They're due at Trials, you know."

Yazz sat forward on his bench and rumbled, "Move!"

All this while there was frantic movement by the front door, partially screened by the crowd of family. Mieka hopped up to the top step of the wagon and peered over everyone's heads just in time to see Blye and Jed helping Jez inside. The door closed behind them. Mieka located the bronze-gold head of his wife and jumped down to the cobbles. He dug the wadded cloth from his pocket, slithering between Cade and Crisiant and Kazie and Petrinka, and pressed the wrapped glass into her hand.

"Give this to Blye—she'll know what it is," he said urgently.

"Miek!" Yazz thundered. "Wagon! *Now!*"

"Why?" she asked. "What is it?"

"Just give it to Blye. That's me darlin' girl." He kissed her hard on the lips and wove back through the crowd to the wagon.

The hack driver had obligingly moved his vehicle. Mieka made a leap for the steps. Cade caught his hand and hauled him up as the wagon jerked forward.

"What was all that about?" Cade got the steps folded inside and shut the wagon door. "What was that you gave her?"

Mieka flopped into one of the chairs and looked up at Cade. "Something Jinsie found in the rubble. She gave it to me that night, remember? It's the crimp end of a withie. One of Splithook's."

Cade understood at once. "You mean one of Black Lightning's."

Rafe turned from the window where he was getting his last look at his wife and son. "If they've found any glass—or if someone was obviously injured by flying glass—"

"Blye's a glasscrafter," Jeska interrupted. "And they'll say it's hers."

"No glass in the building yet," Cade argued. "She was there to take the final measurements. Mieka, are you sure it's identifiable as Master Splithook's work?"

"His hallmark's there for anyone to see."

"But not to prove where Jinsie found it," Rafe said. "And before you have a seizure, Cade, and order Yazz to turn around so we can go back, consider this: If nobody can find anything wrong with Jed and Jez's work, they'll find something wrong with their work anyway." When Mieka opened his mouth to protest, Rafe pointed a long finger at him. "It can't be an accident, not if a withie was used the way a withie isn't s'posed to be used—the way *we* use them, or near to it, every time we shatter one at the end of a show. So if it's not an accident, and no other cause can be found—and *won't* be found, because there's a withie involved—then it'll have to be the Windthistle Brothers' fault."

Cade was nodding slowly. "Sheer chance that Jinsie found it. Any other piece of glass—there's a specific formula for a withie, they all use it by law, so there's no identifying whose it was but for the crimp end."

"And it's not just Black Lightning uses Splithook's work," Jeska said. "Some of the newer groups—"

"But the point," Cade interrupted, "is that to use a withie like that requires a Wizard or an Elf. And only theater groups use withies, and theater people are mainly Wizard or Elf, no matter what else may be rattling around in their backgrounds."

"And the person who dreamed up using a withie like that was your very own grandmother," Mieka said. "How many people know how to do it?"

"Hundreds, for all I know. And not all of them in the theater. You're wrong about blaming Blye, though, Rafe. It wouldn't make any sense. Why would she wreck her husband's business? Same thing goes for any of us. We're known for exploding the damned things, but why would we do such a thing to Mieka's brothers?"

"So, as I said, the blame will fall on Jed and Jez, because it can't fall on a withie made by Master Splithook. That would mean that somebody had deliberately set it to explode. The only people who could do that are Wizards or Elves, and *that* would call up too many bad memories that nobody wants to talk about. So Jed and Jez will be held responsible."

"But that's not fair!" Mieka cried. "And who'd want to do such a thing?"

"Oh, use what brains the Old Gods gave you!" Rafe snapped. "Anything that touches somebody we love touches *us*."

"If we're fretting ourselves over this," Jeska added, "we won't be as good at Trials. And who benefits from *that*?"

"So it does come back to Black Lightning," Rafe concluded. "Although why they'd be stupid enough to use one of their own withies—"

"I think you're wrong," Cade said softly. He turned from the cupboard where his things were stored, paper and pen and ink in hand. Rafe pulled out the table and kicked the supporting leg into place. Cade sat and as he began writing, said, "I'm telling Blye to stall. Not to answer any questions, and especially not to reveal that withie. What did you tell your wife, Mieka?"

"Only to give it to Blye. She doesn't even know what it is. And why are we wrong?"

Rather than reply, he wrote rapidly for a minute or two. By the time he'd finished and folded the letter, Rafe was looking enlightened, Jeska was looking worried, and Mieka was looking from one to the other of them in total confusion. Rising to his feet, bracing himself with one hand on the wall as the wagon rocked slightly over uneven paving stones, Cade got a stick of sealing wax from his cupboard, then sat down again.

"While it's true that the Archduke forbade Black Lightning from playing any more tricks on us like that meddling fettler two years ago, it's also true that, as Rafe says, hurting people we're close to hurts us. Withies are used by tregetours and gliskers—Wizards and Elves, in other words. So if anybody was obviously harmed by flying glass, or if a bit of it was found and could be identified as a withie, since Blye hadn't put any glass into the building, and bottle glass and so forth are different from withie glass, the logical inference is that a Wizard or an Elf, probably somebody in theater, primed a withie to explode and damage the scaffolding. But I think that's what everybody's *supposed* to think. I think we're *supposed* to blame Black Lightning even if the crimp end of that withie hadn't been found."

"Why?" Mieka demanded.

"Because if it's made public—if, for instance, we talked to Tobalt Fluter about it and he published something in *The Nayword*—then what Rafe said about things nobody wants to remember being remembered will hold true. Which directs a lot of suspicious eyes at theater folk in general and me in particular. It was my grandmother, as you so delicately reminded me, who thought up that use for withies, and there's plenty still alive who suffered the results of her inventiveness. Now, who doesn't like theater folk?"

Mieka was completely lost. He didn't have to say so; he knew it was clear enough in his face. Cade lit a candle with a flint-rasp and held it to the stick of sealing wax, then smeared a dark red glob onto the folded letter.

"Oh, come on, Mieka. Who arrived quite inexplicably at the scene with Lord Piercehand?"

Jeska's chiseled jaw was hanging open. "*Princess Iamina?*"

Mieka began to see some of it. "You said she denied ever having seen a play—and she's been flagrantly religious the last year or so."

"She's thief-thick with the Archduchess these days." Cade looked round for something to press into the hot wax, and came up with a chess piece from the box on the shelf. He upended the piece and pushed its crown into the wax and went on, "I keep waiting for my mother to drop them, you know. For all that she turns up every week at High Chapel, religion bores her. And both the Archduchess and Princess Iamina are just a little too pious these days even for her to stomach."

Jeska took the chess piece and began picking bits of wax from its carved wood. "The Archduchess had to forswear her own religion in order to marry the Archduke. It's said that under Iamina's influence, she's become very enthusiastic about certain aspects of ours."

Mieka was still scowling. "So you're saying Iamina just had to come along and admire her handiwork?" He shuddered. "People could've *died*!"

Rafe cocked a satirical eye at the chess piece and said, "How inappropriate of you, Cade, not to have used a highly symbolic pawn."

Cade grinned at him. "Feeling just a little used, are we?"

Seeing nothing funny about this, Mieka demanded, "Who would she know that's able to prime a withie that way?"

"I'm sure there are quite a few left who remember what my grandmother taught them. And since when does a highborn like Iamina or the Archduchess give the tiniest shit about the common folk?"

"Iamina hates us," Jeska murmured. "We've made a fool of her more than once." He looked hard at Cade. "Did you see this? Do you know for sure because of—?"

Mieka almost blurted it out. He actually bit both lips together to keep from saying it, from saying that Cade was refusing his Elsewhens these days.

Cade was shaking his head. "I don't have to see it. Pull the bell, would you? We have to stop and find somebody to run this back to Wistly Hall. Anybody got any change to give the lad?"

A street brat was found who looked relatively clean, if not entirely trustworthy. To Wistly Hall, he was told, double-quick, and there was a nice shiny royal waiting for him there to add to the coins pressed into his palm along with the letter.

While this transaction was being completed, Mieka puzzled through Cade's reasoning. Archduchess Panshilara and Princess Iamina had arranged for a withie to explode at the Gallery work site—how? Black fucking Lightning used Splithook's withies; Thierin Knottinger would be delighted to do a favor for the Archduke's wife. Unless that was a ruse to make them *think* it was Black Lightning, known to loathe Touchstone, while the real culprit went unsuspected. But how could anyone have known that the crimp end would be found and identified? Sloppy work; when Mieka shattered a withie, nothing was left but tiny stardust shards. So if they hadn't intended for the glass to be found, then they couldn't have intended the blame to fall on Black Lightning specifically or theater folk in general, which canceled out Cade's notion about Iamina's new piety and ostentatious disapproval of the theater. Yet it remained that a withie had been used, and in the way invented by Cade's grandmother, Lady Kiritin, which nobody wanted to talk about and which had been the purpose behind the laws forbidding Wizards to work with glass. If those responsible thought the means would go undetected, then all that stuff about Wizards and Elves and theater folk and withies used as weapons was naught but nonsense.

Which left the question of why anyone would want to stage such a dangerous "accident" in the first place. Was it to destroy Windthistle Brothers as a business? To cause such anguishing in Touchstone that their performances suffered and they were relegated to third flight on the Royal—or perhaps taken down to the Ducal Circuit? *That* pointed once again to Black Lightning. But if so, why had Princess Iamina come along with Piercehand to view the calamity?

Good Gods, his brain was getting as twisty-turny as Cayden's.

The wagon had started up again. Everyone was sitting down, frowning over his own thoughts. Suddenly Mieka burst out, "Lord Piercehand!"

"What about him?" Rafe asked.

"It's his Gallery, ain't it? What if it's naught to do with Jed and Jez or us or Iamina or Panshilara or anything else? What if it's to do with *him*?"

5

Cade looked long and hard at Mieka. "Why would Black Lightning want to do him an injury?"

"Who says it really was Black Lightning?" Mieka challenged. "All we know for certain sure is that the withie was made by Master Splithook. And that Piercehand owns the building that parts of it fell down."

"Hmm." He sat back in his chair, knees splayed. "Didn't they sail on one of his ships to the Continent last year?"

"And the year before," Jeska put in. "Just to Vathis, for a dozen or so shows. That makes twice they've gone to the Continent. The Shadowshapers flat-out won't set foot there, but the Sparks did for a fortnight or so last year, and there's talk that Hawk's Claw will be invited soon."

Rafe had by now hooked up his hammock and was stretched out in it, arms folded behind his head. "Did their cabins on board his ships not please them?" he inquired acidly. "Not grand enough? Slops not emptied more than twice a day? Food and wine not what they expected?"

"Auntie Brishen," Mieka said, as if that solved the whole puzzle.

Cade snorted a laugh. "So now it's Auntie Brishen who used a withie to make such a mess at Piercehand's Gallery?"

"Don't be such a quat. One of her letters to Mum complained that she can't get a contract to export her whiskey to the Continent. Most of the demand there is for rumbullion from the Islands."

Rafe began to look interested. "And who is it imports most of the rumbullion? Lord Rolon Piercehand."

"Not everything's to do with *us,*" Jeska mused. "Plenty of private begrudgements going on."

Cade frowned at him. "Are you saying I'm obsessed with plots inside plots and all of them to get at us?"

"Well," Rafe pointed out reasonably, "you didn't see anything about it in advance, did you? We've always taken that to mean that nothing you can do will change what will happen. There's a good chance, then, that it's naught to do with us at all."

Once again, at the oblique mention of the Elsewhens, Cade felt Mieka looking at him. Kind of him, Cade thought with a mental sneer, not to reveal that the Elsewhens were a thing of the past.

"Both the rumbullion and Black Lightning have sailed on Piercehand's ships," Rafe was saying. "Both are in demand on the Continent."

"But the one preceded the other!" Jeska exclaimed. "Kazie hears from her people from time to time, and the news these days is that they're planting more and more sugarcane in the Islands, and production of rumbullion has got really brutal because of the demand. When did the demand start? Right after Black Lightning played Vathis!"

Cade shook his head. "You're reaching for something that isn't there." But the memory came to him, unbidden—and it really was a memory, something that had really happened. Mieka, bristling with outrage: *"You think I'm some sort of backspanger hired by the management to waft a bit of dry-mouth around the tavern?"* Jeska, explaining the trick: *"Those of us Elves as has a bit of glisker magic, but too young or not good enough, tavern owners hire them—but not too often, mind, or it'd give the game away. Easier if you're kagged, of course. That way, nobody suspects Elf when all of a sudden they're perishin' for another drink."*

What if Black Lightning had created during their Vathis shows a preference for rumbullion? Cade knew they had another ploy: an ability to direct specific magic at specific types of people. Anyone but Wizards and Elves would feel the shame and the stain of their Goblin or Gnomish or Piksey or Troll blood. Did that match up somehow with this? Assuming that *this,* the lingering suggestion that one sort of drink was superior to another—no, that wasn't right. It would be an inclination, and mayhap more than an inclination, for one thing over another. Did Black Lightning know how to create a desire in their audiences? Not just a preference, but a need and a want and—and even a *compulsion*?

"Not possible," he said aloud, and the three stared at him. "What we make of emotion through magic lasts only as long as the performance. It can't go on for days or weeks at a time."

Rafe lifted his head slightly. "If you've never tried, how can you be certain?"

Cade heard himself spluttering. "It's not—I mean, it just isn't—I don't know how it would—" Then, with a glance at Mieka's fiendish grin, everything resolved itself into a simple, "I absolutely forbid it!"

The Elf shrugged, magnificently unconcerned. "But we could, y'know. Might take some effort, but I'll wager it could be done."

Cade shivered and shook his head again. "No. It's not—it's not *honest.*"

"Is *anything* we make them experience during a show 'honest'?" Jeska asked. "Fabricated feelings, contrived sensations—"

"But that's what they've come for!" He surged out of his chair and rummaged through the cupboard again. "Here—I wrote this a while ago, I wasn't going to work it up into anything for a goodly while longer—but you have to read it, and even if we don't perform it—well, there's nothing, really, to perform, but—"

"Give it here," Rafe said, maneuvering himself into a sitting position, hammock swaying. He read rapidly through the pages, looked at Cade for a long, hard minute, then began to recite the words aloud.

Cade heard only some of them, phrases here and there. He'd forgotten about this piece, deliberately forgotten, because it had come to him in an Elsewhen.

BUT TO FEEL IS WHAT YOU CAME HERE FOR. YOU KNOW IT, WE KNOW IT. . . .

In an abrupt panic, he wondered what other things he might have missed these past two years that could be worked into a play. So much of "Treasure" had come to him as an Elsewhen, as a dreaming, but he had stopped dreaming. What might he have lost by denying the Elsewhens?

YOU ARE SAFE HERE. WE WILL LET YOU FEEL ALL THE THINGS THAT FRIGHTEN YOU, ELUDE YOU, COMPEL YOU, SEDUCE YOU. THE THINGS YOU CANNOT ALLOW YOURSELF TO FEEL IN THEIR ENTIRETY, IN THEIR REALITY, IN THEIR MAD INTENSE AWFUL PURITY. . . .

What had Mieka said on his Namingday? That not all the Elsewhens had to hurt?

IT'S WHAT YOU CAME HERE FOR. IT'S WHAT YOU WANT. WHAT YOU NEED. . . .

What had he missed? What had he deliberately turned away from, rejected, refused to see and feel?

BUT DO NOT SAY, LATER, THAT YOU WERE TRICKED. YOU WERE NOT. YOU KNOW IT, WE KNOW IT. YOU WANT THIS. AND WE WILL PROVIDE.

Into a long silence he heard Jeska say softly, "We'll do this at Trials. We have to. There's so many these days looking sideways at the theater, ever since women began attending openly. This tells them why they need us. We have to do it, Cade."

"When did you write this?" Rafe asked in the same hushed tone.

"A while ago." He held out a hand for the pages, and Rafe gave them back.

"Don't you dare throw that away," Mieka warned.

Cade gave a guilty start. How had the Elf known how much Cade was regretting the impulse that had led him to share this vision?

"How does the rest of it go?" When Cade shook his head, helplessly this time, Mieka got up and took the pages right out of his hands. "Just us four standing there, and Jeska saying the words? That feels right, doesn't it, Rafe?"

"The plainest stage-clothes we've got," Jeska mused. "No backdrop, no effects. Just the words. But which play could possibly follow it?"

"It doesn't come at the beginning of a performance," Mieka chided. "It comes *after*."

"Something to take home with them," Rafe agreed.

Cade listened as they worked it out amongst themselves. For all that none of them had realized about the Elsewhens, professionally they knew him all too well.

"Speaking not just for ourselves," Mieka went on, "but for all players. Isn't that what you wanted, Cade? Isn't that what you saw?"

Before you stopped seeing anything? He could hear it as clearly as if Mieka had said it aloud. He couldn't look at him, nor at Rafe nor at Jeska. He could only stare at his hands that had written those words in a frenzy after having seen the whole of it in an Elsewhen. No, they didn't all hurt. This one hadn't. But so many of them had been agony, and him so powerless to know what actions of his would or would not make them come to pass that he was better off not seeing them. He was better off walling his conscious brain away from the Elsewhens that had been his torment, and looking at the world from a safe distance.

"I suppose that's what I meant by it," he said at last.

Trials at Seekhaven; Touchstone's sixth. It was difficult for Cade to remember how excited and scared he'd been that first time, how eager to prove himself and Touchstone. He had no doubts now about how good they were, and it really had nothing to do with Trials. Everyone knew that they would again come in second to the Shadowshapers. Mayhap next year, or the year after, Touchstone would come out on top. In a career that had seen triumph after triumph (with that one mortifying exception), this was Cade's secret striving: to best the Shadowshapers.

Both groups stayed at the Shadowstone Inn, as usual. Vered had left Bexan at home this time, and Mieka was fool enough to comment upon it that first evening in the taproom over dinner. The chill that descended over the table could have frozen the blood solid in their veins. Rauel began babbling about how dull it was for her when they were rehearsing or performing, and the weariness of the trip, and how this year they'd not be going back to Gallantrybanks before heading out on tour. Vered cut across this helpful speech with, "Someday women won't just be in the audience, or making suggestions to their husbands. They'll be on the stage."

Cade understood this to mean that Bexan had taken to interjecting her own ideas into the Shadowshapers' work. He tried to imagine Crisiant or Kazie or Mieka's wife giving advice on how to write or perform a play. The absurdity of it made him decide to make a little mischief.

"There've been lady poets before, y'know. Published, giving public recitals, and all that. Quite good, some of them."

"Writing's one thing," Sakary said. "Performing? And in

some of the places we've played through the years?"

"Not my daughters, that's for certain sure," Chat announced. "Look at the life we lead! A girl of eighteen or so, slogging round Albeyn on the Winterly Circuit?"

Rafe was smiling beneath his beard. "Seems to me we'll have to improve the reputation of theater folk before fathers will risk their daughters in so scandalous a profession."

"You're doing your part," Mieka told him. "Married, faithful, don't drink half what you used to—are you getting old, or just boring?"

"You might give it a try, old son," Rafe replied amiably.

Cade held his breath at this indirect reference to last year's misdeeds. Jeska, as he did so often, saved the situation by saying in his sweetest voice, "Especially the drinking. Running out of belt to put extra holes in, aren't you, Mieka?" He directed his gaze at the Elf's midsection.

"Not a bit of it," Rafe said as Mieka flushed crimson. "The leather shrunk in the wash."

They all laughed, and conversation meandered off in other directions. The third round of ale loosened Rauel's tongue enough to produce arch hints of spectacular plans for the Shadowshapers' final-night show.

"Finally finished your bloody—and I mean that in every sense of the word—play, then?" Cade asked Vered.

He pushed his drink away and looked sour. "Six different ways, all of 'em done so wrongly that not even I can get it sorted. Those books I borrowed of you were so much help that I've no notion what really did happen."

"And if not for you," Chat added, "and your stickler-ness for historical accuracy, he'd simply write the thing the way he thinks it ought to go, and be done with it."

"Historical accuracy," Mieka said amiably, "has little to recommend it. You tregetours, your problem is that you think too much. And thinking just gets in the way."

"Angels forfend that anybody should ever catch *you* thinking," Chat teased.

"You know as well as I do," Mieka shot back, "that the best players don't play the play—they *are* the play."

Sakary smirked. "A good thing, then, that Black Lightning is nowhere near the best."

"Heard aught of what they've come up with this year?" Jeska asked.

"Nothing new." Rauel lifted his glass to his partners in turn. "All the creative vision in Albeyn was with *us* this winter. Nothing left for anyone else."

The Shadowshapers grinned; Touchstone groaned; Cade took the opportunity to mention that their early rehearsal tomorrow meant they really ought to get some sleep. He didn't mention how much they needed the time in the rehearsal hall; they hadn't been onstage together in over a month. A review of all the Thirteen would be followed by a preliminary discussion of what Rafe had named "The Avowal." After a winter of few performances and a spring of almost none, Cade knew he ought to have had a whole new play ready. But he didn't. And the first person who remarked on it would get a withie right up his nose.

The day following an adequate if not inspired rehearsal, they were bidden to lunching with Princess Miriuzca. This had become something of a tradition at Trials. Other groups hid their envy behind jokes and sneers, but the fact of it was that Miriuzca liked each member of Touchstone and enjoyed their company. They were, after all, some of the first Albeyni she had ever met, and had done her nothing but kindnesses. Cade wondered occasionally whether or not she had forgiven him for performing the play that had seemingly made Prince Ashgar weep, thus convincing her that he was a sensitive, gentle, tenderhearted man and their marriage would be unadulterated bliss. Still, as

Mieka had told him several times (with increasing exasperation), nobody forced Miriuzca to believe what she'd believed, let alone marry the miserable cullion.

"She really shouldn't be inviting us," Jeska said worriedly as they presented themselves at Seekhaven Castle. "She's just had a baby, and her father died a few weeks ago—"

"And she's probably looking for a little distraction from both those things," Rafe interrupted. "Between the congratulations and the condolences, between the happiness and the grief—she won't know what to feel from one minute to the next. Crisiant didn't."

Cade trusted Rafe to say all the right things. He had experience, after all, of a woman who had given birth and lost her father all in the same month. A tregetour was supposed to be able to imagine what such things would feel like; he was supposed to be able to project himself into any sort of person in any situation. But lately Cade had come to believe that the only feelings he could feel were his own, and those he got rid of as quickly as he could into the withies. And perhaps the lack of performances that used up his emotions was causing his sleep to be even more fractured than usual. He'd observed long ago that Mieka became tense and uneasy if denied the release of a performance. Mayhap he was made the same way. He'd always thought that he sluiced out all his emotions when he was writing—and that outlet had been closed off for a goodly long while, too.

The Princess awaited them inside a charming white summer-house, octagonal in shape, with curtains on four sides made of multicolored ribbons. These blew and tangled in the slight breeze, but the table was set far enough from them so that Miriuzca and her guests wouldn't be constantly picking silk out of the soup. The footman who had escorted Touchstone across the lawns announced them, bowed, and departed, and it was left to the Princess herself to make introductions.

"My brother, Tregrefin Ilesko," she said, indicating with a

smile and a nod the young man seated beside her. "He's so eager to meet you—I write much in my letters. Do please sit down and be comfortable, won't you?"

Tregrefin Ilesko didn't look eager. He looked sullen, which suited his narrow features admirably. He shared with his sister the somber dark gray of mourning and a pair of very blue eyes, but that was all. When his sister said *please* to a group of nobodies, his pencil-thin black eyebrows nearly disappeared into an unruly thatch of black hair. He was handsome in a brooding sort of way, and looked to be about eighteen or nineteen years old.

Commonplace civilities were exchanged as food was set before them—slices of cold roast chicken and three sauces to dip it in, a salad of fruit and walnuts, and mazey-cakes baked with yellow ground meal from some foreign land or other. Wine was poured, the servants effaced themselves, and it became evident that Miriuzca was the eager one, asking questions about Trials designed to acquaint her brother with the whole process of theater that she adored. Jeska provided answers and charming smiles; Mieka contributed several stories of life on the circuits suitable for Royal ears; Rafe explained the functions of masquer, glisker, fettler, and tregetour. Cade said very little, for he was busy disciplining his mind against an Elsewhen that battered and howled at him like a hound frantic to come in from a thunderstorm.

Ought he to let it in? Despite what Rafe had said about the accident at the Gallery—that unless Cade could have changed something, he wouldn't have seen anything about it in advance—that day had been enough of a shock to make him question, just a little, his decision to banish all Elsewhens from his mind. Mieka's words kept coming back to him: *"My brother's likely crippled, all because you think your Elsewhens are a bore."*

"Yes," the Princess was saying, "I'm only a half-sister, and we look nothing alike except for our eyes—that's Father, and all of us have his eyes. So do my children. And so will Ilesko's," she said, fondly teasing, "if he ever finds a girl who suits him to becoming their mother!"

"Is that what brings you to Albeyn?" Rafe asked. "Apart from visiting Her Royal Highness, and finding comfort in your mutual grief, that is."

"A girl from this place?"

The young man did not elaborate on his obvious distaste, for Miriuzca swiftly interrupted with, "I've warned all my ladies not to lose their hearts to him, Master Threadchaser."

Cade watched the Tregrefin's lip curl before a smile was forced to the corners of his mouth. So: he did not like the ladies of Albeyn. He probably did not like the gentlemen of Albeyn, either, nor Albeyn as a whole. Why, then, was he here? Surely not to console Miriuzca. Anyone less likely to provide solace in her sorrow could not be imagined. Well, her husband, perhaps—but Cade knew himself to be prejudiced.

The sweet was served. Some whimsical pastry cook had concocted two towers of cake on either side of a river of blue frosting meant to represent the Keeps and the Gally. Windows were picked out in candied fruit, and the green whipped-cream lawns were dotted with yellow and purple sugar sprinkles representing flowers. How they were to eat this elaborate creation was beyond Cade but, perhaps predictably, not beyond Mieka. He snatched up a knife and decapitated one of the towers, placing it on Miriuzca's plate, then lopped off the top of the other one for her brother.

And at that point, the Elsewhen shrieked at Cade, breaking through the chinks of doubt. A hundred screaming voices; a feeling of horrible panic; the crashing of stone onto stone and into deep water; the smells of fire and the smoke of black powder exploding—

No! I won't! Leave me alone!

He recovered himself and glanced quickly around him. Everyone was laughing at the way Mieka was carving up the Keeps. No one was paying any attention to Cade. It hadn't been a full-on Elsewhen, but all the same it left him with a taste of sick dread in his mouth, and when Mieka offered him a plate of cake and frosting and candies and whipped cream, he thought that he'd vomit.

"My brother," Miriuzca said, "brought with him people who will interest you. They are players in the theater, from—where are they from, Ilesko?"

Cade swallowed wine and commanded himself to pay attention. The word that answered the Princess's question might have been anything. He didn't recognize it, couldn't even sort out its syllables in his head. Derien would have known, he told himself. Derien, who loved maps and knew more about where Touchstone had been on the Continent than Touchstone did. If anyone found out what Derien's magic could do, he'd be seeing all those places and dozens more on a quest for gold. Could an Elsewhen warn Cayden about who might have designs on his adored little brother? He repressed a shiver.

"Will they be performing for the Court?" Jeska asked politely.

"I think yes," the Tregrefin said. "Plays differ here. Not only the making and doing, but the meaning."

"Indeed? May one ask how they differ from what we perform?"

"No magic, of course."

Cade understood then the source of his stiffness, his disapproval. He ought to have known. Miriuzca had taken a while to become accustomed to the magic practiced every day in her new country—but she was used to it by now and more than used to it, for had she not given Blye the Gift of the Gloves, signifying her Royal patronage? All at once he wondered when, if ever, Miriuzca would ask him to seal the little glass box Blye had made and he had given her back in her own country, a box to hold a keepsake safe forever.

With that thought, another Elsewhen hammered at him. He escaped most of it, but for a quick vision of that glass box gleaming at its edges with magic, and a tiny lock of golden hair, tied with a forget-me-never blue ribbon, inside.

Mieka was saying, "D'you know, back when we were in Vathis, a boy tried to steal one of our withies—thought it would give him the magic he needed to be a player." He sighed sadly. "It's there or it's not, and there's no stealing it."

"But how do they manage?" Rafe asked. "Without magic to set the place and feel of the thing—?"

"Words," Cade said. "They do it all with words."

"But *how?*"

"Beautiful words," the Tregrefin agreed. "Words to honor the Lord and the Lady. Words of faith. Words to say that right is right and wrongness is wrongness."

And magic, Cade assumed, was a wrongness. "I'll be interested to see them perform," he said, meaning it more than the young man could ever know.

Ilesko took that as encouragement to elaborate. "Words to make mind again of truth. All are birthed with—" He broke off, asked his sister something in their language, and nodded his gratitude when she replied. "All are birthed with inborn bent to sin. Sometimes one, sometimes many. No escaping from inborn sin."

Cade had never heard anything so sad in his life. He didn't think much about religion; he went to Chapel when he couldn't avoid it, and knew all the stories from the *Consecrations,* but the subject wasn't anything that took up long hours of sleeplessness. Lord and Lady, Angels, Old Gods—people believed as it suited their characters and lineages. But nobody talked about innocent children being born not so innocent at all, children born with inherent sin that they could never escape.

A swift look at Mieka and Rafe showed him that they weren't exactly charmed by that notion, either. Jeska went on smiling slightly, nodding slightly, thoughts and feelings hidden behind his beautiful golden face.

"Plays," concluded Ilesko, "are for showing the sin, and how it is punished, and what to do for the earning forgiveness."

Miriuzca was looking a little desperate. Cade imitated Jeska, knowing the smile to be infinitely less effective on his infinitely less beautiful face, and said, "Our theater was once much the same, you know. Plays were made to encourage people to behave honorably towards each other, and to educate them about history, and the ways of the Lord and the Lady and Angels and Old Gods—"

"That is a very great wrongness," Ilesko interrupted severely. "There is the Lord and there is the Lady and that is all. The other things—they do not matter. They do not exist." He turned to his sister, who looked uncomfortable. "You are now believing these things that you should not."

"It is the custom of Albeyn, which is now my home," she said with simple dignity. "And in Albeyn the theater has expanded beyond plays about morality, and now a tregetour can write about anything. Is this not so, Master Silversun?"

"Your Royal Highness is perfectly correct. Theater has and indeed must move on from the traditional plays, and explore what every person thinks and feels. Has Your Royal Highness ever seen the Shadowshapers' play, 'A Life in a Day'?"

"Oh, yes!"

The more she praised it, the less her brother liked it.

Jeska explained the difficulties of having two masquers onstage at once, and how it complicated the work of the glisker and fettler; Rafe expressed himself grateful that Cade and Jeska were too much the individualists to permit more than one tregetour or more than one masquer into Touchstone's plays, because he and Mieka had enough trouble with the pair of them as it was.

"How many masquers appear in plays on the Continent?" Rafe asked.

"For the play they perform, five." He ticked them off on his fingers. "A learned man named Vaustas, a nobleman and his wife, and the Lord and the Lady."

Rafe grinned across the table at Mieka. "You hear that? Five of them onstage!"

The Elf gave an exaggerated shudder. "I'm good, but nobody's *that* good! I'd get so confused, I'd dress the nobleman in a ball gown and his wife in full armor!"

"The Lord would have long blond curls and a feathered fan," Cade said deliberately, unsurprised to see the Tregrefin's flinch of disgust.

"And the scholar would smell of the stables!" Miriuzca laughed.

"The masquers," the Tregrefin said humorlessly, "do not become confused. They are knowing the importance of their roles and the words."

"*All* done with words." Rafe sighed. "Well, Mieka, that's us out of work!"

The Tregrefin looked as if he thought that would not be a tragic turn of events.

By the time a last round of tea was served, Cade considered that he had the boy's measure. Snobbishly confident, self-righteous in the way only an eighteen-year-old could be (from the vantage point of his twenty-four years, Cade was honest enough to admit that he was living in the skin of the perfect priggish pattern for this attitude); pious, and militant in his piety; wary of magic, and giving Mieka's ears many nervous sidelong glances. Condescension and disapproval competed to a standstill on his dark face. Cade wondered suddenly if the Tregrefin had met Princess Iamina yet.

Miriuzca turned her face to the spring sunlight and smiled. "I so enjoy Seekhaven," she said. "Not as formal as the Palace or even the Keeps. Though it's fun to be there on tour days."

When her brother looked blank and baffled, Rafe said, "There are days for schoolchildren to visit, and days when the Keeps are open to the public." He smiled over at Cade. "Site of our first foray into theater, wouldn't you say?"

"I never looked at it like that before, but you're right!" He laughed—it felt good and genuine to laugh. "We escaped our teachers and ran up and down the halls and stairways—the Keeps have a lot of stairways!—battling horrible monsters who had a beautiful princess captive high in the tower. Twigs broken from bushes in the garden made lovely swords. We made it almost to the top before some guards caught us. But seeing as how we were only ten or eleven at the time, we weren't clapped in irons and tossed into the dungeons."

"So your kind of theater is a pastime for children?" asked the Tregrefin.

Cade considered being insulted, but then realized that the boy hadn't the wit to disguise this rudeness in a seemingly innocent request for information. So he smiled amiably and replied, "Only now that we're all grown up, we use withies instead of swords, and the monsters are made of magic as well as imagination."

"Though of course," Jeska put in, "they couldn't have imagined a princess so beautiful as the one Albeyn was lucky enough to welcome four years ago."

Miriuzca laughed. "If I am needing rescue from monsters, I know who to call on!"

Later, on the walk back to the Shadowstone Inn, Rafe muttered, "Our sort of theater is for children—bah! I'd like to see him call it that once he sees our 'Dragon'! Adorable little naffter, isn't he?"

Cade shrugged. "Well, you know what they say. The firstborn son gets everything the father owns, and the only thing the others get is a choice of clothing."

"Clothing?" Jeska asked. "What would clothes have to do with it?"

"A bright, pretty uniform with gold braid, a gray cassock with a pair of bracelets, or plain trousers knee-deep in cow shit."

"Soldier, Good Brother, or farmer," Rafe explained further.

"You might have said so," Jeska complained.

"State it plain, like?" Mieka snorted. "A tregetour?" When Cade turned down the wrong street for the Shadowstone, he called out, "Oy! Where are you off to?"

"Same place as you. Unless you think we worked out all the rusty lines and creaky transitions after only one rehearsal." Cade laughed as the three of them moaned. "I signed us up for teatime to dinnertime. Nobody else wanted the hours at the rehearsal hall. Mistress Luta is bringing our folios and a bagful of withies, bless her."

"I hate you." Mieka stalked past, scowling.

"You'll get over it."

6

Baltryn Knolltread, an apprentice Steward about thirty years old, smiled all over his broad freckled face as he welcomed them to the rehearsal hall.

"When I saw that Touchstone were asking for more time here, I says to meself, 'Touchstone might be putting together something new,' I says. Now, I won't be telling a soul, but I couldn't be passing up the chance to see it first!"

"Sorry, nothing special happening," Mieka told him. They'd got to know Baltryn last year, when Touchstone's unquestioned excellence had brought the invitation from the Stewards: *Help us train up the new ones by giving them a challenge.* Rafe and Mieka had had a fine old time throwing all sorts of wild and weird magic at the man, who handled it all with aplomb. Baltryn and others like him were in charge of the keys to the rehearsal hall, and sometimes stayed to watch—either from interest, friendship, or caution, if a group was new and inexperienced and needed monitoring.

Rafe greeted him with a genial smile. "How's the family?"

"The bigger and happier this year by a wee girlie. The wife's dark skin, praise be, but my ears!"

Mieka laughed. "Are you sure she didn't get your freckles and they just merged all together?"

"To keep each other company, like?" Knolltread grinned and shook his head. "You do have the oddest notions sometimes."

"Well, if she has your ears, then mayhap she'll have your gift as well, and grow up to be a Steward, just like her father."

Baltryn looked round to make sure no one else was in the hall. Empty of all but himself and Touchstone—still, his voice was low and soft as he said, "I'm thinking that it might not be impossible, y'know. Women in theater audiences—how long before they're trained as Stewards, or even onstage?"

Thinking of Lady Megs's ambitions, Mieka smiled. "Give it time."

"He means," said Rafe, "give *him* time and he'll work something out."

"I've every faith in it!" Baltryn looked up, startled, as someone knocked at the side door. "Are you expecting anyone?"

"Our inn's Trollwife," Cade said.

A few minutes later, Mistress Luta was seated composedly in a chair by the far wall, work-roughened hands clasped neatly in her lap and a huge hamper of food at her feet. Her lovely lavender eyes had acquired a sparkle at the sight of "her boys," but she was deaf to their pleas for the contents of that hamper now instead of later.

"The Princess fed you on naught but smiles and talk, did she?"

"Lunching was very nice," Mieka said, "but it would be a crime and a shame to call it 'cooking' in your presence."

She snorted. "Tea when you earn it."

He tried his best pout, knowing in advance it wouldn't work. So he sighed a tragic sigh, accepted the velvet bag of withies from her, hopped up onto the stage, and settled into a chair. "Right. What shall we do first?"

Cade said, low-voiced, "We'll do nothing until Baltryn is out the door."

Jeska's blue eyes narrowed in puzzlement. "Why not let him watch and listen?"

"For all I know, he's a spy for Black fucking Lightning."

"Baltryn?" Mieka started to laugh. Cade glowered at him. "You're not serious!"

"I am perfectly serious."

Rafe caught his eye and frowned slightly in warning. "Baltryn," he called, deep voice carrying easily from the stage to the back door, "we really aren't doing anything new and spectacular. You can skive off if you like."

"Well . . . there's a bit of botherment going on over some new boys—they can't agree on what to call themselves!" He laughed. "I saw them at rehearsal yestere'en, and it's not likely that anybody will want to remember them, whatever their name is."

"Go get them sorted, the poor silly sods," Rafe said. "We're fine here."

When he was gone, with a genial wave for Touchstone and a bow for Mistress Luta, Cade finally sat down, sprawling long legs, and said, "Let's run through the first five Perils, shall we?"

"Mightn't we do something for Mistress Luta?" Jeska asked. "She was kind enough to bring the withies and our tea."

Mieka thought for a moment, then said, "How about the dear old 'Dragon'? Haven't done that one in half of forever."

Jeska stood, and Mieka used the magic in a withie to clothe him in the Prince's velvet tabard and tall leather boots. They went rather quickly through the play, though Mieka gave the dragon most of the usual flourishes and a particularly piercing roar.

At the end, Mistress Luta applauded politely, then heaved herself to her feet. "If it's dinner you're wanting tonight, I'd best go cook it. Remember to fetch the hamper home." And with that, she was gone.

Touchstone stared at itself in bewilderment. Rafe said hesitantly, "Well, it's only a rehearsal. Not as if we played it full-on."

"I held back on everything except the dragon," Mieka said. "But still, she should've—"

"—should've leaped to her feet and worn out her hands clapping, just because it's us?" Cade smiled a crooked, sardonic smile. "For one thing, if I were a Troll—or at least more Troll than I actually am, so it showed, I mean—if I were, I'd find it a bit difficult to care much about the problems of a Human Prince fool enough to go out and fight a dragon."

"But now that you say it," Jeska mused, "we don't see many Trolls at our giggings. Not obvious ones, anyways, like Mistress Luta and Mistress Mirdley. I wonder why that is?"

Cade shrugged. "Mayhap Troll magic is just that much different from Wizard or Elf or Piksey or any other that they're not affected."

Mieka chewed that one over for a time, then shook his head. "That horrid play Black Lightning does—'The Lost Ones'— where everybody feels just exactly what they are—"

"And if it's not Wizard or Elf, they're ashamed," Jeska added grimly.

"Yeh. Point being that you felt it, Cade."

"I did," he affirmed. "But magic that picks out Troll blood and magic that actually *affects* a Troll might be two different things."

They went on to quick run-throughs of the Thirteen Perils, wondering idly which they'd draw in competition this year. Mieka was bored by the time they reached the Eighth. Cade snarled at him for sloppiness in the Tenth. When the Thirteenth was, praise be to all the Old Gods, finished, Mieka said, "*Now* can we do something interesting? Rafe has an idea about that grand statement thing of yours, Cade."

"Yeh?" he asked warily, turning to the fettler. "What?"

"Well, when you talk about the emotions that it's safe to feel in the theater, we could give them a flash of each. Just a tickle, nothing more."

"There and gone in an eyeblink," Jeska said, nodding. "Just to remind them what we can do."

Cade eyed the three of them. "That makes it into rather a braggarty piece, doesn't it? 'See what we can do, and how good we are at doing it!'"

"We *can* do it," Rafe said. "That's the point. You say so yourself at the end of it. 'We will provide.'"

Mieka studied Cade's expression. "You're thinking about what His High Tregrefin-ness said, aren't you? Using naught but words in a play. No magic at all." As guilt quirked the long mouth into a reluctant smile, Mieka went on, "Next you'll be saying something about how the words ought to make a magic of their own. Fine, then—*you* go onstage and recite the whole of it, and we'll be off drinking the Shadowstone dry!"

"My throat's a bit gravelly, now that you mention it," Jeska said. "And doesn't that poor hamper look desperate lonely all by itself over there?"

It was part of Mistress Luta's magic that when water was poured from the jug in the hamper over a strainer of tea leaves into pottery mugs, the liquid heated to the perfect temperature. Which was bespelled: the water, the strainer, or the mugs? None of them knew.

"Troll magic?" Rafe speculated.

"I've never seen Mistress Mirdley do it," Cade said. "But she's never shown me much by way of her own magic. Hedge-witchery, mainly, with herbs and things. Medicine."

"There's more to Troll magic than that." Mieka contemplated a baked sugar-crisp, studded with raisins, giving it full artistic appreciation before taking a large bite. After swallowing, he said, "Bridges and cookery. All the Trolls I've ever met or heard of specialize in one or the other."

"Mistress Tola at the markets?" Cade reminded him.

For an instant, he couldn't think of anything to say. This was the first time Cade had ever referred to that awful day two years ago when they'd visited the market and then Ginnel House after

Mieka had struck his wife—for the first and last and only time, he vowed again. He'd been back several times to Ginnel House, delivering supplies or just money, but never since went beyond the front hall. Once was enough, to have seen all those women and children looking at him with terrified eyes, simply because he was male. While he was away on the Royal Circuit, he delegated Jinsie to make the contributions for him. And this reminded him that in the worry surrounding Jez's injury, he'd forgotten to write out a note to the bank authorizing Jinsie to withdraw funds.

Aware that Cade was looking at him expectantly, he gathered his wits back together and said, "Deals in foodstuffs, doesn't she?"

"Hmm. Good point."

"They're secretive, though, aren't they?" Jeska mused. "Trolls. As secretive as the Fae. The only difference is that the Trolls chose to stay in this world, and the Fae removed themselves to the Brightlands. Ever been back to that dell where you met your great-whatever-grandmama?"

"Every time we're near the place for a day or two," Cade said. "Time's not the same to the Fae as it is to the rest of us. I mean, there I was in snowy winter, and there she was in a field of summer flowers."

They arrived back at the Shadowstone Inn—hamper duly emptied and remembered—to find an uproar in progress. There were only five people in the taproom, but it sounded more like twenty-five, all shouting. Rauel and Sakary flanked Vered, holding him back from a tall hollow-chested man of about sixty. His dark skin and white-blond hair were proof enough of kinship to Vered even if he hadn't been yelling, "You be keeping a civil tongue in your head when you be talking to your father, boy!"

"Father!" Vered snarled it as the foulest word he knew. "I told you last time that if I ever saw your ugly face again, I'd be peeling it off your bones with a rusted razor—all the Gods damn you, Rauel, be letting me at him!"

Chat leaped between them as the older man surged forward with fists clenched. "Stand back now, just stand back and you won't get hurt." He caught the man by the shoulders, struggling to hold him.

"Hurt, is it? I could take all four of you poofters with one hand!"

"Ah," Cade said softly behind him, "but could you take on eight of us?"

Vered's whole body winced with humiliation. Cade glanced quickly at Mieka, and at the velvet bag of withies in Mieka's arms. The Elf's expression changed from bewilderment to understanding in an instant.

Vered's father had shaken off Chat's restraining hands, backed up a pace, and righted his rumpled jacket. "I made you, boy!" he sneered at Vered in the broad accents of their hometown. "I put you in your mother's belly! You'll be showing your father some respect or I'll be teaching you some, now, won't I?"

"Mm, no, I rather think not," Cade went on. In the voice that always reminded Mieka of Lady Jaspiela, he added, "In fact, I very much believe you're about to vacate the premises."

"Who're these shit-wits?"

Mieka had by now got a hand on one of the withies. He'd never tried this when the glass was wrapped in velvet, but that shouldn't make much difference. A moment's concentration, the withie aimed at the old man, and—

"Oh, we're just a few friends looking for an ale before dinner," Cade was saying. "And here, in excellent time, is Mistress Luta to draw the pints," he finished with a smile.

She didn't look at him. Fists on hips, she snapped, "Leave! Now! Or I'll have the constables on you and the King's Guard as well! There's no such fighting and bellowing will go on in *my* establishment!"

Mieka blinked a bit at this; he'd always thought that the entirely Human couple who'd first welcomed Touchstone here six years ago were the owners of the place. Vered's father, who had subsided with a blank look in his eyes, roused again, and Mieka gripped the withie a little harder, pulling the last shards of magic from it.

"Well, I—that's to be saying, I want . . . no trouble . . . no, no trouble at all." He looked vaguely puzzled to hear such words coming out of his mouth.

The others looked even more baffled. Rafe took the opportunity to assist Chat in coaxing the man out the door. "That's right, come right along now, everything's fine."

"What the—?" Vered demanded of Cade. "What'd you let him go for?"

"I'm thirsty. So must you be. Mistress Luta, if you would?"

"Hells with it!" Vered exclaimed. "Hells with you all!" And he swung round, striding for the stairs with much clatter and many curses and, eventually, an emphatically slammed door.

Rauel sighed. "I'll go look after him." He hadn't taken more than two steps before they heard something smash upstairs. "One of those little night-tables, I think. Be sure to put it on our bill, Mistress Luta. I'd better calm him down before we have to pay for a few windows as well."

The Trollwife arched a heavy brow, hitched an unconcerned shoulder, and set pints of ale on the bar. Mieka put the bag of withies on a nearby chair and went to drink his reward for understanding what Cade's glances had meant.

"His father?" Jeska asked Chat, who rolled his eyes and groaned.

"Last time he tried this, Vered nearly killed him. He left Vered's mother, y'see, about two days after he learned she was pregnant. Wants money, of course."

Sakary gulped down half his ale. "He's got ambitions, I'll give him that. This time it's also a house of his own over to the western coast where the fishing's good, and a boat complete with crew to do all the work while he lolls about with a bottle in one hand and a whore in the other."

Mistress Luta growled a little, low in her throat, and departed for the kitchen. Rafe nodded agreement. "Sounds a real charmer."

"You didn't hear me say this," Sakary murmured, "but it's a pity Bexan isn't here to calm Vered down."

"How often does he have an attack of paternal enthusiasm?" Cade asked.

"Every few years." Chat sighed. "I'm thinking mayhap it's more often than that, but he goes to Rommy Needler instead of Vered."

"Better that way," Sakary mused. "After one of his visits, the power Vered puts into the withies that Chat and me have to control—Lord and Lady, it doesn't bear thinking of."

Time to change the subject, Mieka told himself. "I'm glad Mistress Luta got rid of him. Any more of his muck would spoil our dinner."

"Doubtless that's why she was so . . . emphatic. Nobody faces down a Trollwife!" Cade said. Mieka hid a smile. They did work well together, he reflected; always had.

Talk turned to the news that the theater group from the Continent would be performing for the Court at Fliting Hall the very next evening. Chat, on an afternoon stroll, had encountered a few of them. Being from the Continent himself, he could speak with them in their own language.

"In fact," he told the others over dinner, "they're from the country as sent the Princess's mother to be the bride of the Princess's father." He grinned his endearingly lopsided grin. "Shall I amaze and astound you by my ability to pronounce the name of the place?"

Mieka pulled a face. "Not impressed. It's naught but a gargle and a grunt, with mayhap a whine or two thrown in."

His fellow glisker pretended to be insulted. "I'll not have you talking down my dear old homeland! Or as close to it as makes small difference."

"Miss it much, do you?" Mieka asked with wide-eyed innocence. "Weep into your pillows by night?"

Chat made a face at him. "There's enough in common, speech-wise, that we understood each other."

"Ah, but how will *we* understand *them*?" Sakary asked. "There's the trouble."

"We managed, over on the Continent," Rafe said.

"Took everything I knew to do it, though," Jeska reminded him. "Gesture and expression, tone of voice—with Mieka working the emotions to emphasize what I was doing."

"It'll be interesting to see if they can manage anything a tenth as good," Cade remarked.

"If sheer numbers could do it, they might have a chance." Chat poured himself more ale. "Go on, have a guess at how many there are in this company of players."

"Five," Jeska said promptly.

"Masquers," Rafe reminded him.

"Total?" Cade sipped ale, then said, "They have to do everything we do without the means by which we do it. I'd say at least twenty, not counting those onstage."

"Not a bad guess," Chat admitted. "There's those as sets up the scenery and takes it all down again, and those in charge of the stuff onstage—swords and lamps and chairs and pretend fireplaces and the like. Three costumers who dress the masquers as needed, plus an assistant to clean all the clothes after every performance."

"Poor sods," Rafe said. "When I think of some of the things you and Mieka come up with, Cade, with all the silks and laces and leathers and feathers—"

"Plus the decorations," Chat added. "Jewelry, belts, shoes, crowns for royal heads—and that reminds me that there's two who do nothing but hair. Real *and* wigs. Then there's a worrier to keep track of all the scripts. He was one of those I met today. Can't be much older than me, but with lines carved into his forehead as if a sculptor had scratched them there at birth. There's those what takes care of sound effects, and five for the lighting—which is as dangerous as you'd ever imagine it to be."

"Are you saying they work with real fire?" Mieka shuddered. "It's a wonder and a marveling that they haven't burned down half the Continent!"

"Three for the actual work of lighting and positioning the lamps," Chat laughed, "and two with buckets of water near to hand!"

"It all sounds a bloody nightmare," Jeska said.

"I'm not done yet. There's a manager who's in charge of everything and everybody, and sees to it that nothing and nobody are permitted to lose themselves." He paused for a drink. "And—you'll love this—somebody called an invigilator."

"A *what?*"

"He tells the masquers what to do and when to do it onstage."

Jeska was as unimpressed as Mieka had been. "How's that different from what Cade or Vered or Rauel do?"

"Once the thing is planned out and rehearsed to his satisfaction," Chat said, "he does nothing but sit there."

"Again," Jeska persisted, "how's it different?" He laughed and ducked as Cade aimed a playful fist at him.

Sakary said, with entirely spurious sincerity, "But our lads sit there so *decoratively.*"

"That they do, that they do," Mieka replied. "But what about the writer, then?"

"There isn't one."

Mieka sniggered as Cade expressed his outrage with a single vehement curse. Everyone in a group—tregetour, glisker, fettler, masquer—always considered himself the most essential part of the performance. Without the tregetour's words and his magic in the withies; without the glisker's ability to use that magic; without the fettler's strength and judgment in dispersing and controlling the magic; without the masquer's skills of interpretation and expression . . . Though, truth be told, Mieka knew very well that Touchstone could never have been Touchstone without his own charming self.

"All the plays are about a thousand years old, y'see," Chat explained. "If they mucked about with so much as a sentence, they'd be hauled off the stage and quodded for a month. You, Cayden old son, would never have got away with changing 'Dragon' like you did at your first Trials. And as for what you did with 'Treasure'—"

Mieka spoke up hastily, knowing that any mention of "Treasure" put Cade into a horrible mood. "But what if the masquers forget a line, or change the words about?"

"They don't," Chat said flatly.

"So how many in all?" Rafe asked.

"Forty-two."

They all crowed their disbelief, and Mieka shook his head in amazement. "Imagine what it'd cost the King to trot that many people round Albeyn every year!"

"Forty-two times nine," Jeska corrected. "All three circuits, three groups each."

"It'd cost much more than just multiplying what's spent on each circuit," Chat said. "They're used to the best beds at whatever castle they're sent to visit. That's why they're stopping at Seekhaven Castle, and not locally inned like the rest of us. And at home, the lord or princeling who owns them makes sure they're kept happy. Otherwise, somebody richer than he might do a bit of pilfering. Skirmishes have been known over things like that, and grudgings that last three generations."

Mieka frowned. "So these cullions make much more money than we do for doing much less?"

"More to share it out amongst," Sakary said.

Cade was frowning, too. "You mean they actually fight over who gets to own a group?"

"Yeh. But once that group goes out of fashion—like Kelife and the Candlelights two years since—they're cast off and through. It isn't as if they're not immune to the sort of fighting we do, either." Chat grinned and speared a chunk of succulent roast goose on his fork. "F'r instance. There's the tale of a man in charge of the sounds—anything from running water to hunting dogs belling in the distance. He had a fine new way of doing a rainstorm, and hid himself behind more screens than usual when his players were onstage, so nobody could suss out how he did it. One evening as he was going into the theater, he saw a ragged little orphan boy begging in the street. The sounder, who was known as a kind man, had pity on him, took him inside, gave him some food, and said he could watch the performance from the wings. After the show, he went looking for the boy but couldn't find him. He searched all round the theater. Not a glint of luck. So he went to pack up his various contrivances—and the sheet of metal and soft hammer he used to make the thunder was gone! In its place was a note from a rival group's sounder, grateful for looking after his son for the evening, apologizing sweet as you please for stealing his thunder."

"Mieka, make a note," Rafe said, chuckling. "All withies to be kept in a locked box from now on, with only you and Cade knowing how to open it."

"Better would be a way to make the withies unusable for anybody but those they were made for," said Chat. "Shall we put the idea to our darlin' Blye?"

The clock above the fireplace chimed the hour, followed a moment or two later by the local Minster. Sakary glanced at the staircase, shaking his head. "We'd better take them something to eat, Chat. Vered furious is bad enough, but Vered hungry *and* furious isn't to be contemplated."

"We'd best go up, too," Rafe said. "The draw's tomorrow morning, earlier than usual."

They all bade each other a good night. Upstairs in the room he always shared with Cade, Mieka said, "Well, it has been a day, hasn't it? Now we know where the charm doesn't come from in Vered's bloodlines. Gods, what a scene!"

"Anything that makes the rest of them long for Bexan's presence . . ." Cade rolled his eyes and grimaced.

"Yeh. I give his horrible old sire full marks for cheek, anyways. Remind me to send me own sweet Fa a present to show him how much I appreciate him."

Cade's head reappeared from the snowy folds of his nightshirt. "You know," he said thoughtfully, "I might do the same for my own father, for gratitude that he hasn't so much as spoken to me in about five years."

Mieka waited until the room was dark and they were both in bed before asking, "What did you think of what Miriuzca's brother said? About everybody being born with a sin already inside them?"

"I thought he meant that everybody is born with a *propensity* to a certain sin."

"Whicheverway, it's all rot," Mieka stated. "How could anybody look into Jindra's eyes and believe there's the least little thing wrong in her heart?"

"I was thinking the same thing," Cade admitted. "As we get older, and get to know how the world is, and how it works, and everything—" The sheets rustled as he shifted in bed. "—I think we learn how to be nasty. I don't think it's inborn."

"Things we pick up from other people, you mean? Can't help learning that sort of thing while learning all the rest of it, I s'pose. Some people being good examples, and others—"

"Exactly. But he seems to think that we're all born with wickedness or corruption inside us. I wish he had more of our language so I knew if that's what he really meant."

"Oh, I think it was clear enough." Mieka shoved a fist into his pillow to rearrange the feathers. "But I never heard anything so sad and so hopeless."

"Actually, it's in some of the staggeringly old plays, from before Albeyn had more than a smattering of magic folk living here. Everybody's born flawed—sinful, if you like—and it's only belief in the Lord and the Lady keeps us reasonably clean."

Mieka stared up at the slatted shadows on the ceiling. The breeze shifted the leaves of the oak tree outside the window, throwing patterns from the streetlamp down below. "The only time I ever felt dirty because of what I am, what I was born, I mean, was—"

"—during Black Lightning's play. I know. Me, too."

"Well, that, of course. But on the Continent, when they kept staring at my ears . . ." He turned onto his side, squinting in the darkness, but he couldn't see Cayden's face. "D'you think that's what His Whateverness was really saying? That it's those of us with magic, who aren't Human down to our last hangnail, who're born wicked?"

"Seems so. I hope he betakes himself and his religion home soon."

"Me, too."

As Mieka punched the pillow again and settled down for the night, he smiled; no matter Cade's absurd notion about refusing his Elsewhens (something Mieka would have to talk him out of somehow), and no matter how different they were as people, their thoughts chimed together. Always had. Always would.

7

Usually there were one or two new groups at each Trials, young men eager to prove themselves worthy of any of the circuits. This year, however, there were four. Gone were most of the old familiar names—the Spintales, the Enticements, the Cobbald Close Players, the Shorelines. Redprong and Trinder had finally given up the annual audition for their masquer and fettler; Kelife and the Candlelights had retired as well. There were now, by common consent, five truly important groups: the Shadowshapers, Touchstone, the Crystal Sparks, Black Lightning, and Hawk's Claw. Considerably behind in talents and accomplishments were the Wishcallers, the Smokecatchers, and the Nightrunners. As for the new groups, those invited to Trials for the first time . . . Tobalt Fluter had written up a terse analysis for *The Nayword*. The masquer of the Kindlesmiths hadn't much vocal range, and all the characters sounded pretty much alike. The Flashcrafters lived up to their name: good with the big, loud, showy pieces, but rather awful at quieter and more thoughtful plays. Keeping with the theme of fire, popular these days with young theater groups, the Torchwrights tried to make up in passion what they lacked in subtlety. Lastly, the Blazing Hornets—named after their tregetour's family crest—

had mastered the art of the quick, concise playlet, but longer pieces revealed a lack of training, for glisker and masquer were visibly exhausted after only half an hour. *A little more practice and a lot less alcohol would serve them well,* was Tobalt's scathing conclusion, adding, *With time and experience, any or all of these four groups might well surprise us, but this year's Trials hold scant promise of startlements such as were given by the Shadowshapers and Touchstone in their initial performances at Seekhaven.* Reading that, Cade had wondered if anyone else besides him would notice that Tobalt rather pointedly didn't mention Black Lightning.

Thus there were thirteen groups gathered at Seekhaven Castle for the drawing of tokens that decided who would be doing which playlet. The new young ones clustered over in a corner, pallid and sweating, to the amusement of the old hands (who conveniently forgot that they had done their fair share of sweating their first time out, too). With the departure of Kelife and the like, *old* these days meant about thirty years of age. Yes, it truly was a young man's game, though Cade did retain just a fragment of that Elsewhen of his forty-fifth Namingday, and its promise that Touchstone would still be performing to huge, enthusiastic crowds. He'd lied to Mieka about that. He hadn't been able to let that one go completely. Not that one; not completely.

He knew Mieka was worried that they'd draw "Treasure" again, worried that Cade would react badly to yet another performance of the play he had rewritten to such horrible results for Briuly and Alaen Blackpath. But it wasn't "Treasure" this time, nor "Dragon." Once more, Touchstone managed to avoid the lethally dull Second Peril. That one went to the Shadowshapers, who proved themselves accomplished masquers all by revealing not a hint of dismay. Touchstone drew the Third. Not their favorite amongst the Thirteen, but better than the Second.

On their way back to the Shadowstone Inn, Mieka put forth his opinion that they had rehearsed the Third often enough in the last five years that they had no need to go through it yet again. Rafe disagreed. Jeska didn't care much one way or the other. Cade startled them all by siding with Mieka.

"What?" Rafe exclaimed. "You're not going to make us change up half the play to suit your ideas of how it really happened?"

"Let's put it this way," Cade said. "Everybody knows that the Shadowshapers will be First Flight on the Royal. Even with a performance of the dreaded Second, they'll be better than anybody else. Our only real competition is the Sparks and Black Lightning. And they drew the Fifth and Thirteenth."

In the Fifth, the heir to Albeyn's throne went a-wooing a foreign princess. The "peril" part of it happened when three other suitors tried to kill him in various ways. He survived. The princess, captivated by his courage and cunning as well as his matchless good looks and exquisite manners, fell wildly in love, as princesses were obliged to do. In the right hands it could be a fun piece, but there was nothing of either flash or subtlety about it. The Sparks would do it just fine, but not fine enough to unseat Touchstone from Second Flight. As for the Thirteenth—that one dealt with a clever diplomatic victory that prevented a war. Lots of talk, and some interesting costume choices if the tregetour had done the research (needless to say, Cayden had), but no opportunity in it for an exhibition of Black Lightning's signature brute force.

The Third Peril was just the sort of thing that Mieka delighted in. Cade had long since investigated the playlet and discovered that it wasn't a Giant that the king defeated at a tournament; it was just a regular knight. Nothing he could rework with fresh meaning, so they stuck to the usual script—and Jeska did love stomping about and roaring in his deepest voice as he played the Giant. Mieka had come up with an entertaining twist when first they'd discussed the Third: rather than cloak their masquer in magic that made him ceiling-tall as the Giant, why not shrink everything else? Horses, lances, pennants, spectators in the stands, all dwindled down to the size of a child's toys—it came very close to being a comedy of skewed proportions, and Mieka enjoyed making visual jokes. The Giant would, for example, pluck up a miniature sword from the King and use it to clean his fingernails. There wasn't much else to be done with the straightforward plot, but at least doing it from the Giant's perspective was more interesting than having the King walk onto the tourney field with magic providing only the Giant's massive legs and feet, which was the way everybody else always did it.

Rafe frowned as he thought it over. "We've never done it for an audience, but our Third is better than anybody else's I've ever seen—and different, too, which at Trials seems to be the main thing."

"How outrageous can I get?" Mieka wanted to know.

"Well," Cade said, considering, "we don't want it to be a full-on howler. Just some giggles here and there. This is purportedly King Meredan's ancestor we're portraying, after all."

Jeska gave an inelegant snort. "Since when has that stopped us?"

They spent the rest of the morning on a long stroll around Seekhaven, shopping, greeting the citizens, and idly trading other ideas on how they'd do the Third. Then they repaired to the Shadowstone Inn for lunching. Waiting for them, and for the Shadowshapers, were invitations to Fliting Hall that night for a performance by the theater group from the Continent.

"Here's betting that they take more than an hour to do what we can in a half," said Vered, who seemed to have forgot all about his father's visit. Everyone else was more than willing to forget about it, too.

"Now, now," Rafe teased. "Play nice."

"We can't really judge them by our standards, can we?" Jeska asked, frowning earnestly. "And who knows but that in their circumstances, we'd be terrible."

"Terrible? *Us?*"

They all took up the shouts of abuse. Roundly chastised, he laughed and wrapped his arms around his head, crying, "Mercy! Mercy on the poor player!"

But what he'd said got Cade to thinking, and Vered as well. When the others had departed on various errands—a nap, more shopping, writing letters, or polishing withies—Vered accepted the innkeeper's wife's offer of chilled fruit juice served in the sunny backyard and asked Cade to join him.

When they were seated in the shade of an elm, Vered lost no time in getting to his point. "The audiences on the Continent must get something out of this sort of theater, or it'd not be thriving as it seems to be."

"But it's all they've got, innit? It'd be a bit like amateur theatricals, the sort people do on long winter evenings when they've run out of books and conversation and all the lute strings have snapped."

"Children dressing up in mummy's gowns and grandfather's boots. But from that sort of playing come players—if they grow up with the magic for it. And if they do, it's not the back wall of the drawing room they'll be playing to. They'll play to the gods."

Cade smiled. It was an old expression in theater, not much used anymore: *playing to the gods* meant making sure the entire audience heard and saw and felt everything to the very back rows and beyond, where the Old Gods gathered to watch.

Vered brushed a buzzing insect away from his face. "I hear you've been fooling about with removing one or the other of the tricks we all use during a play."

"Just as an experiment. Mieka's sister Jinsie has friends at Shollop who challenged us, more or less, to leave out the sounds. Theater for the deaf. Yet you've done the same—more or less!— with 'Life in a Day,' and no emotion until the ending."

"Is there more of honesty, d'you think, in that way of doing it? Words and sights that reach into men and drag their own emotions out of them, rather than making them feel what the scene's supposed to make them feel?"

"Men *and* women," Cade corrected, smiling.

"Because of your mad little glisker, yes."

"And the Princess." And Lady Megs, he reminded himself, memory distracting him with a picture of her in trousers and jacket alighting from Miriuzca's carriage. He dragged his thoughts back to the subject at hand. "Would you have Black Lightning take it all one step further, and do nothing on the stage at all except stand there and send out bludgeoning after bludgeoning of emotion?"

Vered laughed harshly. "Great Gods, Cade, don't ever say such a thing in their hearing! Yeh, they make sure everyone feels what's intended to be felt, thus assuring themselves that they've been spectacularly good even if the play itself is shit." He scrunched down in his chair, scowling. "There's not a decent sentence in any of their original pieces. They fool everyone with their intensity. Take away the magic, and they'd be laughed off any stage in Albeyn."

Cade sipped his drink, then said, "It's rather like falling in love with a beautiful woman. I mean, a man sees the outward flourishes, he's knocked all agroof by the way she looks, and thinks only with his cock."

"But when the beauty fades, as it always must . . . there he is, staring at her across the breakfast dishes and wondering why he married her. Yeh, I see that. The magic is the beauty, and if you take it away, there'd best be something else to give the audience or you're back playing for trimmings in taverns." He raked one hand through his white-blond hair, suddenly laughing. "We'll be doing that, we Shadowshapers, if we're not careful!"

Cade snorted his derision. "First Flight on the Royal for how many years now, and how many years stretching ahead? And

I don't like to think what you can command as your fee for a private performance."

"Ah, and that's just it, me lad," he replied merrily. "There's two choices: be a free man or be a thrall. Let other people tell you what to do, where to go, how to play a play, what to think or whether you're allowed to think at all—or tell 'em all to go fuck themselves."

"What are you talking about?" But then he remembered a conversation of several years ago, and how the Shadowshapers wanted to be quit of the circuits, and become their own masters. "Vered," he said, instinctively lowering his voice and instantly disgusted with himself because of it, for why couldn't they talk of such things out in the open? "You're not seriously thinking—?"

"It's the choice we *don't* have, as players. There's no guild for the likes of us. If there were, we could deal with people like that Prickspur lout up near Dolven Wold, and nobody like that could touch us without serious consequences. What happened to him in the end? Lord Fairwalk complained, Rommy complained, all of us refused to set foot in his miserable old inn—but what really happened to him? Sweet fuck-all. There's no guild for players. There's nobody to protect us but ourselves."

"The King—"

"The King and all his little minions, they don't give two shits about us. We're sent out on the circuits, we get paid, we get transport and bed and board—and who collects the profits from those as bids highest to present us, eh? Not us!"

"Our fee is set," said Cade, "but if the Bexmarket Smithing Society outbids the Merchants Ladies League, the Crown pockets the excess."

"True as true can be. Look at this life we lead. Five shows and a break. Three or four days on the road, no matter the weather, then another five shows and a day off. 'Cept that day gets used up in a private booking, so we can actually make ends meet—

because who survives just on what they earn on a circuit?"

Cade frowned at an inoffensive flowering bush. "But to go out on your own? That's quite the risk, Vered."

"Not so much as you'd think. If we do nothing *but* private bookings, they want us, they pay us. *Us,* not His Majesty's Revel-rouseries."

"But the venues," Cade objected. "Where are you going to play?"

"Almost everywhere we do now—besides, d'you have any idea how many castle courtyards there are in this Kingdom? How many great halls that hold three or four hundred? How many guild halls? They can't pay what's needed to book a circuit performance—but what they *can* pay comes all to us."

"Hundreds of royals a night," Cade murmured.

"Hundreds upon hundreds. And none of it goes to anybody but us."

"But—the scheduling—won't you be competing with whoever else is in town?"

"Compete with *us*? Do me a favor!" Laughing again, he teased, "Be sweet to us, Cayden lad, and we'll *think* about not playing the same town Touchstone's playing!"

"Only," Cade replied serenely, "because you don't want to find out who'd win."

"You should consider it, y'know," Vered said, swiftly unsmiling. "Going out on your own, without the bother of the circuits. You've that wagon now, just like us, and enough of a following to pack your giggings full."

"What does Rommy Needler say about this?"

"Hated the whole idea at first. Got all stroppy about the extra work in keeping everything straight—the scheduling could turn up a right disaster, unless it's done careful-like. But he'd been to dinner with your Lord Fairwalk a few nights before we told him our plans, and they were both gnawing over how much the Crown takes by way of profit. So for lacking of a better way, he's got used to the plan."

Immediately Cade knew how it had really happened. When Kearney Fairwalk arrived late that afternoon, Cade took him aside in the taproom and made him admit it.

When discussing business, all His Lordship's affectations and mannerisms vanished; even his voice changed pitch, became deeper and softer by comparison to his usual fluty, fruity tones. "Why shouldn't the Shadowshapers make the experiment for us? They're already rich, they can afford it."

"But if it doesn't work out—"

"Cayden, tell me this, please. How long do you think Vered Goldbraider and Rauel Kevelock will continue to tolerate each other's ambitions? Each is a Master of two disciplines, tregetour and masquer. They've competed with each other since they formed the Shadowshapers. I'm surprised they're still speaking to each other. Good Lord and Lady, I'm astonished they haven't slit each other's throats by now—or that Rommy hasn't taken a knife to his own neck!" He sniggered in his well-bred way. "I told him once that it seemed rather a war of nerves betwixt him and Vered, and d'you know what he said? That Vered hadn't got any."

"Any what?" Cade asked, aware that Kearney was waiting to deliver the payoff line.

"Nerves." He sniggered again, then went on more seriously, "Vered and Rauel haven't actually done deliberate damage to each other's plays during a performance, because they're still dedicated to the Shadowshapers as an entity. But once their loyalty to the group as a whole wanes, as quite honestly it looks to be doing in the next few years—"

"Why?"

"Because their personal identities are changing. They have wives, homes, children—they're not just players anymore. Husband, father, householder, those are *adult* words."

"Rafe's married," he challenged. "And Jeska and Mieka, too."

"Touchstone hasn't the inbuilt tensions the Shadowshapers have. *You* are the driving force, the inspiration behind the group. Rafe, Mieka, and Jeska all see themselves within the group in relationship to you. But Vered and Rauel are constantly switching back and forth, so the group's structure is always changing. Chat and Sakary juggle this very well, but one day Vered or Rauel—or mayhap both—will want to be in complete and permanent control of everything."

Cade had witnessed enough of their sniping at each other to acknowledge the truth of that. Still— "You mean they'd do what Trinder and Redprong used to do, and advertise? Because you can't tell me that one or the other would take either Chat or Sakary with him. The Shadowshapers as they are—" He shook his head helplessly. "They're the best, and everyone knows it. How could they ever be as successful individually as they are together?"

"One day we'll all find out, won't we? But, Cade, listen to me closely now. It's your work that makes Touchstone something extraordinary. Yours is a gift in a million. It's an honor and a privilege to help you make the most of it."

Cade knew, in his secret soul, that he was first amongst equals in Touchstone. But the notion that Rafe, Jeska, and Mieka were there only to do as he told them—

Kearney said it out loud. "The rest of Touchstone exists to serve *your* vision."

He gave a short, cynical laugh. "I can just imagine how well that would play with them!"

"But it's true. You're the one with the ideas and the words, and the magic that makes it all into art."

"I could do it just the same with any other glisker, fettler, and masquer, you mean?" He thought he was saying it just to see what Kearney would reply.

"Not *just* the same," the nobleman said at once. "But perhaps it might be even more yours. If you didn't have to do battle with them over every little thing . . ." He finished with a shrug.

But those jeering, sniping, shouting battles honed his ideas. Made them better. Made *him* better.

All the same . . . not having to fight over the wording of a speech, the intensity of a sensation, the scenery and pacing and emphasis and—

To work without Rafe? Without Jeska? Without Mieka?

Kearney was wrong. The rest of Touchstone didn't exist solely to serve his work. They were an essential part of the work. Whenever he wrote, he kept in mind their talents, their strengths and limitations, their styles of stagecraft. He wrote *to* their gifts, and because those gifts were prodigious, they were in effect challenging him to make it better before they even heard about the piece. Simply put, he was writing for the best masquer, glisker, and fettler in Albeyn.

He tried for an instant to visualize others in their places—Sakary, for instance, as his fettler, or Lederris Daggering of the Crystal Sparks as his masquer—and shied back like a scalded cat.

Whatever their battles with each other, Touchstone was a thing greater than the four of them. They were each a part of something worth being part of, as Mieka had said years ago. Or as Cayden had phrased it in "Doorways": *This life, and none other.*

Cade saw at once that there were no ladies in the audience at Fliting Hall for the Continental group's performance. Touchstone had walked over with the Shadowshapers, and as they found their seats, he nudged Sakary with an elbow and gestured round. Sakary whispered to Chat, who leaned over and murmured, "Women aren't allowed in their theaters, so I'd be betting they refused to perform if women were present tonight. They've no Mieka Windthistle to overset their boring old traditions."

"Gods in Glory," Cade whispered back, "don't mention that anywhere near him!"

"Oh, no fear of it, old thing," Mieka said at his other side. "Enlightening them would mean another trip on a ship with a yark-bucket slung round me neck!"

"By the bye," Chat said, "I have the answer to our puzzlement over who exactly owns the Shadowstone Inn. I asked the Human couple about it, and he said they were hired about thirty years ago, and the ones who had the pleasure of the place before them had been there at least forty years. Mistress Luta is indeed the owner."

Sakary turned to his partner with a frown. "But why does she need someone to pretend otherwise?"

"Who knows why a Troll does anything?" Chat countered.

"How old is Mistress Mirdley?" Mieka asked suddenly.

"It's awfully bad form to inquire as to a woman's age," Cade chided with a wink.

Somebody two rows ahead of them turned with a terrible scowl, and was about to reprimand them for making noise when everyone hurried to stand for the arrival of King Meredan. He was accompanied by Prince Ashgar and Archduke Cyed Henick and selections from their assorted retinues. Cade saw his father's gaze find and dismiss him as smoothly as if he hadn't been recognized at all, and felt his lips twist wryly with the thought of sending Zekien Silversun a gift in gratitude for so reliably ignoring him.

The King planted his plump posterior in the chair specially placed for him in the exact center of the front row. Everybody else sat down. The curtains slowly opened, and the play began.

The basics were easy, and required no words. The lead character was a learned man, his learning signaled by the setting, which was a library thick with books (shelves and volumes painted on canvas; not a bad attempt, Cade thought, but not all that convincing, either). He paced the stage, lighting candles and drawing chalk patterns on the floor. Soon enough, with a clap of thunder (Cade grinned to himself, recalling Chat's story of stolen thunder), a being appeared from a truly amateurish gout of smoke.

So far, so boring. All this masquer had to work with was the physical appearance of the being, identification by way of costume: red robes swirling round a very tall and thin body, red close-fitting hood shadowing the face, and a three-tined hayfork. A theater group in Albeyn would have added noxious smells and a tang of fear, the better to indicate that this was Mallecho, a spirit bent on malicious mischief.

Evidently someone had taught the players enough words to get the salient points across, for Mallecho asked in perfectly understandable Albeyni, "Who summons me?"

"I am Vaustas," replied the scholar, "and I want all goods of the world!"

Now, this could be interpreted as wanting nothing but good *for* the world, or as a desire to possess all the good things the world could offer. It was only when Mallecho answered, "All riches are yours!" that the meaning became clear.

Cade would have done it with conjurings onstage—Mallecho summoning up gold coins stacked halfway to the ceiling, a score of beautiful women, a dozen barrels of fine wine, and so on—to which Vaustas would have cried, "Yes!"

But these players had no magic, and very few Albeyni words. "How long?" asked Vaustas. And Mallecho held up one hand, fingers spread. "More!" cried Vaustas; the other hand, to make ten. "More!" Both hands fisted and opened again: twenty. Eager and greedy, Vaustas shouted, "More!" but this time only the left hand was held up. "More!"—and the thumb curled into the palm. Vaustas was evidently no fool; he nodded, and Mallecho drew a scroll from inside his robes, and Vaustas signed it in his own blood. It was a nice little trick, Cade thought, with the masquer pretending to prick his own thumb and let the "blood" drip into a bowl which was then used as an inkwell; the drizzle of red liquid came from a vial hidden up his sleeve.

A skeletal finger pointing at Vaustas, Mallecho cried out, "Now mine!" and the stage went dark.

The audience shifted restlessly. This was, of course, nothing like what they were used to. Neither was the next bit of stagecraft, which Cade appreciated for its imagination in getting round limitations. The lights went up again, directed specifically to what looked like a large, rectangular painting in the middle of the stage. In Albeyn, painters who used magic—such as the one who'd done the mural on the wall of the Kiral Kellari—could make the scene change with a spell. Having no such ability, this scene changed with the turning of sections of the painting. Eight panels, when locked together, gave at first a rendering of a large, fine brick house; then an interior of silk furnishings and beautiful carpets, gold fittings and a table laden with delicacies, at which Vaustas sat enjoying his meal. Finally there was a landscape of a gray castle on a green hill, with black tiles roofing its many graceful towers.

Gods, how easy it would have been for him and Mieka to do so much more! He pitied these players the inadequacies of their craft.

Darkness again, and the sound of the changeable painting being rolled away out of sight. Someone in the audience snorted scornfully. Light came gradually to the stage this time, in a pretty demonstration of a skill with lanterns no group in Albeyn would ever need. The scene was the interior of the gray castle, walls covered in mounted shields and tapestries, with a wide, frost-rimed window to the left. Three people were now onstage: Vaustas, and a man and woman finely dressed in yellow velvet and white fur cloaks, with small coronets to indicate noble status. The woman pouted and sulked; the man gestured to the iced-over window. The woman pulled the fur more closely around her, shivering. Vaustas smiled, bowed to the lady, and waved a hand at the window. Cade bit his lip against laughter as one panel of painted scenery slid from the window to reveal a sunshine day "outside" and a view of green hills. It wasn't the masquers' fault that the frost window got stuck for a moment just at the bottom, and someone had to yank it down out of view.

Clumsy, clumsy, Cade thought. Some of the audience thought so, too. There were sniggerings throughout Fliting Hall. Touchstone, or the Shadowshapers or the Crystal Sparks—or Hawk's Claw or even Black fucking Lightning—would have done it all in a soundless instant, and added birdsong and a growing warmth inside the castle as well. Hells, it could all have been done in an exterior scene, a garden mayhap, where with one flick of a withie the snow would melt, the grass would turn lushly green, flowers would bloom, and fruit would burgeon on the trees. One obviously needed magic to simulate magic.

The lady went to the window and flung it open—there was another painting just beyond it, of the same blue skies and summertime glory. She clapped her hands with pleasure and threw off her fur cloak. The lord grinned and nodded like anything, and Vaustas folded his arms across his chest, smugly satisfied.

Now what? Cade thought. *And what does any of it have to do with selling his soul to Mallecho for twenty-four years? And why twenty-four?*

He came nearer than ever to laughing aloud as a grapevine came slowly into view. Where Mieka would have sent it sinuously twining round the window, the vine thickening and the grapes purpling to ripeness, all that happened here was somebody below and behind the window slid an artificial assemblage of leaves and bunches of grapes higher and higher.

Vaustas reached into his pocket and produced—flourished, actually, to make sure the audience saw them—a pair of gleaming silver sickles. He gave both to the lord, gesturing him over to where the lady caressed the vine leaves. When each held a sickle, Vaustas said, "Choose and cut grapes. But only when say I— when I *say*," he corrected himself swiftly.

The lord and the lady, half-hidden now by the growing grapevine (which the masquers had not quite unnoticeably pulled around their necks and across their shoulders), selected bunches of grapes and positioned their silver sickles. Vaustas laughed softly and said "Now!" But before they could slice off the grapes, the "illusion" vanished (through the simple expedient of the person behind the wall yanking the fake plant down—the lady was nearly throttled when the vine was momentarily stuck around her neck) and it was seen that they were about to lop off each other's noses.

"Illusion!" Vaustas cried, laughing uproariously as the pair flung away the sickles and backed hastily away from each other, the lady screaming in little gasps all the while. "All illusion! Magic is all illusion from which all evil comes!"

The lord snatched up his sickle and made for Vaustas with murder in his eyes. Vaustas only laughed louder, and fled stage right. Darkness again descended on the stage, and Cade wondered if this was the ending. Evidently not; Vaustas's laughter kept echoing through Fliting Hall, until Cade began to worry for the masquer's voice. There was a rustle of garments, and a single light illumined Mallecho in all his fiery red finery.

A huge clock appeared on one side of the stage, its hands moving to count off the first hour. On the other side was a large rectangular painting of a river meandering through green hills, an apple orchard nearby and tall mountains beyond. This scene's outlines stayed the same through a series of other paintings, stacked like playing cards one behind the next: the apple tree in bloom, and then the fruit heavy on the boughs, and then the trees bare of both fruit and leaves, and then snow covering everything. As the hour hand moved, marking off the quarters, these four scenes kept succeeding each other. *Oh,* Cayden thought. *That's why the twenty-four. Each hour is a year. Or something like that.*

Vaustas walked onstage again, visibly older—gray in his hair, his posture a bit stooped. But his clothing was, if anything, even more luxurious, with many golden chains and the glisten of jewels at his neck and fingers and on the buckles of his shoes. Mallecho pointed to the clock, which showed barely a quarter of an hour left in the day, and then to the painting of winter.

"More—please!" Vaustas begged.

Mallecho laughed and brandished the parchment with Vaustas's signature in blood. He flung a heavy black chain around the scholar's shoulders and started towards the darkness to the left side of the stage, a darkness in which a single red light burned. The pathway to all the Hells? Probably.

All at once two people arrived stage right—the same masquers who had played lord and lady, but clothed this time in the blue and green of the Lord and the Lady. There had been no attempt to translate the words they and Mallecho flung back and forth; there was actually no need. They battled for Vaustas's soul. What Cade would have done with flashes of light and wild imagery, they did with tone of voice and gesture. He had to admit it was effective.

Infuriated, Mallecho flung back his hood. As one, the audience gasped. In the tales of Albeyn, Mallecho was merely a very naughty Elf, a rascal and a troublemaker to be sure, but not really malevolent. On the Continent, evidently, he was no Elf at all. His height and especially the large pointed ears marked him as Fae.

Vaustas writhed on the floor, on his knees in penitence, hands reaching to the Lord and the Lady in their cool blue and green robes. Mallecho waved the parchment contract, shrieking incoherently. Stalemate.

Cade's lip curled in derision as an entirely new character walked out from the wings. The other four froze in place as he took center stage, settled his black robes, and said in very careful Albeyni, "The bargain struck. Though twenty-four hours is as twenty-four years to a Fae, likewise a mere turn of the hourglass for a breed that counts life in centuries. And thus Vaustas was given over to the Fae for that length of time—a brief taste of Hell before the Lord and the Lady in their mercy claimed his soul for their own."

The counting up of hours, days, years, whatever, made no sense to Cade. He was too busy watching the slow fade-out of all the lights but one, marveling in spite of himself at the skill of the specialist. All alone the fifth character—Cade surmised him to be the Continental equivalent of a Good Brother—stood saying his piece, while behind him came the rustle and flurry of painted scenery being changed. Well, Cade thought, one worked with what one had. There was more about the kindness and benevolence of the Lord and the Lady, and how no man was so lost in evil and sin and malicious magic that he could not be saved if he were truly penitent. Then the stage suddenly lit up in a vision of paradise. Rolling green hills, snowcapped mountains in the distance, a cool blue lake, trees, flowery meadows, everything as lovely and idyllic as anyone could wish. Vaustas meandered onstage wearing a rather sappy smile, meant, Cade supposed, to convey relieved delight.

The curtains whisked closed, and the audience began to applaud: politely, but no more than politely, and only for a couple of minutes. There was none of the frenetic cheering Cade was used to after a Touchstone performance (well, with that one mortifying exception). The masquers didn't even come out to take a bow.

As the audience rose and began to file out of Fliting Hall, Touchstone and the Shadowshapers stayed in their seats. Cade eventually leaned across Sakary to look at Rauel, who was looking at Vered, who drawled, "Won't be seeing them on any of the circuits, I s'pose."

Mieka snorted and got to his feet. "If I'm to watch you tregetours break your arms patting yourselves on the back for your cleverness, I need a drink."

8

Sitting in the back garden of the Shadowstone Inn, with drinks and nibbles close at hand, the Shadowshapers, Touchstone, and the Crystal Sparks held a lengthy discussion about what they had seen that night on the Fliting Hall stage. As accomplished players, they snarked and sneered for a while about how they could have done it better with their eyes closed in the middle of a three-day drunk before getting down to genuine analysis.

"It was dead," was Rauel's opinion. "No emotion, no sensation."

Mirko Challender snorted. "They emoted all over the stage! Did you ever see such overacting?"

"But it went only as far as the stage," said Rafe. "Possibly the first couple of rows. You're right, Rauel—to the majority of the audience, it was a cold dead lump."

Lederris Daggering, masquer for the Sparks, began enumerating flaws on his thick, blunt fingers. "Just for starters, the vines should've brought a strangling sensation. The sickles should've felt cold in their hands. Pulling the fur cloaks closer should've felt warm, with softness all along the chin and jawline. That pathetic little red light meant to be the Hells—naught of flames and stench and fear, a *real* Hell. It was all dead, just as you say."

"I disagree," Cade murmured. When the others turned on him, protesting, he smiled and held up one placating hand. "Oh, it was lifeless compared to what we can do, yes. But not all the applause was mere politeness. Some of the audience felt honestly moved."

"Bah!" snapped Jacquan Bentbrooke, glisker for the Crystal Sparks, with a toss of his golden head. "How could they be? Lacking a glisker to quicken their emotions, how could they be feeling what they were supposed to be feeling? Answer me that!"

"And how could it be done," Sakary mused, "with all those people onstage?"

"Total chaos," agreed Jeska. "If the glisker and fettler had to switch emotions each time a different character speaks a few lines—Gods, how maddening!"

"Literally maddening, in all likelihood," Rafe said. "For us and the audience both. There's a good reason why there's only one masquer in our sort of play—or two at the most," he amended, glancing at Vered and Rauel.

"The effects," declared Mirko, "were feeble at best. Did you see the crackles in that painted canvas backdrop?"

"And the little bladder of red paint to simulate blood!" Mieka sniggered. "And the way that revolving painting got all hitched up at one point, and the grape vines half-throttling them, and—"

"And any number of things," Cade interrupted. "Nonetheless, there were people who responded." He turned to Rafe. "You remember the show we did in Shollop that time? Taking out all the sounds, making the visuals and Jeska's face do most of the work?"

"And my glisking!" Mieka reminded him, frowning.

"And your glisking," he echoed dutifully to mollify his vain and volatile little Elf. "My point is that even without all the sounds, and even without Jeska speaking the words, the audience in Shollop *was* affected by the play." He speared a marinated mushroom on his fork and waved it gently in Vered and Rauel's direction. "Your 'Life in a Day' holds back the emotions until the very end. And yet every time I've seen you do it, the audience is responding all through the piece."

Chat narrowed his gaze. "Are you trying to say that mayhap they've got something going, these players?"

"I'm saying that if the story's good enough, it doesn't need all the flash and spangle."

"Don't tell that to Black Lightning," Mieka smirked. "Their whole career is built on flash and Spangler!"

They all grimaced and groaned at his word-play on Pirro's last name. He sat back in his chair, looking sunnily pleased with himself. Cade rolled his eyes and drew breath to continue the discussion, but Vered beat him to it.

"What was so great about that story?" Vered demanded. "Aside from insulting everyone in Albeyn who has even a twitching of magic, that is."

"Consider," said Cade, "how it plays on the Continent." He glanced at Mieka, who nodded agreement.

"Cade's got the right of it. Magic is squinted at sidelong, and anyone with ears like mine had best cover 'em up quick. This play, with magic being evil and spiteful and ending you up in one of the nastier Hells—oh, they eat this Mallecho play up with shovels over there, they do."

"Consider," Cade said again, silky-voiced, "what a slightly different version would do to them, eh?"

Rafe narrowed his gaze for a moment, then sighed his resignation. Jeska took a gulp of his drink. Mirko was chuckling into his glass; he knew Cade rather better than Jacquan, Lederris, and the Sparks' taciturn fettler, Brennert Copperboggin. As for the Shadowshapers—Rauel looked confused, Chat looked resigned, and Sakary looked from face to face to face, one corner of his mouth twitching in amusement. Vered began to smile. But it was Mieka, who hadn't known him longest but somehow knew him best, who laughed with anticipatory glee and poured Cade another drink.

"You're about to suggest something really, truly, appallingly, scathingly awful, aren't you?" the Elf asked.

Cade gave them all his best *Innocent little me?* expression. Rafe plucked a knife from the table and poised it to throw at him. Vered, who was seated next to Cade, wrapped both arms around his head and cowered dramatically—and all at once Cade felt the nagging, clawing sensation of an Elsewhen on the edges of his mind. He pushed it away, adept at rejection by now, and grinned.

"If it's a fiendish thingy you have in mind, me lad," said Sakary, "how can we help?"

The next morning, letters arrived from Gallantrybanks just as they were preparing to head out for the rehearsal hall. They lingered in the taproom, expecting a quick read, but moments into Blye's letter Cade was fuming.

"Mieka!" he snarled, and the Elf looked up from a letter from his wife. "Didn't you tell her to give that glass shard to Blye?"

"Of course I did."

"Well, she didn't." He read aloud, easily interpreting Blye's quick, illegible scrawl; he'd been deciphering it for many years:

The evening of the day you left for Seekhaven, I asked Mieka's wife if she had anything to give me, but she didn't. Nearly as I can figure, it was wrapped in a bit of wool, and when she changed dresses to go shopping, she didn't take it out of her pocket. Whichever of the cousins it is who gathers up the laundry took the skirt downstairs, went through the pockets like she does with everything, and threw away the clump of wool. The cousin and Mieka's wife are both ever so sorry, but it remains that the thing is gone.

"Oh," Mieka said inadequately. "She doesn't mention it in her letter."

"What were you thinking could be done with a crimped end of a hallmarked withie, anyhow?" Jeska asked. "It's not proof of anything, we decided that in the wagon on the way here."

"You remember that spell we were told about on the Continent? The one about a brick suddenly deciding to grow dozens like itself and become a building? I was thinking maybe we could find someone with—I don't know, a Reassembly spell, I guess you might call it—and have it put back together."

"Would such a spell tell you who put the magic into it?" Rafe asked. "More to the point, would it identify that person before it reassembled the magic as well as itself—" He leaned forward, right into Cade's face. *"—and blew up?"*

Cade slumped. "I hadn't thought of that," he admitted.

"It's gone, and there's an end to it," Rafe said, heading for the door. "And we're late for rehearsal."

On their walk, Mieka pulled Cade back a few paces and said, "She says Fa is furious with all the things people are saying about Jed and Jez, that they're incompetent. He went to inspect the Gallery, every part of it he could get to. What she doesn't write in her letter but Jez does in his was that Fa took along one of the Staindrop uncles, or great-uncles, I'm not sure and it doesn't matter, anyway one of 'em who'd actually got caught up in the war and knows what he's looking for by way of nasty magic. The rest of the withie is in a million pieces, but tracing back the shards and the destruction pattern—whatever that means—they found where it had to've been put."

"Where?"

"On the river side of the Gallery, in a room on the ground floor. Anybody could've just tossed it in from the riverbank or even from a boat on the water—no windowglass yet."

"Blye said she was there to take final measurements," Cade

mused. "So we're left with knowing it was one of Splithook's withies, and he makes them for Black Lightning, among others, and somebody primed it and threw it right before it exploded. But the evidence got binned."

"I'm sure she's sorry," Mieka mumbled. "I ought to've told her how important it was."

"It makes no neverminding. It's not as if we could make any accusations, even with the crimp end to hand. We know as much about the accident that wasn't an accident as we're ever going to know—"

"Unless you see something that explains it." Mieka smacked a palm to his own forehead in an exaggerated mockery of recollection. "Oh, but you don't do that anymore, do you? Too *boring*."

Cade lengthened his strides, boot heels emphatic on the paving stones as he caught up to Rafe and Jeska. He was in no mood to quarrel. He'd thought Mieka had given over being angry about the Elsewhens, and simply accepted the situation. Nothing had been said on the journey to Seekhaven, and indeed the Elf had been behaving towards him just as he always did. Cade cursed himself for ever having admitted the truth.

The Shadowshapers and Crystal Sparks were waiting in the rehearsal hall. Vered and Rauel had offered their own time there to work on the response play, saying that the Shadowshapers were more than ready for Trials. Liquor had loosened their imaginations last night, ideas tumbling any whichway, but in the sober light of morning there was practical stagecraft to be organized by professionals, the best in Albeyn.

It fascinated Cade to see how the other two groups worked. He learned as well a new respect for the group from the Continent, and especially for whoever it was who managed the performances of thirty-five or forty people onstage and backstage. Usually it was all he could do to keep track of a single wayward Elfen glisker.

It was easy to see who did the bulk of the work in Crystal

Sparks. Mirko and Lederris went off by themselves in a corner for a while, muttering, gesturing, scribbling, snarling, and final nodding approval. Their glisker and fettler, Jacquan and Brennert, had brought a pack of cards and ignored everyone while Mirko and Lederris thrashed everything out between them. Some sort of signal told them when to join their masquer and tregetour, yet there was no further discussion of what they wanted to do. Mirko and Lederris simply informed them of what was needed. All the other two did was take notes.

The Shadowshapers, on the other hand, worked in shifting threes: Sakary and Chat with Vered, then with Rauel, then with Vered again, and so on until all four got together to squabble a bit before agreeing on a working draft.

Only Touchstone sat together for the whole process. True, Cayden had brought with him a detailed outline and commentary that he'd written on his own, and he read it out to his partners, but in contrast to the other groups, there were suggestions, protests, additions, and corrections from fettler, masquer, and glisker. Cade might not have the total control that Mirko and Lederris did, but neither did he have to compete with another tregetour the way Vered and Rauel had to. If he had to define it, he would have said that Mirko and Lederris told the others, *We've decided that this is the way you'll be doing it;* Vered and Rauel each would say, *My way's better and here's why;* and as for Cade himself—*What do you think? How should this be played?* He had his own ideas about all of it, of course, but he also knew that he was playing with the best fettler and the best glisker and the best masquer in the Kingdom. He had to acknowledge and respect that—and nothing could have lessoned him more convincingly than the disaster of "Turn Aback." They'd told him what was wrong with it. He hadn't listened. It was a mistake he would never make again.

With three masquers working at the same time, the details of blocking out who got which portion of the stage (so the gliskers didn't overlap and confuse the fettlers) took the rest of the morning. The hour for lunching was long gone by the time they'd run through the piece with much-muted magic, and when Baltryn Knolltread came in to tell them that the hall was needed for someone else, they were astonished to find it was nearly time for tea.

"No wonder I'm starving," Mieka grumbled as he tied up the velvet bag of withies. No one had used more than a fraction of what would be done for the real performance; Cade had worried that in the effort to impress one another, the tregetours would prime, and the gliskers use, the withies more forcefully than was standard in a rehearsal. Evidently the importance of what they would perform prevailed over any petty, if playful, swanking.

"One more go-through on the morning of the night we play it," Mirko said as they left the hall, "and that should make everything right."

Rauel laughed. "Or at least as not-totally-wrong as we can make it after only two real rehearsals!"

"We're professionals, we are," intoned Vered, purposefully pompous. "We're knowing what we're about."

"And if we don't," Mieka said, "we can sham it so professionally that the audience won't notice!"

"The Stewards would," Lederris mused.

Brennert, his glisker, gave an elaborate shrug of skinny shoulders. "Ah, but we're not being *judged* on this performance, are we?"

Cade saw the Shadowshapers trade smirks and significant glances. They were plotting something, he felt sure—and for just an instant wondered if an Elsewhen might have warned him what it was.

He hadn't long to wait for the solution of the mystery, but Touchstone was compelled to wait for nearly an hour after the Shadowshapers finished at Trials.

They'd been scheduled to do the Second Peril. They didn't.

They performed "A Life in A Day" instead. And such was the power of Chattim's glisking, and Sakary's fettling, and the magic that Vered and Rauel had primed into the withies, that no one in the audience stirred an eyelash until it was all over.

Cade, finally enlightened about that sly look the four had shared, stood with his partners in the wings of Fliting Hall, listening as murmurings became commotion, and commotion became all-out uproar.

"Oh, dear," Jeska sighed. "I'm guessing it will be a bit of a while before we can be going on."

"My thought exactly," Mieka replied. "Anybody else for a drink?"

The Shadowshapers entered the tiring room just then, grinning all over their faces, to be bombarded with questions by roughly half the twelve other groups there assembled. Vered caught Cade's eye and winked. Rauel was laughing a wild and excited laugh, rather as if he'd just pricked a little too much bluethorn. Sakary replied with stony silence to anything anybody asked him, and pushed through the crowd to the array of drinks in the far corner. Chat paused to supervise the three boys who were carrying glass baskets, lecterns, and withies to a safe place, then headed for Touchstone.

"Well," he said, blue eyes dancing, "we've been and gone and done it now, ain't we?"

"I like the choice of play," Cade remarked. "Subtle."

"We were wondering how many people would catch on."

"With your main character agonizing over a life blindly spent and mostly wasted?" Cade chuckled. "An elbow in the ribs along with a middle finger under their noses!"

Vered joined them, slinging an affectionate arm over his glisker's shoulders. "Free as a bird, that's what I'm feeling right now! Master of me own fate!" He slugged back a gulp of beer and laughed.

"Did you see poor old Rommy?" Chat asked. "We've been telling him and telling him we'd do it, but he had a seizure anyway!"

Mieka arrived with all his fingers and both thumbs wrapped around the handles of seven glass mugs of beer. "Drink up, old son," he said to Chat. "You deserve it. And it's probably the last of the King's free beer you'll ever taste!"

"Listen with those sharp little Elfen ears of yours and tell me if you can hear my heart breaking." Chat relieved him of a mug and drank deeply.

"What I'm hearing," said Mieka as he distributed the rest of the drinks, "is the Stewards shrieking themselves raw in the throat." He contorted his face into a horrible scowl and using six different voices in succession said, "They were magnificent—but they didn't do their assigned piece—no, but they *were* magnificent—yes, but they didn't do their assigned piece! But they were magnificent and how do we justify not giving them First Flight on the Royal? *But they didn't do their assigned fucking piece!*"

Jeska's brows arched. "Not bad. Not bad at all."

Mieka bowed his gratitude. "I watch and I listen and I learn."

"You're in no danger of losing your job to him," Vered said to Jeska. "The voices were all right, but he'd never stand for that pretty face of his to be concealed behind magic."

"*I* manage," Jeska said.

"And brilliantly, too." The Elf smiled serenely. "Still, it's my feeling that since the Old Gods in their ancient wisdom made me the way they made me, hiding me would obviously be a sacrilege as well as a shame."

Rauel came over to them, trailing a few astonished young players who were still trying to get their minds around what the Shadowshapers had just done. He bestowed his most adorable smile on Touchstone and said, "Dreadfully sorry you're having to wait. Shouldn't take them much more than another hour or two."

"No worrying," Cade replied. "Going out on your own this year, I take it?"

A couple of the new young players gasped. Rauel eyed them sidelong and they all blushed.

"We're not going through the insult of Trials anymore. Neither will we be locked into a circuit. We'll make our own giggings when, where, and as we please. Nobody owns us except us."

"Succinctly put," approved Vered. "Once Rommy's recovered himself, he'll calm them down. Wretched old crambazzles, they've been shocked out of their skins!"

"Yeh, the pity and remorse just drip from you, don't they?" Rauel teased.

"What about the King's celebrations in the autumn?" Jeska asked. "For the Royal and Ducal, it'll be the last show of the circuit, and for the Winterly, it'll be the first. But if you're not First Flight—"

Vered smiled sweetly. "If King Meredan wants us, he'll have to pay us."

This might well have been sacrilege, to judge by the reactions of the younger players. But Touchstone and the Shadowshapers—and the Crystal Sparks, who'd wandered over carrying their glass baskets and withies—laughed themselves silly, and drank more beer to toast freedom.

Touchstone, and especially Cayden, ceased to be amused after about an hour of standing about like office clerks waiting for the Gallybanks morning coach while Romuald Needler settled the Stewards. Rafe was just muttering that it would be midnight before the Thirteenth was played and they all learned their places on the circuits when Needler trudged into the tiring room, tall, thin, and drooping.

"You're up," he told Cade, then gathered the Shadowshapers to him with a glance. "Time for some talking amongst us, lads."

Touchstone performed the Third Peril with poise and skill,

much to the relief of the Stewards—who were wondering what in all Hells they'd do if the Shadowshapers' shocking rebellion spread. Cade privately conjectured that Touchstone might have been given a few extra points just for sticking to their assigned play.

The rest of the performances went smoothly, though a couple of the newest groups were a trifle shaky or somewhat overly emphatic in execution—the Blazing Hornets in particular, who sported little polished brass pins flaunting their name. Well, Cade thought magnanimously, they were young. Still, the rest of the Thirteen Perils were played, and the Stewards huddled together in the front corner of Fliting Hall, and for the first time in the history of Trials at Seekhaven, the results were not given the same night. When it was announced from the stage that the Flights would not be decided on, Vered and Rauel shared a triumphant grin.

Speculation and rumor rampaged through Seekhaven for two days while the Shadowshapers sunned themselves in Mistress Luta's garden. On the final evening of Trials, Hawk's Claw graciously relinquished the last performance in Fliting Hall, though it would be their first time for this coveted place. Cade never knew what persuasions were used on them—though he suspected that two pairs of big puppy-dog eyes (Mieka's and Rauel's) had had very little to do with it. Trenal Longbranch and his partners weren't fools. More likely was the fact that they'd traded the last-night performance with the one given the night before that for the ladies at the Pavilion. Few and far between would be the groups who turned down the chance to go on in place of the Shadowshapers. Hawk's Claw made a good showing of it, or so Cade had heard the next day. For himself, he spent the whole evening with the Shadowshapers and Crystal Sparks, working on their new play.

Rumors had got out, of course. Thirteen groups of Trials-invited players in one theater-mad town made for rapid relay of gossip: better, faster, but less accurate than a Gallybanks broadsheet. The rehearsal hall was always empty after the Thirteen Perils had been performed—so what were the three best groups in Albeyn doing there two mornings in a row? Baltryn Knolltread was let in on the plan, and guarded the door against all comers. Pirro Spangler very nearly got in, however, pleading for a brief moment of Mieka's time; it seemed he'd lost a withie somewhere and because the Royal and Ducal would start immediately after Trials, with no return to Gallantrybanks for resupply, he wanted to borrow one. Baltryn didn't let him in. He waited for a pause in the proceedings, then approached the stage.

"Lederris, old son," Mieka warned, "you get betwixt me and Jeska one more time and I'll— What is it, Baltryn?"

He explained. Mieka pretended chagrin as he claimed he hadn't a withie to spare, and Baltryn withdrew.

"The cheek of it!" Brennert shook his head. "Lend him a withie, indeed!"

"Gettin' careless, he is," Chat mused. "Too much thorn and not enough attention to counting his withies."

Cade very deliberately didn't look at his partners. Was it madness to believe that he had a good idea of what had happened to that withie?

9

To the collective shock of the Stewards (who were having rather a rough time of it this year) the Shadowshapers, Touchstone, and the Crystal Sparks all showed up at Fliting Hall a mere ten minutes before the final performance at Trials. They didn't use the front door. None of the players did—and of course every single one of the players contending for a place on the circuits was there, because the places on those circuits had not yet been announced. The Shadowshapers, Touchstone, and the Crystal Sparks went in by the artists' entrance and enlisted the help of a few friends to lug in three sets of glass baskets, three velvet bags of withies, two glisker's benches, six lecterns, and an armful of wood that, unfolded and assembled, turned into supporting frames for Touchstone's glass baskets. All this was set up onstage in a complicated arrangement while the tregetours— Vered Goldbraider, Rauel Kevelock, Cayden Silversun, and Mirko Challender—made it quite clear to the nearly apoplectic Stewards that everything was quite in order, and Hawk's Claw had graciously ceded their place tonight for a special, one-time-only performance. Trenal Longbranch was shouted for, and found lounging in a corner of the tiring room. Appealed to, he confirmed the arrangement. The Stewards were compelled to accept it, for there were upwards of six hundred people in Fliting Hall waiting for a play, and whereas the other three members of Hawk's Claw were also present, they had neither withies nor glass baskets to perform with.

Rauel smiled his adorable big-eyed smile at the furious Stewards. Vered paused to blow them a kiss over his shoulder before walking onstage. Cade sketched a flourishing bow, Mirko waved cheerily, and all twelve players assembled in carefully calculated positions behind the curtains. A quick run-through of the play that morning had revealed a snag or two, easily corrected. Everything they had jeered at a few days ago, about the deadness of the atmosphere and the silliness of all those slapdash backgrounds, they would make happen with magic. Cade knew the timing was still a little off—they'd not worked it out as tightly as it really ought to be, but for the effort of a couple of days, it would be quite good. Not the polished, perfect performance all three groups were accustomed to giving, but it would make their point.

Besides, even if they did experience a hitch or three along the way, they had an option the Continental players did not: They could cover it up with magic.

He worried about the spread of that magic over the audience, though. The three gliskers would work with their own masquers as usual, and it would be up to the fettlers to control what and where and which one would dominate at any given instant. Brennert Copperboggin was much like Rafe and Sakary: as taciturn and watchful in his private life as he was onstage. What he lacked was a sense of humor, as far as Cayden could tell. Earnest and even grim at times, he also seemed to lack the quickness, the agility that made Rafe and Sakary the best in Albeyn. Well, Cade thought to himself with a shrug, as long as he stuck to the plan without trying to elbow aside everyone else's magic so that Lederris shone more brightly than any of the other masquers, things would be fine.

The play had been the easy part. It was the notations for performing it that had proved problematic. Each of the three gliskers had his own little code by now, incomprehensible to anyone else. None of them had studied with the same master, so there was no shared foundation to build on. At length they decided to work the way they always worked, each using his own code, marking the scripts in that code with warnings about which of them would take over at various points in the play.

Cade watched with a smile twitching his lips as Baltryn Knolltread made a respectful bow to his elders in the wings and sidled his way through a break in the curtains. A few moments later his voice rang out to announce the players and the play—and surely it wasn't just Cade's imagination that supplied the buried laughter in his voice.

"Your Majesty! Your Royal Highnesses! Your Grace! My Lords, Ladies, and Gentlemen! The Master of the King's Revelries is pleased to welcome the Shadowshapers—*and* Touchstone—*and* the Crystal Sparks—in a special performance of a new play! 'The Soul-Snuppers'!"

So that's what we're calling it, Cade thought, wondering who had come up with a title. Somehow, in all the discussions and deliberations, wrangles and analyses, not one of them had thought to name the thing. He thought he detected Vered's sardonic sense of humor; *snup* came from *snap up,* as in grabbing something valuable at a bargain price.

Baltryn had included *Ladies* in his greeting, so there were more women here than just Miriuzca, who could be counted on to attend any performance she possibly could. Only one *Your Majesty* meant the Queen was not in attendance. Queen Roshien had dutifully sat through several plays at the last Trials and a few Court performances since, but, it was said, had decided that although theater was charming enough, she wasn't particularly interested. Everyone knew, however, that she had the intellectual prowess of a teakettle and didn't like theater, because she didn't understand it.

The plural *Highnesses* meant that both Ashgar and Miriuzca were here. Iamina, of course, would not demean herself by coming to a play. And, because there were two Your Graces in Albeyn and only one had been mentioned, neither would the Archduchess Panshilara be present. The newfound piety of Princess and Archduchess demanded renunciation of theater and other crude amusements. And, if the stories were true, abandonment of personal ornamentation as well; Iamina's famous yellow jewel had been given to the new little Princess Levenie as a Namingday present, and Panshilara's bulky and vulgar wedding ring had gone into her husband's coffers—possibly against the day when their daughter, Belsethine, would be old enough to wear it, possibly for the future bride of their son, Boltris. It remained that neither woman wore much by way of jewelry these days, which, in its way, was as ostentatious as the gaudiest finery.

Cade drummed his fingers on his lectern, caught himself at it, stopped, and wondered why the curtains stayed shut. Nervous enough about this performance already, the tregetours and gliskers, masquers and fettlers, all looked at each other with varying degrees of anxiety, bewilderment, and annoyance. Then Cade heard a gruff voice rise disapprovingly.

"What's it called? Never heard of it. And weren't we given to understand that Hawk's Claw would perform tonight?"

The King, who had been attending plays for longer than any of these particular players had been alive, was confused. Someone else's voice came soothingly, but His Majesty was having none of it.

"All three in the same play? Never been done. Crowds the stage, what?" Pause; low-voiced explanation. "Goldbraider, you say? *And* Silversun? Hm. Clever boys, both of 'em. But I don't care much for surprises in my theater." Longer pause. Then: "Response to *what*? Oh. I see. Very well. Let's see what this new thing is."

Cade was so astounded to hear himself praised in the same

breath as Vered Goldbraider that he almost missed the opening swirl of shadows. They were of Chat's making; this was, after all, partly a Shadowshapers performance. As for the rest of it . . . Cade smiled to himself and did his usual work of surveying the audience in support of his fettler. Strange, to sense two other fettlers in the mix, and stranger still to have four masquers onstage while three gliskers used the magic of four tregetours to create Albeyn's reply to the Continental players.

Vaustas (Lederris Daggering: nondescript, plainly clothed, and fidgety) was a boy of about fifteen, with mixed Wizard, Elf, and Goblin blood, physical traits indicating his ancestry: height, pointed ears, crooked teeth, and so on. The play opened on him alone onstage in a library that looked just like the one used in the magic-less players' play. It was Mieka's little joke on them to have Vaustas wander over to the shelves and pluck out a book or three to hold in his hand or set on a table or chair. Lederris's own glisker, Brennert, was clothing him, but for this portion of the play, Mieka had control of the backdrop while Chat provided the sensations.

"Vaustas!" yelled Vered, unseen behind the illusory library walls, in a woman's high-pitched tone of demand. "Clean up your clutter, boy, and come downstairs to dinner!"

Lederris called back, "Yes, Mother!" and, surveying the piles of books and papers all over the chairs and table and flowery rug, sighed dismally. He struggled within himself, the emotions clear on his face and in the magic lightly touching the audience. Then Vaustas pointed a finger, and a small pile of books rose from the floor and drifted lazily towards the shelves. Vaustas pointed to another stack of books, but before they rose from the table, he turned away and clenched both fists.

"No. I won't use magic. I won't!"

Cade sensed it, but knew the audience did not: the skilled handoff of the background to Chat, while Mieka readied himself. From the window that opened onto pasture and woods came a whirl of silvery smoke, and from it Jeska appeared, wearing his own gorgeous face, gorgeously robed in blood red: Mallecho.

"My, my! You *have* made a bit of a mess, haven't you? Looks to be the work of an hour at least, and that means your mother will be annoyed and your dinner will be cold. Why *not* use magic on the rest of it, too?"

"I don't want to."

"Really? Why not?"

"I don't like magic!" He hesitated, then burst out, "I *hate* my magic!"

"No need to be so defensive, lad. Magic is a thing that could happen to anyone, you know."

"It's deceitful."

Mallecho snorted. "About as deceitful as having red hair or big feet. It's part of you, and no denying it."

"But I could dye my hair," Vaustas said sulkily.

"And lop off your toes to make your feet shorter?"

"I wish I could do that to my magic! It's wicked, don't you see? It's a cheat, and it's rotten and evil and—and I hate it! I wish I could chop it out or carve it away, and have nothing to do with it ever again!"

"Hm." Mallecho walked slowly round him, and at last folded his arms across his chest. "Well, then. If you feel that way about it, and if that's what you truly want . . . I believe I can oblige. For a price." He smiled, and it was Jeska's sweetly captivating smile, nothing sinister about it at all—but with a smidgeon of mischief wafting over the audience from Mieka's withies and Cayden's magic.

"Anything! If you can truly rid me of magic, I'll pay anything!" Feverishly, Vaustas clasped both hands together. "If I have to work the rest of my life mucking out stalls in the castle stables—cleaning the middens—taking care of the cows or—or stuck all alone on a hillside with the sheep!"

"Oh, it's nothing so dire as that. Truth to be told, it's really nothing much at all, as most people reckon it, if one takes into account what they do with their lives. One can't help but wonder what they're thinking, or if they think at all before they act, but—that's their own business, I suppose." Mallecho shrugged. "The price of your magic, my dear Vaustas, is your soul. You may live your life free of your own magic, but at the end of your life, your soul is mine. Agreed?"

"Agreed!"

"You don't want a minute to think it over?"

"I don't need even an instant to think it over! My soul will be the purer and my life the more virtuous for being free of magic. Do it now!"

"Don't you want to clear up the library first? No? Very well. Brace yourself."

Vaustas struck a pose, arms outstretched, head flung back. Mallecho rolled his eyes and shook his head. He made a coaxing gesture with his left hand, and from Vaustas's chest, there streamed shimmering rivers of light, the blue of a Wizard and the gold of an Elf and the green of a Goblin. Mallecho caught all in his right hand and stuffed it into a pocket of his robes.

After a moment, Vaustas looked at him, frowning. "Well? Is it done? I didn't feel anything."

"Would you like it to have hurt?"

"No—I mean, shouldn't I have felt *something*?"

"Try some magic," Mallecho suggested.

Vaustas half turned, saw a pile of books, and made a gesture as if to brush them all back onto the shelves. The books stayed put.

Mallecho, listening to the young man's joyous laughter, shook his head again and spread his arms wide, as if to say, *Who can possibly understand this idiot?* Then the mother's voice shouted an impatient demand, and Mallecho said, "I told you that you should have cleaned the place up first!"

Shadows wafted once more across the stage. When they

lifted, Vaustas was much older: stooped and white-haired, any age from eighty to a hundred. He wore the same drab clothing, and stood in the same library, with the same books and the same woodland scene beyond the windows. He hobbled about the room, as faded as the flowered rug, mumbling to himself.

Mallecho, young and vigorous, handsome as ever in his dark crimson robes, appeared in a gusting shadow that rippled lightly across the library's curtains and a few loose papers on a table. Vaustas looked at him, blinking and confused.

"You?" he asked at last. "Have you come for me?"

Strolling idly round the library, Mallecho said, "Don't tell me you've read all these books! The work of a lifetime, eh? Have you had enough? Not that it matters. Yes, I've come for your soul." He trailed a finger along a shelf, and held it up, gray with dust. "Ugh. Nasty. Well, it's appropriate, anyway. Dust you came from, and dust you shall be. It's time, so if there's any note you'd like to leave for your loved ones—no? Not a single loved one? Not a single friend?"

Before Vaustas could reply, two more shadows were spun from thin air, and in the next eyeblink had coalesced into the Lord and the Lady (Vered and Rauel, respectively).

Mallecho looked mildly surprised, but unworried. "And what are *you* doing here?"

"He is one of Ours," said the Lord, gathering his dark green cloak around him.

"One of Our children," added the Lady, beautifully garbed in blue and silver. "All living beings are Our children."

Both of them lowered their hoods to reveal ears extravagantly pointed, more Fae than Elfen. Mallecho bowed mockingly and said, "Come to claim him for yours? I assume you know he sold his soul to me, in order to be rid of his magic."

The Lady inclined her head gracefully. "Nevertheless, We claim him."

"That depends on what sort of soul he's got, doesn't it? What he's done with it during his four-and-twenty and four-and-twenty and—" He paused to count up on his fingers. "—and four-and-twenty years. Let's have a look-see, shall we?"

Vaustas limped forward at the Lord's gesture. Hunched and frail, he seemed completely uninterested in this contention over his soul.

"I have everything all ready for him," Mallecho said, and snapped his fingers, and where the window had been, there now was a yawning void that quickly filled with greedy flames. The red glow flared, then settled down like a cat at a mouse hole, complacently waiting for the inevitable kill. "Haven't decided yet which Hell would be the most appropriate," Mallecho went on rather apologetically, "but he can roast a bit while I figure it out."

"We, too, are prepared for him," said the Lady, and waved a hand. Opposite the fires a scene of sylvan peace replaced a wall of books: tender greens, crystalline blues, warmed by sunlight and cooled with a soft breeze.

"Very pretty, my dear," approved the Lord. "Now, where were We? Ah, yes. The soul."

The Lady spread her open hands wide, as if to gather something up. Nothing happened. The Lord attempted the same thing, with the same result.

"What's wrong?" Mallecho asked in a concerned and sympathetic tone at odds with the smile playing around his lips. "Can't you find it?"

"Silence!" the Lord commanded. Both he and the Lady tried again, but to no avail.

"But he has to *have* a soul," the Lady fretted. "Everyone does."

"He's not dead yet," Mallecho remarked, "so it must still be in there. I mean to say, it's not as if it suddenly vanished or anything. You gave it to him, so if not even You can find it, then—"

The Lord, after a horrible scowl for Mallecho, confronted Vaustas and bellowed, "Come forth!"

All at once a thin, shriveled, colorless lump of *something* appeared in Vaustas's place. More substantial than a pallid gray fog, less solid than a cloud of spun white sugar, it drifted aimlessly upwards, then downwards, from side to side, and at last settled a few feet from the library floor.

"That's *it*?" Mallecho asked, staring. "Scarcely worth contending over!"

"Pitiful," muttered the Lord. More briskly, moving around the wan, pathetic lump of a soul, he said, "You know what's happened, don't you?"

"Enlighten me," Mallecho invited.

"It was all your fault," the Lady admonished. "You were the one who took away his magic."

"But he asked me to! Said it was evil and unclean, and wanted nothing to do with it!"

"Without it," said the Lord, "he could not become what he was meant to become. His soul remained a mere nursling. It never grew up. It never grew at all."

Mallecho propped his fists on his hips, frowning. Then, with a sigh and a shrug, he said, "If that's all there is to his soul, it's of no use to me."

"Nor to anyone, most of all himself," agreed the Lord. "It isn't as if any soul, any being, can grow and ripen when so much of it is rejected and denied."

"But what will We do with him?" the Lady asked anxiously.

"Whatever you like," Mallecho said, with a final, disgusted glance at Vaustas's blighted soul. "Nothing in it for me. I bid you good day until next we meet—in more interesting circumstances, I hope, to battle over something worth having!"

He ambled into his fiery preview of Hell and vanished.

There was a brief silence as the Lord and the Lady contemplated the shapeless soul before them. At last the Lady said, "I know what We ought to do, my Lord."

"I was just thinking the same thing, dearest Lady."

They smiled at each other. Standing so that Vaustas's soul was between them, they spread their arms and from their fingertips arced blue and gold and green fire that surrounded and then penetrated the hazy, stunted soul. The light grew brighter and brighter, and the unshapen thing acquired substance, color, identity, and became Vaustas, a young boy again, immobile and silent yet radiant with all the magic that had been his at birth.

"It's no guarantee," mused the Lord, "that he'll do with his gifts that which will keep him from ending up in any or all of the Hells."

"But he is once again a whole being, and his soul is his own, and complete. To use oneself and all the gifts of intellect and magic and spirit and everything else for good or ill, that is every person's choice. He must decide."

"It will be interesting to see if his soul will be worth fighting for."

Vaustas came to life then, stretching his shoulders, looking at the Lord and at the Lady, and saying, "*Every* soul is worth fighting for."

Smiling at him, the Lady nodded. "You've made a start, then. Every soul *is* worth fighting for. Luck to you, Vaustas, and Our blessings."

With that, all the magic onstage abruptly winked out, and the four masquers were joined by their gliskers and fettlers and tregetours, linking arms, standing there in silent challenge to the audience. The applause began an instant later and threatened to shake down the walls. Mieka, in between Cade and Sakary, laughed aloud and tossed a withie high into the air, where it shattered into a million tiny shards that rained down in a shimmering curtain behind the players. If this had been a Shadowshapers performance, it had also been Touchstone's. Cade wondered with a smirk whether Mirko was regretting that Crystal Sparks had no signature move that hallmarked a play as theirs.

His Majesty was grinning broadly. Never the shiniest jewel in the coffers, he nonetheless understood very well what messages his players were . . . well, to be honest, what they were shoving under everyone's nose in letters six feet high while beating them over the head with a pickax. Princess Miriuzca was applauding excitedly, and when Cade caught her eye, she winked. Her brother, sitting between her and the Archduke, was seemingly questioning the latter regarding a matter of such importance that both of them forgot to clap their hands. This was noticed by nobody except those immediately around them—and the players onstage, of course.

Backstage they were congratulated by every other player there—including Black Lightning. Thierin Knottinger approached Cayden and said it had been a real treat to watch them disgrace and discredit those Continental quats, and Pirro Spangler clapped Mieka so hard on the back that he nearly fell over. The tumult in the tiring room, being in a more confined space, was even louder than the applause in Fliting Hall, and with a triumph in it that, for all their competition and rivalry, made them all Players of Albeyn together.

Toasts were shouted and drunk, and all the while, Tobalt Fluter, notebook in one hand and pen in the other, was trying to interview anybody he could get close enough to hear. Cade watched his frustrated progress through the crowd, scribbling a word here and a half a sentence there, desperate for just one coherent, attributable quote. Mieka compassionately offered Tobalt a few sips of his own beer, but somebody bumped into them and the drink drenched Tobalt and his notebook. Cade finally broke down laughing when Mieka attempted to wring out the pages like a soggy stocking.

"Come by the Shadowstone later," he told the anguished reporter. "We'll tell you all about it."

"Somebody said Copperboggin argued for including the twining vines, just to show how it ought to be done."

"Yeh, but we couldn't figure a way to work it into the piece without doing the whole tedious scene with the knives. Take pity, Tobalt—we only had a couple of days. Couldn't do *everything*!"

They had also argued about who would play Vaustas, and Jeska lost against Lederris's point that not only were old men one of his own specialties, but having Jeska wear his own delectable face during the whole of it would let Mieka concentrate on supporting Chat, who had to keep both Vered and Rauel costumed and so on. These two had got into a laughing scrape about which of them would do better as the Lady, centering on who moved more convincingly when fully gowned, until Mirko drawled that it was a shame Mieka wasn't a masquer, because he was the only one with any experience wearing real skirts instead of those created by magic. Those stories and a few more would keep Tobalt happy, Cade felt, but would scarcely divert him from probing into the other staggerment of the evening: the announcement that Touchstone would be taking First Flight on the Royal Circuit.

On the walk back to the Shadowstone Inn, notable for becoming more raucous and chaotic with every step, it was reasonably easy to avoid Tobalt. Things were a little more tense once they stashed their equipment and invaded Mistress Luta's taproom in boisterous triumph. Tobalt stood the first round of drinks (for twenty-one: the Shadowshapers, Touchstone, the Crystal Sparks, and Hawk's Claw, plus their managers, plus himself; considering the sure sales of the Trials issue this year, *The Nayword* could afford it) and when everyone was supplied with a tankard and rose for a toast that Tobalt as benefactor was supposed to give, he looked panicky. The success of the new play? Touchstone, as First Flight? The Shadowshapers, who could be assumed to need a toast to luck now that they were going out on their own?

Mieka solved his problem for him. Leaping up onto a table without spilling a single drop of beer, he yelled, "His Majesty the King!"

The Loyal Toast was drunk. Mieka jumped down—losing nothing but a globule of foam on the way—and settled into a comfortable chair, smiling his blithe delight with the world and all its wonders. Cade snorted, shaking his head, and devoted himself to further avoidance of Tobalt. The poor man couldn't decide if he was more anxious to get the Shadowshapers' reactions to being kicked off the circuit by vindictive Stewards, or Touchstone's feelings at winning First Flight without having actually won it. His readers would be keen for details. There was never much to be had out of Sakary or Chat, though Rauel was always good for a mild joke and Vered could rival Cade in talking the hind leg off a wyvern. But Mieka's jokes were better than Rauel's, and if Rafe and Jeska were reticent, Cade the Eminently Quotable always made up for it.

Cade the Eminently Quotable wasn't the first to leave the celebration, but as soon as he was certain his absence wouldn't be too much remarked, he mounted the stairs to his and Mieka's room. Even with the door closed, the noise from the taproom invaded every plank of the floor and every stitch of his blanket. Blockweed beckoned. He was just about to search for it when Mieka arrived, kicking the door shut behind him and holding aloft two beer tankards.

"Thought you might be gettin' thirsty again," he said, stepping up onto Cade's bed and sinking gracefully down cross-legged with his back to the footboard. Thus arranged, he handed over one of the tankards, took a sip from his own, and cocked his head to one side. "Well?"

"Beholden," Cade muttered, and took a healthy swig of what turned out to be brandy. Choking, coughing, eventually able to breathe again, he glared at his glisker. "You might've warned me!"

"Sure, I might have," Mieka agreed, unrepentant. "But I was thinkin' that mayhap it would give you a start on bein' ireful with me, because what I'm about to say ain't anywhere near bein' close to what you want to hear."

"And what might that be?"

"I saw your face when the Flights were announced."

"So?" He took a defiant swallow of brandy.

"We won, but we didn't really win."

"I'd sussed that out for myself."

"You'd rather beat the Shadowshapers in a fair contest, not because they broke the rules and got kicked out."

"Well . . . yeh," he admitted.

"And now you're thinkin' that we'll never have the chance to beat 'em fair."

"They'll never be asked back to Trials."

"Mm." Mieka sloshed liquor around in the tankard, frowning thoughtfully. "Is it just at Trials, I wonder, where we compete with them?"

"What do you mean?" Cade asked suspiciously.

"Oh, nothin'." He drank again, and Cade began to consider reaching over to shake him by his ears. "It's only . . . I mean, there's other ways of measuring success, right?"

"Money." As he said the word, his lip curled, and Mieka glanced up in time to see it and smile. "Well, it *is* vulgar, isn't it? To judge someone by his bank account?"

"Wasn't thinkin' of that, not at all."

"What, then? That someday we'll be in the same town at the same time with performances on the same night? They'd outsell us in tickets, you know they would."

"No, that's not it, either."

"Mieka, if you don't get to the point—"

"It's nothin' much. Just this." He flashed a look at Cade, then returned his gaze to his drink. "In all the Elsewhens you ever told me about—not that there were that many!—you never once talked about the Shadowshapers."

"What of it? How could anything I do have any influence on what any of them do?"

"The one I liked best," Mieka went on, "was the one where we're old. It's your forty-fifth Namingday but you forgot, and there was a party just starting, and I had a diamond earring. I know you don't remember it, because you deliberately got rid of all the Elsewhens, but that *was* a good one, Quill, a future to look forward to."

"If you say so."

"I do say so. But what I'm thinking is this," he went on, then paused for a swallow of brandy.

Cade noted suddenly that the *g*s were firmly attached to Mieka's words again and those eyes were brightly alert, though half-screened by heavy lashes. He sounded and looked, in fact, much less drunk than he ought to.

"After a few days of watching Vered and Rauel have it out over this play we did tonight, do you really think that with all their snarking and sniping, they'll still be playing shows together when *they're* forty-five?"

10

On the way from Seekhaven—with no stop in Gallantrybanks to celebrate their triumph—the sight of the Tincted Downs was usually an inspirational delight. In spring and summer, the gently folded hills bloomed, seemingly every fortnight, with different flowers: crimson, yellow, blue, orange, pink, purple, as if throngs of drunken Pikseys had danced through the fields flinging gallons of paint across the green carpet of grass. This year a violent wind had blown through, ripping all the petals from the flowers, leaving bare broken stems and not much else. The green undergrowth still clung to the ground, huddling as if hoping the wind wouldn't notice it, but all other color was gone.

Mieka refused to be depressed by the sight of it, or the bare-naked trees in the orchards, or the villages with the cottages' bones pitifully exposed now that all the thatching had blown away. Cade and Rafe and Jeska *thought* he was depressed, because he wasn't saying much. The truth of it was that he was working something out in his head, and before he said anything about it, he wanted to be certain sure he had it right.

In the scant weeks since Cayden's Namingday, he'd felt by turns stunned, furious, ashamed, and disappointed by this refusal to see the Elsewhens. Stunned, because they were so much a part of Cade—and to Mieka, that deliberate forgetting really was a bit like murder. Furious, because Cade might have seen something that would have prevented what had happened at Lord Piercehand's Gallery. Ashamed, because he hadn't even noticed that no descriptions of any Elsewhens had been forthcoming for almost two years. And disappointed because he'd thought Cayden was braver and smarter than anyone else he knew.

These emotions scraped and scratched at him in no particular order at night when he was supposed to be sleeping. Eventually they resolved into simple worry, which lingered, expanded, proposed all sorts of troubling things that struck him anew almost every time he looked at Cade.

Mieka knew that he couldn't rightly question himself on why he hadn't noticed—why none of them had noticed. He already knew why. They hadn't noticed, because it took too much effort to notice. It wasn't that he didn't give a damn, nor Rafe nor Jeska, either. It was just so much easier to trundle along on the Royal Circuit, in Gallantrybanks, rehearsing and gigging and saying nothing to overset anyone's balance. He supposed they had all reasoned that if Cade had seen anything interesting, he would have told them. He'd begun telling them before that terrible night in Shollop, when he'd seen Alaen and Briuly find The Rights of the Fae. And hadn't that piece of Cade's that wasn't really a play, "The Avowal," come from an Elsewhen? If there'd been something interesting or puzzling to tell about an Elsewhen, he would have told it. Or so they'd all thought, and hadn't considered it any more deeply than that.

It wasn't as if all of them didn't have problems of their own. Rafe's constant fretting about Crisiant until Bram was born had turned to a blissful blindness to just about everything and everybody else now that he had a son. Jeska's long, frustrating courtship of Kazie, with all its attendant vexations, had become, now that they were wed, a silent pining for her when Touchstone was on the road. As for Mieka . . . well, he could refuse to admit even to himself that his marriage wasn't perfect, but the facts of its imperfections were there for anyone to see if they looked just an inch or so beneath the surface. And the surface—of anything—was as far as any member of Touchstone had bothered to see for a long time.

Mieka saw things now. He couldn't not see them. Thorn and whiskey took the sharp edges off his worry, but he had grown up enough to know that there wasn't enough thorn or whiskey in the world to let him avoid things forever. The fact that he'd tried to avoid things didn't shame him; it was that he hadn't even noticed what went so wrong with Cayden.

And yet . . . *was* it wrong? Surely the Elsewhens were Cade's to see or not see as he chose. He'd been their victim for so many years, taken by them with heart-stopping suddenness. His mind was his own, wasn't it?

Of course. But the Elsewhens were part of the way his mind worked. Look at what had happened with "Turn Aback." They'd all tried to talk Cade out of it, pointing out this difficulty and that, but he had been adamant, and they'd shared a shrug amongst the three of them, thinking that he'd seen its success in an Elsewhen.

Time and again during long nights in Seekhaven, with Cade sleeping in the next bed with the help of blockweed, Mieka heroically forbade himself the redthorn that would knock him out for the hours until dawn. He *had* to reason all this out with a clear head. And time and again he concluded that it just wasn't right of Cade to refuse the Elsewhens. They were part of him, part of the way his mind worked. Without them, he was as blind to the futures as anybody else. Without them, he wasn't really Cayden Silversun.

They had left the sadly un-Tincted Downs and roofless cottages behind, bypassed Gallybanks, and were well on the road to Shollop when Mieka finally decided what to say. The *clever and mad* that Blye had advised might work in other circumstances. Not now. Not that he had any hope of being as logical and disciplined as Cade with his arguments. But at least he now knew what those arguments would be. His trouble would come in being serious; in convincing Cade that he was indeed serious, and had indeed thought deeply about this. At times it was something of an affliction, having a Kingdom-wide reputation for artful foolery.

But if there was one thing Cade always took seriously—sometimes too seriously—it was his work. Mieka couldn't help a secret grin when he realized that while Cade and Vered and Rauel and Mirko had been congratulating themselves on being so very clever in their response to the Continental players' play, together they'd given him the perfect means to make his point with Cade.

Since the Shadowshapers wouldn't be needing their huge white horses for the Royal Circuit, and there were in fact enough of them in Romuald Needler's stable now to supply (for a fee) anyone with a private wagon, Touchstone was making excellent time. Yazz, as much in love with the beasts as ever, was plotting how to persuade Needler to part with four or more of these beauties permanently, though Kearney Fairwalk blanched at the expense. Leasing them, Yazz pointed out, was more expensive in the long run than buying them outright. As for stabling, there was the mews at Wistly Hall, there was the barn at Hilldrop Crescent, and there was Fairwalk's own manor house in the country, so it wasn't as if they'd have to pay for anything but the feed. Mieka had no idea how much a year's worth of nosebags would cost, but surely it couldn't add up to more than they were paying Needler for the use of the horses. Negotiations might get somewhere, Mieka thought, now that the Shadowshapers could no longer count on the guaranteed income from the Royal—though none of them seemed worried. They probably had enough in the bank to last them through the scandal until people began to realize they could hire the best theater group in Albeyn pretty much whenever they pleased. Rafe was of the opinion that whereas the merchant and craft guilds would be lining up with buckets of money, the higher nobility would avoid the Shadowshapers (for the next little while, at least) for fear of offending the King.

"After all," Rafe had concluded, "he must be rather annoyed that he doesn't own them anymore."

"*Own*?" Cade had asked in a dreadful voice.

"*Own*," Rafe repeated. "For the length of the Royal Circuit, he owns us. Hasn't that got through to you after all these years? We do private giggings along the way, yeh, but on whose authority do we play for the Honorable Brotherhood of Nose-Pickers rather than the Singular Order of Ass-Scratchers? They pay the King for the privilege, he takes his share, and then he pays us. But the King—or, rather, the Master of Revelries—decides who has the privilege of presenting us. And *that,* my dear old lad," he concluded, "is what the Shadowshapers have escaped."

Cade had looked as if he was beginning to contemplate a similar escape, but nothing much had been said about it since. Mieka was still musing on this topic one afternoon just outside Shollop as he walked beside the wagon to stretch his legs. He kept well away from the gigantic white horses that were costing Touchstone a small fortune to lease, and told himself sourly that he didn't want to speculate on the Shadowshapers' nightly fee.

Money. Bothersome subject. His wife had been hinting for over a year about finding a flat in Gallybanks so that she didn't always have to stay with his parents. That she had expected him to present her with the signed lease on her twenty-first Namingday this winter, he was well aware. The trip to Lilyleaf had been an inadequate substitute as far as she was concerned, but he simply didn't have the coin to support both a house and a flat. He knew she had ambitions to set herself up in society, and one could hardly receive the sort of ladies she wanted to entertain in the cheerful chaos that was Wistly Hall. Suppose one of the less presentable cousins traipsed downstairs in the middle of afternoon tea, or someone decided to go for a swim—naked— during lunching on the river lawn? Mayhap Touchstone ought to do what the Shadowshapers had done. He tried to calculate how much they would be making this summer as opposed to what Touchstone would be paid as First Flight on the Royal Circuit, but numbers were Jeska's specialty, not his.

"Deep dark thoughts?"

He turned to find Cayden catching up to him. "Not really."

"When you put your fists in your pockets and walk all hunched up like that, you're always anguishing yourself about something."

He pulled his hands from his trouser pockets and straightened his spine, then rotated his arms like a windmill. "Better?"

Cade smiled and fell into step beside him. "Nice breeze out here. It's hot in the wagon."

"Mm." Mieka fought a mild skirmish with himself, then decided that now was as good a time as any. "I've been wondering. How bored do you get, not seeing any Elsewhens?"

"Bored?"

"Yeh. What I mean is, with you not really being all of you, just part of the you that's really you, the you that you are must get tired of not being really you, and you rather miss the parts of you that the you that's really you is used to being."

By the end of this speech—carefully thought out during a sleepless night in Seekhaven—Cade's jaw had dropped open and his gray eyes had gone blank. Mieka smiled sweetly.

After a time, Cade gave a gusting sigh of defeat. "Why did I try to find a way through that maze? Would you kindly explain what in all Hells you're talking about?"

"Unless you *like* it when you're bored," Mieka went on, frowning thoughtfully. "Do you?"

"Bored?" Cade echoed again, then with a slightly strained laugh: "Around you? Never!"

"Nice to know I'm so entertaining," he snapped. "Any favorite jokes you'd like me to tell? I'm afraid I'm no great dancer, but mayhap you'd care for a song or two? I work cheap."

"I didn't mean it that way."

Mieka nodded as if mollified. "You still haven't answered my question."

"About being bored?" Cade shrugged his shoulders. "It's more peaceful than boring. Quiet inside my own head."

"Sounds deathly dull," Mieka remarked, kicking at a rock in the road. It shied sidewise into the dried mud of the bordering ditch. "You mean you don't chase down words or plots or ideas or anything anymore?"

"No, that still happens."

"But no visions. No dreamings. No Elsewhens."

"No."

They walked on in silence for a time. Heat shimmered the wheat fields, the feeble breeze bending a leaf here and there in trees clustered beside a farmhouse. Insects buzzed and clicked, the horses' harness jingled, Yazz hummed tunelessly to himself up on the coachman's bench.

"Don't you miss it?" Mieka asked.

"No."

Well, *that* was a lie, he thought. "Must've been an adjustment, though," he mused. "Being like everybody else."

"I rather like it. Being ordinary."

Another lie. Cade was the most arrogant man Mieka had ever met. His talents with words, his magic, and his Elsewhens made him more than special. He was unique. Mieka decided it was time to laugh. He did, and Cade shot him an irritated glance.

"Sorry," Mieka said, not meaning it. "It's just trying to see you as *ordinary* is a bit of a stretch, even for a man with my prodigious gifts of imagination."

"I don't see the Elsewhens anymore, because I want to live like a normal person and not have to keep wondering when the next turn is going to take me, and what it will show me, and what I should or shouldn't do to change it or not change it, and—"

"What makes you think you could ever be normal, even *without* the Elsewhens?"

Cade gritted his teeth for a moment, staring at the dry dirt road ahead of him, digging his boot heels in with every step. "Blye said something like that once."

"And she's right, just like I'm right. I'm not ordinary, either—"

The retort came lightly, but with obvious effort. "And just look at the trouble it's got you into!"

Mieka refused to let him joke his way out of this. "—but can you see either of us with a job in the Royal Archives, or—"

"I think I'd enjoy that," Cade broke in. "I can see it would be a problem for you, though. You'd have to learn how to read."

It was an insult Vered had flung at him once, and Cade had lost his temper over it, and now here he was using it himself. Mieka glared at him and went on, "—or a clerk in a bank or a business, or a server in a tea shop—"

"No, that wouldn't suit either of us. For one thing, you'd have to learn how to count."

"—or a courtier like your father?"

He'd saved the best (worst) for last, and it worked. Cade stopped in his tracks and swung round as if to return to the wagon.

"If you never saw another Elsewhen, if you never even felt a prickling of one inside your head, you'd still never have the life of an ordinary person. You're not ordinary. You never could be. What's more, you don't *want* to be." He finished, shrewdly, with: "Did Blye say that, too?"

"Consulted with her, did you?" Cade spat.

Mieka noted with satisfaction that he stayed put, hadn't taken a single step back to the wagon. It rolled on without them, little puffs of dust rising with every massive hoof-fall.

"I didn't have to," he told Cade. "I've got the knowing of you by now, old dear."

The gray eyes sought his. "Don't forget, old dear," Cade said in that silky soft voice that always grated on Mieka's nerves, "that *I* know *you,* too. And what have you been doing for the last few years but trying as hard as you can to be ordinary? To do what everybody's supposed to do? Get married, buy a house, have a child, just as if you were normal! That's one of the masks you wear, Mieka, husband and householder and father—just as if you were an ordinary type of man. Hiding behind that, just the way you hide behind the palace jester mask, so nobody will look any further and start asking awkward questions. Yes, you did exactly what a man is supposed to do, and keep moping and whining because it isn't all perfect the way it's supposed to be. Poor you!"

"At least I tried!" he snarled back. This wasn't turning out the way he'd planned. Did anything? Not even his pranks worked out the way he wanted these days, and now, when he was deadly serious and needed Cade to think in a certain direction, without all these distractions along the way—

"Frustrating, is it?" Cade was smiling a nasty smile. "Hurts, does it? Wretchedly unfair, you think? Welcome to life, Mieka."

He pinched both lips between his teeth to keep himself from speaking too swiftly, and then he saw how to use what Cade had said to steer him back to the road Mieka wanted him to take. So he said, "Exactly. Life. It hurts."

"What do you mean by that?"

"It *hurts,*" he repeated deliberately. "When you do everything you're supposed to do and it still doesn't come right—it's not fair, and it hurts, and there's nothing you can do about it. Except that you *did* do something about it, about one part of it, anyways. You forgot all the Elsewhens and won't see any that have come to you since. Are you any happier for doing that, Quill?"

"Fuck you," Cade spat, and used his long legs to outdistance Mieka. The wagon was well ahead of them now. Mieka knew he couldn't let Cade reach it, climb back aboard, wrap himself in silence, refuse to listen. Refuse to see. So he yelled, and had the satisfaction of seeing Cade stop dead in the middle of the road.

"Coward!"

For many long heartbeats Cade didn't move. It scared Mieka a little, this imitation of cold and unmagical marble statuary. It scared him even more when Cade turned around and looked at him.

"You *are* a coward," Mieka said. "A stupid, blind, bloody coward. You can gripe and moan and deny the Elsewhens—but some of 'em have been pretty damned useful, wouldn't you say? I guess you would've liked it better if I'd sliced my foot open on broken glass and bled to death onstage!" He stalked closer, holding that steel-gray gaze. "You can play the coward in another way and accept the Elsewhens and not tell anybody what's in them—like a fucking pantomancer, seeing omens and portents in everything that happens—going about with a black cloud over your head and whimpering and whining until no one can stand you, and one or another of us—or all three!—ends up slicing out your tongue with a broken withie!"

"That's enough!"

"Not by half! Back when you saw the Elsewhens because you couldn't help it, you had such a lovely time anguishing yourself about them, scared to say or do anything in case it changed, but if you didn't do anything then maybe it changed even more and even worse, so you're paralyzed and no use to anybody. Not the people you might help, or people who might help you, and least of all to yourself."

"I'm warning you, Mieka." Cade took one step and then

another so they were glowering at each other almost within arm's reach. Mieka knew he had perhaps another minute before Cade raised a fist to him, and that had always been what Cade feared most: losing control. He wondered if he should risk it. Just once, just to see what happened.

"What about this, then?" Mieka asked. "What if you actually take responsibility for the Elsewhens? What if you share what you've seen? You started to, before that night when you saw Alaen and Briuly. Don't think I don't know how horrible it was for you. I was there. I saw you, that night in Shollop. But I've seen the other times, too, the ones that came in time to warn us, and the good ones like when it was your Namingday and Touchstone was still going strong and I had a diamond earring and we all of us were happy."

He ran out of air, but not yet out of things to say. Cade stood there, staring at him, a trickle of sweat running unregarded down the side of his neck.

"Quill . . ." Mieka softened his voice and dared another step towards him. "The Elsewhens haven't stopped. They're still there, and real, and you can accept them and use them, and maybe then they won't torture you so much. Some of them will be good ones and some will be rotten, but if you turn your back on all of them, then you'll miss not just the awful things but the wonderful ones as well."

Mieka waited for Cade to say something. It seemed a long, long while before at last he spoke.

"They're different." He walked to the side of the road and stopped, shoulders flinching vaguely as he encountered the runnel of dried mud. "The one about Alaen and Briuly—it isn't that I remember it, because I got rid of all of them. But I remember what it was about. And the thing of it was—" He glanced over his shoulder at Mieka, then returned his gaze to the languid wheat field. "—I couldn't have done anything about it. All the others, they always showed me things I could change. A future that I had a hand in making, and that I could alter. It's always been this dread of not knowing what I ought to do to make things better. But that one—I was too far from Nackerty Close, Mieka, there's no way I could have done *anything* to prevent what happened. I've thought a lot about it, and—"

"—and now you're scared that not only would you not know what to do, but there wouldn't be anything you could do at all." Mieka chewed that over for a moment. He could see how that intensified the difficulties; he could understand that Cade had more reason than ever to fear the Elsewhens. The helplessness would be crippling. Still . . . he couldn't go on crippling himself. It wasn't right. It wasn't *Cayden*.

Mieka dragged in a deep breath full of heat and dust and sun. But Cayden spoke before he could organize his own thoughts.

"What if I see things in the future that are the *result* of something I did or didn't do in the past?"

"In the past," Mieka echoed. "Where you can't do anything about them." Without knowing where the thought had come from, he blurted, "What about Dery? What if you keep on not seeing the Elsewhens and one of them is about Dery, especially now that his magic has come up and—?"

The blank shock told him that this was a thing that, for all his compulsive thinking, had never occurred to Cade. Mieka regretted the pain that began to tremble in his friend's face; he knew it could be worked on; he made a deliberate decision not to do so. Instead, he returned to his original plan. Not that Cade would much enjoy being told that he'd already told himself this next bit in a play without even knowing it. But Mieka had to make him understand.

"Quill . . . don't you see you've been doing just exactly what Vered and Rauel and Mirko *and you yourself* warned against when you reworked that play? You're refusing your magic just the way

Vaustas refused his. You're crippling yourself. How can anyone be everything he ought to be if he doesn't—?"

Cade swung round. "You're saying that to me? About growing up? *You?*"

Mieka nodded with a stubborn set to his jaw that made his teeth hurt.

"If I take responsibility for the Elsewhens, don't you think it's time you took responsibility, too? You've done everything a man's supposed to do, and you feel cheated because it's not perfect. Well, either shut up about it or grow up and make the best of it."

"That's all *I'm* saying, Quill. Except with you, it matters more. Didn't I tell you within weeks of meeting you that your dreams are important? And back then I didn't even know what those dreams really were. You've been living as if what was done to your mother and her sisters had been done to you. A Hindering of your magic. Remember how you described it to me? Like being in a room with a window looking out onto life, but you can't feel the wind or hear the birds sing or smell the fresh bread when the bakery cart goes by—seeing through the window but the window is really like a wall that keeps you from—"

"All right. Enough."

Mieka was only half out of breath, but a searching of Cade's face told him he'd made his point. They resumed walking, and after about half a mile, Cade finally spoke.

"Tell you what, Mieka. I'll stop refusing to see the Elsewhens if you stop behaving like a quat. No more pranks, for one thing—leave Rafe's beard alone! And if you're going to use the black powder, use it on somebody who deserves it."

"Prickspur?" he asked hopefully. "We *still* owe him, y'know."

"Prickspur," Cade agreed with a sigh. "I'll even bring the flint-rasp. And we both go easy on the whiskey and the thorn." After a slight hesitation, he said, "Your marriage is up to you. None of my business. I shouldn't have brought it up."

Mieka shrugged that off, too, too happy with his success to worry about something that he wouldn't have to worry about until they returned to Gallantrybanks in the early autumn.

"And one other thing," Cade said. "If I'm to use the gifts I've been given—all of them—then so must you."

Mieka frowned. "But apart from the glisking, I can't—"

"I'm not talking about magic. I meant that we both stop hiding. We can't become who we're meant to be if we don't let people see us. You don't have to play the clown *all* the time, Mieka."

"Then don't you play the tormented tregetour," he retorted. "D'you have any notion how boring you are when you sulk?"

Cade ignored this. "I mean it. I know you see yourself as the great and grand and glorious purveyor of jokes, and that's fine sometimes. But if you're not careful, people will see you that way whether you want them to or not, and they'll force you into that role until a clown is all you'll ever be."

He was tempted to shrug that away, too, but a certain fundamental and inconvenient honesty compelled him to say, "It's what everybody expects, though, innit? Nobody takes me seriously when I'm being serious." Except, he thought with a slight shock, Cayden.

"You've quite a history of larking about, you know," Cade said more gently. "All the way back to the cradle, I should think. But you don't have to hide from me, nor Rafe nor Jeska, either."

"So we're to grow up, the pair of us?" He made himself shudder, then was ashamed of himself for doing precisely what Cade didn't want him to do: hiding behind a joke. "Growing *up,* all right. I'll give it a try. But don't ask me to grow *old,* Quill."

He smiled. "If I'm forty-five in that Elsewhen you keep talking about, then you're coming up on forty-four. Did I ever tell you what you looked like?"

"Yeh. Gray hair and a diamond earring. Nice of you not to mention the wrinkles."

"Idiot!" Cade grinned. "Elves don't look their age until they're past seventy or so, and you know it. I can just see us all, onstage, in our forties, with you looking like you're still twenty-two years old!"

"Can't wait," Mieka replied. He hesitated, then asked, "D'you think you'll see it again? That Elsewhen."

"And will I tell you if I do? Yes, Mieka. If I see it, or one like it, I'll tell you."

He nodded, satisfied.

When, three days later in Shollop, they did "Doorways" and Jeska got to the final line, Mieka suddenly thought of that Namingday Elsewhen. Was this the life that would take them to that day? If so, he was halfway there. *This life, and none other*—if he had to grow up in order to reach that day, then he'd do his best to grow up.

He just hoped it wouldn't be as boring as he'd always feared.

11

Mile upon mile passed beneath the wheels of Touchstone's wagon; stage after stage echoed with their magic and the wild applause that greeted them even before the curtains swept open. They performed at the assigned venues on the Royal Circuit and at private giggings; their share of the take from the former and their fee for the latter—almost double what it had hitherto been—were deposited in their Gallantrybanks accounts. Occasionally they were invited to spend the night in a lordly castle, to sleep in silken bedclothes; sometimes they stayed at the finest inns Sidlowe and New Halt and Bexmarket could offer (in Lilyleaf they stayed at Croodle's, of course). The Royal Circuit, for those who had reached the pinnacle of First Flight, turned out to be a rather luxurious experience.

It was a real shame that by the time they rolled out of Scatterseed, they were almost too exhausted to enjoy it.

The truth of it was that at the first few shows, the people in charge of the venues weren't exactly thrilled to see them. Which was strange, because they'd played all those places before as Second Flight on the Royal and been greeted with enthusiasm. It was Jeska who eventually realized that these people expected the Shadowshapers. It had been the Shadowshapers for years now.

And Touchstone wasn't the Shadowshapers.

Mortifying. But it steeled them to give the best performances of their careers thus far. To do this, they had to have all the energy and brilliance and flash they'd ever had, and more.

Word that their shows were *almost* every bit as good as the Shadowshapers, and drew the same crowds at the same prices, preceded them out of Shollop. So after those first few shows, nobody looked sidewise at them anymore and silently wished for the Shadowshapers. It was Cade's acerbic opinion that none of them had yet learned that although they'd be able to book the Shadowshapers for giggings, the cost would probably stagger them. "And then," he told Mieka, "they might *really* start appreciating us."

The Royal and Ducal Circuits had been trimmed by a number of days but not by a corresponding number of shows. With the addition of women to theater audiences, attendance was nearly doubled and only the biggest venues could meet the demand for tickets. That Touchstone were themselves largely responsible for this was no consolation to them. They arrived, performed, collapsed into a bed somewhere, got up the next afternoon, did it all again at least three more times, then crawled into their wagon for the journey to the next town.

Bluethorn for energy and alertness. Performance. Alcohol to counteract the bluethorn. Sleep. More bluethorn to wake up. Another performance. More alcohol. More sleep. First Flight on the Royal was a thing Cade had been wanting since he'd decided he wanted to be a tregetour. The first part of it, the long journey from Seekhaven to Scatterseed, he actually remembered most of. But after that he was occasionally too wrung out to enjoy it, or too thorned and drunk to remember it.

Dolven Wold was one of the places very clear in his mind. The Rose Court was outdoors, where nearly a thousand people clapped their hands crimson and yelled themselves hoarse—four shows they played there, but it wasn't until the last of them that he found out why he felt oddly off balance each time they walked onstage. The grating in the center of the stage, presumably for drawing off rainwater, tweaked something inside him. But for fear of what it was he pushed the Elsewhen aside until "Caladrius" was over and they were gathering to take their bows. With one arm over Mieka's shoulders and with Rafe's strong arm around his waist, Cade gave in to the Elsewhen and wished he hadn't.

{ —the strange iron grate in the middle of the stage, in the shape of a full-blown rose—blood flowing, fresh blood, thick bright red blood, spilling through the grate—the audience groaning, ecstatic, participating through magic just as they would if a play was being performed rather than this ritual of slit throats and eager feeding—}

Mieka kept him upright with a shoulder against his ribs. Rafe held him steady with an arm around his back. Somehow they made it into the darkness stage right, where Yazz simply picked him up and carried him to the wagon.

The next thing he knew was the gulping, bloddering sound of liquid poured out of a narrow-mouthed bottle. Not beer, not whiskey from the barrel in the back of the wagon; wine. Smooth and soothing white wine in one of Blye's cool glass goblets. He drank gratefully, then opened his eyes and stretched slowly where he sprawled in one of the padded chairs.

"Sorry. It hit me rather sudden-like."

Rafe took a seat at the table. "I think they'll take you like that until you get used to them again."

"Finish your wine," Mieka advised, crouching at his side.

Cade did as told. He was glad it was white wine; red would have been too much like blood. Setting down his glass, he chose words carefully as he described the Elsewhen, finishing with,

"And I swear that's what it felt like. Feeding time. Only it was a public spectacle, too, with the audience partaking."

"Of the blood?" Jeska's blue eyes were wide with shock.

"No. Oh, no. The sensations. Just as if they were in Rose Court for a play, and a glisker and fettler had spread the magic."

"Wasn't anyone . . . well, *disgusted*?" Mieka asked.

Cade shook his head. "Not a bit of it. It was like a special treat they were given, a favor eagerly sought, that they were allowed to join in."

"But what was being fed, down below the grate?" All at once Mieka turned very pale and sat back hard on his rump. "Oh Gods," he muttered. "*Balaurin*!"

"What?" Jeska exclaimed.

"Like in Vered's play! The enemy warriors who drank blood from their victims' skulls, like Vampires except not exactly, but enough to set Chat to tale-telling that time, remember?"

Cade thought about it, then nodded. "But what were they doing at Dolven Wold?"

"It's where the Archduke was born," Rafe mused. "He doesn't own it anymore. But it's where he was born. And his ancestor came from that part of the world, didn't he?"

They were quiet, all four of them, until Yazz whistled to the horses, and the wagon lurched gently forwards. Wordlessly they passed the bottle, needing the alcohol to offset the bluethorn. Safely in their hammocks, the only light coming from a half moon shining through the right-side windows, they stayed silent until Rafe said, his voice light and casual, "What you saw, Cade—it's not quite the sort of 'communal experience' one expects at a theater."

Cade grimaced in the darkness. "More like what it must feel like at a public execution."

"Which this was?"

Mieka made an inarticulate noise of revulsion. "Shut it, both of you, and right now! Or I'm for some redthorn so I can sleep without nightmares."

Cade didn't remind him of his promise to take it easier on the thorn. How could he, when he and Rafe and even Jeska partook of bluethorn before a performance? And they hadn't even crossed the Pennynines yet. They'd all end up, he told himself glumly, either wild-eyed in thornthrall or very, very dead.

He worried about these things on days when he was sober. Increasingly, he was not. Certainly if he'd been in his right mind, he would never have joined Mieka on a little expedition across the summery green hills. Then again, he *had* been stone-cold sober when he'd offered to bring the flint-rasp.

Mieka had planned it as carefully as he planned the arrangement and use of his withies. Perhaps fearing that Cade would renege on his promise, he'd kept it secret until the morning of the great day. They had spent the night in the wagon, and a little while after dawn reached the inn where everyone on the circuits but themselves and the Shadowshapers stayed on the way to Sidlowe. Here, after an excellent breakfast, Mieka vanished. Everyone thought he'd gone upstairs for a nap while the horses were fed and rested.

But it seemed he had only changed clothes. He reappeared in coarse woolen trousers tucked into high brown boots and a vivid blue shirt. In his hand was the knitted cap Jeska had bought for him on the Continent.

Rafe glanced up from writing a letter to Crisiant, and whistled. Mieka made a face at him and said to Cayden, "I've hired a horse, but I don't know how to drive it. And you said you'd help."

Grinning, Cade snatched the cap from Mieka's hand and stuffed it into his own jacket pocket. Knocking back the last swallows of his breakfast ale, he said, "See you lads at the next stop!"

Mieka added, "Probably somewhere on the Sidlowe road—"

"If we don't get lost," Cade interrupted.

"In either case," Mieka finished, "don't wait up."

"What are you doing?" Jeska demanded. "Where are you going?" He turned to Rafe. "Where are they going?"

"A little journey back in time, to a rotten, filthy night ringed with Wizardfire torches."

The masquer's puzzled frown became a radiant smile. "Oh, excellent! Have fun!"

"I intend to," said Mieka.

It was a ways to their goal. Mieka provided directions, clinging to the back of the saddle, sitting as straight and tall as he possibly could so he could rest his chin on Cade's shoulder to see where they were going. The route taken by the circuits had changed, and because of that, the inn served naught but locals. Farmers, herders, tradesmen, the occasional traveler, all these drank in the taproom and slept abovestairs, but without the circuits coming regularly to the inn, profit was chancy at best. That was what you got when you snubbed an Elf, if the Elf you snubbed was one of the King's players. One could only hope that the pristine racial purity of the establishment was compensation.

A s they crested a rise and saw the outlines of the inn atop the next hill, Cade asked, "What were you thinking of destroying? The garderobe?" He shifted uncomfortably. "And quit digging your chin into my shoulder, will you?"

"Sorry. I was thinking mayhap the taproom hearth. 'Twould make a lovely noise and take a long time to repair, yeh?"

"Just make sure everyone's out of the place."

"There'll be no murder done, I promise."

"I was thinking more about witnesses. I don't want my glisker brought up on charges in the middle of the Royal Circuit."

"Such *foresight*, Master Silversun!"

Cade grunted a laugh, and they rode on. A few minutes later he drew rein in a stable yard he hadn't seen in nearly five years. The torches he'd lit with magical fire were still in their brackets, but the walls were a trifle crumbly and the yard was inches deep in foul straw and horseshit. The stables needed painting; so did the sign above the front door. He smiled, deeply satisfied. He waited until Mieka had jumped to the cobbles before dismounting and handing the reins to a wide-eyed boy who could barely gather up courage to approach close enough to take them. Though Mieka's ears were hidden by the cap, certain things about Cayden screamed *Wizard*. Evidently magical folk were rare and suspect at Prickspur's.

They mingled with the other customers in the taproom, getting slowly through a pint of quite good ale, keeping mostly to themselves as they listened to the desultory conversations around them. Farmers, herders, tradesmen, crafters—anyone who could leave his work for an hour or so for a drink did so at noon. Mostly they brought their own food. The smells coming out of Prickspur's kitchen were not encouraging. Cade managed not to gag when a pot of something purporting to be stew was brought around with a couple of bowls. Mieka smiled and ordered another drink. They were the only ones who weren't locals; nobody was staying upstairs. An idle question or two informed them that just Prickspur and the stable lad lived here full-time, which suited Cade and Mieka down to the ground—which was where Cade surmised a lot of this place would be once Mieka got through with it.

There had been a few suspicious looks directed at Cade when he and Mieka entered. Prickspur himself was rude enough when he delivered the drinks to their table, but gave no sign of recognizing them. A little while later, a large, balding, ferociously muscular man came in still wearing the leather apron of his calling, and upon spotting strangers looked as if he wished he'd brought his anvil or at the very least his hammer.

"Prickspur!" he bellowed. "Be it three year or four that no

Wizardy git's crossed yer threshold?"

"Three, innit?" someone replied.

"Nah, goin' on four," countered someone else. "And liking it that way, each and every one and all of us!"

"Left Sidlowe, I did," said the blacksmith, smacking one meaty fist into his palm, "ten years since, to get clear of the Gobliny smiths and the filthy Gnomish Elferbludded Trolling Wizardly bastards who went to them instead of me."

Cade felt his spine stiffen. Mieka clunked his beer down on the table and, wide-eyed with shock, exclaimed, "You don't mean to say you think he's—"

"Has the look of it, don't he," said Prickspur. "With that height, I might've said *Giant,* but the spindliness of him says *Wizard.*"

"Well, I *never!*" Mieka stood, kicking back his chair, and glared down at Cade. "When my carriage lost a wheel and I accepted your offer of a ride, my good man, I'd no idea!" Turning to the rest of the taproom's patrons, he spread his hands in a gesture of helplessness. "I simply thought he was *tall,* don't you see."

Cade struggled to keep a straight face, as always when Mieka used his *Lord Fairwalk with a bigger stick than usual up his ass* accent. But he knew his part in the farce now, and stood up, saying, "Can I help it if me mother's sire was six feet and a half and a bit and another bit, and me fa's old grandsire was said to be muchlike the same? Yeh, I'm bein' *tall,* but it ain't my fault!"

The blacksmith scowled, looking Cade over. "Well," he said at last, "if tall is all you're being, then I s'pose this is as good a place to drink as any."

"Beholden," Cade said, and sat down again.

Mieka pretended to hesitate, then shrugged, righted his chair, and sat down to finish his drink. The faint and distant chiming of the local Minster announced the hour past noon. The farmers returned to their crops, the workmen to their trades, the herders to their animals. Cade felt rather sorry for them. When they returned for a dinnertime drink, there'd be nothing to return to.

When the place was nearly empty, Mieka rose, stretched, and ambled over to inspect the fieldstone fireplace, professing admiration for the workmanship. All at once he turned to Cayden and snapped, "Well? What are you sitting about for? I must be in Dolven Wold by sunset! Go do whatever it is you need to do with the horse to make the poxy thing ready to ride, and do it quickly!"

Cade stumbled to his feet, dipped his head, touched his forehead, and tried not to snigger at the wicked gleeful gleam in those eyes. He was halfway to the door when he heard Mieka say, "Frightfully clever. I mean to say, how does one get all those round stones to fit together just as snugly as if they were square bricks? Must be this whitish stuff in between them, don't you think?"

Dead silence greeted this imbecility. Biting his lips together did Cade no good; a snorting giggle escaped him, and he lunged for the door and stumbled outside into searing-bright sunshine, where he clapped both hands over his mouth and leaned against the wall, shaking with laughter.

Eventually he reckoned that haste might be advisable, so he fetched the horse, checked the girth, mounted up, and guided the animal nearer the inn's front door. And waited.

And waited.

The last noontime customers exited. Cade began to worry that Mieka had forgotten the flint-rasp, or couldn't get rid of Prickspur long enough to dump the black powder where he wanted it to go, or—

The horse reared up and shrieked an instant after detonation. The upstairs windows blew open, scattering glass like the ending of a Touchstone performance. Cade hunched his shoulders against the slicing shower and struggled to stay in the saddle. When all four hooves were grounded again, he fought the animal's dancing nervousness and wheeled around towards the front door again. This had burst open, disgorging smoke and a stunned and stumbling Mieka.

Cade heeled the horse nearer and yelled. Mieka didn't hear him; Cade scarcely heard himself. His ears were ringing like a Minster on Wintering Night. Mieka waved his arms about, trying to clear the smoke so he could see. Cade urged the horse nearer just as Prickspur staggered from the door, coughing.

Cade panicked. Kicking the horse, he leaned precariously over and grabbed Mieka by one elbow, hauling him up even as Prickspur scuttled towards them. Mieka flopped across the horse's hindquarters like a sack of grain, arms dangling on one side and legs on the other. Cade reached behind and tugged frantically as Mieka scrambled himself around and finally got the horse between his knees, hanging on to Cade for dear life.

They passed Prickspur at a dancing trot, nervous hooves clattering on the cobbles. Mieka hollered something indistinct but undoubtedly obscene and flung his knitted cap in the man's face. Cade reined the horse through the gates and within moments they were fleeing at the gallop.

After a mile or two, the grip around his waist crushing the breath out of him, Cade slowed and stopped. Mieka tumbled to the road, whooping for air. He tried to stand, knees wobbly, and sat down hard on his rump.

Cade couldn't help it. He started laughing.

Mieka glared. "Don't—*ever*—do—that—again!"

Though he'd heard perfectly well, he cupped a hand beside one ear. "What?"

The Elf pushed himself upright, looking over his shoulder. "Oh, shut up and help me back on before he comes after us!"

"Eh?"

Swearing fluently, Mieka clambered back up behind Cade and resumed his hold on the saddle.

They caught up with the wagon around dusk, and over a

simple dinner of bread, cheese, fruit, and wine treated Jeska, Rafe, and Yazz to a spirited description of their triumph. But later, as the others sat up late playing cards, Cade stretched out in his hammock, hoping he wouldn't be too stiff in the morning (he wasn't used to riding for that many hours), and thought over the things he'd heard at Prickspur's. He started to worry. He lay there listening to the banter and the bidding, and the soft *clip-clop* of the hired horse, tied to the back of the wagon, due to be dropped off tomorrow at the next circuit inn. So normal, so usual: two mostly Wizards, two mostly Elves, and a Giant sitting up on the coachman's bench—but not usual for those ordinary rural men who'd eyed him askance today. Was it common throughout Albeyn, that away from the cities and larger towns, prejudice against magical folk flourished almost as malevolently as on the Continent?

He told himself he'd keep his eyes and ears open for signs of it from now on. Though it was true that even in Gallybanks there were people who turned their faces away when a weathering witch passed by, and shopkeepers who were obviously relieved when a Gnome paid for his purchases and departed, intolerance was considered by most people to be dishonorable.

Suddenly he tried to sit up, forgetting that he was in a hammock. Swaying dangerously close to one of the witching spheres that had been a gift from Rafe's parents (handed down in the family for generations, or they would of course have gone to Blye to craft them), he managed to turn onto his side. The others glanced over.

"Mieka," he said, "that night in Gowerion, when we did 'Silver Mine'—how did you know they'd react the way they did? We were on the Archduke's old lands, and everybody'd either been in the war or knew someone who had, but how—damn it!" An incautious movement of emphasis set him to swinging again. Rafe unfolded himself from his chair and helped put him right.

"Go on," the fettler said. "But I think I can guess what you're getting at. Why was it, with all the damage that magic had done in the war and with all the people who died, especially there on the Archduke's former lands, whyfor didn't those people treat magical folk as badly as Prickspur and his ilk do? After all, this whole area is near to Dolven Wold, and was once owned by the Henick family, right? So why is there such a difference in attitude?"

Mieka looked from one to the other of them, sighed his exasperation, and returned his attention to his cards. "How the bloody Hells should I know?" he said, and played a double pair atop Jeska's single.

Rafe sat down again. "I'd be willing to bet that the chirurgeons around here do a brisk business in kagging ears too obviously Elfen, and even though we've full houses at all our shows, there's a significant portion of the population that steers clear of theater because of the magic."

"Is it only because Gowerion is so much closer to Gallybanks?" Jeska asked. "I mean, *here,* they can get away with being intolerant."

"Could be," Cade mused. "Could be. Or mayhap there really are fewer of us in the north than in the south."

"Or it might be," Mieka said, "that they like the Archduke less here, or there's more of the sort like Jeska's grandsire— brought over from the Continent to fight, like Prickspur's father or whatever it was. Rafcadion, old thing, are you going to play that set of roses in your hand, or wait for them to take root?"

That was the end of the conversation and the speculation as far as they were concerned, but Cade worried it over in his mind until at length he went to sleep.

The next day they left the extra horse behind, and by the next morning they were at Sidlowe. Cade didn't remember a thing about those few days. But on the last, just as they were packing up to leave the inn and get a good start for Scatterseed, Mieka received a letter.

He said nothing about it until they were in the wagon. Clouds were threatening, and Yazz's consultation with a local weathering witch informed him that the weather wouldn't hold beyond tomorrow afternoon. Cade was just sorting through the books he'd brought along, wishing he'd made a few selections that were guaranteed to send him to sleep rather than perk up his ever-overactive brain, when Mieka settled himself at the table with a decided air and said, "Somebody has to write to Fairwalk."

The letter was from Jinsie. In it, she wrote that Jez was healing very nicely and was determined that the cane would become more of an elegant accessory, as Mieka's wife had suggested, than a needed prop for his bad leg. All the children were thriving. Jindra and her mother had returned to Hilldrop Crescent, but not before Jindra had sewn another little pillow for her uncle's leg, all on her own, without sticking herself with the needle even once. Tavier had taken up the lute, Jorie had made off with a ream of the best paper to fold into houses and castles for a school project, and Cilka and Petrinka were being pursued by the same boy. (Neither of them liked him.) King Meredan and Queen Roshien had started off on their progress to the acclaim of most of Gallantrybanks, who had turned up to see them off. Prince Ashgar was now said to be in charge, but rumor had it that Princess Miriuzca was present at more meetings of ministers and the like than her husband was. The Archduke and Archduchess were at Threne, presumably cuddling their new little son. The weather was brutally hot, the Gally River was sluggish and stinky, and the bank had turned down Jinsie's request for money.

Here Mieka paused in his reading aloud to say, "I don't understand it. We do this all the time. I leave a note, she takes it to the bank, and the money goes to Ginnel House. But the bank won't honor the note. And what's more, they won't say why."

"And you think Fairwalk has something to do with it?" Jeska asked.

"He handles the money, doesn't he? Whatever we get paid goes to him, and he divvies it up. It's the same bank he uses—same one we've all used for years now."

"You must've worded the note wrong or something."

"I wrote for a third time what I've been writing for two years," Mieka said flatly.

Cade was surprised, and suspected he oughtn't to have been. That little rainy-day outing to Ginnel House had evidently made an even deeper impression on Mieka than Cade had dared to hope. He could still see the Elf, curled into a corner of the hire-hack, weeping helplessly for those battered women and bruised children and, it must be admitted, for himself. For shame.

"Write to Fairwalk, then," he said. "Let him know the trouble. I'm sure he'll fix it."

"Hmm." Mieka folded the letter and sat back in his chair. "Yeh, all right. But this isn't the first oddity, y'know. In Lilyleaf earlier this year, I ran short on cash and went to the bank there that acts for our own bank, and they made me wait two whole days."

"Maybe they're not theatergoers, and didn't know Who You Are," Rafe said, his voice supplying the capital letters.

Mieka made a face at him. "*Everybody* knows Who We Are," he retorted.

It was, perhaps, an indication of how seriously Mieka took his self-assumed obligation to Ginnel House that it was not the incident in Lilyleaf but the difficulty in Gallantrybanks that had made him broach the subject. He was growing up. Some, anyway.

Cade had every reason to doubt that two days into their stay at Scatterseed.

An interesting and often gratifying (personally as well as professionally) result of women's attendance at the theater was that no longer was the admiration of young ladies confined to the placards advertising a group's performance. There was always a collection of them at the artists entrance, and Touchstone's wagon was more often than not greeted by a dozen or so girls (if the arrival was anytime before dark). The more mature, and presumably more dignified, ladies contented themselves with sending notes, bottles of wine, and occasionally an invitation to sup (at home, with their husbands, for the less adventurous; at a discreet local tavern, alone, for the daring). The young and giggly thought themselves frightfully bold by gathering in groups to invade the tiring room after the show. Mostly they were intercepted by the chucker-out before they could outrage their modesty and infuriate their parents by consorting with theater players. Cade and Mieka were known to take a personal interest that often led to a private encounter. Rafe smiled and flirted and went to his own bed alone. It was Jeska who was in demand, and in agonies, for his popularity among females had only increased with the years, and dalliances in haylofts were definitely a thing of the past—dalliances anywhere, in fact, for as much as he appreciated girls, he loved his wife more.

Every so often the after-performance drinks and relaxation got interrupted by a respectable young woman with her father or elder brother in tow. So it happened that second night in Scatterseed.

It was clear from the first moment of the pair's arrival that Darling Papa hadn't the least wish to be there. His daughter, aged about twenty-two and dressed in the more ridiculous excesses of the current fashion, had obviously pestered him into escorting her to Touchstone's performance. Darling Papa was a big, broad, bluff country gentleman, uncomfortable in his velvet jacket and fine polished shoes, much happier in a homespun woolen shirt and stout boots. He suffered through introductions and then addressed Cayden with a scowl.

"Don't know what I'm doin' here, but for the nagging of this filly." He nodded at his daughter, who had fixed her large brown eyes on Mieka. "Good show, I s'pose. Not my glass of ale."

"I quite understand," Cade soothed. Ordinarily he would

have curled his lip and left the tiring room, or told someone to get these people out, but the look in the girl's eyes amused him as she slowly backed Mieka towards a corner. "Not really a profession for grown men," he went on, correctly judging the man's views on theater. "But the pay's decent, and one gets to travel."

"Load of poofters," growled Himself, then coughed and colored up, and blustered on, "Not but what you don't get a good experience of the whole country, what? Interesting, all the travel. Glad to have you here, in fact. My girl's Namingday present, you see. Hasn't clapped her trap shut about it since you placed First Flight and not those others. What's their names? Shifty-shins?"

"Shadowshapers," Rafe supplied. "I hope your very charming daughter had a very charming evening. Won't you have a drink, sir?"

"I wouldn't mind one. Decent of you, boy." He winked, perking up. "Need it in this line, do you? All these silly fillies lolloping about." Rafe led him over to the table where wine, ale, and beer were on offer. Jeska wandered after them, keeping an eye on Mieka and the girl, and Cade heard him ask, in his best Lord Currycomb voice (the one he used when the rain washed the black horse gray), "And shall we see you at the races down in Gallybanks this year, sir?"

Meantime, the girl's acquaintance with Mieka was progressing famously. The Elf had his back to the wall, a chair on one side of him, a table on the other, and the girl right in front of him. He was still smiling, but something a trifle desperate had seized up his face. Cade ambled towards them, sipping at a glass of ale.

"—the very first time I ever saw a placard," the girl was breathing huskily. "All my friends are wild for Jeska or Rafe, but I—"

"What about me?" Cade interrupted, making a face of piteous hurt.

Without looking over her shoulder at him, she said, "Sindalee thinks you're splendid. She'll be here tomorrow night. But right now—" Her fingers approached, darted back, stole like little white snakes towards Mieka's face. "—*I'm* here right now," she whispered.

"Your father—" Mieka began.

"Give him enough to drink and he won't notice we've gone." She leaned in, head tilting up, lips parting. "I bribed the manager to let us have his private room. Just the two of us."

Cade smiled pleasantly at Mieka. Mieka gulped. Then, with fresh and awful cunning lighting those eyes, he reached around the girl and hauled Cade to him, stood on tiptoe, and kissed him full on the mouth.

The girl giggled. "The *three* of us, then? It hadn't occurred to me, but—sounds wonderful!"

Mieka was saucer-eyed. Another joke that hadn't worked out as planned. Cade shook his brains loose and said, "I'm sorry, truly I am, but—Mieka and I—well, I'm sure you understand." He put an arm around Mieka's shoulders and felt him snuggle close. "Isn't he just the most adorable little thing?" Cade went on. "I feel for you, my dear girl, I really do. Irresistible, that's what he certainly is."

"You can pretend I'm your wife," she coaxed. "The way you must do at home in Gallantrybanks or Hilldrop Crescent."

Cade almost choked.

"Oh, nothing of the kind," Mieka piped up. "At home, I'm all hers. But when we're out on the road . . ." He wriggled closer.

Cade took his cue. "Away from home, he's all mine. Aren't you, lumpling?"

"Oh." She sighed, disappointed. "Well, all right, then. I must say, you *are* terribly cute together." Another giggle. "I'll have to warn Sindalee!"

Once she and her father were gone, Mieka fell into the nearby chair, laughing himself silly. Rafe was right beside Cayden with a drink, which he tossed back in three long swallows.

"The things I do for you," he accused the Elf.

"Regretting the delicious Sindalee?" Jeska asked.

"Poor Quill!" Mieka accepted the ale Jeska proffered, drank, then smacked his lips and grinned up at Cade.

"You've ruined his bed-sport for tomorrow night," Rafe observed. "I trust you're willing to provide proper consolation."

Mieka looked startled for just an instant, then pretended to inspect Cade, head to toes. "Nah," he said at last. "He'd never survive me."

Cade arched his brows. Then he said, "Your pardon, old friend," and took Rafe's glass. More satisfying if full, but there was quite enough in it to leave Mieka nicely soaked, hairline to collar.

12

Making Prickspur finally pay for refusing to allow Touchstone—or, more accurately, Mieka—into his establishment that first Winterly Circuit was a deeply satisfying thing. But the delights of retribution reminded Mieka that further retributions were certainly in the offing. Rafe had yet to retaliate for the incident with the beard. The incident with the beard had been retaliation for the incident of the missing clothes in Lilyleaf. Farther back than that, Mieka could not follow the back-and-forth of the pranks. Whoever had started it (most likely himself, he had to admit), it was by no means finished. It was, after all, a matter of honor—and of Rafe's insufferable pride in his beard.

So Mieka kept a wary eye on him, when he remembered to. Generally he was occupied on this, their very first Royal Circuit as First Flight, with tending his withies, performing, getting some sleep, liberally sampling the best liquors that the inns and taverns could offer (and Auntie Brishen's barrel of whiskey while on the road), and making sure his thorn-roll was replenished at convenient intervals. Auntie Brishen had obliged in this, too; packages had been waiting for him at Sidlowe and Scatterseed, the latter with a note saying she'd send the next on to Bexmarket. Dear Auntie Brishen; she didn't even question the increase in his use of

bluethorn. In any event, it wasn't really his own use of it, it was
Cade's and Rafe's and even Jeska's. Though the masquer usually
shook his head when offered a thornful, he had recently taken
to not shaking his head. And who could blame him? Because
King Meredan wanted all his best players back in Gallantrybanks
to celebrate the twenty-fifth anniversary of his ascending to the
throne, the schedule of performances and travel was punishing,
sleep was a precious commodity, and Touchstone was determined
that no audience would suffer through a lackluster show because
Touchstone had the bad taste to be exhausted.

The problem was that with such determination came tension.
Cade might deplore his constant clowning, but Mieka felt he
had no choice other than to do his best to relax everyone before
a performance with jokes and capers. *Clever and mad* was even
more necessary now. Still, the only thing that reliably worked was
reenacting his grand entrance into the Downstreet of two years
ago. With Jinsie's help he had gathered up a motley assemblage of
ladies' clothing from Wistly Hall, and from time to time scorned
the artists entrance in favor of flouncing in by the main doors.

Swanning down the aisle, he would call out, "Open the
curtains! Start the show! I have arrived!" Jeska would peek out
from between the swagged curtains, snort a laugh, and haul
the heavy velvet aside himself to reveal Cade on one side of the
stage and Rafe on the other, glass baskets snug in their wooden
frames at the back. Cade would roll his eyes and they'd go into
the routine of *You're late!* and *What is that awful thing you've got
on?* and *Play nice, Cayden—I borrowed it from me mother-in-law!*
and *You just try and start without me sometime!* Cade always went
along with it, but after the first few times he tended to get a look
on his face as if wishing Mieka would behave like every other
glisker and just do his job. What he would never understand was
that such things were part of Mieka's job—as he saw it, anyway.
And when had he ever been anything like every other glisker?

It was also part of his job to do what he'd done all his life for family and friends and schoolmates: keep everybody entertained, lighten the mood, ease the tension with laughter. To that end, he'd invented a game. Each player had to come up with a clue to the name of a tavern or inn, and the others had to guess which was meant. They'd all been in so many such places by now that there was a practically endless list to work with. Points were scored for and against, the winner of each round had to begin the next, and the ultimate loser had to buy the drinks at the next stop.

Two days out of Scatterseed, on an afternoon of broiling heat remarkable in the Pennynines, Mieka judged that it was time to begin the entertainment or they'd all be snapping at each other. After explaining the rules, he started it off with, "Top of me mother-in-law."

Various increasingly obscene suggestions led them to guess *Nag's Head,* and Jeska won the point. In between guessing, there was a great deal of silence while brains worked furiously, but as little as Mieka admired quiet, this part of the exercise was his gift to Yazz. There was nothing the Giant liked better than a nice, quiet spell of guiding the horses and appreciating the scenery.

It took Jeska a while, but he finally came up with, "One for the bonce, one for the bum." This time it was Rafe who eventually got *Crown and Cushion.* He was ready for the next round, promptly offering, "Three-and-a-half cold men." Then he sat back in his chair, folded his arms, and to all appearances composed himself for a nap.

After a long silence, many frowns, and no guesses at all, they yielded. Rafe refused to tell, claiming the point and the right to use the clue again in future. After some grumbling, Cade volunteered the next round.

"Where a married man should never be again after his wedding night."

Mieka stuck out his tongue at him, then replied, "*Maiden's*

Arms. You'd think a great whirring powerful brain like yours could think up something better!"

"I'm saving my best efforts for later," Cade said haughtily, gray eyes dancing. "Your point, and back to you."

"That's hardly fair," Jeska complained. "He's the one who thought this up. For all we know, he's been inventing them for weeks."

Cade snorted. "You're assuming he has the mental capacity to remember anything other than a play. Come on, Mieka. Your turn."

"Mine," he announced, "needs a very big mouth."

After a time, Jeska asked, "We've been to all these places, right? You're not tossing in some tavern we've never seen?"

Before Mieka could reply, Cade teased, "Oh, just look at those big innocent eyes! Would anybody with those eyes cheat?"

Rafe answered, "Every chance he gets. And it's *Cock in the Bottle,* by the way."

"How did you guess?" Mieka complained.

"As well as being exceedingly handsome, I'm exceedingly brilliant. Hadn't you noticed?"

Cade smiled his sweetest. "Seven Blue Balls."

"Huh?" Jeska looked from one to the other of them, confused.

"Three-and-a-half cold men. *Seven Blue Balls.* My point, I think."

And so it went until they arrived at a place they'd never been before and never even heard of. Just outside Scatterseed they'd been compelled to take a detour by a ferocious spring storm that had loosened a hillside onto a section of the usual road through the Pennynine Mountains. The obstacle had not yet been removed. The alternate route was longer and more difficult for the horses. Thus it was necessary to rest them for a full day at an inn on the outskirts of Wooldridge—the sources of its name evident in the living fleeces covering the hills. It was a town of perhaps a thousand souls, most of whom had never seen theater performed. To show their gratitude for the hospitality of the Fleece and Froth tavern, Jeska proposed an outdoor gigging, for free. Polite interest was expressed, but the general attitude was a collective shrug. There was nothing much else to do in Wooldridge of a summer night, so why not see a play?

The general attitude changed to wild applause once they'd seen "Dragon." After a swift consultation among themselves, and some quick replenishment of the withies, Touchstone then gave them one of the oldest and silliest of the Master Fondlewife comedies. It wasn't their fault that someone in the audience had been suspecting his own wife of being fondled by someone who was not himself this past fortnight and longer. Neither could they be blamed for the fight that broke out in the middle of the throng and spread in all directions. And it certainly wasn't their fault that the local physicker was up to his hairline in bruised jaws, black eyes, and cracked ribs for the next two days.

The sooner Touchstone got out of town, the better. The wagon rolled out a little past midnight. At midmorning, after a rotten night's sleep jouncing over rutted roads—Mieka had forgotten to renew the spell his mother taught him that smoothed the road—they mumbled awake when Yazz stopped the wagon.

"Where the fuck are we?" Rafe demanded.

"How the fuck should I know?" Mieka countered, and then forgot that rolling over to go back to sleep was a much trickier maneuver in a hammock than in a bed. By the time he had uncocooned himself, swearing, from netting and mattress and sheets, Yazz had opened the back door and was smiling with each and every one of his large white teeth.

Mieka, still upside down but no longer strangling, squinted at him and moaned. He knew that smile. It was the one Yazz wore when a visit with his kin was in the offing. Mieka had never been able to understand it; liberally supplied, and one might say oversupplied, with relatives himself, the prospect of seeing more did not thrill him. He supposed it was different for Giants and part-Giants, there being so recognizably few of them these days. Look at what Prickspur had said about Cade's height arguing for Giant blood. Well, yes, he was indeed tall, but how anybody could mistake those long bones and narrow ribs for anything but Wizard was beyond Mieka's comprehension. Still, Prickspur hadn't exactly proved himself the shiniest withie in the basket.

"Who is it this time?" he asked, extricating himself from the hammock.

"Cousin on Mam's side," Yazz said happily. "Only an afternoon, Miek."

"Yeh, yeh, all right." He explained to his partners that Yazz rarely ran across his kin, and surely they could spare a few hours for a reunion.

"You had only to say so," Cade told Yazz. "Take the afternoon, and the evening as well, if you like."

Yazz shook his head. "Back before sundown toasting. Beholden!" He slammed the back door shut and went away whistling happily.

"What happens at sundown toasting?" Jeska asked Mieka.

"More Giant-brewed mead than you could drink in a year. More than even I could drink in a year. It's a real sacrifice, believe me, and shows his devotion to us, for him to miss it. So what'll we do for the afternoon?"

"If we are where I think we are," Cade said, a slow smile on his lips, "then this ought to be fun."

"So where are we?"

"Boggering."

Mieka scorned the obvious punning question, merely raised his brows. Cayden acknowledged the restraint with an eye-roll.

Yazz had taken care of the horses—unhitched, provided with nosebags—and the wagon was neatly parked in the corner of an inn yard. A few questions asked of the stableboy—a dark, stumpy youth with Gnome written all over him but for the incongruity of Elfen ears—and they were heading up a side street that went from rough cobbles to plain packed dirt within twenty paces.

"Boggering," Cade announced as they climbed a gentle rise towards a low building lacking any sign at all, "has something not even Lilyleaf can boast."

"And that might be?" Jeska asked.

Their tregetour grinned broadly. "Mud."

"Mud?" Mieka frankly stared at Cade. "You want to spend the afternoon looking at mud?"

"Not looking at it, you quat. Bathing in it."

"Bathe. In mud." Rafe sighed mournfully. "Tragic, it is, seeing a fine brain go all aflunters."

"No, really," Cade told him. "The waters at Lilyleaf are supposed to be healthful, right? Minerals and suchlike."

"Yes, but one bathes in them and drinks them. I do hope you're not suggesting—"

"Try not to be a bigger fool than the Lord and the Lady made you. There's a whole chapter in a book my grandsire bequeathed me—"

Mieka looked over his shoulder at Rafe. "You've known him since childhood, right? Well, then, it's all your fault. You should never have let him learn how to read."

Cade decided to ignore them for the rest of the walk in favor of searching his pockets for appropriate coin. Once inside the building, its weathered wooden door clicking shut behind them, Mieka blinked to see a rather good painting of a curvaceous young lady clad in nothing but a scanty green towel and her own long black hair, laughing as she dipped a dainty toe into what looked like a bog of bluish dung.

And damned if what looked to be the original of the painting didn't walk out from behind an inner door—wearing, unfortunately, a perfectly respectable skirt and shirt with a colorful scarf draped around her shoulders. She smiled up at Cade.

"Been seein' your wagon, I have, down to the town," she said. "Touchstone! An honor it is for us, and no mistake!"

Mieka was astounded that she'd heard of them in this tiny village at the back end of nowhere. Cade played the gallant, introducing them and complimenting her on the facilities, of which he had read much, and so forth and so on through the paying of the fee and the distribution of towels and the entry into a side room where the vat of the painting, set deep into the wooden floor, bubbled and steamed. A wary, experimental sniff told Mieka that the mud smelled of herbs he couldn't identify, with a mildly metallic tang.

"I don't know why this place isn't more popular," Cade was saying after the girl left and they were exchanging their clothes for towels. "Look at Lilyleaf."

"In Lilyleaf, you end up *clean*," Rafe pointed out. "That's the whole purpose of a bath."

"Oh, but we'll be getting clean, too," Cade told him. "There's oil you slather on before the mud bath, and that way it all washes off. You saw how beautiful that girl's skin is. The locals come here after work. And think how warm it must be in winter, instead of washing in a barely heated tub! But I guess this place is just too remote to become fashionable."

Rafe had selected the oils, with the girl's assistance. After generous application, Touchstone—renowned throughout Albeyn, esteemed by the Princess, revered by all, and cooped up in their wagon for days on end—shed half their years along with their clothes and promptly engaged in a mud fight. It started when Mieka plopped a double handful of the stuff on Cade's head, and ended quite some time later with what seemed like half the contents of the vat on them, on the walls, on the floor, and even on the ceiling.

Submersed to their necks in the vat, they relaxed and agreed that this had been a wonderful idea. Mieka wriggled deeper, then packed a pound or so of mud on his face, closing his eyes to enjoy the tingling sensation all over his body. The mud was surprisingly soothing to the thornpricks inside his elbows. All he lacked was a nice flagon of ale, or mayhap a pricking of some interesting sort of thorn, to make him perfectly happy.

He didn't know how long it was before Rafe, seated beside him in the vat, moved suddenly and violently. Mieka opened his eyes to find that Cade, opposite them, had slid to his chin in the mud and looked to be sliding deeper. Rafe got a slippery grip on his shoulders and pulled him upright again, but said nothing. Mieka knew why. The large gray eyes had gone blank and blind, the way they always did during an Elsewhen.

The three of them waited it out. Eventually he shivered slightly, looked around, and realized what had just happened. But instead of shrugging it off and refusing to tell, the way he'd done before, he drew a breath and said, "This was a nasty one."

"Are all of us safe?" Jeska demanded. "Us and ours?"

Cade nodded, and Jeska relaxed. "It was just me—no, nothing happened to me, I was just there to see it."

He told them of sitting with the Princess in a river garden at the North Keep, her favorite of the two, drinking tea and nibbling on cakes. Then there was an explosion, and fire and flying glass and smoke, and the grind and shatter of tumbling stones. Not a hundred feet away from them, the Keep began slowly to collapse. He grabbed the Princess and carried her bodily down the riverwalk towards safety.

"There were people everywhere, some of them screaming, some of them bleeding, guards running all over the place, boatmen coming in to shore to help. I carried her along, and there was a little cottage for the man who takes care of the Royal barge or whatever. Her brother was standing nearby, with the oddest look on his face as he watched the North Keep fall—as if he was surprised, but—I don't know, a sort of *gratified* surprise, as if he hadn't expected things to turn out that well."

Mieka chewed his lip for a moment, then asked, "You didn't get anything when we had lunching with them at Seekhaven, did you? Looking at him didn't trigger an Elsewhen?"

Cade looked startled. "When . . . when you were cutting up that cake—you remember, the one shaped like the Keeps, there was a twinge— No," he said, interrupting himself, "it's not possible. He wouldn't dare. Not his sister's own kingdom!"

"Hers, not his," Rafe growled. "I didn't like that little ferret the instant I clapped eyes on him."

"But why would he—?" Jeska slapped the surface of the mud bath. "You remember all that shit he spewed about religion? They don't much like us over on the Continent, you know. We scare them, with our magic." Then, eyeing Cade narrowly: "How much did this explosion at the Keep remind you of what happened at the Gallery?"

Cade didn't answer. The girl had returned, ushering three gray-haired ladies (who admittedly had perfect complexions, not a wrinkle on their faces) through to another vat in the adjoining room. By the time they had bowed and smiled their way past, and the door had shut behind them, Mieka was shaking his head. The mud clinging to his long, shaggy hair annoyed him.

"That was done with magic," he said, low-voiced. "A withie. We found the crimp end, remember? And anyway, if the little git wanted to blow something up in the name of religion, why not one of the Minsters?"

The girl came back and gestured that it was time for them to be moving on to the other room. "Elsewise it's mortared you'll be, and chipped at with a chisel!"

They obliged her with a laugh, and extricated themselves from the thick, sucking mud. They'd left on their underdrawers for modesty's sake—the girl's, not their own—and followed her into a large warm room paneled in fragrant wood. She indicated that they were to stand in the middle, then hauled away at a wheel over in the corner—and suddenly they were standing under a veritable waterfall, as if they'd been fools enough to swim underneath the Plume.

But for some reason, the mud didn't wash off Mieka the way it did the other three. It caked all over his face and most of his body. He stood beneath the deluge twice as long as the others. He scrubbed, he scraped, he picked.

The girl began to frown. "Of the oils, which did you use?"

"I don't know! It smelled nice." He pried a dollop of mud off his arm, and yelped as hair came off with it. "A green bottle, I think."

And then he looked over at Rafe, who had handed him the green bottle of oil and helped to spread it down his back. Rafe, for whom he'd performed the same service, wincing a little at the thin scars of a willow switch used on him by a cruel teacher in littleschool, against whom he'd had his vengeance. Rafe, who was thoughtfully stroking his thick, luxuriant beard.

"You!" he bellowed. "This is *your* fault!"

"Mine?" But the blue-gray eyes were dancing and he could barely keep his lips from twitching.

"Green?" The girl shook her head. "That is for *after*."

Cade and Jeska were trying to look sympathetic as Mieka stood there, pummeled by the waterfall, sopped as a clumsy puppy, and still bedecked in bluish mud. But when Rafe said, "Oh, was it? Sorry, Mieka," his sincerity was so overplayed that they doubled up in laughter.

They weren't laughing when the girl began stripping off her clothes, right down to a pair of short pink pants and a loosely laced corset that barely contained her breasts. She tied back her long black hair, kicked off her shoes, and joined Mieka under the cascade. Together they spent many long minutes working mud off him, and when most of it was gone, she stood back and eyed him.

"Luck it was, that you kept on your smallclothing."

Mieka, who had been congratulating himself (between moans of pain as mud and hair and even some skin came loose) on all the attention, felt himself turn pale at the thought of having to—having to—oh, he was going to *murder* Rafcadion Threadchaser.

At length the water was turned off and she led him to a private room, where she smoothed the green oil all over him while the other three had to fend for themselves. Mieka would have enjoyed it more if it all hadn't stung so much.

Three days later, as the wagon rolled the last few miles to New Halt, Yazz was still chuckling, Rafe was still grinning, and Cade and Jeska were still picking odd bits of dried mud off Mieka, like plaster from a decaying wall.

They were also still discussing Cade's Elsewhen.

Mieka had his own thoughts about that, keeping them to himself until the wagon had been secured and the horses stabled, and Touchstone was upstairs at their usual inn at New Halt. He shared with Cade, as always, and when they had organized their shaving gear and stage clothes, he brought out his thorn-roll and tossed it onto his bed. Cade looked round from hanging up the shirt he would wear for tomorrow's performance.

"I've been thinking," Mieka said, "about that time you saw me with the diamond earring. Remember? If you think about what you want to see just as you start feeling the thorn—and I'll be here the whole time, I won't let you—" He shut his teeth over the rest of it. He'd been about to say *"I won't let you get too lost, I'll always come find you,"* but that brought up the memory of Cade sneering, *"How do you like what you've found?"*

Cade had the decency to remember it, as well, and to look embarrassed. He said nothing about it, replying only, "But it wasn't a real Elsewhen. I don't think so, anyways. It could have been just the thorn."

"How can you tell the difference?" Mieka asked shrewdly.

Cade opened his mouth, shut it, and scowled.

"Do you want to try? I've got some. Auntie Brishen was thorough, as usual."

"Maybe tomorrow night."

"We've shows every night here but this one. You'll be too tired." He held up one hand. "I know what you're about to say, but after the bluethorn you'll probably have tomorrow night, you won't want to try anything else. And you know you hardly ever react the way everyone else does, whichever thorn you use."

Cade pursed his lips. "I don't know, Mieka. . . ."

"C'mon, Quill." He risked saying, "I'll be here."

"All right, then," Cade conceded. "Tonight."

13

Yazz joined them at dinner downstairs, giving his customary report about the health of the horses and the state of the wagon. Except for a loose strut in the retractable steps, everything was fine. Repairs would be the work of a morning, after which he'd be free to do as he liked until it came time to leave New Halt for Castle Eyot and three days of rest.

Cade wondered sometimes whether or not Yazz got bored, sitting around waiting with nothing much to do but tend the wagon and horses. Or did he find other things to do? Visiting friends and relatives happened quite seldom. He'd never stuck Cade as a great reader. He drank, of course, but despite Mieka's frequent efforts to prove the opposite, it really wasn't possible to spend all one's time sloshing back whiskey or wine or ale. Yazz seemed perfectly happy in his duties and life on the road, and if anyone in any of the towns they passed through or the cities they lingered in had a problem with Giants, Cade never knew about it. Which was only logical, of course. It was easy to have a prejudice against Elves or Wizards or Goblins or Gnomes. They were all Human-sized or smaller. Even so, Cade had the feeling that even if someone directed insults at Yazz, he'd only shrug and look pityingly at the offender. Such intolerance was entirely beneath Yazz's notice.

Except when it came to Mieka. When they'd returned from their little jaunt to Prickspur's, once they'd told their tale and received Jeska's and Rafe's congratulations, Yazz chided Mieka using more words than Cade had ever heard him utter at one time. The gist of it was that Mieka was an idiot; he should have taken Yazz with him; Cade, Wizard or not, was no protection; what would Yazz have said to his wife and his mother and his father, leave alone to Cade's parents and brother and Mistress Mirdley, if anything had happened?

Mieka took all this in a submissive silence that startled Cade almost as much as the scold. Later, once the wagon was on the move again, Mieka had said, "You'd think I was still eight years old, and he'd just caught me stowing away on the whiskey wagon halfway to Auntie Brishen's. Of course, it *was* halfway to Auntie Brishen's, so maybe having taken me all that way without noticing was what made him angry." After a moment's thought and a stifled chuckle, he added, "Y'know, of all those people he mentioned just now, I think Mistress Mirdley scares him the most!"

Sitting opposite Yazz at the dinner table, Cade wondered idly what the Giant actually thought about all this. He liked to watch them perform, but surely he was bored beyond tears with their folio by now. Cade tried to think of all the others he knew with Giant blood—a very short list—and realized that none of them mixed very much with the rest of Albeyni society. They kept to their homes in the hills and mountains. Every so often they appeared in Gallybanks for purposes of trade or amusement, or to petition the King for one thing or another. But ever since the end of the Archduke's War, they had mostly stayed put. It might very well be that Yazz had been born with greater curiosity than most Giants, and was with Touchstone purely for the constant change of scenery.

The innkeeper, whom they knew by now on this, their

fourth Royal Circuit, had waited until they were bathed, rested, fed, and watered before presenting them with the letters that had arrived over the last few days. The most important was the one from Lord Kearney Fairwalk to Mieka. The Elf read the relevant portion aloud, a frown on his face.

I am most dreadfully sorry about the difficulty your sister encountered at the Emberward Bank. This past winter I directed that no money should be paid out to anyone without my own written permission, and further that all tradesmen's bills be sent to me for settlement. This was done to protect Touchstone, for, in conversation with Romuald Needler, I learned that several times persons unknown have attempted to draw on the Shadowshapers' various accounts using forged signatures. Unhappily, this custom of signing placards, while excellent advertising and doubtless delightful for admirers, has produced hundreds of copies of their signatures, and now, of course, of yours. I have satisfied myself that no unauthorized persons have been able to steal from you in this manner, but it seemed prudent to take precautions. Please know that I have apologized to your sister and spoken to the Bank, where her future requests will be promptly honored.

Mieka glanced round the table. "Well?"

"It never even occurred to me," Cade admitted. "We're lucky he had that talk with Rommy Needler."

Jeska's frown had started out deeper than Mieka's and stayed that way. "I'm thinking that this might be the reason my accounts don't tally every so often. But I'm also wondering why he didn't tell us all this before."

"With all the other things he has to do for us?" Cade asked. "He probably just left it to one of his clerks and forgot about it. Pass the chicken."

That night, upstairs in their room, he donned his nightshirt and got into bed, relaxing back with a sigh into the soft mattress. He was lying on more than forty pounds of feathers, grateful that it wasn't yet high summer, when the feathers would begin to stink. In his career thus far, he'd slept on mattresses filled with everything from down to wool to sea moss to sawdust, and more blankets-over-bare-straw than he cared to recall. All of these were heaven to bedbugs, fleas, mice, rats, and moths, but the herbs Mistress Mirdley packed into his clothes kept him safe. At this inn, one of the finest in New Halt, he doubted there'd be so much as a wayward spider to scurry off once it got a sniff of protective herbs. Did spiders have noses? He laughed softly to himself at the absurd direction of his thoughts, knowing it covered apprehension. It had been a long time since he'd tried this particular thorn.

Schooling his brain to consideration of what little he'd seen of the explosion at the Keep, he waited for Mieka to prepare the thorn. His brain, however, did not seem disposed to take the lesson, and before Mieka had even touched his arm, an Elsewhen came.

{ He'd looked for Kearney in four of the shim taverns in Gallybanks, with no luck. Finally he tracked him down to a rather elegant establishment three streets off Amberwall Square. A well-dressed crowd danced on polished wooden flooring to the music of two lutes and a drum, and those who were not dancing draped themselves in attractive attitudes on dark blue velvet upholstery at dozens of little round black tables. Still more stood by the room-wide copper bar. All the men were definitely men, and so were all the ladies.

There was a difference, though, between these people and the costumes Mieka got himself up in, or the way Jezael and Tobalt and the others had worn their gowns and shawls that memorable night at the Downstreet. Cade looked around him, puzzled, and at last he realized: it had to do with sincerity. Mieka and the rest had worn women's clothing as a joke. These men were in earnest.

Kearney, catching sight of him, flushed scarlet with mortification. His embarrassment amused Cade, who joined him at the bar and ordered a drink.

"I thought your tastes ran more to the intellectual, like Drevan Wordturner."

Kearney mumbled and stammered.

"Or are there noteworthy scholars here amongst the embroidered codpieces and—" He squinted through the gloom. "—leather masks? Ought I to have worn one? Am I well-enough known to want to hide my face like that man over there in the corner?"

"No," Kearney said incautiously. "He's nobody famous. He just wants people to think he is."

"Ah. I see."

Low-voiced, Kearney asked, "You don't mind? You're not shocked?"

"Should I be?" Though in truth he was, a little bit. This annoyed him. Here he was, Master Tregetour for Touchstone, famous throughout Albeyn, leading the wild mad life of a traveling player, with excellent drink and prime thorn and girls aplenty at his fingertips, high living and not quite respectable . . . he realized that despite what Blye had told him, he *was* rather ordinary in some respects.

"Did you have some reason for seeking me out?" Kearney asked, gathering up the tattered shreds of his dignity.

Cade's drink appeared on the beaten copper bar, and instantly half a dozen coins joined it. He glanced around to find four gentlemen and two shims clustering nearby, all of them eager to pay for his drink and his company. He cursed himself for blushing as deeply as Kearney had done, shook his head, and reached into his jacket pocket for coin.

"Much beholden," he said to his admirers. "But—"

"He's not available," Kearney growled bluntly, all at once looking more threateningly Gnomish than Cade had ever seen him. "Be gone!"

Cade blushed anew as the implication provoked (variously) annoyance, regret, disgust, resentment, skepticism, and a resigned sigh. Somehow he managed a smile as he took Kearney's arm and steered him towards a vacant table. When they were seated, he said, "I wouldn't have come looking for you if it wasn't urgent. I don't care what you do in your private life, Kearney, truly I don't. But there's a problem with Derien's school fees, and—"}

He barely had time to register the panic in Fairwalk's eyes before the Elsewhen abruptly ended and he was looking at Mieka.

"There's something about money," he blurted. "My brother's school hasn't been paid—or won't be paid, I'm not sure how far in the future this is—I went to Kearney to ask him about it, and . . . and I think there's something wrong, Mieka."

"Diddling the accounts? Let's have Jeska go through *all* our finances when we get home." The Elf was seated in a chair beside Cade's bed, the thorn-roll open on his knees. He toyed with several of the packets, scowling. "That bilge about signatures being copied—that doesn't listen quite rightly to me."

"Well, there's nothing we can do about it at the moment. And I want to know about Tregrefin Ilesko."

Mieka finished preparing the glass thorn, warning, "This can be dodgy stuff."

"Just get on with it."

If Mieka was surprised, or possibly amused, by Cade's

eagerness to see more Elsewhens, even though he'd spent almost two years denying and rejecting them, he gave no sign of it. Cade, alert for the tiny pinprick, waited for the familiar warmth and then heat to spread up his arm and through his body. He closed his eyes and pictured Miriuzca's shifty-faced little brother in his mind. He heard Minster chimes as if from very far away, unsure if the sound were part of the burgeoning Elsewhen or part of real life. Suddenly the Elsewhen *was* real life.

{ "But she told us it would work."

"She told us, she told us," the young man mimicked in a high singsong voice. He laid both hands flat on the tavern table before him, glancing once over his shoulder to the tall bearded man who could not have been more obviously an armed guard if he'd been dressed in chain mail and carrying his knives in both hands, rather than a plain shirt and trousers with a light cape of dark green silk concealing the blades. Returning his attention to the pair of robeless Good Brothers opposite him at the table, he spoke again, this time in his own voice, pitched low even though the tavern was nearly empty, and in very good Albeyni. "Whatever she told you, she was wrong. Haven't you learned yet never to trust a woman? Look at my dear sister! Gone over to the enemy for the chance to become a queen! If you want to help the cause of the Lord and the Lady in this sinful land, you had best come up with something and someone else."

"We wanted to use magic to destroy the place," one of the Good Brothers said, rubbing mindlessly at the pale circle of skin at his wrist where the silver bracelet bespeaking him to the Lady had been removed for this encounter. "To show how wicked magic can be."

The other one, taller and with a mouth too wide for his narrow face, contributed, "The girl stole the withie from

Black Lightning's glisker competently enough. Pity her father wasn't so competent at bespelling it. However, what's done is done, my lord, and if this is to succeed, the method must be chosen quickly. It isn't long until the celebrations."

The Tregrefin's fingers slowly curled into fists. "I should think the method would be perfectly obvious."

The pair of disguised Good Brothers traded looks, and the tall one said, "It's not as if one can walk into a shop and order up half a hundredweight."

Ilesko brought his clenched fists down onto the table. "Had it occurred to you that ten times half a hundredweight will be in Gallantrybanks to make the fireworks for King Meredan's festivities?"

"But how will we—?"

"The how of it is your problem. And I assure you that you will solve it. The Lord and the Lady will inspire you to success."

The edgy Good Brother abandoned rubbing his wrist and looked at his friend, light dawning in his dark eyes. "Isn't Sister Audelon related to one of the apprentice Firemasters?"

"As I say," Ilesko interrupted impatiently, "how you accomplish it is your concern. But accomplish this you must, for the sake of the Only Faith."}

Cade came awake slowly, conscious of feet and legs, hand and arms, one by one. His eyes opened. Mieka sat waiting with a patience entirely foreign to him. Cade cleared his throat a couple of times, then smiled ruefully.

"I can tell you one thing right off," he said. "Tregrefin Ilesko speaks Albeyni *much* better than he let on at lunching."

"Then he's behind it." Mieka nodded his satisfaction.

"The explosion at the Keeps—using black powder, by the way—*and* what happened at the Gallery."

Instantly he knew that telling Mieka that last part had been a mistake. Fury flared in those eyes, turning them a bright blue-green that Cade had rarely seen before. "You mean that little shit is responsible for what happened to my brother? I'll pull his guts out through his throat with my bare hands!"

"He's got a couple of Good Brothers working with him— being Naughty Brothers, actually. All sorts of stuff about the Only Faith, and the Lord and the Lady. On second thought, they weren't anything more than Nominatives. The one kept rubbing his wrist where his bracelet should've been. They can't take them off after they're fully accepted into a Minster. They're sealed with magic, just like wedding jewelry. Neither of these men were wearing theirs, but they did have them, so I'd guess they were Bespoken Nominatives, one step away from being Good Brothers." He knew he was babbling, but he was trying to distract Mieka from the vengeance glowing in those eyes. When the Elf met his gaze again, he knew that Mieka knew what he'd been about, and that whereas it hadn't really worked, Mieka was allowing it to work.

"Could you recognize either of them again?"

"Probably not. But it was definitely the Tregrefin. They were talking about how they'd fucked up the explosion at the Gallery, that the magic hadn't been worked right, and black powder like the kind used in fireworks was the only thing to use at the Keeps. And somebody called Sister Audelon has a cousin or something who's an apprentice Firemaster."

Mieka chewed his lip for a minute, then asked, "Do you know when the Elsewhen happened?"

"A little while before the big celebrations for King Meredan and Queen Roshien. I can't be sure exactly when."

"Well, by then we'll have thought something up to stop them. Right now you have to sleep."

Cade would have said that right now sleep was as far from him as the Vathis River, but, strangely enough, the mere mention of it set his eyelids drooping. Forcing them open, he looked suspiciously at Mieka, who snorted.

"Do you see me holding a withie?" he asked, spreading his arms wide. "I'm not doing anything, Quill. You *are* tired. Sleep sweet."

Cayden woke early the next morning, tired but satisfied. How could he have been so foolish as to have rejected the Elsewhens for so long? Mieka had been right: They were part of what he was, and without them he was a fraction of who he had to be. Not even he was arrogant enough to think that there was a reason for them greater than himself, and if such a reason existed, he didn't care. He felt real again. No, that wasn't quite the right word. Lying there on his back, staring at the low beams of the ceiling, he searched for a way to describe it. And at last he had it.

He felt *visible*.

For almost two years he had done everything he was supposed to do and many things he shouldn't have done. He had moved into his own lodgings, he had written or rewritten plays, he had primed withies and performed at Seekhaven and on the Royal Circuit and throughout Gallantrybanks, he had dined with friends and visited castles and shared lunchings with the Princess, he had bedded girls and forgotten their names (if he'd ever even known them). All those things had been real enough. Yet it was as if he had closed his eyes to almost everything he was doing, or—no, not closed his eyes but looked away, unwilling to watch. He knew that all these things were happening to him, and that they were real, and that they had consequences—the disaster of "Turn Aback" might have ruined Touchstone if he'd insisted on performing it over and over again, and he was more beholden than he could ever admit that Rafe, Jeska, and Mieka had flatly refused to keep on with it. Himself, he hadn't been paying attention. If he'd heard the reactions of the audiences, he hadn't really been listening. If he'd noticed confusion and boredom on their faces, he hadn't really been seeing. And he certainly hadn't been watching himself as he sulked for weeks after his partners laid down the law.

The only times he'd felt entirely present in his own life had been onstage. *That* was where his life meant something; *that* was what he had been born for. He had this in common with Mieka, that they both felt totally alive only when they were onstage. Theater demanded everything of them, all their resources of mind and magic, rigorous alertness and swift reactions. Cade was too much the professional not to give his all in performance—but his all had not been all of him during those two years of denying the Elsewhens. Seeing them again now, he was seeing himself, whole once more. Visible, not just to himself but also to those around him.

It was no wonder that Jeska and Rafe and Mieka hadn't noticed the disappearance of the Elsewhens: walling himself off from that unique (as far as he knew) magic had set up a similar wall between him and them. They hadn't been able to see him. Granted, he resented that none of them had really bothered to look very closely. They had their own lives to contend with, after all. But if they had looked, what would they have seen? Portions of Cade, not the entirety. He had presented more or less what they had come to expect. But that version of Cayden was a man whom not even he had wanted to see.

Derien was the only one who had looked close and hard, and had not liked what he saw. Cade swore to make it up to his brother. To Mistress Mirdley. To all the people he loved.

Derien, whose futures Cade had to go seeking, the way he had sought the Tregrefin Ilesko.

"Hungry?"

He was so startled that he sat halfway up in bed before he realized that it was just Mieka with a tray of tea and toast and scuffled eggs. He plumped pillows behind his back and drew his knees up, watching as Mieka stepped up onto the bed and sank down cross-legged, the tray between them atop the counterpane.

While they ate, the Elf chattered away in his usual fashion—about the chilly wind off the sea that was spoiling New Halt's summer, and the nice welcoming note sent by the ladies of what Rafe called the Needles and Nosebags Society for whom they would play a private gigging tomorrow afternoon, and which of their many coordinated but not identical outfits Touchstone would wear onstage tonight. Listening, it seemed to Cade that he was seeing Mieka for the first time in a long time. That irresistible grin, full of mischief; that tumble of shaggy black hair; those quick, clever hands; those eyes, brown and green and blue with an elusive glint of gold sparkling when he laughed. All these things were familiar, and unchanged. Yet something *had* changed. Something was different. A certain tilt of the head, a sidelong glance, a quirk at the corner of the mouth—these combined with an expression in those eyes that wasn't older, exactly, or more thoughtful, but . . . more *aware.*

"Finished?" Mieka asked.

"Umm—yeh. Are we in a hurry to go somewhere?"

"I thought for certain sure you'd want to walk out to the Chalk Dragon again. Last year you couldn't find the Faerie Vale you keep saying has to be close by. Mayhap you could use Elfen eyes and Elfen ears to help."

"It's too far to walk."

"I am *not* riding bitch again!"

Cade laughed. "Wouldn't dream of asking. Maybe they have a little horse-cart we could hire." He paused. "You really want to come with?"

Mieka shrugged and threw Cayden a shirt. "Got nothin' else to do."

Cade almost asked if he hadn't noticed the barmaid's giggling regard of last night, then recalled that with the letters had come a tightly wrapped package from Mieka's wife: a new pair of trousers, dark blue with green and yellow interlocking patterns embroidered down each side seam. Evidently, Cade thought with a snide interior smile, she had decided to go right to the source of his infidelities. He got dressed, watching Mieka from the corner of his eye as the Elf preened in front of the mirror like a lady-in-waiting about to attend a Court ball, fussing with his hair, tightening his belt a notch. These past few years on the Royal Circuit, he picked up weight during the winter months at home that he lost during summers on the road. Cade didn't know how much of that was due to the quantities of bluethorn he pricked, although he was well aware that his own clothing was getting looser. Not too many days before a nice bit of rest at Castle Eyot, he reminded himself. No performances, no worrying, no travel, nothing to do but sleep and eat and laze about in the warm summer sunshine.

Mieka had told Rafe and Jeska where they were bound. He had also done some asking, and heard about a farmer who came regularly in to New Halt to see the first show of any Royal Circuit. His lands were in the direction of the Chalk Dragon, and if he and Cade waited at a particular crossroads in midafternoon, they were more than likely to get a ride back to the city. They were just in time to catch the morning coach out of the Brindled Brach, an inn several streets over from their own, and jumped out when the driver obligingly halted the horses for about half a minute at that same crossroads. It was a long walk up into the hills, made longer by Mieka, who strayed now and then to pick daisies that he wove into a chain to drape about his shoulders, but finally they crested a rise and saw across a narrow valley the Chalk Dragon.

Cade had used up most of his breath in the climb. He stood in silence, staring at the gigantic creature drawn on the side of the hill, white outline against green, as if limned with strokes of a broad and heavy pen. This local point of interest wasn't worth trying to see in winter, covered as it was with snow. But in summer, as he'd learned last year, it was magnificent. The wings spread from the crown of the hill almost to the row of hedges at the bottom, and the stark white lines of the body from nose to spiked tail reached at least three hundred feet across the hillside.

"Do they know who did this?" Mieka whispered. He had never seen it before, and it was one of those sights, like one's first view of the Flood or the paintings in the Great Royal Minster, that demanded a hushed voice. Even the stream sparkling through the valley seemed quieted by awe.

"Not sure. It's tremendously old, of course."

"Fae, d'you think?"

"Could be. Some sources say they rode dragons, but how would you control one? Can you imagine trying to rein one in? And where would you put a saddle?"

"I'll have to ask Tavier when we get home," Mieka said, chuckling. "He'll know. He knows everything about dragons." He waded a few paces into the tall grass to pick more flowers. "And that remembers me, I promised Mum that for his Wintering present he can come to a Touchstone performance and we'll do 'Dragon' for him."

"A pleasure." He watched the quick, clever fingers begin weaving more daisies: splitting the green stems, interlocking them into a continuous chain of yellow eyes and long white petals. "What in all Hells are you doing?"

He grinned and struck a pose. "I have proclaimed myself a Knight of the Most Excellent Elfen Order of the Daisy. If you're very nice to me, I'll invest you the same."

"I'd rather go have a closer look at that dragon."

Mieka squinted across the narrow valley. "There won't be anything to see. Not if it's Fae you're after."

"How do you reckon?"

"They always come from the west. That hill *faces* west. So if they're around here at all, they'll be on this side of the valley. In a cave or a hedgerow or something."

He didn't congratulate Mieka on his insight, too annoyed with himself for not having realized it before. He led the way down a narrow track through knee-high bracken, skidding and slipping but managing to keep his feet. Mieka gamboled down after him, trailing the unfinished daisy chain, and about halfway to the stream below misjudged his footing and landed on his backside.

"Clumperton!" Cade accused with a laugh, extending a hand to help Mieka up. A moment later, when the Elf was standing next to him, he exclaimed, "You're bleeding!"

"Mm? Oh. Nothing to signify." He hung the uncompleted chain over one elbow and brushed the dirt from his hands. After a brief inspection of the scrapes on his palms, he asked, "This is the way most people take, innit? Those as come to see the Chalk Dragon."

"What of it?"

"So this is about as far as anybody ever goes, right? Not much of a trail, and it doesn't go all the way to the bottom." He pointed to a cluster of yellow-flowering bushes strewn across the path about twenty feet ahead of them, six or seven feet high, very thick, blocking the way. "I'll wager you that this whole place is a Faerie Vale."

Cade inspected the scratches on Mieka's palms with more attention that they deserved. "The first time, I fell down a hill from winter into summer."

"And met your great-great-whatever granny—yeh, I know." Mieka looked grim. "If you think I'll let you stumble back into the Fae world, think again! It could be hours or years before they let you out—*if* they let you out!"

"Why wouldn't they?"

The flowering bushes rustled, and from them a high, harsh voice said, "Good question."

14

Lagging a half instant behind his body, which had flinched and spun towards the voice, Cade's brain registered the presence of a tall and elegant Fae emerging with graceful dignity from the bushes. His hair and his robes were made of green leaves, his eyes as yellow as the blossoms. He inspected Cayden and Mieka frankly as he took a few delicate steps towards them, gaze lingering on Mieka's pointed ears that were a sort of child's version of his own, which were extravagantly large and decorated at lobes and tips with emeralds set in gold. At first he appeared to be handsome, but as he neared, Cade felt a stinging sensation in his guts, for the finely drawn features had in them a hint of cruelty. It wasn't quite fear, and it wasn't quite revulsion, but the sensation held elements of both, and the shock of unfurled wings did nothing to comfort him. Those wings also seemed made of leaves: long, slender, translucent leaves like feathers, one overlapping the next, palest green and shimmering in the sunlight.

"It's not many of the Blood who come this way, this far," the Fae said. "Mostly they stay up there, staring at that brazen bit of self-congratulation the Giants carved into my hill. As if they ever let us forget who it was who rode the dragons, and left *us* with naught but the land and water beasts!"

Questions clogged Cade's mind: *What do you mean,* your *hill?* and *Giants rode dragons?* and *Land and water beasts like the ones in the Vathis River?* and *I know* I'm *partly Fae, but—Mieka?*

Before he could figure out which he wanted answered first, the Elf spoke.

"Your pardon for disturbing you," he said with a jaunty bow. "We've come seeking someone you may know, or may have heard of. A Wizard—with some Fae blood for good measure—who arrived in your part of the world two Midsummers ago as Humans reckon time."

"Friend of yours?" The Fae arched a mocking brow, as amused by this drawing room civility as Cade was appalled by it. Everything he had ever read about—and the one encounter he'd actually had with—the Fae cautioned wariness in dealing with them. But this one's wings folded themselves against his back, their upper curves framing his face, as if he were settling down for a teatime gossip.

Mieka didn't skip a beat. Neither did he directly answer the Fae's question, which indicated to Cade that he had at least a little sense. "Curious fellow, he is—curious in the way of wanting to find things out, I mean, though the other kind of *curious* applies as well, now that I think on it. A bit strange sometimes, you know. Anyways, he has very dark skin and curling hair. Rarely seen not cuddling a lute in his arms. Goes by the name Briuly Blackpath."

In the next instant, Cade knew he'd been right to fear the Fae. Wings shuddered with a clicking, rasping sound as muscles tensed and leaves shifted. The yellow eyes lit with sudden fire. "He who stole the King's Right!"

"Oh, you know him, then?" Mieka smiled winningly. Cade wanted to tell him that he'd lost before he'd even opened his mouth. "At your Royal Court, no doubt, delighting all with his music?"

The Fae's features had sharpened, his bones like razors beneath skin pale as parchment. All the beauty was gone, leaving something almost feral: the face of a predator. A killer. Cade gripped Mieka's elbow, but to what end he could not have said. They could never outrun an infuriated Fae. However decorative the wings were, they could not be used for flight; Fae soared and swooped like dragonflies by manipulating the very air around them, and they were rumored to do it with indescribable swiftness. They couldn't fight him, not with fists or with spells. Perhaps he got hold of Mieka just for the comfort of knowing that Mieka, bone and muscle and warm skin, was real.

"I know of him," the Fae said harshly. "All the True Folk know of him, after the tribunal."

"Really?" Mieka sounded mildly intrigued. "And what was the outcome of this tribunal?"

"Witless, chattering Elf! Scant wonder your kind stayed amongst the Humans—the only race even more witless than you! Can you not reason it out? On the one side were those who demanded his death for daring to touch and even to place upon his head the King's Right. On the other, those who discerned in him the Blood, and argued for sparing his life despite the desecration, for the King's Right had at last been recovered."

"Desecration," Mieka repeated thoughtfully. "It must've been rather muddy, I agree. How long did it take to clean the thing?"

He was scornfully ignored. "The Crown may be only slightly less crucial than the Carkanet, but neither are worth anything without Sealing. Our King quite properly refuses to wear his Right until the Queen wears hers again."

"So why not go get it?" Mieka asked as calmly as if they were indeed sitting in velvet-covered chairs over cinnamon tea and buttered muffins. "If it's as important as all that . . ."

Cade astounded himself (and, from the looks of him, the Fae) by saying, "The Oakapple lords—Briuly's family—once owned Nackerty Close. One of their ancestors stole The Rights. Only someone of that blood could take them from where they're hidden."

"Such a clever Wizardling," snapped the Fae.

"He is that," Mieka said fondly.

"The Crown," Cade pursued, "is basically just something fancy to put on the King's head. It's the Carkanet that really matters, because it's the Queen's Right, and the Fae are matriarchal."

"'Dancing Ground'!" Mieka exclaimed.

Cade nodded, and would have said more—though not about the Shadowshapers' play—but the Fae's blazing eyes stopped him. "What you do not know, stupid Wizard and stupid Elf, is that this ancestor who stole The Rights was a halfling. Begrudging his place in the Brightlands—lowly, as befitted a half-Human—he purloined Crown and Carkanet in the mistaken belief that he could bargain with them for a high place in the Seemly Court. And when the Humans learned they had been stolen, they began a war to retrieve them that killed many thousands, and—"

"No, they didn't!" Mieka interrupted. "'Twas the Fae who made war on the rest of us!"

"Is that the tale they tell in your portion of the world? *I* say that this halfling was hunted down by Fae and Human alike, and at last he hid The Rights—"

Cade's turn to interrupt. "And the Humans caught him at it, and before they hanged him, he said that no one but a Fae would ever wear The Rights, and if a Fae—meaning himself, of course—if he couldn't, no one would."

The Fae scowled at him, wings rustling. But he made no correction.

So *that* was how it happened. Cade was delighted. He could use this new information to change "Treasure"—no, he'd write an entirely new play, incorporating what the Fae had told him—no, he'd write *two* plays, one about the initial stealing and the second about the finding, and put "Treasure" in the middle, and perform all three on the same night—if he wrote fast enough, he'd present this innovation of connected tales in the same show before Vered Goldbraider could finish his play about the *balaurin*—but Vered had been working on the damned thing for the better part of two years, and still hadn't finished, so it was more than likely that Cade and Touchstone would be credited with a revolutionary new concept in theater, and—

It seemed he had been very far away, because he heard Mieka's voice, as if from a distance, say, "What about Briuly?"

Briuly. Good Gods, he had completely forgotten that the third play of the group would be about Briuly and Alaen, and the vengeful Fae, and death. Abruptly present in the here and now, and with more of a shock than any time he'd ever come out of an Elsewhen, he looked at the Fae.

All the menace had faded; the eyes were flat yellow again, lightless. Sullenly, like a five-year-old caught raiding the sweets canister, the Fae said, "Deep into the Brightlands he was taken. The Seemly Court was gathered from far and wide—"

"Quite the spectacle, I take it," mused Mieka.

With a glance of annoyance, the Fae continued, "His crime was weighed against recovery of the King's Right. *I* was in favor of killing him."

"He's not dead?" Cade blurted. "You didn't kill him? He's alive?"

With a smirk: "If you'd care to call it that."

Cade was scared to ask what that might mean. The Fae was maliciously eager to explain.

"Ask him a question, and he'll sing you a song. Remark that it's a lovely sunny day, and he'll sing you another song. Songs are all he knows. Not even his name. Not a single spoken word leaves his lips. He opens his mouth only to drink and sing—"

"At the same time?" Mieka interrupted.

"Elf!" spat the Fae. "How I have always hated Elves! Rude and foolish—utterly undeserving of the ears of the Blood—"

"Oh, but they look so pretty on me," Mieka said earnestly. "Everyone says so. Well, much beholden for the information. We really ought to be on our way. Lovely meeting you. Do please give our best regards to Master Blackpath when next you see him!"

The wings rustled angrily. "I'll have my Tithing first."

"Sorry, no idea what you're talking about." Mieka had hold of Cade's arm, pulling him backwards one step, then two. "Must toddle off home now."

"I'll have my full Tithing of Fae Blood!"

He lunged forward, leafy wings widespread and snapping. Mieka hauled Cade to one side, flinging the second daisy chain over his head. The Fae recoiled, his eyes flaring gold flames once more. But he didn't back off. Indeed, he took one step forward, then another, wings chittering like the wings of a thousand angry insects.

Mieka dug his free hand into his trousers pocket and came up with a coin, rather large, about two inches across. He tossed it into the air and caught it again. Cade watched the Fae's yellow eyes follow the dull gray disk and acquire a look of confusion that Cade was pretty sure matched his own.

Mieka smiled with all his teeth. "I really don't want to lose this," he said. "But if it's a tithing you're after . . ."

And then the Fae gasped as Mieka threw the coin right at him. Cade, utterly bewildered, yelped as Mieka yanked at his arm again and cried out, "Run!"

They gained the top of the hill, thighs aching, lungs heaving, and at last they stopped. Bent over, hands on his knees, gasping, Cade looked down the path to the bushes. They were simply bushes again, lushly green, frothed with yellow flowers.

"Fucking Hells!" Mieka panted. "That was close!"

Getting his wind back, Cade asked, "You want to explain all that?"

The Elf flopped a hand in the air, still whooping for breath.

Cade waited him out. At last he managed, "Daisies are protection against Fae."

So they were. Something else he'd forgotten. "How did you know?"

"Had a talk with Mistress Mirdley, didn't I? Back last winter, when I told her about your little side trip to see the Chalk Dragon. Trolls don't much like Fae. She gave me fair warning, and a gambit or two in case you got foolish and wanted to have another look."

It shamed Cade that he had not remembered this vital piece of information himself. A laughably simple bit of protective magic that had protected them from—what?

"He wanted our blood!"

"No, just yours. I already gave some." He held up his scratched palm. "It summoned him, I think. Strictly by accident, of course, when I tripped on that rock. But I didn't much fancy watching him open one of your veins." Frowning at the reddened skin on his hand, he added, "You could've been quicker on the uptake, y'know."

"Forgive me if I didn't quite believe that a Fae was so insulted by the thought of accepting money instead of blood that he'd—" He stopped. Mieka was looking insufferably smug. "All right, I give up."

"Too easily," Mieka scoffed. "'Tweren't just any old coin, but I don't s'pose Mistress Mirdley will grumble much at losing it to save your life. I tossed him an ironslip, my dear old Quill," he explained at last. "From the early part of the war. The only danger was in me forgetting, and spending it!"

As a precaution against the Fae taking advantage of the conflict spawned by the Archduke, King Cobin had ordered iron coins struck, under the theory that if the Fae thought to hide their wings by magic and mix in with everyone else and cause further havoc, daily life necessitated the use of money. And although iron, properly bespelled as in the rings Cade's grandfather Isshak Highcollar had worn, interfered with a Wizard's magic, it was pain and poison to the Fae. The *slip*, of course, would be a Fae's taking the coin and inevitably reacting to it.

Not that it had ever really worked. There'd been a few anecdotes, mostly suspect, about a Fae's burned fingers or cries of agony. What the ironslips had really done was make the general populace feel a bit safer from any encroachments by the Fae in a war that wasn't their own. Most of the coins had been culled from general circulation. Though they were still legal tender, they were rare these days, kept mostly by those who had been in the war, or whose fathers or grandfathers had; the coins served as a convincing prop for implausible tales of outsmarting a Fae.

"Could've just used a nail," Mieka went on. "But the ironslip had more flash."

"And the Old Gods forfend that you should do anything that lacks genuine style," Cade teased. He paused, then straightened his posture and settled the daisy chain more evenly around his shoulders. With a low bow, he said, "I am honored, Master Windthistle, to have been invested with the Most Excellent Elfen Order of the Yellow Eye." After a moment he added, "Though one might have wished—not that I'm complaining, mind you— but it would have been less strain on the nerves if the ceremony had been just slightly less spectacular. You do tend to go for the grandiose, don't you?"

Mieka pretended puzzlement. "What's the point, otherwise?"

Even as he burst out laughing, Cade reflected that Mieka had done it to him again. The Elf could always make him laugh, whatever the situation. And this one, anybody would admit, was purely ridiculous.

Daisies. And a coin. A big bad beastly yellow-eyed leafy-winged Fae had been flummoxed by two chains of daisies and a rusty old coin. Had he put it into a play, not only would nobody believe it, but the audience would pelt the stage with whatever came to hand.

Back at the crossroads, they hitched a ride with a farmer who was thrilled to be conveying such illustrious young men and plied them with questions about the theater for at least ten miles. Unhappily, he could not take them directly to their inn, for his wagonload of cabbages was destined for a market on the other side of New Halt. Cade expressed their gratitude and asked his name, and told him that two free tickets would be waiting for him at the theater. The man never asked about the daisy chains both wore.

Rafe asked. Cade shook his head and invited him and Jeska into his and Mieka's room, there to regale them with the whole story. Rafe was incredulous ("Daisies?"), but Jeska was appalled.

"Why did they do that to Briuly? He got them back the Crown, and they punished him by taking away everything but his music!"

"He's probably happier that way," Rafe said with a shrug. "You know him—never had time for anybody or anything but his lute. I'd swear that even in his sleep he was fingering songs on his blankets and pillows."

Cade, who had been trying to avoid thinking about Briuly, seized on to this idea and liked it. But then he thought about Alaen, thorn-thralled and morose all this long while. The notion that Briuly was most likely living a life of perfect contentment, only himself and his lute and his songs, eased some of Cade's guilt. Still—what would Alaen say when he was told what had happened to his cousin?

He had deliberately forgotten the Elsewhen that had showed him Briuly and Alaen's discovery of The Rights. Glimpses lingered, nothing substantial—and he wondered if he could track down the rest of it inside his mind for use in the new play. He had the feeling that the cold calculation of it should have disgusted him more than it did. What kind of man was he, anyways?

"You're wilting," Rafe said to Mieka, pointing to the daisies still draped about his shoulders.

Eyeing the drooping petals, he sighed. "If Cilka or Petrinka were here, I could get them to do a preserving spell. As it is . . ." He lifted the chain and gathered it all between his palms, then crushed the flowers together and dropped them into the bin by the door. "Cade?"

Part of him wanted to keep it on, a reminder of how foolish he had been today. To have forgotten that the Fae always came out of the west, that Briuly had been captured and Alaen traumatized by the Fae because Cade had insisted on their listening to "Treasure," and that something as common and innocent as a daisy and a coin could halt an enraged Fae in his tracks—actually, what miffed him the most was that Mieka had remembered all those things.

Mieka, who never opened a book, and read a broadsheet only if Touchstone was mentioned.

Mieka, whose education was best described as *sketchy*.

Mieka, who was worried enough to ask Mistress Mirdley how to defend him from the Fae if necessary.

Mieka, who had bullied and shamed him into accepting his Elsewhens again.

There was more than one type of intelligence in this world. Cade had never doubted it, but neither had he ever given any of the other sorts much more than scant acknowledgment and grudging respect.

He handed over the daisy chain. "You didn't tell me you were Fae enough to make your blood interesting."

"*All* my blood is perfectly fascinating." Flowers disposed of, he raked both hands back through his hair and grinned. "Wait until I get hold of Yazz! All this about Giants riding dragons—I'll grill him like a pork chop!"

The performance that night went brilliantly. They gave the audience "Troll and Trull" and "Dragon." Cade had a glimpse of the farmer, seated front row center as befitted someone with a free pass, rapt with fascination and applauding wildly.

That night, lying under a light sheet with the breeze from the open window cooling the bedchamber, he broached with himself the topic of the Elsewhens. Though he had purposely forgotten their content, he retained a fair idea of what most of them had been about, and—his stupidity today seemed limitless—he finally realized something that he ought to have figured out long before this.

He'd thought that the Elsewhens were almost always visions of things that could happen in the future—weeks or months or years in the future—that he could influence. There had been a very few exceptions, or so he had to tell himself, cursing his own arrogance and cowardice up one side and down the other for deliberately getting rid of them. They might have confirmed this new idea of his—something Mieka had proposed and that Cade had, shameful to admit, not considered seriously: that the Elsewhens could also show him things that would happen in the very near future, within days or hours or even minutes, because of something that he'd already done or said. And that sometimes, as with the one about finding The Rights, they were events about which he could do nothing at all. Events he had in large part caused.

The others, of months or years into the future, no longer frightened him. It was the prospect of more Elsewhens like the one about Briuly and Alaen that sent waves of cold sickness through him. In common with everyone else in the world, he feared being helpless. But the Elsewhens held a particular cruelty. He understood now that sometimes he would see them not because there was something he could do or say to change them, but because something he had already said or done had brought them about and there was nothing, *nothing*, that would alter them in the slightest.

He was well aware of why Briuly and Alaen had gone after The Rights. He'd nagged Alaen into it. As for other Elsewhens of the kind—he might or might not know how they had come about. He might or might not realize which decision of his had led to them.

What he had to acknowledge, if he was to continue accepting and keeping the visions, was that sometimes he would be utterly helpless. He was well acquainted with worry, confusion, anger, fretfulness about what he ought to do to bring about or to avoid a certain Elsewhen. Now, for the sake of his sanity, he had to resign himself to the fact that there would be times when he could do nothing at all.

"Oh, for fuck's sake! Give it a rest, would you?"

He nearly fell out of bed at the sound of Mieka's annoyed voice.

"You're thinking too loud! Stop it and get some sleep!"

"Sorry," he mumbled, and turned over, and tried to compose his brain for slumber.

A rustle of bedclothes from the opposite side of the room made him sit up and light the bedside candle. Mieka was rummaging in his carrysack. Cade knew why.

"Just enough so you can sleep."

"It's all right, I don't—"

"Shut up and hold out your arm."

He began to roll the loose sleeve up his right arm, then quickly switched to the unmarked left. He knew he needed bluethorn for the energy to perform, and blockweed to be able to sleep, and the occasional exotic mixture concocted specially for him by Auntie Brishen for interesting dreams such as those he'd had last night. But he couldn't help feeling ashamed of the red pinprick marks on his right arm.

* * *

The rest of their stay at New Halt was unremarkable, as was the drive to Castle Eyot. They did not perform at the mansion outside New Halt, and had not for two years now. The substantial heft of the bags of gold they earned wasn't worth the terrible drain on their energies and the sheer creepiness of the place.

They had only three days at Castle Eyot, rather than the six or seven that were usual on the circuits. The visit was memorable for the presence of Lord Rolon Piercehand himself, master of the place and of a fleet of ships. Most of these were sailing about somewhere, but he was on none of them because of the anniversary of King Meredan's accession. Long a favorite with Queen Roshien, it was unthinkable that he would miss the celebrations.

Now that his Gallery was almost finished—with no further mishaps—he had repaired to Castle Eyot to greet Touchstone personally. His patronage, encompassing Windthistle Brothers and Cindercliff Glassworks, had expanded to Cilka and Petrinka for their expertise in hedge sculptures to be placed in decorative pots all around the new Gallery. Lord Piercehand welcomed Touchstone practically as family.

"Everything's going frightfully well at the Gallery," he told them as he escorted them up the stairs to their chambers. "All the walls up, all the windows in, all the roofs in place, and all that remains is to sort everything into the rooms for display. I really hadn't realized I'd brought back so much from all my travels!"

At the top of the stairs waited someone familiar: Drevan Wordturner, looking rumpled and woebegone, a bedraggled goose-feather pen stuck behind one ear. He smiled to see them and while Piercehand showed Rafe and Mieka to their rooms, Drevan led Cade and Jeska down another hallway.

"How are things out in the world?" the scholar asked.

"How long have you been here?" Jeska countered.

"Too long," Drevan returned morosely. "'Twas enough,

so it was, cataloging His Lordship's books and sorting out the duplicates, but then the Archduke took it into his head to compare this collection with what's in his own library *and* the Royal Archives. I'm up to my gullet in lists, with no two entries giving the same information, so that I have to find and examine each book to see which edition is here or not here—and there are times when I think a particular volume doesn't exist at all."

Cade laughed. "Cheer up. It can't be all that bad. I remember a few years ago, somebody had arranged all the books according to the color of the binding."

"Who do you think had the *re*arranging? And there are times when I'm almost sure that that's much the smarter method." He gestured to a door. "This is you, Jeska. Tea downstairs in an hour or so—you'll hear the gong. Cade, you're this way."

The chamber was as lovely and luxurious as always. Cade unslung his carrysack from his shoulder, went to the window to admire the view of the river, and turned to find that Drevan lingered in the doorway.

"Come in, sit down. I haven't seen you for an age. What have you been doing, besides cataloging books?"

The young man hesitated, then shut the door and paced a few determined steps into the room. "Cayden—if I tell you something, can you make sure it gets to Vered Goldbraider?"

"Of course. It may be a while, though. I don't think we'll be seeing the Shadowshapers until we return to Gallybanks. I'm not even sure where they are, now that they're booking their own giggings. I'm assuming," he added, lowering his voice a little, "that it's not to be trusted to a letter?"

Drevan twisted his long, ink-stained fingers together. "I hardly dare to trust *you*. Not that I don't trust you," he went on hastily. "That's not the issue. You're absolutely trustworthy, I know that. But it's so—it's such a—"

"Sit down and tell me about it."

"Close the window first, please?"

Cade felt his eyebrows attempt to connect with his hairline. His room was two floors up from the garden below. He shut the window anyway and gestured to the couch and chairs in the far corner of the room.

When they were settled, Drevan balled his fists into knots and began.

"As you say, I had to go through the whole library when I got here—I purposely didn't ask who put all the books into the shelves by color, because I didn't want to have to find him and kill him." A faint smile touched his lips and was gone. "I don't even know how long it took to sort everything out by subject. Then by author. Then I had to decide whether to keep translations together with the originals, or make a separate section, and then the Archduke wanted me to go through all *his* books and compare them with those here and those in the Royal Archives, and— well, I said all that before, and you're not interested anyways.

"There's one section of about seventy books that deals with the part of the Continent the Archduke's forebears came from. A lot of them are pretty worthless. Bad poetry, doubtful histories. But there are half a dozen that mention the *balaurin*. I'm assuming you know about them, from the Shadowshapers' play."

"And the Knights of the Balaur Tsepesh."

"Who had as their symbol a red dragon on their shields and tabards. Well, they were real. I mean *really* real. Only what they were originally meant to do—fight the invading army with their own kind of magic—did you know that the only way to kill one and make sure it stays dead is to cut off its head?"

" 'It'? They were *men*, Drevan. Not things."

"They became *things* when they became Balaur Tsepesh," he stated grimly. "Things so horrible, I can't even—" Breaking off, he shook his head. "Look, Cayden, I shouldn't even be telling you this much. It's all terribly secret, and the only reason I know about it at all is that I can read the language those books are written in. But what I wanted to tell you to tell Vered is this." He paused for a deep breath, gaze nervously flickering all round the room as if searching for someone who might overhear. "There's one book that shows up in Lord Piercehand's collection but not in the Archduke's. And it's also in the Royal Archives. Vered wouldn't be able to read this copy—but the one in the Archives is a translation. My grandfather or great-grandfather did it for a friend of his, who left his whole collection to the Crown when he died, and it's been there ever since. And it will tell him everything he wants to know."

Cade thought this over. "Would it be safe to say that he shouldn't just walk into the Archives and ask to see it?"

"That's the problem. I don't think they know what they've got. But on the chance that they do—"

"Someone like Vered, without a history of scholarship—"

"—except in this one area," Drevan interrupted. "He spent weeks last winter and the winter before pestering them for books and old scrolls, and you can be sure the Archduke knows all about it. If he asks for this one, they'll know what it deals with even if they don't recognize the title or know what's really in it."

"And that, too, would get back to the Archduke. Why is he so sensitive about it? I mean, he's generations removed from the original Archduke who married one of our Princesses."

"If you'd read this, you'd know. All I can tell you is that the name 'Henick' shows up as one of the Balaur Tsepesh."

This time Cade felt as if his eyebrows were within inches of the nape of his neck. "One of his forebears was one of them?"

Drevan nodded. "Vered hasn't been able to finish the second play, because he doesn't know what happened. He won't finish it until he does—" Another tiny smile twitched his lips. "—and that's *your* fault, what with your example of 'Treasure.' Oh, yes, I believe your version. I know a lot of people think you made it up, but I've read enough to know better. Anyways, tell Vered that the book he needs is in the Archives, but it can't be known that he's looking for it."

"What's the title?"

"I'll write it down for you to give to him. Just please tell him not to be obvious about it. The Archduke doesn't have a copy, and I don't think he knows that such a book exists. If he did, he'd see to it that it found its way into his own collection or was destroyed."

"What's so dire about it? It's not his fault that one of his forebears became one of those *things,* as you call them. In fact, he ought to be proud. If I understand correctly, it was a magnificent sacrifice."

"At first, yes. They saved the Continent and, by extension, Albeyn. But that kind of power—and the way it was maintained—" He actually shuddered. "Believe me, Cayden, if everybody, or even a small fraction of everybody, knew what really happened—and that's another thing. I'm telling you this because I think you might be able to convince Vered to let the whole thing drop. I'm taking the chance that if he sees that book, he'll understand why. He's drawn enough of the Archduke's attention with his researches so far. The play they perform, it only hints at what came next. The second play, the one he can't finish—it shouldn't be finished or performed at all."

15

In a low, intimate drawl, Lord Rolon Piercehand murmured, "It has come to my attention that you and I share certain tastes."

He said this with one arm slung companionably about Mieka's shoulders, leaning down from his great height so that his words could not be overheard. Mieka hated it when really tall people loomed over him like that (well, not Yazz or Cade, except when they were angry with him). Lord Piercehand made things worse with the sharp curl of his fingers into Mieka's right shoulder. But worst of all was the truly astonishing smell of the man's breath, caused in part, as he had learned last night when Piercehand opened his mouth wide to roar with laughter, by several back teeth that were succumbing to black-rot. Mieka forced himself to smile rather than screw up his face in disgust at the odor of bad teeth, stale liquor, the spices from last night's dinner, and the sickly scent of sweet violet candies. Like an unwashed whore who soaked herself in strong perfume instead of a bathtub, His Lordship mistakenly believed that the violets masked any other smells.

"And those tastes might be?" Mieka asked politely. A wink was the only answer. He was propelled by that powerful, heavy arm along a hallway from the breakfast room to a staircase, up to another hallway, around several turns (one of which took them past the library), and at last to a painted wooden door. Every time Mieka parted his lips to speak, Piercehand hushed him with a shake of the head or another wink, conspiratorial now, as if some delicious secret awaited him.

The arm was removed as Piercehand delved in both jacket pockets, muttering about a key. The door was painted with the scene of the family name's origin: a battle, a king in armor, a young squire with one palm held out at the level of the king's chest, and an arrow shot through the middle of that palm. The dripping blood was made of dark crimson rubies set into the wood.

Noting Mieka's interest, Piercehand said, "Yes, saving a king's life turned out quite profitable in terms of lands and castles. I wonder that more people don't do it. Here we are—it always takes me half of forever to find the damned key." Applying it to the lock, he flung open the door.

The room was long and rather narrow, paneled in pale wood, lit by three hanging candle-branches of a dozen lights each, and cluttered with wide couches, deep chairs, spindly tables, glass-shaded lamps, thick carpets of violent and mutually antagonistic designs, tall shelves displaying a thousand different trinkets and trifles, and a deeply carved wooden desk below the middle window. All three windows were festooned with ropes of fat, shiny glass beads. The outer two were done in patterns of gold, blue, green, and purple, arranged in squares and rectangles and diamond shapes. The middle window, above the desk, was hung with scarlet only, as if someone had strung together solid drops of blood. Mieka looked away from it, uneasy somehow, and saw that on the desk were all the things appropriate to the elegant pricking of thorn.

"Our other shared interest is the company of beautiful girls," Piercehand chuckled as he walked towards the desk. "But we'll save that for tonight! Now, I wonder if you'd care to sample one or two interesting things I've picked up on my voyages. And would it be too much of presumption to ask if I might call you 'Mieka'?"

"Please do." Mieka took a few steps into the room. With one exception, he'd only ever used thorn provided by Auntie Brishen Staindrop. That exception had been a horror provided by Pirro Spangler, glisker for Black Lightning and, after that incident, former friend. It had been in this very castle that he'd taken the thorn that had so tangled his mind that he ran frantically through the halls, seeking Cayden and safety.

Still . . . he admitted to himself that thorn nowadays was rather usual. A bit boring, actually. Blue, white, green, purple, red, yellow, combinations of two or more . . . he was familiar with all sorts of thorn and knew what effects they would produce. Auntie Brishen hadn't sent him any new mixtures for quite a long while. It might be entertaining to experiment for an afternoon with whatever Piercehand had discovered out there in the wider world.

"You must and shall address me as 'Rolon.' Rather a silly name, but all the eldest sons have had to endure it. The original Piercehand—the one on the door—labored under it, which often makes me wonder why he didn't step his whole body in front of the king to receive that arrow!"

Mieka smiled politely, watching as His Lordship made preparations. He didn't use thorns made of glass; his were silver, delicate little things lined up in a specially made silver rack on the desk. Likewise the flask of brandy, the bowl he poured the liquor into, and the pincers he used to remove the cleansed thorns were all of silver. A few drops of water from a silver pitcher were dripped into a silver spoon, and a pinch from one of the small silver boxes laid out in rows was mixed in with a thin silver stick.

"It began in this room, you know," he said as he worked. "My original wonder cabinet. Other men have them to display interesting objects or little collections of things. My collection

232

grew beyond this room, and then beyond this house *and* the house in Gallybanks. Princess Miriuzca's suggestion to put much of it into a gallery was most fortuitously timed, for I really was beginning to run out of space! And while sorting through what ought to be at the Gallery, I ran across some things I'd forgot about. A chain, for instance, made of teeth. Oh, not *people* teeth—although somewhere around here there's a set of buttons . . ." He waved aimlessly.

"I ought to show Jeska. Our masquer used to have a collection of teeth from people foolish enough to challenge him to a fight. His wife made him get rid of it, though."

"A reason I never married! What woman would put up with all this in her home? Anyway, talking of dentistry, this particular thorn is called Demon Teeth—such an exciting, provocative name isn't it? They grow it in—oh, I've forgotten exactly where, except that it was so hot, I was near to expiring! My personal apothecary tells me it had all the qualities of Dragon Tears, but without the slighest danger to Elves, I assure you, Master Windthistle, not the slightest. I'm quite a goodly mix of Elf, you know, though I missed out on the ears, and it's never done me any harm at all." He poured the brownish mixture into the silver thorn, holding it out to Mieka with the pincers. "Do give it a try. It's really remarkable. This little taste won't last more than an hour, I assure you."

He hesitated. The last time he'd used someone else's thorn . . . here in this very castle . . . but Pirro had given him some sort of wicked warping thorn on purpose. Piercehand wasn't likely to do the same to an honored guest who was moreover the brother of his builders. And there was something else, something he'd never admitted even to himself: a tiny sneaking part of him had always wondered what Dragon Tears might be like. This was everything Dragon Tears was, but without the danger. Without the risk.

"Oh, you needn't be frightened of it," Piercehand went on. "I hope you're not frightened. Are you?"

Mieka snorted. How stupid of the man, seeking to goad him by querying his daring as if he were still fourteen years old and desperate to prove himself all grown up. Of course he wasn't frightened. Even if this thorn turned out strange, Cade was nearby in the library with Drevan Wordturner. Cade was close, so he was safe.

He rolled up a sleeve and held out his arm.

The hanging candle-branches grew feathers, and the feathers grew into wings, and the wings flared from the backs and shoulders of almost the most beautiful girls he'd ever seen. Pink and green and blue and orange they swung back and forth, back and forth, wings beating lazily, long hair and filmy silken skirts trailing behind them, nearly long enough for him to reach up and grasp a handful. Silvery bells chimed and rainbows twinkled in the wake of their passing, as if they enchanted the very air around them, these lovely Fae birdies with their languid smiles and sweet bells and drifting silky skirts.

He laughed softly, enjoying the show, which surely was finer and more magical than anything the most elegant of gentlemen's private guilds could offer. Not even the Finchery, with its vast and voluptuous reputation—the Finchery—the—

He struggled to his feet, bellowing incoherently with rage. Did one of those bird-girls have gold-and-bronze hair? Did she? That one on the farthest swing—with rainbows wrapped round her dainty fingers—wearing silks exactly the shade of plum that turned her iris-blue eyes dark purple, her favorite gown and his as well and was that her, was it, *was it?* He could smell the violets that were her favorite perfume and he could hear her high trilling laughter and was it her, was she here, swinging amid the rainbows and the candlelight with these whores from the Finchery—their wings couldn't be real, no Fae would ever demean herself to prostitution—but it paid well, didn't it, being a whore, and she was forever asking for more money and more money and the Finchery paid very well indeed because the little birdies were favorites of Zekien Silversun who picked out the finest of them for Prince Ashgar's entertainment and—and there it was at last, the reason for the Finchery card! She had given up trying to make him use friendship with the Princess to their advantage and she planned to become a highly paid whore to attract Ashgar's notice and get into Ashgar's bed and thereby gain riches and jewels and a fine house in Gallybanks and mayhap even a castle because these days there were no opportunities to save a king's life and thus become landed nobility with an arrow through your palm—all you had to do was spread your legs—

Staggering, infuriated, he tripped on a cat's tail and fell flat on his face. When he found the energy to roll over, the candle-branches were plain silver-gilt, unlit, and the room was empty of everyone but himself and the cats and Lord Rolon Piercehand, who was bending over him with a worried expression on his handsome, dissipated face.

Then the cats began to yowl. He pushed the nobleman away and clambered to his feet. He had to let the cats out—he knew that note in their voices, the one that meant *The walls are closing in and I need to be outside! Now!* He knew there must be a door someplace, he had no idea where, but there were three windows and so he shoved aside the bead curtains on the left-side window and then on the right, and was just about to climb onto the desk to get at the cascading blood-beads when the cats swarmed out both open windows. One of them got caught in the glinting curtain of glass. He untangled it gently, whispering to soothe it. The shiver of white and gray fur nestled into his neck, meowing faintly. *Hungry,* he thought, and looked around for food.

Over in a corner of the long room that he hadn't noticed before was an alcove, badly whitewashed, with a sink and a counter and shelves. He carried the cat there and began rummaging through the shelves. It turned out that the whitewash wasn't poorly done: it was crawling with tiny black things that gathered into larger black things and became wriggling black maggots that slid off the walls onto the floor. He cuddled the cat closer and backed away, nausea cramping his stomach. The maggots were everywhere, clustering on the white walls and thudding to the floor in great writhing heaps. Sickened, he kept backing up until he felt soft carpet beneath his feet again. He knew the maggots would not swarm across the carpet. Something about the color, but he didn't bother to chase the thought down. The cat cried softly against his neck and he stroked it, thinking that it would have better luck hunting for itself, and walked towards the windows. The beads were all red now, flinging blood rainbows across the floor.

"You have to change everything, Mieka. You have to change everything."

He didn't recognize the voice. There was no one else in the room with him—just the cat, not even Lord . . . Lord . . . what was his name? Mieka couldn't remember.

"You have to change everything, Mieka. You have to change everything."

Deep and compassionate, as if hoping he would heed the warning—but quiet and sad, too, as if only too aware that all warnings were pointless.

"Why?" he asked.

The cat burrowed more deeply into his neck, purring. Behind him he could hear the slither and plop of more and more maggots falling to the floor. He must get out of here somehow. But there was no door—no door? How had he gotten into the room? He didn't know. But there was no door. Only the windows, all of them dripping blood.

The cat dug its claws into his shoulder as thunder bellowed in the distance and the sunny gardens outside were quickly awash in cold gray rain. Lightning flashed and the cat hissed. And then he saw, dimly through the lashing rain in the garden and the drops of blood at the window, a tall man dressed in gray. Cayden. He called out, hopelessly: the window was still shut and the maggots shirred threateningly behind him.

Suddenly he was ankle-deep in squirming maggots and the cat hissed again and clawed his shoulder and the ropes of glass beads in his hands were bubbles of blood that burst and stained his fingers and he cried out for Cade again, and again, and down in the garden Cade looked up and Mieka couldn't even get hold of the window now because the blood made his fingers slick and clumsy but if he could only get outside where it was raining clean cool water he could wash off the blood and the yowling hissing cat would abandon him because of the wet and the maggots couldn't crawl up his legs and despite the pounding rain and the ragged lightning and the deafening thunder, Cade was there, and with Cade he was always safe.

"Mieka? Mieka, come on. Look at me. Open your eyes."

How had Cade got into the room? The windows wouldn't open, there was no door—

"Mieka!"

—and how had he ended up on the carpet, anyways, when just an instant ago he'd been at the desk clutching at the blood dripping from the window, trying to escape the maggots—

"I do apologize, Master Silversun. I'd no idea it would produce this effect on him."

—and none of it mattered, because Cade was here. He huddled inside the warmth where nothing could hurt him.

"Mieka. Open your eyes and look at me."

"He might be asleep, you know," said the other voice,

unwelcome. "It takes some people that way. They sleep it off, rather like too much whiskey."

"Mieka. I won't ask again."

So he opened his eyes and looked up, and Cade was frowning down at him, his skin ashen beneath the sun-glossing of summer. With the wrinkling of his forehead and the strain around his eyes and mouth, he looked twice his age and then some. Mieka felt horribly guilty. But he'd apologize later. For now—

"Don't let go," he said, or thought he did. It came out sounding like *dunnlekko*. He tried again, very carefully. "Don't. Let. Go."

The lines of tension and worry mostly smoothed from Cade's face. "Can you stand? I can't carry you, Mieka. I'd call for Yazz, but he's across the river in the village. Come on, get up." Then, sharply: "No, Your Lordship, we don't need your help. Beholden all the same. He can walk."

There was that in Cayden's voice that told Mieka he'd better be able to walk, or something a lot worse than a roomful of maggots would happen to him. So he got up and walked. More or less.

He must have fallen asleep on the way to his chamber. The next thing he knew, he was tucked up beneath a blue silk sheet as light and delicate as a cloudless sky. Cade was nearby, folding his shirt. As Mieka grouked himself awake, slow as always to return to full consciousness, he sighed and grunted softly, and Cade turned round.

"Your wife won't be happy," he said. He held up the new trousers, the braid down each leg tattered and straggling, as if someone—or something—had been clawing at the material. "I won't ask what happened or what you saw, and I won't tell you what you already know—that of all the stupid things you've ever done, this probably tops the list. But I will tell you one thing absolutely, Mieka, and you'd bloody well better take heed. Whatever kind of thorn that was—"

"Demon Teeth." He hadn't meant to interrupt. Doing so when Cade was in this mood was invariably dangerous.

"Demon Teeth. Charming. If you *ever* prick that kind of thorn again—"

"No—don't say it," Mieka blurted. "I won't. I promise."

An unpleasant smile twitched the corners of Cade's mouth, and suddenly Mieka knew he was about to say something like, *And what are your promises worth these days?* He couldn't have borne it. Mere moments ago, he had been treasuring the warm security of being with Cade; how could that feeling change so quickly into fear and foreboding? An unexpected flush of anger flared. How dare Cayden be so nice to him one minute and rip him apart the next?

But once more the mood altered, and Cade nodded, accepting the promise. He plucked at the tattered hems of the trousers. "How did this happen, anyways? Do you even remember?"

Mieka shrugged and pulled the sheet up to his chin. "No." Wary of the lie that must be in his eyes, and the fright, he didn't look at Cade, for he did remember the maggots. Reason told him that all of it had happened inside his own thorn-befuddled head. Like a dream while sleeping, it must have been—yet here was evidence otherwise. A horrible idea occurred to him and he squeezed his eyes shut, knowing Cade couldn't possibly miss the new horror that filled him. It was this: What if Demon Teeth stimulated magic? Glisker's magic? What if the cats and the maggots and the bloody ropes of beads had been real?

He felt the skin of his shoulder where the cat had sunk in its claws, ran the instep of his right foot along the ankle of his left leg. No blood, no tenderness, no bruising, no damage at all. And it made no sense to him, because if the trousers were half-shredded, then surely his leg must be as well.

With other thorn, he could and did work magic onstage.

Skill, training, instinct, and experience had taught him how, for example, to make a breeze luffing a ship's sails ruffle Jeska's hair at the same time. The sails were the products of magic; so was the wind; Jeska's golden curls were real. Magic acted upon magic, and—when Mieka willed it through the withies—upon reality as well. Bluethorn and whitethorn never interfered with his work. What *was* Demon Teeth, that it could merge with his magic this way?

"You probably ought to sleep this off, as His Lordship said."

Mieka frowned at him, annoyed that his thoughts had been interrupted. He'd been on the verge of something; he knew it. "Wake me in time for tea," he replied, trying to sound as normal as he could.

Cade had a strange expression on his face. "That was over an hour ago."

Good Gods, how long had Demon Teeth had a grip on him? It had been shortly after breakfast that Lord Piercehand had ushered him into that awful room. Mieka gave another little shrug, as if it didn't matter, and said, "Dinner, then."

Cade began to fold up the trousers. "She won't be pleased, all that work going to waste."

And then he remembered his insight regarding the Finchery. But he could never tell Cade. Never. The humiliation of it wasn't that she had tried to provoke him and had succeeded. It was that he had married a girl so shallow that all she wanted from life was money and social position, and so unscrupulously scheming that she'd do anything to attain her goals, even sell her own body. Mieka clenched his fists around the silken sheet, renewed fury firing his blood. She was his. Her body belonged to him. He tolerated people looking at her, and even enjoyed it—up to a point. But she was *his,* no one else's—certainly not Zekien Silversun's to look at and evaluate and select for a night in Prince Ashgar's bed.

"Get some sleep," said Cayden.

Mieka was relieved to see the back of him as he left the room. Turning onto one side, he stared at the beige and crimson stripes of the wallpaper and thought feverishly.

The only explanation for the torn trousers was his own magic. The maggots hadn't been real, but the damage was a fact. He had spent years by now onstage directing his magic to affect real things. And when he did, he was in control of it. This had happened without his conscious volition. Though his skin bore no signs of the maggots or the cat, mayhap the shirt he'd been wearing did. With a sick chill in his belly, he wondered if the maggots had left their marks on the walls or the floor or the carpets—and if the sparkling red beads had left smears of blood on the desk. His hands must be clean, or Cade would have said something. As for his shirt . . . perhaps the pinpricks of sharp claws hadn't actually torn the fabric.

The Minster across the river had chimed the hour before he got up courage enough to rise, find the shirt, and investigate. No evidence on the shirt, no matter how hard he squinted at it. He picked up the shoes he'd been wearing, looking for slime or scratches or *something*, but they were unmarked as well. He settled back into bed, pulling up the sheet, then gasped aloud. There were blotches of blood on the sky-blue silk. His arm, where Piercehand had pricked him with the silver thorn of Demon Teeth, was openly bleeding. And with the rush of shock came a pounding of his heart and the thorn took him back to itself, screaming.

"Mieka!" Cade was here with him and he clung to thin shoulders, babbling.

"Maggots, Quill—there were maggots and they're back and one is inside me head—"

"Mieka, no, it's all right. There aren't any maggots."

"Yes, there are! And—and it's growing, I can hear it—a

241

brainsnake, it's thinking and I can hear it thinking and it's *horrible*, what it's thinking—"

Cade lifted a hand as if to slap him, then shook his head and gathered Mieka tight. "Shush. It's all right. There's no brainsnake, Mieka. It's just the thorn."

"It got in through my arm," he whimpered. "I thought I got away from them—they ripped up my trousers and she really did want to be a whore so the Prince would give her everything she ever wanted—" He sobbed once, fingers clenched in Cade's shirt. "No, it can't—it's the brainsnake telling me that, she'd never— she *couldn't*—help me, Quill, please!"

"Mieka, try to settle down. I don't know what to do other than wait it out. There's no brainsnake, it's just the thorn, I promise it'll be all right. I'm here, Mieka. I won't let go."

"Talk to me. I'm scared, please talk to me!" When he listened to Cade's voice, he didn't hear the whispering and muttering inside his own head.

Sighing, Cade settled them both against pillows, and Mieka huddled close. "I'll remind you of this the next time you tell me I talk too much."

How could he be so calm? How could he make a joke out of this? Well, there wasn't anything inside *his* head, was there, making him think such vile things about his own wife—

"What do you want me to talk about? How I spent this afternoon? Drevan and I were in the library again, looking up some old books about theater. He swears he saw them a few months ago, but he hasn't cataloged them yet and forgot exactly where he put them, so we had a merry old time of it, sneezing our way through stack after stack of paper and leather held together with dust and spiderwebs."

He paused, and Mieka, whose muscles had begun to relax, tensed again. "More," he whispered. "Please, Quill. Just keep talking."

"All right. I was looking through a couple of books while Drevan was rummaging through a crate that he'd unpacked and then packed again for the Archduke. And for some reason, I don't know why, I began wondering what my mother's been up to these days, whether she sees anything of the Archduchess now that Her Grace has joined Princess Iamina in conspicuous displays of piety. She guested at Threne, of course, but I just can't see her attending Chapel twice a day and all that. Then, and I *really* don't understand this at all, I remembered that time you tried to magick her and I told you about the Hindering, how her magic was locked away. Do you remember how I explained it?"

"Y-yes . . . I think so—but tell me again."

"Like being inside a room with a huge window looking out onto the world, only you can't touch or smell or feel or hear anything of what's happening out there. And that's when I started thinking that it might make an interesting play—something about a boy who's been locked inside that room, and he can see out but nobody can see in, because his parents are afraid of magic and there's magic out in the real world but they want to protect him from it. Sort of like what we did with that Vaustas play at Seekhaven, remember? I thought, What would daily life be like for someone who'd made that bargain, or had that bargain made for him? It might make for some interesting magic, deliberately muffling the audience's sensations. Anyway, I wondered how he'd get stuck inside the room, and I thought mayhap his parents had done it to him, and died before they could have the spell lifted—"

"No," Mieka heard himself say. "They knew they were about to die—they were sick—you could have it be the same thing that killed Blye's father. That way, they'd have a reason to hate magic."

"That's good. I like that."

"They've protected him all these years, but now they're dying, and before they die, they have this spell done to him. To keep him safe."

"Excellent!" Cade hugged him briefly. "That works much better than what I'd thought of to begin with. Anyway, at first he's content to watch but not really experience—but after a while he sees something that makes him wonder what it would be like to—oh, I don't know, mayhap it rains outside and some people are annoyed at being caught in the wet, and some people turn their faces up to it and smile. He can't even imagine what it might be like, but he grows more and more curious. Watching as someone bites into an apple, or—"

"—or a street musician comes by but he can't hear the music. We could have Alaen play something for us offstage for that." Mieka had by now loosened his death grip on Cade's shirt, and had snuggled comfortably against his side, breathing in Cade's scent: Mistress Mirdley's sage soap, clean sweat, ink and paper, a faint tang of cinnamon from afternoon tea. To Mieka, whatever Cade wore or drank or had washed in, he always smelled like magic. "There's all kinds of things to be done with it. But how does he get out? Because he *has* to get out, Quill. Otherwise, what's the point of the play?"

"Well, I'm not terribly sure about that part of it. What do you think? Any ideas?"

He built the images in his head, the way he did whenever Cade proposed a new play. The familiar practice of one part of his craft soothed him. "No matter how curious he is about life beyond that glass window, he knows he's safe inside, right? And outside—there's magic out there, that his parents always told him was wicked and dangerous."

"What could motivate him to break the window and go outside and start living life?"

"'This life, and none other,'" Mieka quoted softly, and Cade chuckled and hugged him again. "I'm sure you'll think of something." He yawned mightily. "You always do."

"Sleepy, are you? Glad to know I'm so fascinating."

"Shut up, Quill."

He burrowed closer. When Cade made a slight movement, as if to let him go and rise from the nest of pillows, Mieka held him in place with an arm across his chest. He subsided, and Mieka gave a long sigh of contentment, feeling sorry for that boy behind the window wall, looking out at people to whom he was invisible, who had to hide from the world to feel himself safe. All Mieka needed was Cade.

And all Cade needed . . .

Oh, of course. Why hadn't he understood before? "That boy," he mumbled. "He *is* like Vaustas. Books to hide in, not a room with a window."

"Hmm? Yes, I suppose he is. But we can't use the same trick to end the play with, y'know."

"You'll think of something," he said again, nearly asleep. "'Cause they're you, Quill."

From very far away, he heard Cayden's voice. "Yes . . . I suppose they are. Get some rest, Mieka. I'm here."

16

Visibly chastened, Mieka behaved himself perfectly for the remainder of their stay at Castle Eyot. It was perhaps fortunate for him, and for the rest of them, that they were there for only one more day. A quiet, sensible, unadventurous glisker might have been too much for Touchstone's collective peace of mind. Still, it was a relief to Cade that Mieka confined himself to pursuits less risky than thorn: walking in the gardens and over the bridge to the village, catching up on his sleep, lolling in a hot bath for over an hour, joining the others to hear Cade's new idea for a play: "Window Wall." Lord Piercehand was seen at lunching and dinner, and twice took Mieka aside to suggest another foray into exotic thorn. The Elf was polite but firm in his refusals. Cade was proud of him.

On their last night, Drevan Wordturner suggested a before-bed brandy up on the roof. Piercehand did not join them, but his most trusted ship captain did. Frolian Webstitch had come to Castle Eyot only because he'd had to track His Lordship down following the latter's hasty departure from Gallantrybanks. There was business to discuss, and Captain Webstitch was annoyed at having to traipse all over the countryside during days he had much rather spend with his wife and family. So he was slightly less discreet than usual after two or three brandies.

"I'd not say it," he remarked as they sat under a moonless starry sky, "if Rafcadion here wasn't Clan-kin. And it goes no farther than us, right?"

"Sworn eight times," Rafe agreed, as a good son of the Spider Clan ought. Cade rolled his eyes at him, and he grinned.

The captain was satisfied. "Well, then. All these voyages His Lordship brags on—" Lowering his voice and leaning forward in his chair, he confided, "In twenty years, he's never been farther than a cottage on an island beach just t'other side of Yzpaniole."

Drevan muffled giggles behind his hand. The others simply stared.

"Oh, it's true enough," Webstitch went on. "We set him down with his personal servants, a goodly supply of whiskey, and a crate full of presents for the local whores. While we're halfway round the world, dodging pirates and damned unfriendly locals, he's lazing on velvet cushions in the sand."

"But how," Jeska wanted to know, "does he account for all the things you collect? I mean, this castle is *crammed* with everything anybody could think of, and then some!"

"When we pick him up again, we captains have lists waiting for him. On the way home, he picks out about a dozen of the most interesting bits, finds out where and how they were found, and when we dock, he makes sure those crates are sent to his house at once so he can study them." Webstitch held out his glass and Drevan refilled it. "Tell me, Master Wordturner, have you ever asked about a particular piece, and had him scrunch up his face as if he's trying to remember on which of his voyages he found it?"

"Several times. So that's why he says what he says!" In a deep voice with an exaggerated highborn accent, he intoned, "'Well, you know, my boy, it's shocking, but I've been so many places and acquired so many nice things, it's quite impossible to remember them all!'"

Rafe snorted. "I always knew the nobility was a fraud—saving your presence, Cayden," he added with a little bow in Cade's direction. "But he seems to have diddled the whole country!"

"No offense taken," Cade told him, chuckling. "But that's not the whole of it. You know the story about the origin of the name?"

Mieka hunched his shoulders like a scolded puppy. "It's painted on a door someplace. Heroic squire saves king's life by taking an arrow through the hand. What's the real story, Quill?"

"The squire was one of the king's drinking companions. One night he got very, very drunk and tried to juggle knives—one of which went right through his palm. He was so drunk, he didn't even notice until the king started laughing and dubbed him Sir Rolon Piercehand."

Captain Webstitch gave a mighty guffaw. "That's one to tell my crew! And afore anyone asks, none of them tattles on him, because he pays very well indeed."

"I thought it'd be something like that," Rafe said. "Forgive my tastelessness, Drevan, but I assume you're being paid plenty, too?"

"I wish," he replied, glum-faced. "I'm still working off the shame of how drunk I was the night of the wedding."

Cade remembered very well how Drevan had made a disgusting display of himself, and how frightened poor Miriuzca had been. But in a way he owed the man, for the incident had begun the friendship between the Princess and himself, and eventually all of Touchstone. Drevan, whose real ambition was to be a member of the Horse Guards, had certainly paid for his folly by now, immured with thousands of books here at Castle Eyot or at the Royal Archives or at the Archduke's residence at Threne.

Minster chimes across the river reminded them how late it was, and after a last few swallows of brandy, they all started down the stairs to their own bedchambers.

Webstitch hung back a little, putting a hand on Cade's arm. "A small word, if you please," he said.

"What can I do for you, Captain?"

"You realize why His Lordship is here, and not in Gallybanks?"

"Directing the pack-up of things for the new Gallery, I'd imagine."

"I suppose that would do as an excuse. But listen here, Master Silversun. In tracking His Lordship down, I found he'd spent a night at Threne before traveling at speed here to Eyot. In time to catch you here, I'm thinking."

Cade said mildly, "Noblemen pay visits to each other all the time."

"'Twasn't just the usual, or so says my wife's cousin, His Lordship's Master of Horse. It seems the pair of them had long and private talk, and His Lordship came away with a locked case made of green leather, kept with him at all times on the way here. Had it tied close to his knee while in the saddle, and at his side while he slept."

"That sounds important," was all Cade could think of to say.

"That it does. And here's another oddity as got mentioned to me yesternight by my good girl's cousin, after word of your glisker's misadventure. In the courtyard at Threne, the Archduke bade His Lordship farewell, and was heard to say Master Windthistle's name. Not the names of his brothers, who are doing so much work on the Gallery, nor of his brother's wife, the glasscrafter. 'Mieka Windthistle' was the name the Archduke spoke. His Lordship patted the case at his knee and smiled."

Cade wanted to cringe. Everyone in the castle and probably the village and ten miles beyond it must know what had happened to Mieka yesterday. On the other hand, if no one had gossiped about it, Captain Webstitch wouldn't have been told about the locked case—all too obviously supplied with thorn meant for Mieka. Cade expressed his gratitude to the captain, and on their way downstairs said, "I do wonder, though, that he took the trouble to provide something that must be very expensive.

The Archduke, I mean. Demon Teeth, it's called. Isn't it from somewhere quite far away?"

Webstitch nearly lost his footing on the spiral stone stairs. "Is *that* what it was? By all the Gods in the Briny Deep, that lad's lucky to be breathing!"

"It's like Dragon Tears, isn't it? Only not dangerous to Elves." *Just stupid, easily bored Elves with overactive imaginations,* he reflected sourly.

"Who told you that? It's dangerous to anybody and everybody. 'Tis not the first taste, nor the second, that binds a man. But by the third, he'll sell his own wife and daughters to the nearest whorehouse for money to buy the fourth."

"Why would anybody want to prick that sort of thorn even a *first* time?"

The answer was so close to what he'd just been thinking that he winced. "Because," said Captain Webstitch, "not excluding bored young lordlings with more money than sense, stupidity is in my experience the commonest failing of any race— Human, Wizard, Elf, Goblin, Gnome, and all the rest, and any combination of any or all of them."

Cade lay awake half the night thinking about it. This was the second time someone connected to the Archduke had provided Mieka with treacherous thorn. The first had been Pirro Spangler of Black Lightning—and Mieka had pricked what Pirro had given him in this very castle. Cade struggled to recall whether the Archduke had already bought and paid for Black Lightning at the time, or whether they had simply been trying to impress him, then decided it didn't matter. This time it was pretty clear. A locked case, with whatever was inside meant for Mieka Windthistle, and the grim results yesterday—yes, it added up.

He spent quite a while silently cursing Mieka for being so reckless. The mad little Elf hadn't the slightest acquaintance with anything resembling caution. But if he had, he wouldn't be Mieka. Cade had concluded years ago that pushing him to change was an invariably doomed effort. All one could do was work him into a position where he could see for himself, the way Cade had done on the visit to Ginnel House. Left to himself, he might have kept his promise never to hit his wife again, but seeing those terrified, battered women and children at Ginnel House made certain of it.

And that led him to what Mieka had said about his wife—thorned to the tips of his ears, of course, so it wasn't entirely to be trusted—but could money and position have motivated her? Had she really been angling to become Prince Ashgar's mistress? He could have named a dozen kings, princes, grand dukes, and other noblemen whose relationships with their official mistresses had furnished the stories for a dozen plays and twice that number of poems and songs. He just couldn't see Mieka's wife casting herself in a similar plotline. For one thing, she did truly love Mieka—

—which hadn't prevented her from groping Cade's crotch at the races.

Well, she wasn't his problem, he told himself. Except that she *was,* because she was Mieka's wife and Jindra's mother. Leaving aside the havoc she might wreak on his glisker, Cade was aware of an odd anxiety whenever he thought about Jindra. She seemed happy and healthy, and in all respects was a darling. His unease was probably the aftermath of an Elsewhen, he told himself, accepting at last that he had been a rank fool and a craven coward to have purposely forgotten all of them.

Of those Elsewhens, there remained what amounted almost to a compulsion to protect Jindra from her own parents. The Gods alone knew what her mother might have in mind, but at least this little episode at Castle Eyot had crossed off the list of Mieka's possible stupidities a potential addiction to Demon Teeth. Not that there weren't scores of other things he could prick into his arms, and scores more mistakes he could make.

Someone had said something to him once, long ago, when he'd known Mieka less than two days. The wagon driver who'd taken them all back to Gallybanks . . . what had he said? *"You'd do well to keep him, in spite of the trouble he'll be to you."* Cade fell asleep cataloging all the separate and distinct sorts of trouble Mieka had caused. But when he met his partners downstairs for breakfast before climbing into the wagon for the drive to Bexmarket, one smile, one burst of laughter, one joke, and Cade realized yet again what he'd known for years now: that Touchstone would never have become Touchstone without their mad little Elf.

And that was why the Archduke had chosen Mieka. Cade heard someone say in a memory, or a memory of an Elsewhen, he couldn't be sure: *"When Touchstone lost their Elf, they lost their soul."* Cade himself was their brain, thinking up the words. Jeska was their heart, giving voice and feeling to those words. As for Rafe—he was their conscience, ever watchful. And Mieka, dancing behind his glass baskets, weaving Cade's magic with his own, giving everything of himself night after night—yes, Mieka was their soul.

Towards morning he had dreamed that he was in the clock room at Castle Eyot. The hour struck on hundreds of clocks at once, ticking, whirring, thumping, chiming, whistling, tapping, ringing—like the pulse beats and the mocking laughter of spiteful beings that scorned all those persons, with magic or without it, who lived in the real world. *This* life, and none other—not the haughty hidden lives of the Fae, or the despised and shunned Gorgons or grinning bloodthirsty Redcaps or any of the malicious races who begrudged all others the freedom of the light. Cade had woken himself with his own voice—not that what he said made any sense. What he muttered, just as the sun rose, was, "The window is out of time."

Lounging in his hammock while the wagon rolled smartly towards Bexmarket, he wondered what his mind was trying to tell him about that dream and the new piece, the one about the boy trapped in the room with a window on one wall. What did clocks have to do with anything, other than telling and tolling the time? Was it a warning that he ought to hurry and write this new play? He knew he had interesting and mayhap even important things to say in it, but was there any reason he should rush to write it? Was he treating an honest dream, one that came while sleeping like the dreams other people had, the way he would have examined an Elsewhen?

The boy in the room with the window wall, separated from life and magic . . . Vaustas, sheltering in the safety of books, rejecting his own magic . . . *"You'll figure something out. 'Cause they're you, Quill."* Damn the Elf for his perception. But he hadn't got to the very core of it: Through that window, the boy saw other people who never saw him. Denying magic, Vaustas's soul was a stunted, ungrown thing. Denied life and magic, the boy was invisible.

He wished suddenly, passionately, for an Elsewhen that would show him how "Window Wall" ended. "The Avowal"—which, oddly enough, they had yet to do onstage—had come straight out of an Elsewhen of a performance. Why couldn't "Window Wall" do the same?

Yet the Elsewhens, it became clear to him on their arrival in Bexmarket, were not to be relied on for warnings about the future. If they could be, he wouldn't have been so thoroughly gobsmacked when they encountered the Shadowshapers after Touchstone's last performance at the Smithing Guildhall. And even then, it wasn't that the Shadowshapers were in Bexmarket, on their way to a series of lucrative giggings in New Halt and points north. It was what Vered and Rauel and Chat and even Sakary told them about over drinks late that night.

"You hadn't heard?" Rauel asked, eyes wide with innocence—
too wide, Cayden thought, frowning slightly, aware that whatever
came next would in all likelihood be something he'd have to force
himself to laugh at.

He was right.

Black Lightning had a new playlet. Not even a playlet,
actually, for there was nothing even remotely resembling a plot.
It involved the frustrated efforts of a tiny Elf with huge floppy
ears to kiss an immensely tall, extremely skinny Wizard with a
huge nose. There was much capering about on chairs and tables
and stepladders, and attempts by the Wizard to fold his gangly
limbs so that he was an approachable height, and snippy dialogue
about the nose and the ears getting in their way, and a speech
from the Wizard about being unable to find any girl willing to
bed him because he's so ugly which ended with, "What's a man
to do when he's in need of a lick and a tickle?" Things became
truly obscene from that point, and the Shadowshapers kindly
spared them the details.

The Elf and the Wizard were, of course, unmistakable.

Cade knew where the thing had come from. Mieka's famous
adventures dressed in women's clothing had provided a start—
and Touchstone on occasion repeated the before-performance
scene of Mieka showing up late and swanning up to the stage in
voluminous skirts while Cade berated him. Audiences loved it.
And then there was the little farce he and Mieka had played for
the overly amorous young lady in Scatterseed. Her father might
have talked about it; she undoubtedly had done, to excuse her
failure in attracting Mieka to her bed. Cade knew she had talked
because a fortnight or so ago he'd received a letter from Blye,
playfully demanding to know when she ought to craft the loving
cups for the wedding, and chastising him for breaking so many
female hearts. It was a very funny letter, and he'd laughed when
he read it to his partners.

He laughed now, too. So did everybody else. Mieka blew him a kiss that Cade pretended to catch in his two hands and press, sighing, to his heart. And thus the evening ended, with everyone pleasantly drunk and singing an old ballad on the walk back to their respective wagons.

It was only when they were alone that Cade felt he could vent his disgust. "Black *fucking* Lightning," he muttered as he hooked his hammock up for the night.

Jeska snorted. "Don't tell me you give a shit?"

Mieka turned from the cabinet where the blankets were stored. "But I owe them such a great debt!" he exclaimed. "They've managed to get the message across! Gods know *I've* never been able to!"

"Aw, poor little Elf," Rafe said, patting him on the head.

"Oh, give over!" Cade snapped. "It's not *you* getting laughed at, is it?"

"Yes it is too!" Mieka declared. "I can't blame you for being a trifle peeved by the description of your nose, but *I'm* the one who was grossly insulted."

"How do you reckon?" Jeska asked.

He flourished a finger at the tip of one ear. "How could anyone think that these ears aren't absolutely *perfect* specimens of Elfenhood?"

They all grinned at him. He stroked the tips of both ears with admiring fingers, then delved into the cabinet for the velvet bag of withies. He picked through it for a moment, then came up with a long, slender glass twig colored a faint green.

"I think *we* ought to do a playlet," he announced, holding the withie at arm's length and pointing it at himself. "Prominently featuring someone we all know." Whatever magic was left in it after the night's performance was enough to give him the semblance of Thierin Knottinger: tall, thin, dark, sneering. "And what *we* show the audience will be the truth!"

Wearing Thierin's sharp-boned face and prominently displayed crotch, he frowned elaborately, wriggled like a puppy, and with his free hand undid a few trouser buttons. From his—Thierin's—crotch he produced a pair of balled-up stockings. And another. Letting them drop to the floor of the wagon, he twisted again, reached, and drew a shirt from his groin. And a towel. When Mieka gave another spasming squirm and began to pull a sheet from his pants, Cade simply gave up and collapsed onto the floor beside Rafe and Jeska, howling with laughter. Their mad little Elf had done it to them again.

He didn't dream that night, but a few minutes after waking in the morning, an Elsewhen took him completely by surprise.

{ Cade stretched out across the seat of the carriage, boots propped against the closed window and head resting on a green velvet cushion. Pleasantly tired, still thrumming inside with the triumph of *Window Wall,* he squinted in the dimness at Mieka, sprawled in the opposite seat. Despite the lines crossing his forehead and framing his mouth, and even despite the silver in his black hair, he looked at least fifteen years younger than his age. Cade, who daily glared at his receding hairline, glared now at the Elf.

"What?" Mieka asked, catching the look.

"Stop looking seventeen years old. It's despicable."

He snorted. "With all this gray in me hair?"

"At least you still *have* hair."

"Are we gonna go through this again? You're boring me, Cayden."

Pushing himself upright, he peered out the window at the lamp-lit street. "I thought we were headed for a drink at the Keymarker, and see that new group Rauel likes so much."

"They're on for tomorrow, not tonight."

"Oh. Well, then, why aren't you out with that pretty little Elfen girl? And don't pretend you didn't notice her in the front row, fluttering those big blue eyes."

"Not in the mood. C'mon, off your lazy bum, we're almost home."

The carriage came to a halt beneath the central archway that divided the building in half. On one side was Mieka's share of the house, and on the other was Cade's. Long gone were the nights when they'd tiptoe in so as not to wake Jindra, supposedly sleeping upstairs but almost always waiting for them in the kitchen with Mistress Mirdley, a pot of tea, and eager questions about the evening's performance. Even though she hadn't lived here for years—first away at school and now married with a house of her own—Cade missed her.

Tonight Mieka led the way through Cade's door, seeking the ground-floor room decorated like a very exclusive tavern. Arrayed on the bar—built from the same gray-veined marble that had gone into the Royal Theater—were bowls of berries dipped in mocah powder, a silver ice bucket with a bottle of sparkling wine, and a pair of crystal glasses that didn't match the rest of the barware.

"You didn't remember, did you?" Mieka challenged.

"Remember? What's all this, then? Remember what?"

Excited as a child, he gave a little bounce of delight that his surprise had turned out a surprise after all. "Happy Namingday, Cayden!"

He was right; it was past midnight, and that meant it was his Namingday. "Forty-five!" Cade groaned. "Holy Gods, Mieka, I'm too old to still be playin' a show five nights out of every nine!"

"Oh, *I* know that," Mieka said with his most impudent grin. "But try telling it to the two thousand people out there tonight screaming for more!"

"You're crazy, Sir Mieka."

"I am that, Sir Cayden." He unhooked the little wire cage from the bottle and carefully popped the cork. "Pity His Gratuitous Majesty can't see us now—we'd be Knights of the Bar instead of—oh, whatever it is we're Knights of."

"The Most Noble Order of the Silver Quill. Why can't you ever remember?"

"You remember only because you're the only person in the Kingdom with a whole entire Order of Knighthood named after him. And don't say it was a coincidence. Miriuzca's heard me call you that often enough." He poured wine, and the crystal sang with their silent toast. Blye's work was more exquisite every year.

"Forty-five." Cade sighed. "There's times, lookin' at you, when I feel a hundred. You don't get older," he accused. "It's un-fuckin'-natural, even for an Elf." His gaze went to the framed imagings behind the bar. "There's the proof."

"All I see is proof that you keep opening the best door."

Laughing, he toasted Mieka again. "Every single morning."

"This life?" His head tilted to one side, shaggy hair shifting to reveal the tip of one pointed ear where a tiny diamond gleamed.

"And none other."

There came the clatter of many footsteps in the courtyard, and voices calling out their names. A door slammed open, and Rafe roared, "You started without us!" and all at once they were in the middle of a party that Cade knew full well would last until dawn. }

"What're you all grinagog about?" Mieka demanded.

Cade came back to himself. The sun was well up. The wagon had stopped so that everyone, including the horses, could have a peaceful morning feed. Rafe and Jeska were helping Yazz set up chairs outside. Mieka, who grouked and grumbled and took at least half an hour to wake up every morning, stood at the head of Cade's hammock, scowling. When Cade smiled, those eyes lit with excitement.

"Was it a good one?"

"The best one."

"The one where it's your Namingday and you're forty-five? Really? That one again?" He laughed and pushed at the hammock so it rocked alarmingly. "See? I told you! Didn't I tell you? And if you had that one again, it *must* mean it will come true!"

Grabbing for handholds, Cade stilled the swaying hammock enough to climb down out of it. He put a worried expression on his face as he said, "It was *almost* the same. I think some of it changed. And I did learn something pretty awful."

Mieka stopped celebrating and looked at him. "What? Tell me."

"I don't know if I should."

"Damn it all, Quill! You said you'd tell me—you promised you wouldn't keep them to yourself anymore!"

"I don't remember that I actually *promised*."

"As good as. Tell me what happened."

"Well . . . it seems . . . I mean, I kind of gathered that I . . . well . . ."

"Quill!"

Judging by the threat in Mieka's voice that he'd drawn it out as far as he could, he gave a great gusting sigh. "I'm losing my hair."

Prepared for something horrid, Mieka simply gaped at him.

"It might not matter to *you*," he went on as if affronted by the Elf's lack of sympathy. "But it upsets *me* rather a lot. Not that I saw myself in a mirror or anything, but there were some words exchanged, and that's how I know that I'm going bald."

Mieka still didn't react. Cade shrugged and moved to the washstand, fitted with a big glass bowl and water pitcher nestled securely into the wood, and a shaving mirror and a towel rack and a little shelf for their razors. He couldn't help pushing his uncombed hair off his forehead to scrutinize his hairline in the mirror. No signs of it yet, but he wished he'd caught a glimpse of himself in that Elsewhen.

A comforting hand patted him on the shoulder. He shifted his gaze to look at Mieka's face in the mirror. The Elf was smiling sweetly.

"Don't let it worry you, Quill. After all, considered very logically, if there's more face to your face, it'll look like there's less nose to your nose!"

17

Elsewhens came to Cade rarely from that day until their return to Gallantrybanks. He took this to signify that Mieka was right. If, as he'd said, that Elsewhen—twenty-one years into the future, which meant he was over halfway there—was still possible, then they must be doing *something* right and therefore ought to keep on doing it, whatever it was. Not actually knowing what it was bothered Mieka not at all. Cade gave the notion some consideration now and then, always ending with a shrug. Should the future be altered in some way by what he did or didn't do, an Elsewhen would show him. Until such time as that happened, he would keep on doing whatever it was that he was doing right.

This indicated to him that he didn't have to be so scrupulously careful, so anxiously self-questioning, with every decision he made. It was surprisingly liberating, much better than getting rid of all the old Elsewhens and refusing to see any new ones. Life was headed in that best of all possible directions, and he could relax. It didn't matter, for instance, that all of Touchstone, not just Cade and Mieka, used more thorn and drank more whiskey than mortal beings ought to bear; they had to get through the last few weeks of this Royal Circuit and back to Gallybanks, and whatever they had to do to accomplish it had no effect on that

Elsewhen. Neither did it matter much that several times in those last few weeks they had to go searching for Mieka.

Sometimes he vanished until just before a show, turning up less than an hour before they were due onstage. Twice, however, they had to scour the streets for him. In the first instance, someone who'd seen their show the night before directed Jeska to a hayloft, where Mieka lay curled up, sound asleep, with a cat and her seven half-grown kittens. The other time he was discovered in a cutler's shop, trying to convince the man to make him a sword. He was so angry when Cade canceled the purchase that if Yazz hadn't been there, he probably would have taken a swing at Cade. Afterwards, he didn't remember a thing about it.

Thrice they had to go looking for him because they were due to depart for the next town. The first time, he was finally located well after midnight, climbing a forty-foot Minster bell tower, hampered only slightly by the half-empty bottle of Colvado in one hand. Rafe ordered him to come down. Mieka laughed. Jeska pleaded with him. He laughed harder. Cade sat on a bench in the torchlit Minster garden, folded his arms, said, "Wake me if he falls and breaks anything," and pretended to go to sleep. Deprived of his favorite audience, Mieka turned back and somehow made it down safely, though he did manage to fall the last eight feet or so. Cade knew he had been right to trust in the loose-limbed resilience and the insane confidence of the very, very drunk. By that time, the Good Brothers had been roused by all the yelling, and Touchstone barely evaded a stay in quod by running for their wagon as if the Sentinel Fae were after them.

The second time Mieka went missing was on the way to Lilyleaf. They'd paused for dinner in a small town, where a tavern featured a local theater group, both recommended by Rauel Kevelock. The food was as good as promised, and the group was surprisingly accomplished for scantily trained amateurs. Cade agreed with Rauel's opinion: They were nearly ready for some giggings in Gallybanks and an invitation to Trials. When Jeska, Rafe, and Mieka left for the wagon, Cade lingered awhile to talk with the tregetour. He had to buy the boy several drinks to cure him of awestruck paralysis at being addressed by the great Cayden Silversun. At length Cade departed, only to find nobody but Yazz at the wagon.

"Gone again," Yazz said with a shifting of massive shoulders.

"Stupid bloody little Elf," Cade muttered. "If he doesn't show up until morning, can we still make it to Lilyleaf on schedule?"

Another shrug. "Gained a day this week. But there's rain in the air. Smell it?"

Jeska approached up the street, lamplight glinting on his golden curls. "Is he back yet?" When Cade shook his head, he snorted. "That would be too easy, wouldn't it?"

If they'd gained a day, it mattered little whether or not Mieka showed up tonight or tomorrow. But something nagged at him. He didn't figure it out until Rafe returned without the Elf in tow, declared himself fed to the back teeth with Mieka's antics, and went to bed.

When Rafe kicked Mieka's clothes out of the center aisle of the wagon, Cade caught sight of the shirt his wife had sent about a month ago, and said to Jeska, "I know where he is."

"And that might be?"

"Where's the nearest whorehouse?"

Jeska frowned his confusion. "But he's not had a woman since—well, at least in the last month."

"Exactly," Cade said. "Yazz, come with us, please?"

What he didn't say, as they went a-hunting whorehouses, was that whatever magic had compelled celibacy had worn off by now.

They found him at the second brothel they tried. Yazz brought him back to the wagon by the scruff of the neck, yelping with outrage, dangling a foot off the ground. He refused to speak to anyone for the rest of the drive to Lilyleaf.

At Croodle's, a surprise was waiting for them. When Touchstone tumbled out of the wagon midafternoon, grateful to escape the heat inside and not expecting the heat to be almost as bad outside, Croodle met them with cool drinks and a wide grin. They went inside, slurping beer, and two paces through the doorway got all tangled up, for Jeska had not only stopped short but also dropped his mug shattering onto the floor. Cade bit back a snarling reprimand, because Kazie stood there, plainly pregnant and lovelier than ever.

That Jeska had had no inkling that his wife was pregnant was scrawled all over his face. He managed to keep his feet, but had to be guided towards Kazie's laughing embrace and then into a handy chair. Cade instantly decided that tonight, rather than the tragic "Silver Mine," they'd be doing something light and funny. Bubbling-full of elation as Jeska was, it would be simple kindness to let him express it in a rollicking Mother Loosebuckle farce—or mayhap "Hidden Cottage," so Mieka could have fun doing his beloved pig. He also decided to make it a short night so that Jeska could spend as much time as possible with his wife. He would have done the same for Rafe if Crisiant had shown up unexpectedly, and his mood was such that he might even have done the same for Mieka.

Lilyleaf was also the location where Cade began to lose track of things in general. So many performances in so many places in so brief a period of time compared to the usual round of the Royal Circuit—and so much thorn and alcohol to get him through it all—it was no wonder that on the morning they arrived at Coldkettle Castle he was convinced that Yazz had made a wrong turn and they were at Castle Biding instead. Later on, priming the withies was more difficult and took more energy than at any time in his career. And that night, even though he was bone-tired and they had been invited to stay in comfortable rooms within the castle (real beds that didn't sway and rock even when the wagon wasn't moving), he could get no sleep. So he put on a shirt over his nightshirt, gathered up pen and paper, and left Mieka snoring in the other bed, careful to close the door quietly.

It was a gorgeous summer night, warm and clear, the full moon so huge and bright that Cade had plenty of light to write by. He chose a corner of the upper walk that ran two-thirds of the way round the castle, pushed up his sleeves, and sat down. No table, no chairs, but the crenellations were such, and he was tall enough, that he could comfortably sit cross-legged at the wall and use the stone shelf as a desk. "Window Wall" had been nagging at him ever since Castle Eyot, though he couldn't have said how many days or how many performances ago that had been. If he couldn't sleep, he may as well write.

He had no idea how long he'd been there when a voice spoke behind him and he gave such a start that he nearly lost the ink bottle and his scrawled-upon pages over the wall.

"I suppose that when inspiration commands, you're quite a slave to it. Or is it just that you have so little time to yourself, while you're out on the circuit?"

Megs—Lady Megueris Mindrising, whose father was richer than any other ten nobles combined—stood there, looking badly put-together as usual. In fact, she looked as if someone had rather sloppily packed her away for the journey from Gallybanks, unpacked her in haste, and forgotten to shake her out and iron her. Her blond hair straggled from its braid, her plain white shirt was coming untucked from her plain brown skirt, and the fringed turquoise shawl bunched around her shoulders could have done duty as a table-drape. And she was barefoot.

Scrambling to stand up, awkward as ever, the scrape of uneven stone on one ankle and his own bare feet reminded him that he was even more ill-clad than she. A shirt due to be washed, a nightshirt the same—and his legs bare from the knees down.

Her amused glance made him grit his teeth.

"Do you often wander about other people's castles at strange hours of the morning?" He tried to keep the question casual, fully aware that in the wrong tone of voice, it could be very rude.

Rude or not, she didn't seem to mind. "Oh, quite often, yes. I like getting up early, even before the servants are awake. Don't let me interrupt your writing."

"No, I was finished," he lied. Then, ridiculously: "I didn't know you were here. At Coldkettle, I mean. Not here on the walls. Here at the castle."

"I'm on my way to Lilyleaf."

"To see Croodle?" He seemed to remember something about her getting lost as a child and somehow meeting Croodle; he wasn't sure how.

"Just for a week or so. The Princess is organizing part of the celebrations, and wants me back at the Keeps, or I'd stay for a month."

Celebrations? Oh, yes—the reason why they were tearing around the country at a breakneck pace. They had to be in Gallybanks for King Meredan's twenty-fifth anniversary celebrations. If he worked very hard, he might have "Window Wall" ready by then, or, rather, the two plays that the piece had become. He'd realized tonight that he had to chop it in half, with the first part telling why the boy was imprisoned behind the glass, and the second getting him out of it. Could they have both plays ready in time?

He became aware that he had said nothing for at least a minute, probably longer. Not holding up his end of the conversation; deplorable manners. What had she been talking about? The Princess, Croodle, Lilyleaf—

"May I plead a favor?" he heard himself ask, not quite sure what he was about to say. His brain seemed to be lagging behind his mouth. He waited until she nodded permission, and flogged his thoughts to catch up. Ah—yes, of course. "Jeska's wife is Croodle's cousin, and—"

"Oh, yes, I know. She's with child. How did he take the news?"

"Stunned, staggered, and stupefied," he told her with a grin, and she laughed.

"If you're about to ask me to escort her back to Gallybanks, you're too late. That was the plan from the start."

"I am very much beholden to you, my lady. And so will Jeska be. Your carriage will be much more comfortable than one of the post coaches."

"It's not the slightest trouble at all."

And with that, they both ran out of things to say. Cade wondered why he was glibness personified with the girls who clustered backstage in tiring rooms, but around highborn ladies, he invariably made a fool of himself. *Unmarried* highborn ladies, he corrected himself, thinking of Lady Vrennerie. And that gave him something to say.

To his inquiry, Lady Megueris replied, "Yes, Vren's with the Princess. And serving dreadful duty, I'm afraid. Tregrefin Ilesko is forever underfoot, and Miriuzca is constantly busy with the celebrations, so Vren is delegated to keep him entertained and out of the way."

"We—Touchstone, I mean—we had lunching with him and the Princess at Seekhaven."

"So I'm told. She says you were all exquisitely polite, even though Ilesko was exquisitely rude. Betwixt you and me and the wall over there—and your ink bottle—she'll be as pleased to see the back of him as all the rest of us."

"Flirting with you, is he?" Again words had popped out of his mouth before he could think. Paralyzed by his own tactlessness, he flushed crimson and couldn't even begin to stammer out an apology.

She only laughed again. "Once he found out how rich I am!

For now it's funny, but I have a plan if he becomes a bother."

"Magic," he said.

"Magic," she agreed. "Obviously. He's rather ferocious on the subject, isn't he? I wish I'd seen that play you and the Shadowshapers and the Sparks did at Seekhaven. He's still frothing at the mouth."

"Good," Cade said, and they smiled smiles of perfect accord.

A few moments later she said, "Well, it's getting on for morning, and we're leaving today, so I won't be seeing your show tonight." A slight frown darkened her bottle-green eyes. "Do try to get some sleep between now and then, won't you? There's a tale making the rounds that the Kindlesmiths' tregetour rode thirty miles there and back to visit his mother, and barely returned in time for the night's performance—and instead of 'The Princess and the Snowdrop' he primed the withies for some obscene thing they used to do at some of the more raucous gentlemen's guilds."

"I'm careful." He hid his annoyance. He was a professional, for fuck's sake. He knew what he was doing. He could prime withies perfectly for anything in Touchstone's folio even when drunk to the earlobes. "I'm always careful," he said again, trying not to sound belligerent.

"I didn't mean to imply that you aren't. But one can't help noticing those." She gestured to his right arm, where the rolled-up sleeves of shirt and nightshirt revealed a dozen or more slightly reddened thornpricks.

He bit his tongue between his teeth, not daring to open his mouth for fear of what might blurt its way out. Something angry and insulted and guilty and rude, something unforgivable, he was sure

She looked up at him, and whatever she saw in his face thinned her lips. "Good morrow, Master Silversun," she said coldly, turning for the stairs. "My thanks for your time."

The word made him flinch as perhaps nothing else could

have. *Beholden* was the usual, ubiquitous expression of gratitude (sincere or not). But it implied a debt, whereas *thanks* was considered payment enough, nothing owed beyond that single syllable. Nobody he knew used the word; it was more common among those who had so little to their names that they tended to avoid even the polite implication of indebtedness that *beholden* suggested.

Years ago Cade had explained to Mieka why a shopkeeper's assistant had no business saying *beholden* to Kearney Fairwalk: that there was no conceivable service such a person could possibly perform for a highborn, wealthy lordship that could compare to the simple honor of his presence in the establishment. But Megs had deliberately disdained using *beholden,* for she was so wellborn and so rich that her *thanks* was a reward in and of itself. And the Lord and the Lady forfend that she should even imply that she was beholden to somebody like him for anything.

Oh, yes, it was a splendid morrow. Just the sort he liked: no sleep, Mieka in a snit because the girl he usually slept with at Coldkettle had got herself married this spring, Jeska fretting over Kazie, and Rafe—Rafe just looked at him with those too-perceptive blue-gray eyes. And besides all that, half the pages he'd written made little if any sense. He'd thought them quite brilliant while scribbling. How lovely it would be, he told himself, if Auntie Brishen could come up with a mixture of thorn that stimulated his creative mind *and* his interior critic.

Their next stop was Castle Biding. There was no fair to swell the local audiences, so they were mercifully spared having to perform more than twice. Then they were off to Frimham.

Cade remembered only one thing about Frimham, and it occurred on the day they left. They were in the wagon, half a block down the lane from the inn they'd stayed at, when Mieka leaped to his feet from his chair and bellowed, "Yazz! Stop!"

"What?" the Giant yelled back. "Why?"

"I forgot! We have to go back!"

It was impossible to turn the wagon in this lane. Mieka jumped out the back door and ran. Cade roused himself to follow at a more leisurely pace.

Rafe called out the window, "What's he doing? Did he leave something behind? The withies?"

"How should I know?" He ambled along to the inn and was in time to hear Mieka call out from the upstairs window.

"'Ware below!"

Cade took a second to react, and then lunged beneath an awning that belonged to the shop next door. The contents of a chamber pot, followed by the chamber pot itself, came flying out the window onto the street. Nobody was hit, either by showers of shit or shards of ceramic, though in some cases it was a near thing. Mieka came racing out the door, saw Cade, grabbed his arm, and hauled him back to the wagon. When they were inside, he shouted, "Let's go!" before collapsing into his chair with a wide, satisfied grin.

"What in the unholy fuck did you do that for?" Cade demanded.

The grin widened. "I'm Mieka Windthistle—what's *your* excuse?" When Cade frowned at him, he relented. "Don't you remember that great long gabble of a lecture the innkeeper's wife gave us about emptying the chamber pot ourselves every morning? That she and her maids weren't our adoring wives or our doting mothers, to clean up after us?"

Cade remembered nothing of the kind.

"I was just doing what I was told," Mieka finished, vastly pleased with himself.

"That's a first," Rafe commented, and ostentatiously opened a book, fully prepared to ignore them all.

Cade had had enough. Enough of Mieka, of Rafe, of Jeska, of the wagon, of performing, of not knowing what town he was in, of having no time and peace to write, of everything. He hopped out the back door with the wagon still rolling and ran up to the front, where Yazz, startled but amenable, reached down a massive hand and hauled him up to the coachman's bench.

"Naught but Stiddolfe," he said by way of comfort.

Cade grunted assent and settled himself on the padded leather seat, one hand on the railing. Stiddolfe would be their last stop before Gallantrybanks. The university town, rival to Shollop for several hundred years, was full of brilliant students and even more brilliant teachers. In the past, he'd felt himself intellectually inferior to the young scholars who were his own age; now he was older than all of them and still an academic straggler. *Imposter* was more like it, he thought glumly. Oh, he could hold his own in conversation, and he was accustomed to their admiration, but that regard had altered subtly in the last couple of years. Those first Winterly Circuits, the students had looked upon him with awe. He'd found this embarrassing at the time. In retrospect, and in all honesty, he rather missed it. Now they treated him with respect—as if he were eighty and had threescore publications in learned journals to his name, instead of twenty-four and at the very least a mention, and often a whole article, in every issue of *The Nayword* for the past five years.

Cheer up, he told himself sourly. If that Elsewhen was correct, then by the age of forty-five, he'd be a Knight and they'd have to call him Sir Cayden—if they dared speak to him at all. Or had any interest in speaking to him, age-weary old relic that he'd be, and losing his hair besides.

He regretted leaving the interior of the wagon, where the whiskey and the thorn were.

To distract himself, he asked Yazz if he'd had a nice time with his friends at . . . at that place with the mud puddles, he couldn't recall the name. The Giant nodded. In another attempt at conversation, Cade said that the wagon had behaved very nicely this circuit. Yazz nodded again. He was trying to think up something for his third and final venture when Yazz cleared his throat, a sound like a gravel landslide.

"Skinny, all of you," he said. "Mistress Kazie worries."

Cade reflected on this idea. It was true that all four of them had taken in their belts a notch or three. Scant wonder, when they survived on thorn and whiskey and little else for six or seven days of each fortnight. "We'll rest up before the celebrations."

"And after?"

"I'll have to ask Lord Fairwalk to hold back on the giggings this winter. Now that you mention it, Yazz, I could do with a rest."

During the next few miles the sun's heat and the rhythmic *cuh-clop* of hooves lulled Cayden to a doze, and that was all he remembered about Frimham.

He would just as soon have forgotten Stiddolfe, too.

It was their second night there—or mayhap the third, he wasn't sure and didn't bother to ask later on. Jinsie and Jezael Windthistle were waiting for Touchstone at a nice, respectable little inn on the outskirts of town. Jinsie was there to consult with some scholarly friends about a project she had in mind for teaching the blind and the deaf. Jez was there not because his sister required an escort but because he had had it up to the eyeballs with their mother's coddling. He used his cane only sparingly, the injury having healed quite nicely under Mistress Mirdley's supervision. But he did bring along the cane for the sake of his leg when he got tired, and the little green pillow his niece Jindra had helped to sew for the sake of sentiment.

They all met for dinner—Touchstone, Jinsie, and Jez—on that second night (or mayhap third), and when Jinsie asked Cayden if he'd be willing to meet with her friends, he rolled his eyes and said, "Only if nothing even remotely resembling the philosophy of *anything* is discussed."

"Snob," Rafe commented, helping himself to more lamb stew.

"Not a bit of it," said Mieka. "He'll talk enough if there's a reporter there to note down his every golden utterance and publish it all in the next day's broadsheet."

"Quat," Cade said.

"So will you or won't you?" Jinsie asked impatiently.

Before Cade could reply, Mieka said, "He's been thinking great thoughts for weeks now—a new play, don't you know. Angels forfend that anything or anyone should interrupt him while he's being matchlessly brilliant!"

Cade heard the note of resentment and frowned. It was true that he was working on the two plays that "Window Wall" had become, and not having more than a couple of hours a day to himself for writing annoyed him. But he knew what Mieka referred to: an incident at Castle Biding. Mieka had burst in on his solitude, wild-eyed, a polishing cloth bunched in one hand and a withie held by the crimp end in the other, babbling about how the withies had all grown thorns. The only thorn in question, of course, was whatever Mieka had pricked that after-noon. Cade told him so. In a fury, Mieka threw the foot-long glass twig at him. He caught it, wrapped his fingers round it, then set it on the table and held up his palm to show Mieka that there was no injury and thus there were no thorns. Mieka insisted that he was wrong. Losing patience, Cade told him to get out and stop bothering him with such nonsense. Mieka swore at him and stalked from the room, and didn't speak to him for two days.

Mieka was glaring at him now, renewed hostility in those eyes. Cade opened his mouth to snarl at him, but all at once he couldn't seem to get any air. His heartbeats thundered irregularly in his ears. He felt cold all over, as if his skin had acquired a riming of frost that thickened with every passing moment. He heard someone say his name and could not reply. Blearily, his vision swirling with wisps of fog, he saw Mieka race from the taproom. And wasn't that just like that fucking little Elf, running out on him, vanishing just when he was needed? What he could be needed for was unclear to Cade and he couldn't track down the thought, because his brain was slowly revolving inside his skull and his heartbeats had subsided to one thump and a long pause, one thump and a longer pause, and of all the times for an Elsewhen to slide into his head, this was undoubtedly the worst—but it wasn't just one Elsewhen, it was four, a dozen, a score, he couldn't tell how many, because they all overlapped, versions of himself at various ages all moving within his vision, uncounted numbers of Archdukes and Rafes and Blyes and Jeskas and Miekas and Princesses and different rooms and an exploding tower and the burying ground at Clinquant House but how could he know that because he'd never been to the Windthistles' Clinquant House and what was Megs doing there, and there, and there again, and if only he could get some air into his lungs he'd be able to sort all these cascading Elsewhens—

—and suddenly he *could* breathe, in great greedy whoops that filled his lungs and spread precious air all through his body. The frost sloughed from his skin, his heart beat strongly and regularly, and the distant roaring in his ears faded.

"—all right now, Jinsie, he's breathing just fine."

Jeska's voice. He turned his head and saw Rafe standing over him.

"Wh-what happened?"

At least that was what he thought he'd said. Whether it came out as he intended was problematical. Either Rafe understood the mumble, or he guessed what Cade wanted to know—an obvious query, after all.

"Lost track, didn't you?" the fettler said. "Blue, white, blockweed, who knows what all, with dinner and two pints of beer on top—and only you and Brishen Staindrop know what she cooks up for you special. That was thorn-shock, and if you ever scare us like that again, I'll break your skull open and wash out your brains with lye soap."

"He should be upstairs," Jezael said calmly. "Shall we call Yazz to carry him? I don't think he can walk."

The Giant was duly found, and within ten minutes Cayden was in a soft, scented bed. He lay back and closed his eyes, and asked, "Mieka?"

"He's the one gave you the thorn that got you breathing again." Rafe picked up Cade's left arm and pushed back the shirtsleeve. "See? The fresh one. Right here."

He heard Rafe's disgust at the number of tiny scabs and reddened marks on his arm. The humiliation was even worse than what he'd felt when Megs had had the same note in her voice. A feeble quiver of pride made him say, "You do it, too."

"I have," Rafe agreed. "To get through a performance or to get some sleep. But this—this is insane, Cayden. It's dangerous. I never would've thought you could be this stupid. Or—no, you *are* that stupid, now that I come to think on it. What I don't believe is that you of all people could be so pathetically unoriginal."

He squeezed his eyes shut. Yes, it was true. He'd thought himself trite when he realized that refusing to feel was a thing thousands had done before him. This was worse. Using thorn and liquor so foolishly—wasn't it precisely what he deplored in Mieka? And hadn't he seen what thorn-thrall was doing to Pirro Spangler of Black Lightning? He suspected the same of Thierin Knottinger and perhaps Mirko Challender and Lederris Daggering of the Sparks. He knew for a fact that Vered Goldbraider, who reacted badly to more than one or two drinks, substituted thorn for alcohol and sometimes indulged quite lavishly. And here was Cade, so intellectually superior, so wise, so prudent—he was just like any other man who thought himself smarter than everyone else when it came to thorn.

But he needed it. There was no conceivable way he could have got through this Royal Circuit without it. Thorn gave him energy, it helped him sleep.

It made Mieka see the withies grow thorns.

It had stimulated his mind to a score and more Elsewhens, all at the same time.

It had nearly stopped his heart.

When he opened his eyes at last, the feel of the bedchamber had changed. Rafe was long gone. Instead: Mieka, white-faced by the light of a single candle. He sat on the floor, knees hugged to his chest, staring at Cade.

It took a moment for him to realize how terrified Mieka had been, how scared he still was. Cade knew that kind of fear. Shame warred with anger and a contempt that included both of them.

"Now you know how it feels," he said.

Mieka flinched as if Cade really had hit him this time. Cade promised himself that if Mieka said anything, anything at all, any words of regret or apology or blame or any damned bloody thing at all, Cade really would hit him this time.

Mieka said nothing. He got to his feet and doused the candle and closed the door quietly behind him.

18

After what happened in Stiddolfe, nobody talked to anybody else more than was strictly necessary for their performances' sake. Rafe was angry; Cade was angry and humiliated; Mieka was angry, humiliated, and hurt; Jeska, who felt none of these things and wanted only to get home to his pregnant wife, decided that the wisest course was to keep his mouth shut.

The atmosphere in the wagon, those last long miles to Gallantrybanks, became so intolerable that their second-to-last night on the road, Jeska went to the nearest posting inn and hired a horse and rode the rest of the way home by himself. Though Cade considered doing the same thing, he'd spent almost all the coin allotted to him for the circuit. The few private shows they'd had time to do had paid well, but the money had gone into the local branches of their bank to be credited to their Gallybanks accounts. For the first time he regretted not having played the weird old mansion outside New Halt. Payment for that had always come in the form of individual purses fairly bursting with coin.

So he gritted it out those last two days, and when the wagon finally arrived at Wistly Hall, he slung a satchel of his personal belongings over his shoulder and went looking at once for a hire-hack. He knew Mishia and Hadden Windthistle would be puzzled and disappointed, mayhap even insulted, that he hadn't joined in the welcome—hadn't even stopped long enough for more greeting than a nod and a wave—but he simply couldn't face several hours of the merry story telling that would be expected of him. Even less did he want to watch Mieka effortlessly fulfilling the role of family clown.

It was getting on for dusk when he arrived at his flat. He had enough in his pockets to pay for the hack, with some left over to spend on two meat pasties and a bottle of beer sold by a street vendor. Had he gone to Redpebble Square, there would have been a hot dinner and clean sheets, and he couldn't face Mistress Mirdley or Derien, either. So he trudged up the many flights of stairs, jerked down the door handle, and went inside.

Empty.

Not just empty of people other than himself. All his furniture and clothes and books and the glass dinnerware Blye had made for him and his Trials medals and those silly peacock feathers Mieka had given him on his last Namingday and everything else he owned was *gone*.

He stood in the center of the room, stupid with shock, unable to comprehend what he was seeing. Physically, mentally, and emotionally exhausted, feeling the need of bluethorn as a quick insistent demand, he turned slowly round. *Empty*.

Footfalls and gasps announced a new arrival through the open door. His landlord: red-faced with the climb, scowling, sucking in a great wheeze of air and using it to provide an explanation.

"A fortnight and a fortnight again I waited to be paid, my fine young sir, and could I get in to my own property—my own property, sir!—what with that illegal lock you put onto the door? Yes, illegal, and well you know it, but that's in the past, and so is your time here! All your belongings went to your mother's house, and it's lucky you are, young sir, that the Trollwife came along just a day or two before I would have found someone to un-bespell the lock and sold off the lot! She took on herself the packing and the moving of it all, and the cost of it, though I ought to've charged for those weeks and weeks of storage here, which deprived me of any income on the place at all! And what she's done with your things I neither know nor care, and even less do I care what you do with yourself, sir, once you're away from my premises! Great and grand tregetour famous throughout Albeyn, my ass! Naught but a bully-rook, a cheat, a lying young cogger! Away with you, now, and good riddance!"

Cayden surveyed the room again. Rent unpaid. All his things back at Redpebble. He looked down at the landlord, wondering suddenly what had become of the cat. No, that was foolish; Rumble was at Redpebble Square, where Derien had taken care of him during the circuit. And Redpebble Square was the only place Cade could go. He didn't question how this had happened. It didn't matter. It was a fact. He had best get home before dark, because he'd run out of funds and would have to walk the whole way.

"Well?" the landlord snapped. "Anything to say for yourself? Well, sir?"

A thoroughly hilarious notion seized him to answer that one day, people would use that *sir* in earnest, for real and true, in Royal recognition of honor and accomplishment. He started back down the stairs, munching on the cold meat pasties, and paused at the food vendor's to ask him to pull the cork from the beer. His corkscrew was of course gone along with everything else to Redpebble Square. His big comfortable chair, the bed-and-desk Jed had made for him, his books—a shudder went through him as he realized how close he'd come to losing his grandfather's books. He drained the beer down his throat, tossed the bottle and the remains of the food into the gutter, and started walking.

It was full dark in Criddow Close when he knocked on the kitchen door of his mother's house. Mistress Mirdley let him in without a word, but with eloquent eyes. Jeska was waiting for him, and soup and bread and wine. Derien must have been listening for the slam of the back door, because he flew into the kitchen, threw his arms around Cade, and hugged hard.

He clasped his not-so-little brother close, meeting Jeska's limpid blue eyes. All he could think of to say was, "Kazie's well?"

Jeska nodded. Derien drew away and looked up at him—not nearly so far up as when Cade had left in the spring, and how had he grown so much and so quickly?

"All your things are in your old room, or down in the undercroft," Dery said in a rush. "You mustn't worry. That awful man didn't steal anything. He couldn't, because he couldn't get into the flat until I came. And he was so horrible while we were getting your things downstairs that I shut the door again while the magic was still working so he couldn't get in even after everything was out of there."

"I suppose he found somebody to bespell it open," Cade said.

There was an awkward pause. "You and Jeska have to talk, I know. I'll get out of your way now."

"You're never in my way." He wrapped his arms around the boy and held tight. But only for a moment, for he was disgusted with himself: his defense against whatever was in Jeska's eyes was a boy scarcely twelve years old. Letting go, he managed a smile. "But I'll wager you've lessons to be done, yeh?"

Dery shot a glance at Jeska, then at Mistress Mirdley. "Um— yeh, I do. I'll just go upstairs, then."

Cade sat beside Jeska at the kitchen worktable. Pages were spread neatly across most of the surface. Many of them bore the remains of Lord Kearney Fairwalk's ribbons and seal: deep blue ribbons, outlines of oak leaves pressed into broken plum-colored wax. Mistress Mirdley set fresh glasses of wine and a decanter within their reach and departed for her stillroom. She hadn't yet said a single word. Jeska handed him a glass of wine.

"I s'pose," Cade said with a pathetic attempt at casualness, "I'm going to need this. You're about to tell me why my rent wasn't paid."

"And my rent, and my daughter Airilie's support, and debts belonging to Touchstone as a whole and each of us personally." He paused, then forced out the words, "And Derien's school fees."

School fees . . . from an account that only he and Kearney Fairwalk could access . . . all his grandfather's legacy, gone. He knew it even before Jeska said it. Emptiness spread through his body as Jeska explained what the figures and notations on all those pages meant. When the masquer finally stopped talking, Cade felt as hollow as the rooms that were no longer his home. His brain went slack, like loosened reins just before a horse surged to a gallop. It wasn't possible. It just simply wasn't possible that all the money was gone.

Not just gone. Owed.

The wainwright. The wainwright's painter. The wheelwright. Imagers, engravers, paper-makers, printers. Tailors, shoemakers, glovers, hatters, drapers, mercers, and lacemakers. Goldsmiths and silversmiths and coppersmiths and jewelers. Wine merchants and greengrocers, butchers and fishmongers, fruiterers and florists. Blacksmiths, ironmongers, cutlers, coopers, stonemasons, brickmasons, glaziers, wallers, joiners, carpenters—he had the wild thought that the only profession that seemed to be missing was grave-digger.

His mind skittered about, trying to avoid the disaster of it by finding something else to think about. Who had bought so many knives from the cutler? Whose walls had the wallers walled? Blye made panes of window glass, but it wanted a glazier to install them—and whose windows? Where? And talking of windows, what about the windows Touchstone had shattered in the Princess's father's palace—was there a bill here for those, too? Were carrots and lettuce and beans and celery really that expensive? Who had bought so much jewelry? How many placards had been ordered, that they owed so much to printers and engravers and papermakers? The only bills he accepted without question were from the wine merchants. They'd done a lot of drinking, these last few years . . . .

The list was endless and terrifying, for all their creditors been paid just enough to keep them from seeking redress in the law courts. Individually, the bills weren't much. Cumulatively, they were crippling.

It would take Touchstone at least two years to pay them all off, and that was if every other expense was cut at least by half.

A cold, sick panic began in his guts, replacing the hollowness, feeding off the hard lump of meat and pastry in his stomach. His mind scurried in every direction, desperate for a source of funds. What could he sell, where could he borrow, who could lend him money, how could he keep Derien in school—when would any or several or all of the creditors demand final and complete settlement of their accounts?

He was no nobleman, like Kearney Fairwalk, to wave a lazy hand as he strolled out of any shop in Gallantrybanks with the assurance that his custom was worth more to the proprietor than actual payment of the bill.

He owned nothing of sufficient value to sell.

He had no wealthy relations.

What he had was a thick folio of plays, and a beautiful lectern inlaid with dragonbone, and his Trials medals, and his books, and a little brother whose education would be calamitously curtailed if the school fees couldn't be found.

The fear spread all through his veins, thick and ice-cold, clogging his thoughts and stuttering his heart. What was he to do? How could he find his way out of this? A trapped rat at least had teeth to savage the cat that had cornered him. He had nothing.

"Cade," Jeska said quietly, "we have to do something."

A weakening wave of gratitude flooded him. At least he

wasn't alone in this: "We *have to do something*—" They were, Gods help them, in this together.

Performances. Private performances that paid well. All this autumn and winter, when he'd hoped to work on *Window Wall,* they'd have to go wherever they must for whatever money people were willing to pay them.

But they'd just come off the Royal Circuit—what if people had seen enough of them for one year? There'd been intimations and more of disappointment that the Shadowshapers hadn't won First Flight on the Royal, and never mind that the Shadowshapers *had* won and rejected the circuit. Touchstone had felt the need to prove themselves time and time again. What if they'd failed to convince people that they deserved their position on the Royal?

And what if no one wanted Touchstone's particular kind of theater? If they'd been Black Lightning, patrons would be lined up the length of the Gally River from the Flood to the Westercountry, eager for the chance to experience over and over the dangerous turbulence of emotion, the blunt force of sensation—what had he said once? That Black Lightning was a group for addicts?

Touchstone could outdo Black Lightning. Easy. It wouldn't take long to establish a reputation for that kind of shocking performance. Touchstone could—

—could betray everything they were. Could sell themselves. Could whore their art and their craft.

"We know enough people now," Jeska was saying, "to organize our own schedule. Kazie and Jinsie will keep track of it all for us. I've already spoken to them. I'll have to give up my lodgings, of course, to provide for Airilie, but Kazie says she'll be glad to live at Wistly, especially now that she's pregnant, and Mishia says they'll be glad to have her. Crisiant and Bram will go on staying with the Threadchasers. Crisiant runs the bakery now, anyways."

And Cade would have to live at Number Eight, Redpebble Square.

And Mieka . . .

"Mieka's house is paid for—his father made sure of it—so his family will be all right at Hilldrop. Not that he'll be there much, of course. We'll either be traveling or in Gallybanks doing the rounds of all the theaters and taverns."

Of course. The Windthistles would adore having Jindra at Wistly, but as for the wife and mother-in-law . . .

"What we have to decide, Cayden, is whether or not to bring suit against Fairwalk."

"He's a nobleman," Cade rasped, the first thing he'd said since Jeska had shown him the books. "D'you think we'd get a fair hearing in the courts?"

"We might." The cleft chin set stubbornly.

"We're nothing and nobody. We signed a contract. What he ended up doing with the money we earned—it's our own bloody fault. That's how the law court will see it, and I'm not sure but that's the truth."

"We trusted the wrong person." Jeska sighed. "We were young, yeh, and inexperienced—and he, as you say, is a nobleman. Well, we can decide later." He gulped wine and set the glass down. "I haven't yet sussed out exactly where all this went—but I'm guessing that a goodly clump of it went to Fairwalk Manor, and his own house here in town."

"How did you get hold of all this in the first place?"

Strong shoulders shrugged. "I went to our bank."

"Did they say—? I mean, do they know—"

"They had a stack of papers authorizing withdrawals, signed by each of us with Fairwalk as witness, and Fairwalk's signature with one of the bank officers as witness."

And who would question the word of a nobleman, and a distant relation of King Meredan's into the bargain? How could they have been so stupid?

"He did best with that scrawl of Mieka's," Jeska went on.

"Mine wasn't very good. Rafe's was all right. Yours was perfect."

And he could hear Mieka's scathing explanation for that: *"Writing your name over again and over again like a lovesick thirteen-year-old girl! Didn't I always tell you he was looking for more from you than a smile and a handclasp?"*

Cade had never really seen it. Just as he'd never seen that Fairwalk wasn't truly rich. He only behaved as if he were. Reputation alone would keep most creditors from hounding him, for the bragging rights of having Lord Fairwalk's custom were worth more than what he bought and never paid for.

No wonder Kearney was always telling him not to bother his head about so vulgar a thing as money. *"It's your job to be brilliant and create masterworks, Cayden. Let me take care of everything else."*

Oh, he'd taken care of it, all right.

"If I'm hearing this correctly," he said with an attempt at practical reasoning, "Kearney took out cash for whatever he was supposed to be buying for us, and used it for himself. The bills—*our* bills—went unpaid."

Jeska nodded, and raked the limp blond curls from his face. It was hot in the kitchen, Cade realized with a start. Yet he felt so cold, shivering-cold. "There's something else," the masquer said reluctantly.

Of course there was something else. Of course. Cade cocked an eyebrow at him and he cleared his throat.

"When Blye paid off her debt to Touchstone and bought back the last few shares we owned, Kearney had her write the bank draft out to him. He told her he'd break it up into equal shares and deposit it in our separate accounts."

"Instead, he used it all himself."

"Yes. And Blye can't ever find out, Cade. She'd want to pay us a second time. I told you only because it shows how long all this has been going on."

Had it all been just to steal from them? All the encouragement, the praise, the introductions to important highborns and merchants and officials, the private performances he'd arranged—the commission from Lord Oakapple to write the real story of "The Treasure"? They'd all four received fat purses from the grateful nobleman afterwards, but where had the advance got to? Their accounts, or so Cade had assumed.

"Do you remember when he told us that there'd be nothing more for the journey to the Continent? Because of the windows we broke and had to pay for?"

Cade knew what was coming. "We didn't have to pay for the windows, we did get the rest of the money, and he pocketed it. Jeska, is there anything left?"

"We can pay down most of these." He waved a hand at the bills. "Some here, some there, just so they don't haul us before a justiciar. But from now until Trials next year, we have to play as many shows as we can."

It would take years of shows to replace his grandfather's legacy—which was supposed to pay for Dery's schooling until he reached the age of eighteen, by which time Cade had intended to be so rich that his brother could attend a university. "I was thinking about Derien's school fees."

Jeska didn't look at him as he said, "You seem to have more in your personal account than the rest of us. But the other account, the one that needs your signature and Fairwalk's . . . that's almost all gone. And you'll have to settle with the King's College quick. Derien hasn't been allowed to attend since the term began about a week ago. Your mother put it about that he's unwell."

Lady Jaspiela must be livid. But why hadn't she paid the fees herself? She cared fervently about her younger son's education and prospects. Couldn't she have forgone the regular autumn refurbishments to her wardrobe, or sold a few jewels? Neither, Cade realized, would even have occurred to her. After all, such things would be *noticed* by the society she so avidly cultivated.

The school term was only a week old; an "illness" could be stretched another fortnight or so, and if Derien had trouble catching up with the work, that was his problem. No, she would much rather have this disaster to berate Cayden about once he returned home. It was Cayden's responsibility to pay the fees, and pay them he would. Lady Jaspiela would have no interest in how.

Jeska was smiling slightly. "You can imagine how much Dery's liking it, having to stay inside every hour of every day."

So that was the meaning of that glance they'd exchanged. Dery hadn't any schoolwork to do, because he hadn't been in school.

"The first thing we have to do," Jeska was saying, "is confront Kearney and empty whatever's in his accounts into our own."

Cade thought of Fairwalk Manor, and the town house here in Gallybanks, crammed with books and decorations and rugs and tapestries and the family silver. "He can sell off whatever he's got and hand over the proceeds. Highborn or raised in a gutter, he won't much like seeing his reputation crushed."

"Well, there's that, of course. But they tend to stick together, all those toffs." He began gathering up papers into five tidy stacks. "These are yours, this one's mine, there's Rafe, and Mieka, and this one's Touchstone. Do you want me to leave them with you, or should I take charge of all of it?"

"You take it. You understand it."

"Most of it."

"You can add and subtract, which is more than the rest of us ever managed to learn." He helped Jeska load everything into a flat leather case and watched as he folded the flap over and snicked the little brass lock shut. "Go home to your wife. We can all meet here tomorrow—around noon?"

"Noon," Jeska agreed. He went to the kitchen door, then turned. "Cade . . . I know how hard this is for you. But nobody blames you. We all trusted him. Hells, we were thrilled when he took an interest. We're none of us businessmen, to know or even suspect—" He ended with a final shrug of his shoulders.

Cade made no reply. Jeska wrapped his arms round the leather satchel and left. The door shut with a familiar clack behind him. Cade poured himself more wine and slumped at the kitchen worktable. Despite what Jeska had said, he ought to have seen it. He ought to have known. He was supposed to be the smart one, wasn't he? The cautious, perceptive, rational one? A tregetour owed it to his group to look out for them, not just onstage but in matters of payment and bookings as well. He'd left all that to Kearney for five years now.

Touchstone would have to make a huge splash—or shatter—at the celebrations of King Meredan's accession in order to attract enough giggings to begin paying their debts. They wouldn't be paid for that performance; loyal congratulations and all that, happy to demonstrate their gratitude and esteem. If they worked it right, half a dozen noble lords and wealthy merchants would bid for their appearance at Wintering parties. The Downstreet, the Kiral Kellari, the Keymarker . . . where else, where else? his mind nattered at him. Lady Megueris's father had paid very handsomely. How many properties did he own that Touchstone could perform at? And Vrennerie's husband, Lord Kelinn Eastkeeping—he'd hire them if she asked. Did he have more than one castle? Cade knew he ought to cringe at using his friends that way, but he was past humiliation.

Yet if Touchstone went on a circuit of their own this autumn and winter, they wouldn't be available to play in Gallantrybanks. Would the money from Lord Mindrising and Lord Eastkeeping offset the expenses of so much travel? Would it be worth it to go out on the road instead of staying close to home, where the Downstreet and the Kiral Kellari and the Keymarker and other venues would be glad to have them as often as they wanted to show up?

Gods and Angels, how had all this happened? Why hadn't he

seen it? He ought to have known years ago, when performing the traditional version of "Treasure" at Trials had landed them on the Winterly when they knew they were good enough for the Ducal and even the Royal. He'd never really understood that before, but now as he reviewed the incident in light of new knowledge, it actually made sense.

It had been at Fairwalk's urging that they did the standard rendering of the play. A competent performance—and how furious Mieka had been!—had not been enough to win them a promotion to the Ducal or Royal Circuits. They were therefore free all summer and part of the autumn until the Winterly began. And then Fairwalk had shown up with giggings and Lord Oakapple's commission and, amazingly, the invitation to accompany the Archduke to Miriuzca's homeland and escort her back to Albeyn.

The bookings had been settled by Fairwalk before the ink on the final Trials results sheets was dry. He'd *known* they wouldn't make the Ducal or Royal. Further, instead of having them do their own, more accurate version of "Treasure" for free at Trials, he'd got them the commission—and kept the down payment. Somehow, he'd known that Miriuzca had requested Touchstone's presence at her proxy wedding—ah, but that wasn't all that odd, for Kearney was a connection of the Royal Family, wasn't he? Quite a few generations ago, to be sure, but a connection all the same. So he'd made sure Touchstone was free to travel to the Continent, and went along with them.

His absence from Albeyn for all those long weeks had put him beyond reach of his creditors. And as one of the delegation, his enhanced social standing would have made those creditors think more than thrice about demanding payment in the very public precincts of a court of law.

On his twenty-first Namingday, Cayden had come into an inheritance from his father's father, who'd been a fettler back in the day. Lady Jaspiela, more concerned for the future of her younger son than the rights of her elder, had proposed that the money be dedicated to Derien's education. Cade gladly agreed—and then he had done something that must have made Kearney caper like a dog with two cocks across every acre of Fairwalk Manor. Cade had stipulated that his grandfather's legacy go into an account separate from his own, and that only two people could withdraw money from it: himself and Lord Fairwalk. Cade's mother had been mortally insulted, a thing he'd enjoyed down to the ground, but he had been adamant. He'd thought the money was safe. No matter what her ambitions for Derien, it was Cade's opinion that she was incapable of resisting all that money if she could possibly get her hands on it. He'd made sure she couldn't. He'd thought the money was safe.

But not even that had been enough for His Rapacious Lordship. These last years, while Touchstone was away from Gallybanks on the Royal Circuit, he had used his position as their manager, his position as a highborn related to the Royals, and Touchstone's forged signatures to drain their bank accounts. Surely it was ironic that the only one of them completely spendthrift was the only one who owned his own home—but Mieka was in full legal possession of the house at Hilldrop only because his father had been resolute about paying the debt.

Cade knew what Kearney would say about it all, how he'd excuse it. Wainwright and wheelwright—the wagon, of course. All those repairs and additions to Mieka's house required wallers and masons and glaziers and joiners and carpenters—had Windthistle Brothers been paid? Of course they had. If not, it would have started people wondering. Touchstone required advertising placards and handbills—thus the printers, engravers, imagers, and so on. And of course Touchstone must appear in the most fashionable clothing, and eat the best food, and drink the finest liquor. All those places and more, Kearney would say, was where the money had been spent, and all the spending had been necessary. They were *Touchstone*.

That the bills had been sent to the bank for settlement— and for Jeska to be handed when he inquired—would be more difficult to explain away. As for where the money had actually gone . . . Cade had not been invited to Fairwalk Manor for several years now. He had the distinct feeling that if he were to pay a visit, he'd find a new roof to replace the elderly and leaking one, new windows, new floors, new carpets, new furniture, and a new carriage or two in the coach house, with new horses to draw them.

He had a brief, ludicrous vision—no Elsewhen, this, but a deliberate conjuring attributable to fear and hatred—of himself, striding through the Manor, pointing to this table and that sculpture and saying, *"That's mine, and that, and this over here. You bought it with my money, and that makes it mine."*

No, take it one step further, the way Mieka would. Imagine himself and his partners and their wives and children (but *not* Mieka's mother-in-law) taking possession of Fairwalk Manor, choosing bedchambers and private parlors, admiring the elegance of every room and the lovely views from every window, all of which they owned. And Kearney Fairwalk as the lowliest of stable boys, mucking out stalls and tugging his scant, sandy forelock whenever any member of Touchstone happened by.

His musings turned even more ludicrous. Who would be the wife he'd share his portion of the Manor with? How many children would they have? It would be a nice place to raise a family: away from the noise and flurry of Gallantrybanks, safe and serene. They could hire tutors, and if any of the children— his, or Mieka's, or Rafe's, or Jeska's—turned out to have talents like their fathers', four accomplished practitioners of magic would be there to teach them how it was all done. Accomplished and acclaimed, he reminded himself, thinking of their knighthoods. Rich, famous, titled, brilliant—

He became aware that the wine was affecting him, and looked at the decanter. Jeska had accounted for about two glasses; Cade had unknowingly drained it dry.

Well, and why not get drunk? It was a pretty vision, ownership of Fairwalk Manor. Now, if only he could figure out whom he ought to marry. To own so fine a property was one thing. Maintaining it was something else again. That had been His Lordship's problem. Keeping everything repaired and up to date, adding things here and there to increase its beauty . . . Touchstone could put in a rehearsal hall, nearly the size of a real theater, and invite friends to exclusive advance viewings of Cade's latest plays . . . how much would it cost to do that . . . but not the noblemen and representatives of the various guilds who bid every year for the right to present groups on the circuits . . . well, except for Lord Eastkeeping, who was a friend . . . and Princess Miriuzca . . . she'd adore it . . . but to pay for the upkeep of a place like that, they'd need a steady and secure source of income, for no matter how many shows they played, there was no guaranteeing that they'd be paid one year what they'd been paid the year before—

Megs.

The name appeared in his mind and he stared at it. Lady Megueris Mindrising was the richest person he knew. Heiress to a dozen fine holdings—if he married her and brought a quarter of Fairwalk Manor with him, she'd have another property to add to her list, and with both parents possessing the sort of magic used in theater, the children were more than likely to inherit—

Forget Fairwalk Manor, the sober part of him said. Lady Megs—how about it?

If he married her, a goodly portion of her income would be his—it depended on how the writ-rats sorted it in the marriage settlement. But even if he got only half, or even less than half, it would pay off all Touchstone's debts (which were his fault—he'd accepted that, somewhere in all his half-drunken ponderings) and there'd be plenty left over to live on rather beautifully.

True, she usually looked like an unmade bed, and there were times when he suspected she didn't much like him, and she obviously disapproved of his use of thorn, and—

What in the name of the Lord and the Lady and Old Gods and all the Angels was he *thinking*?

Trapped. Cornered. It was a way out.

"Any more of that, and we'll have to send for Yazz to carry you up to bed."

He looked up, bleary-eyed, to find Mistress Mirdley watching him. "I won't," he told her, unsure if he referred to the wine or matrimony. "I really won't, you know."

"Get up to bed, then, while you can still walk."

The number of steps on the cast-iron staircase seemed to have multiplied. Each footstep had a metallic echo, as if his boots had steel soles. When he collapsed fully dressed onto his bed, he spared a grateful glance for his big black armchair over there in the corner, and a half smile for Rumble, who looked up at his arrival, yawned, and went back to sleep.

He stared at the ceiling for a while, every crack and ripple of the plaster familiar in the candlelight. He felt that he understood things now, and the understanding brought no comfort. He ought to have known. From that very first time Fairwalk took him and Mieka shopping, and no bills were presented at the time, and they had both learned that it was almost a dead certainty that no bills would ever be presented—the honor and privilege of serving His Lordship, don't you know—he ought to have known then.

But he hadn't. And now Dery was close to being permanently expelled from the King's College for lack of payment of fees, and Jeska and Kazie had to move into Wistly Hall, and Rafe's plan to buy Crisiant a country cottage like Mieka's was impossible, and Cade had to live at Redpebble Square again—and for a few minutes, he had actually considered marrying Lady Megueris Mindrising for her money—

Dery. He had to concentrate on Dery. The school fees were the most urgent of his problems. Without the Masters at the King's College to learn from, and the social connections that came from attending school with lordlings, Derien's ambition to become a Royal Ambassador would die aborning. He would have to roll up and put away all his beloved maps, and forget about travel and service to Albeyn—and what about his magic? There would be no money for a special school like Sagemaster Emmot's Academy.

Derien's magic . . .

. . . which included an ability to sense gold.

Absurdly, Cade began to giggle. A solution at last! The solution to everything! Send Derien off on one of Lord Piercehand's ships, to return with cargo holds belching gold. Yeh, he could see it just like an Elsewhen: himself, waiting proudly at the docks below the Plume, Derien waving from the deck, flags flying, a brass band playing, their mother and even their father turning out to cheer the triumph and collect a share of the spoils—

Wine and weariness caught up with him before he could decide, still cackling inanely to himself, which idea was more disgusting: using his twelve-year-old brother like a ratting dog, or using Megs as a bank account.

19

The first awful thing that happened was that his wife wasn't at Wistly Hall to meet him.

"I know you're disappointed," his mother said as she hugged him. "But Jindra isn't feeling well, poor darling." She stood back and looked at him. "Good Gods. How long since you had a decent meal?"

Mieka shrugged off her concern. Pointing to Jeska, hovering near the staircase, he asked, "What's he doing here?"

That turned out to be the second awful thing, which made the first fade to insignificance. Jeska was there because, arriving a day earlier than the wagon, he'd discovered Kazie in a fury because of something to do with the bank, and first thing this morning he'd gone round to demand an explanation, and now he was here at Wistly with appalling news.

They all looked round for Cayden, who seemed to have vanished. Jeska said he'd go over to Redpebble Square later, which led to Rafe's asking why Redpebble, which led to Jeska's tale of what he had discovered at the bank.

The third awful thing was that Mieka was the only one who actually owned the house his family lived in. Rafe had been waiting for just the right country cottage; Jeska had been planning to buy a flat in one of the big new buildings down below the Plume; Cade—well, who knew what Cade had in mind, and Mieka didn't care anyways. Now Jeska and Kazie would move into Wistly, Rafe and Crisiant and Bram would continue to live with Mistress Threadchaser over the bakery, and Cade would be back at Redpebble Square before the sun set this evening. Of them all, Mieka was the only one with his own home to go to. It was no fault of his; Hadden Windthistle had arranged to pay off the mortgage as quickly as possible. Mieka and Yazz and their wives and children were perfectly safe. He didn't know why this made him squirm inside with guilt, but it did.

The most awful thing of all was finding out that he should have trusted his own instincts years ago about Kearney Fairwalk.

Jeska described the whole dismal situation and set off for Redpebble to tell Cayden. Rafe went silently home. Mieka glanced into the dining room, where a welcome-home dinner was all arranged, and fled upstairs.

The awful things just kept happening.

His fully depleted thorn-roll could not be replenished with whatever he'd left here, because ten minutes' search revealed that he'd left nothing here. Auntie Brishen would be unable to supply him for another week—it would take that long to send her a letter and for her to send the thorn. After a brief display of temper that no one witnessed, which included the grinding of one empty thorn-roll beneath his boot heel and the flinging of the other against a wall, he bethought himself of the Shadowshapers. Vered was known to savor thorn now and again. But the Shadowshapers were out on their own someplace, and probably wouldn't be back until a few days before the King's Accession celebrations. It took Mieka quite a while to recall the name of their supplier—Master Bellgloss—but he had no idea where to find him.

Worse, taking vengeance on the empty thorn-rolls had broken the little glass thorns themselves.

So, after a horrid night's sleep, he dressed early and headed over to Redpebble Square. Even if Cade didn't know anything about Master Bellgloss, he had his own thorn-roll and could bloody well share. Little as he relished having to speak to the man after that horrible *"Now you know how it feels"* in Stiddolfe, he set his jaw and walked the whole way there, angrier by the minute.

But instead of the front or back doors of Number Eight, he walked down Criddow Close instead. Neither Blye nor Jed had been at Wistly last night. Working, his mother had said. Mieka knew he'd find at least one of them in the glassworks.

The next awful thing was Blye.

She refused to make any glass thorns for him, saying that glass thorns were hollow and she was forbidden to make anything hollow.

Mieka scoffed. She made their withies, and they were hollow. Hells, she had the Gift of the Gloves and could make anything she fancied, now that the Princess was so obviously her patron.

"You're forcing me to say it, so I'll say it." Blye met him look for look, her brown eyes flashing with cold anger. "I *won't* make any glass thorns for you."

"Why not?"

"Because I can see what you're doing to yourself and I won't help you do it."

He was not in the cheeriest of moods when entering the kitchen at Number Eight. Lacking thorn, he'd slept badly. Cade had bloody well better have something left, or he'd—

"What are *you* doing here?"

For a moment he forgot his own worries. Cayden sat at the worktable before a plate of barely touched food. He looked dreadful. Unshaven, uncombed, with bloodshot eyes and a sickly pallor emphasized by two ugly welts of color on his sharp cheekbones, he was so skinny that he'd run out of notches on his belt. It rested at his hipbones rather than his waist, and precariously at that.

"Quill," he began, soft-voiced. How had he not seen how bad Cade looked? He supposed that over the course of the circuit, the changes had been so gradual that no one noticed anything about anybody else. Familiar, and bringing a familiar guilt.

"You can't stay. I'm off to the bank. Have to scrape together whatever I have left and go pay the King's College personally."

Oh, Gods—Mieka had forgot that Derien's schooling would be involved in their collective financial disaster.

"I can help pay it," he blurted. "I still have—"

"You still have a wife and a daughter and a mother-in-law to support."

"They can get by for a while. Dery's education is important, Quill. I don't know how much there is, but whatever's there is yours."

Cade drew breath to continue the argument. Then, all at once, his eyes lost their stormcloud color and softened, and he said, "You're such a miserable little cullion sometimes, and then you say something like that and—" He gave up and shook his head. "We'll talk about it later. I've had the footman run round to Jeska's and Rafe's to come by at noon so we can make some plans."

"Where d'you think we could get giggings that pay the best? How much would we be able to charge?"

"Not sure. Fairwalk took care of all that for us."

Mieka noted, but did not comment on, the fact that not only was the nobleman no longer *Kearney* to Cade, he had even lost his title. "We've all been right little idiots, haven't we?" Mieka asked ruefully. "It's not your fault, Quill."

"Isn't it? You didn't much like him from the first, as I recall."

"No. But I got used to him. We all did. And with his connections, and how he always encouraged you with your writing, and—"

"Stop trying to make me feel better, Mieka."

"D'you think anything could make any of us feel better? I just don't want you to feel *responsible*."

"You'll have to teach me how. It's one of your specialties, isn't it? Avoiding responsibility?"

Goaded, Mieka snarled back, "And why didn't you see this in an Elsewhen, eh? Before the very first time he showed up, when it was your decision to let him work for us or not—it all depends on what *you* choose, doesn't it? Well, then, why didn't you see this?"

"As I recall, you and Rafe and Jeska had all but taken him on before I ever even met him!"

"So now it's *our* fault?"

"It couldn't possibly be, could it? That would mean taking some respons—"

"Stop it!"

Another voice, scared beneath the anger, spoke behind them. They turned to find Derien, trembling, his hands fisted at his sides.

"Stop it! You sound like the play yard at school! Which of you is going to say 'But he started it!'?"

Mieka dragged his gaze from the boy's furious face to Cade's shocked one. In point of fact, it had been on his lips to say exactly that. Cade's shoulders slumped a bit, and he offered his right hand to Mieka: palm outward, the greeting of one nobleman to another. To an equal. Mieka looked him in the eyes as he matched his hand to Cade's. Their fingers laced together, and each held on hard for a few moments before letting go.

"Right," Derien said, relieved. "Has anybody thought yet about renting your wagon to one of the groups on the Winterly?"

Disasteful as the notion was, it would be income. Still—

"They'd have to find their own horses and driver," Cade said. "Yazz will want to be at home when the new baby comes."

"He might want the income," Mieka argued. "Babies aren't cheap."

"On the other hand, we might want the wagon for giggings outside Gallybanks," Cade said. "Jeska can figure out if we'd spend more using it than taking the post coach and putting up at an inn."

Mieka opened his mouth to protest—they were *Touchstone,* and Touchstone did *not* take public conveyances—but just then Mistress Mirdley appeared, cast a withering glance at Mieka, and said, "Another skeleton in a silken shirt. Derien, get down the plates and cups. You, Cayden, stir up the fire. As for you, Master Windthistle—"

"Yes?" he asked apprehensively.

"There's fresh apple muffins in the warming oven."

He found a basket, lined it with cloth, and filled it with muffins. Half an hour later, breakfast—scuffled eggs, slices of honeyed ham, apple muffins dripping butter, and strong black tea—had vanished down hungry throats and everybody felt better.

Until, with the unmannerly insistence of a creditor insisting on payment, the idea of thorn barged into his mind. He could barely restrain himself from jumping to his feet and racing upstairs to Cade's bedchamber. Many long, twitching minutes later, Cade suggested a remove to the drawing room.

"I'd rather your room upstairs," Mieka said. "No interruptions."

Derien snorted a laugh. "Don't worry, Mother had breakfast in bed and she's out visiting all day today."

It was only then that Mieka recalled Lady Jaspiela's dislike of his charming self. His own fault, attempting to use magic on her to . . . he couldn't quite remember why, but she had reacted rather badly. He hadn't set eyes on her since he couldn't remember when. The thorn-hunger reminded him of her utter unimportance.

"We should get your folio," he heard himself say—or mayhap it was the thorn talking. "We can plot out which plays people like best, and set a price on each of them. After all, it takes more out of us to do 'Dragon' or 'Treasure' than 'Cottage.'"

"What about your beloved pig? Would you really be willing to forgo your pig in exchange for more money?"

"Poor pig," he sighed. "I'll miss him." Rising to his feet, he pulled Cade along out of the kitchen. "C'mon, we ought to get started."

It was difficult to think up a good reason to ask Cade about his thorn-roll, for the unrelenting need made his thoughts skitter. By the time they were at the top of the five flights of stairs, he had his excuse.

"You must be as low on thorn as I am. Why not make a list for Auntie Brishen? I can send it to her along with mine."

As they entered the bedchamber, Cade cleared his throat nervously and wouldn't look at him. His long, thin hands fidgeted towards his satchel, where Mieka supposed the thorn-roll was.

"Er . . . in fact, I was thinking that with all the thinking we have to do, and how badly I slept last night . . . I'm always tired after a circuit, and this one was pretty brutal, so I thought it might be a good idea . . . only a little, I mean, not really very much at all . . ."

So Cade was feeling the same thing. Mieka made no reply, simply took the thorn-roll Cade handed him and began preparing the little glass thorns.

They worked steadily for a couple of hours. Derien clattered up the wrought-iron stairs to tell them Rafe and Jeska had arrived, and they spent another couple of hours down in the drawing room, batting ideas back and forth like a four-sided game of shuttlecock. By the time Mistress Mirdley brought in a belated lunching, many things had been agreed upon. The wagon ought to be rented out, but it was Yazz's decision whether or not to go with it. This notion of charging more for specific plays wouldn't wash. They would write to the Shadowshapers to get an idea of what performances fees ought to be. Rafe's suggestion of asking Romuald Needler, who managed the Shadowshapers and was moreover resident in Gallybanks and therefore could be contacted much more quickly, was turned down flat by Cade. It was his opinion that Needler would either name a figure so outrageously high that the Shadowshapers would be a bargain by comparison, or a figure so low that everyone would think that Touchstone would perform practically for free, so desperate were they for money.

"Well, aren't we?" Jeska asked, smiling his gratitude to Mistress Mirdley as she came into the drawing room with a tray of tall glasses and a huge pitcher of ice-cold lemonade.

Mieka shook his head. "Yeh, but we can't let on that we are. Cade, write to Vered and tell him you've found a book he'd be interested in—doesn't matter whether you have or not—is this your special recipe, Mistress Mirdley? With the pinch of juniper berries? Beholden! Anyways, Cade, you just have to remind him that he owes you for the books he's borrowed so far, then ask him all casual-like what the Shadowshapers make. He'll likely be more honest that way."

"Vered's not stupid," Cade said. "Wouldn't he try to do what Needler probably would?"

"They'd both assume," said Mistress Mirdley, "that you're to be setting yourselves independent, just as they have, and in direct competition with them. That's *not* a kick towards honesty, to my way of thinking. I have another idea."

"Say on," Rafe invited.

"You might send him a present—him or all of them. Matching scarves or suchlike."

Mieka heard Cayden suddenly catch his breath, and didn't understand the quick, swift, almost guilty glance in his direction.

Mistress Mirdley replaced the pitcher on the tray and turned to face Mieka. "Your wife and her mother could sew them."

"They could," Mieka agreed. "But—"

"It's what they could sew *into* them that matters."

"I don't understand," Mieka complained. "What are you talking about?"

"You really don't know?" Rafe asked, earning himself startled looks from the Trollwife and Cade. What did they know that Mieka didn't? And about his very own wife!

Cade said quickly, "Or we could just do the practical thing and ask the owners of the Keymarker and the Kiral Kellari and the Downstreet what they pay the Shadowshapers, and find out that way—yeh, that's what we ought to do."

Mieka knew a desperate diversion when he heard one. "Will somebody please explain what my wife and her mother have to do with—?"

"He really *doesn't* know," Rafe observed.

"Neither do I," said Jeska. "What are you talking about?"

At the same time, Mieka bellowed, "Know *what*?"

Now Cade looked truly guilty but also annoyed. Rafe looked mildly intrigued, as if the scene and its possible resolution were interesting, but really nothing to do with him at all. Mistress Mirdley looked the way Mistress Mirdley always looked: composed, skeptical, watching the follies of all these silly, ignorant people who could live to be a thousand and not have one-eighth the wisdom of the Trolls.

Cade opened his mouth to speak, and closed it again. And then, timed as if he'd written the script to get himself out of an awkwardness, Derien ran into the room, skidding to a stop that rumpled the carpet, and announced breathlessly, "Cade—Lord Fairwalk is here!"

"Excellent. Let's have him in."

"Why's he here?" Jeska demanded.

"Because I sent for him."

Cade wore his *I Can Be Snootier Than Any Highborn Ever Born* face. Mieka could just imagine the note that had summoned His Lordship. The demeanor Cade had inherited from his mother (and possibly his father; Mieka had never even met the man, so he couldn't know for sure), but the words were all his own. Knowing that he'd get no explanation about the scarves and his wife and her mother for quite some time, he pushed the matter aside and prepared a few choice phrases of his own. Pity Mistress Mirdley was still in the room; he'd have to mind his language.

Fairwalk swanned into the drawing room, fashionably dressed and smelling of lilacs. The smile dropped off his face like a withered leaf from a dying tree when he met Cade's eyes. But he put a brave front on it, seating himself in one of Lady Jaspiela's spindly chairs, and apparently not noticing that he was not offered a glass of cold lemonade.

"I'm so pleased that you asked me to come by today, Cayden, I have such excellent news! That wonderful new theater that's been so long in the planning is finally going to be built, don't you see, and you—that is to say, Touchstone—has been asked to contribute ideas."

"The Archduke's theater, you mean?"

"Yes—with the additional patronage of Princess Miriuzca!"

Fairwalk was beaming as if he had personally done something exceedingly clever. A quick glance round the room told Mieka that, like him, nobody else liked this development. Cade looked not only displeased, but disgusted, too. Mieka asked, "How'd she get mixed up in it?"

"Well, don't you see, she can't really say anything about it officially until after her brother leaves for home—his being so disapproving of theater and all—but the Archduke tells me that she's thrilled to be a part of it, and because you're all such friends and she shows you such favor, he says that your participation is crucial, and—" He broke off, bewildered that they weren't in ecstasies. "I thought you'd be pleased—flattered—"

In silken tones, Cade asked, "How much did he offer you to get us involved?"

"Offer me?"

"You know. Money. Coin. Our accounts are pretty much depleted, and you must be frantic for a new source of funding. Come on, Your Lordship, what price does His Grace put on us?"

Slowly, like soft foggy clouds melting from a mountain crag, the real face of Kearney Fairwalk was exposed. The civilized mask gone, the true nature of a Gnomish past glowered on his thick features. Mieka understood at last why long-ago kings had set Gnomes to guard Albeyn's borders. The frustling, chattering lordship had vanished, and in his place was something fierce and threatening.

"Say it, why don't you? Say that you believe I stole it all from you! Say it!"

"You *did* steal it."

"Money you never would have had if not for me! Who found you, shaped you, taught you, sponsored you? Showed you how to discern the best so that everyone knew you knew it, and never tried to foist third-rate on you ever again? Who hushed up the intolerable offenses of that stupid little Elf before they landed him in quod? Who kept your insufferable excuse for a father out of your way? Not to mention that Harpy who calls herself your mother! Who arranged the journey to the Continent so that the new Princess would look on you with favor above all other players?"

Cade stood up, drawing himself to his full six-foot-four, and glared down at him. "Who did all the work of writing and performing the plays?"

"Who gave you the confidence to *write* those plays? Who took care of the advertising, and the articles in the broadsheets? Do you think Tobalt Fluter and his ink-stained kind simply heard your name and queued up to interview you? Who created your reputation before you even knew a reputation was necessary? Who paid those first few audiences at the Downstreet to come see you—even after your success at Trials that year, why else would they come to see a group that barely even had a name?"

Mieka felt that one in his guts. He saw Jeska's fists clench and Rafe's expression freeze. Cayden had turned white to the lips. Everything else they could shrug away; this got them right where they lived.

Fairwalk was still raving. "Who saw to your bookings and your travel, your wagon, your lodging? Who made certain that you were always dressed in the first word of fashion? Who took care of your families while you were gone for months at a time?"

Cade had recovered by now. "Who stole from us and our families, and took most of my grandfather's legacy besides?"

"Do you think that ten out of a hundred is adequate compensation for everything I did for you?"

Jeska spoke for the first time since Fairwalk had entered the room. "I've been through the books. You left us the ten and took the rest of the hundred for yourself."

Rafe nodded slowly. "And now," he murmured with gentle menace, "we want it back."

The nobleman gestured this away, like casually swatting a fly. "You can't have it. It's gone."

"Fairwalk Manor still stands, doesn't it?"

He sucked in an outraged breath. "My ancestral home? Are you mad?"

"No. Just poor. I should think the horseflesh alone would bring a tidy sum. And there's all the decorations, rugs and furniture and all that. As near as I can figure it, you'll need a bed to sleep on and a pot to piss in," Rafe concluded, "and that's about it."

Fairwalk pushed himself to his feet. "I refuse to listen to any more of this. Whatever grievances you think you might have, you may address them to my lawyers. I can prove that every expenditure was in Touchstone's behalf, either as a group or individually, regarding your wives and children and parents and all the rest of your greedy tribes who came to me for money while you were traveling on the circuits, and were paid out in cash, and—"

"Gather your so-called evidence," Jeska said. "I know what we have to hand, which proves what you *didn't* pay for. Where did all that money get to?"

"As I said—expenses incurred in your behalf—"

"Get out of this house," Cade said quietly. "Get out on your own two legs before we throw you out."

"You wouldn't dare."

Cade smiled. "I believe the appropriate platitude in reply is 'Try me.' But I've always deplored formulaic writing. So my answer is this: Get out on your own two legs while you still *have* two legs."

Fairwalk was crimson by now, every stubby inch of him trembling with fury. "You," he grated, "all you damned superior Wizards—Elves—you think your magic and your heritage put you so high above the rest of us that the only direction you can possibly look is down! I know who your grandmother was, boy!" he shouted at Cade. "I know what she did! I know how many she killed! Oh, but not with her own delicate Wizardly hands, oh no! It was the rest of us, all of us lowly Gnomes and Goblins and simple unmagical Humans, we're the ones who did her killing for her! And as for *you*," he spat at Mistress Mirdley, "you *Troll,* knowing so much and living so long and keeping more secrets than even the Fae! You none of you have any idea how much the rest of us hate you—all of you! Money's the least of what you owe us!"

Rafe unfolded himself from his chair and stood beside Cayden. The two tall Wizards didn't bother to menace the Gnome with fists. They merely looked down at him. He turned on his heel and stalked out.

Rafe was the first to speak when Fairwalk had gone. "Well, that was fun. Cade, is there anything in this house stronger than lemonade?"

When the brandy bottle had made the rounds, Jeska sighed

back into his chair. "I went to see my little girl this morning," he said. "She's beautiful, and growing apace, and I'm thinking that we'll be working so hard for the next few years that the next time I see Airilie, she'll be in long skirts and giggling about boys."

Mieka was momentarily distracted by application of this thought to Jindra. He was unsure whether he was more amazed or appalled.

Cade had an odd expression on his face. Not the Elsewhen sort of look, but as if an idea had come to him from he knew not where. "Rafe," he said, turning to their fettler, "is your children's play done?"

"In basic form, yeh. It wants you lot to fill it in and plan the changes and things, but—"

"How soon could we get it ready?"

Rafe considered. "Mayhap a week. Less, if we really work at it."

"Then let's really work at it. Because if we're to be hired more often than anyone else, including the Shadowshapers, we have to have something that nobody else can give."

"Children," Rafe reminded him, "are notoriously short of spendable cash."

"But their parents aren't. An afternoon show—one adult ticket at a smaller price, accompanying two or three children at half-price—you can get more small bottoms onto a bench than grown-up asses—and then the adults come back at night for our regular show—theater owners will be filling the seats twice in one day, they'll love that—"

"And how exhausted will we be by the end of it?" Jeska asked.

"Not you," Mieka retorted. "All you need do is remember your lines. It's me and Rafe will be doing all the work, with the animals and noises and things. And who's going to bring little ones to a theater?"

"They'll queue up a mile long," Cade said with a shrewd smile, "if Princess Miriuzca does it first."

20

Leaving the specifics of their troubles with Lord Fairwalk to Cade and Jeska was both easy and justifiable. Mieka and Rafe had enough to do with planning out how the new play would go. For the first time in their experience, Cade was not involved in the writing or the staging. Once they were done, they'd tell him what was needed by way of magic, which he would prime into the withies, but in truth, the production rested almost entirely on Mieka and Rafe.

It felt weird, but it was working.

For one thing, they didn't have to contend with Cayden's griping and grimacing at every other thing anybody said. His voice yelling (often), *"No! Not like that, like* this*!"* and (less often but more forcefully), *"Are you fucking* kidding *me?"* were things they had become used to, especially this past year. It was odd not hearing them, but more than that, it was a relief. Both of them knew that once they presented the nearly finished product to their partners, Jeska would study the piece, make a suggestion or two, and learn his part—but Cade would have quite a bit to say. He always did. At least they weren't hearing it from the first run-through.

As for contacting Princess Miriuzca, they had several methods of approach. First was Cayden himself. He refused, and refused as well to let them use Lady Megueris Mindrising, who was one of the Princess's ladies-in-waiting. So they ended up going to Blye, who obliged them by making, in record time, two small round plaques, one for each of the Royal children, with real forget-me-nevers pressed between two panes of glass. Wooden frames were made by Jed, painted in thin concentric circles of all the Royal colors: blue and buff for Prince Ashgar, brown and sea green for the King and Queen, and blue and more brown for the Princess herself. Blye fretted for hours about the placement of the colors—a combination that didn't please her artistic eye in the first place—but because they had to have the pieces as soon as possible, she shrugged away her qualms and let her husband get on with it.

It was Jinsie who composed the note that went with them. In fact, the whole was quite the Windthistle production. Cilka and Petrinka supplied the flowers, and the bedding of ferns and moss cradling the plaques in their box, which was made by Jez with wood contributed by Hadden. Mishia found some very old and very beautiful embroidered ribbon to tie the box with. All that Mieka, Cade, Rafe, and Jeska had to do was sign the note and send it off to the North Keep, which Miriuzca had made her own. Away from the Palace with all its noise and traffic, with a garden and plenty of lawn for children to run about on, the North Keep was as close as she could get to a real country home. Ashgar had been promising that very thing for several years now, but it was said that he couldn't decide which of his father's many properties to ask for. Gossip had it that he'd simply wait until he inherited the lot and then let her choose for herself. Gossip also said that he resisted making a choice because the North Keep was only a half hour's ride from the Palace. He could present himself as both a good husband and father who visited almost every other day, and a conscientious prince who assisted his father in running the Kingdom. A country home, many hours or even days away from Gallantrybanks, would demand that he be one or the other place because at that distance he couldn't be at both. Staying with his family in the country would open him to criticism regarding his duties; staying at the Palace would incite charges of neglect. When Rafe remarked that the poor silly git couldn't win for losing, Cade pointed out that the Palace was also much more convenient for indulging in amusements that living all the time in the same place as his wife—city *or* country—would make impossible. He didn't look at Mieka as he said it.

Whatever, Mieka thought. The note was signed, the plaques were sent, and within a day there was a return note from Princess Miriuzca's own hand saying how delighted she was with the gift, and wouldn't they please do her the favor of taking lunching with her very soon? Cade's smile was one of deep satisfaction as he penned his reply, reading it to his partners as he wrote.

"'*Touchstone individually and collectively would be honored to attend upon Your Royal Highness at whatever time and place is desired. We have, in fact, an idea we would very much appreciate your opinion on—*' No," he said, taking a fresh piece of paper and recopying the first sentence. "That's not quite right. More like this. '*And we would very much appreciate Your Royal Highness's opinion of an idea we've been working on. With all gratitude, and as always beholden to Your Royal Highness—*'" He passed the page around for all of them to sign. "How's it coming along?" he asked as they scrawled their signatures. "Will we have something definite to tell her?"

"If she wants us there next week, we can show her the whole play," Rafe said, "if we bring along a withie or two. Though I'm thinking that the invitation included Blye and Jed as well, don't you?"

Mieka had the unworthy, if accurate, thought that his wife would be in tears of sheer frustration that Jindra's illness kept her from claiming a seat at the Princess's lunching table. The child was on the mend, but not yet well enough to do without her mother's care. He had hired a messenger—finances be damned—to deliver the stuffed animal he'd bought for Jindra in . . . well, wherever he'd bought it; he wasn't terribly clear on a lot of where he'd been the past month or two. Or, rather, he knew where he'd been, but wasn't entirely sure when he'd been there. At any rate, he had included a note to his wife, saying he missed her, would see her soon, and please don't let the fuzzy brown velvet doggie anywhere near the pet fox. Something regrettable had happened last winter to a stuffed toy Cade gave Jindra, and she'd been inconsolable for days.

They were all at Wistly on the afternoon the Princess's note arrived, taking tea out on the river lawn before resuming rehearsal, when Cade brought up a new idea. It had to do with making money, of course.

"You're wanting to do a picture book to go along with this play, right?" he asked Rafe, who nodded. "Are the drawings done? Have you talked to a publisher?"

"No to the drawings. I thought it'd be best to wait until we know what we'll be doing onstage, and then get some artwork done to match it. As for publishers—just Tobalt. He's the only person I know who knows anything about printing and suchlike."

"What do you think he'd say to publishing pamphlets? Our own original plays in script form. None of our notes on performance or anything," he went on hastily when Mieka scowled, "so we wouldn't be giving away any secrets. The idea is that if people can't go to see a play, at least they can read one."

"We couldn't use 'Dragon' or 'Treasure,' could we?" Jeska asked. "Our versions are very different from the traditional scripts, but the stories themselves aren't ours to make money from, if you see what I mean."

"Hadn't thought about that," Cade admitted. "But until we can figure it out, we can publish our original stuff."

"Which is to say *your* original stuff," Rafe observed. "You wrote the things. The bulk of the money would go to you."

Mieka was, quite simply, gobsmacked by Cade's reply.

"The plays are by *Touchstone*."

"Well, yes," Rafe said. "But—"

Cade interrupted him. "How many days have we spent just like today, thrashing things out, making changes and working in new ideas? Ideas that *you* three have. Look at 'Doorways'—every time we do it, it's different. Glisker's choice." He winked at them over his teacup. "There's times when I stand there knocked all agroof because I actually heard one of my original lines!"

"But 'Doorways' is mostly visual," Jeska argued. "Unless we made it into a picture book as well, it wouldn't make any sense."

Mieka paid little attention as they ran through Touchstone's folio of original plays, trying to find two or three that wouldn't need illustrations. He was still wrapping his brain around the fact that possessive, snobbishly intellectual, controlling, arrogant, my-work-is-Art Cayden Silversun had actually said that authorship of Touchstone's plays belonged to all four members of Touchstone.

He thought perhaps this might have something to do with what Fairwalk had said a few days ago. The staggering revelation that their first audiences had been paid to go see them still burned in his gut like a bellyful of stinging nettles. He suspected it always would. Not that anybody had to be paid nowadays; Touchstone was hailed as second only to the Shadowshapers in creativity and skill. And maybe that had something to do with sharing the credit as well, he mused—they were *second* place, no matter that they'd been First Flight on the Royal this year. They'd earned the position, he knew they had, but they'd got it only by default.

Mieka studied Cade's face as the conversation went on around him. It wasn't just that he'd voluntarily divided authorship with his partners, it was also that he had tacitly acknowledged that their contributions made his work better. Cade wrote for Jeska's prodigious abilities; he wrote for Mieka's distinctive style of glisking; he wrote for Rafe's steady, unfaltering control of magic. Cade's words were brilliant (well, with that one mortifying exception, Mieka reminded himself, wondering if Cade would ever go back and tweak "Turn Aback" for performance and rather hoping he would not). Would those plays be as good if someone else performed them? If his glisker or masquer or fettler were different people? Cade had admitted without actually saying it that as fine as his work was, Mieka and Jeska and Rafe made it superlative. Touchstone was greater than the sum of its parts—it was a thing worth being part of.

Mieka felt pleased that Cayden had finally remembered that. All that time spent denying and rejecting his Elsewhens had separated him not only from that crucial portion of his magic but from his partners as well. Nobody had noticed, not because nobody cared, but because they'd been doing quite well (except for "Turn Aback") and couldn't be bothered to be better. Now that imperative had awakened again. Fairwalk's horrid words, and getting First Flight only because the Shadowshapers removed themselves from the scene, had kicked all of them into that need to make the work the best it could possibly be.

Well, those things, plus another overwhelming need: money.

Last night they'd played the Keymarker to huge applause. Tomorrow night they'd be at the Kiral Kellari. And there was a brand-new theater—a real one, with rows of seats instead of tables and chairs, and the bar in the entrance hall—opening soon south of the Plume. Added to whatever private performances they (or, more properly, Jinsie) could schedule, there were venues enough to keep them busy all winter. They would need everything in their folio, including several of their least-loathed Thirteen, to keep people coming back for more. This new play for children, though, that would ignite chavishing from here to Scatterseed, and that would be a very good thing—

"Mieka? You haven't said what you think."

He shook himself free of his ponderings and looked at Rafe. "Whatever you like."

"I thought Cayden was the only one who went all blank-eyed and otherwhere," said Jinsie, and Mieka was stunned to find her seated just beside him on the grass.

"Elsewhen," he corrected. "And why should he be the only one to Think Great Thoughts?"

His voice supplied the capital letters. Jinsie elbowed him a good one. "Fool! Do you have a clean shirt to go to lunching in?"

"Someplace or other. What did we decide about the pamphlets?"

"Not much. We're all just sitting about, waiting for Jez." Cade picked up the last of the fruitcake. "New recipe, Rafe?"

"Chopped plums. Huge crop this year, so they're cheap. What's Jez got to do with anything?"

"He went to see Black Lightning last night with his new girlfriend." Jinsie glanced towards the house and waved. "And here, in happy hour, he is."

"His limp isn't bad at all," Mieka observed gratefully.

"Oh, it's always worse when Ardyssian is around."

"The better for leaning on her?" Cade asked. "Or to turn her all sympathetic and solicitous?"

"Well, you can't expect somebody his size to conjure up the mothering instinct without some help," Jinsie observed. "She doesn't coo over him, I'll give her that. In fact, I like her quite a lot."

Jezael greeted everyone, complained over the total lack of anything to eat or drink, and sat down on the grass. Mieka offered him his own plate—naught but crumbs—and Jez playfully threatened him with his cane.

"I hear you've been—well, not consorting with the enemy," Cade said, "but going to see them perform."

"And a good thing, too." He stretched out his bad leg and placed the cane beside his knee. "Their new piece is a rework of something called 'Winglets.' Ever heard of it?"

"It's pretty old," said Cade. "Nobody's done it in a long while, but I remember reading about it in *Lost Withies*. One day a couple's new baby is seen to have sprouted wings. They're astonished—can't figure out what happened, because they can account for the Elfen ears but not for wings. Husband suspects wife of indecent colluding with a Fae."

Jez nodded. "Turns out the Fae baby was substituted for the couple's own child, only the Fae forgot to do something about the wings. And the Human baby turns out to be a real screamer, which annoys the Fae so much that he gets stashed in the hayloft and abandoned. The couple raises both children, emphasis on the Fae child who in spite of his wings can't fly until he comes into his magic."

"The wings are just for show," Cade said. "It's magic that lets the Fae soar about as they please."

"Remember the wings on that one we met, Cade?" Mieka asked. "All leafy-like, not enough heft in them to lift a daisy off the ground."

Cade snorted a laugh that told Mieka he remembered becoming a Knight of the Most Noble Elfen Order of the Daisy.

Jinsie looked from one to the other of them, frowning. "You're serious? You met a Fae?"

"Long story," Mieka assured her. "Tell you some other time."

"Yes," she said emphatically. "You will."

Cade grinned. "Better you than me! Anyway, as for 'Winglets'—the lesson is that sometimes you have to wait to do the things you're meant to do until you've the wherewithal to do them. One version adds the idea that everybody has wings of some kind, and you just have to figure out exactly how you were meant to fly. A bit sicky-sweet in the wrong hands, but I'd imagine there would be some interesting visuals."

"'Twasn't the visuals last night," Jez said grimly. "'Twas the words. Right at the beginning—and believe it or not, it got worse and worse all the way through—when the husband is told that his son now has wings, he plays out the bewilderment and says, 'Wings? Whatever shall we do with a baby that has *wings*?' " He drew in a long breath. "And someone in the audience yells out, 'It's Fae-born! Kill it!' "

The shocked silence was eventually broken by Mieka, who indeed had some trouble kicking his brain back into action. But it was his job to lighten dark moods, ease tense situations, and go as far as he had to for a laugh. So he said, "It's a right shame, it is, that Princess Miriuzca's brother wasn't there. Sounds like the sort of thing that would suit him down to the ground." He waited a moment, then sat up straight as if something horrible had just occurred to him—which, in a way, it had. "Good Gods—you don't think he'll be at lunching again, do you?"

He wasn't, though not for lack of his sister's invitation.

"He went to the horse fair today," she explained when Rafe made a polite inquiry about her brother's health in this wretched summer heat. "He'll be taking back a dozen yearlings for the stables at home." She fanned herself with what looked like a huge clamshell made out of painted sticks and lace. "How he can rush about in this weather, I truly do not know. I have been hoping this part of the garden would be cooler, but the shade is making very little difference, don't you think? And the cook wanted to be serving hot soup! Anyway, if my brother had been here, we would have been fourteen at table, rather than lucky thirteen."

These thirteen—the four members of Touchstone, Derien, Crisiant, Kazie, Blye, Jedris, Jinsie, Jezael, the Princess, and Lady

Megs—were seated at a large, square table in a garden retreat walled on three sides by blue-flowering hedges. The fourth side was a long expanse of grass to the river. The table was just the right size for everyone to join in the same conversation without raising their voices or straining to hear. Lunching consisted of cold meats and cheeses, chopped vegetable salad, iced drinks, flatbread, and bowls of berries dusted with mocah powder. A very casual meal, and very casual talk round the table—but Miriuzca was chattering away as if she'd just pricked bluethorn mixed with whitethorn and a little something else on the side. Ridiculous to think she would ever do such a thing, but Mieka was at a loss to understand her somewhat fevered vivaciousness.

It was a relief not to have to carry the conversation all by himself. In fact, it hadn't been necessary for him to say much at all. That left him free to observe Cayden and Megs, who were deeply engrossed in not looking at each other. Mieka found this infinitely entertaining, but he knew better than to tease Cade about it in front of the others. Truth be told, he also had a healthy respect for Lady Megs's equally sharp tongue. And besides all that, Jinsie was here, and any breach of manners would be reported to their mother. One would think, he mused as he speared another bite of carrot with a golden fork, that Mishia Windthistle would have given over scolding him—or simply given up—by now. He was almost twenty-three, and she had four children much younger than he to lesson as she saw fit. He had a moment of shock when he realized that Cilka and Petrinka were fourteen and Tavier and Jorie were nearly seven. How had the time gone by so fast? This Wintering, his own Jindra would be four years old. Astounding.

"Mieka!"

His twin sister's voice shook him out of his thoughts. Jinsie had turned to the Princess, saying, "He's taken to doing that. Must be premature old age setting in." Then, to Mieka once more: "Her Royal Highness had the kindness to ask about your wife and daughter. Are you back from wherever it was you went, or should I be a good elder sister and make a reply for you?"

"Elder?" He made a face at her. "By a scant half minute, and only because I kicked you out first so I could finally have some room! How was I to know the birthing-wife would yank me out by the ears just as I got comfortable?"

Jedris shook his head at the foolery of his younger siblings and told the laughing Princess, "Not a word of it true, of course. What really happened was that our poor long-suffering mother called in the birthing-wife and told her that she absolutely refused to be burdened with those two for one more day. Little did she know they'd be even more trouble to her once they were born!" When Mieka and Jinsie both began to complain, he said, "Hush up. I was there."

"And so was I," Jez put in. "And you weren't. Hush up."

Mieka and Jinsie traded glances, and Jinsie said to the Princess, "We wouldn't accord them half so much deference, being our oldest brothers, if they weren't so uncouthly tall."

"Your house must have been lively!" Miriuzca looked as if she would ask more about growing up at Wistly Hall, but something or someone coming into the garden caught her attention. Her soft mouth thinned for an instant before she stretched her lips into a smile; she couldn't hide the mingled worry and annoyance in her blue eyes.

Mieka looked round. Tregrefin Ilesko and, of all people, Archduchess Panshilara were approaching the lunching table.

"Oh, splendid," Cade muttered so quietly that only Mieka and Blye, seated on either side of him, heard.

All the men got to their feet and bowed to the Archduchess. Servants leaped forward to offer chairs. It was difficult to tell which it gave her more pleasure to ignore—the men of the working class or the men of the servant class—in favor of greeting Miriuzca almost as a sister, with a clasping of hands that she continued even when the Princess began to pull away. Mieka smirked inwardly, wondering if she would officially notice that none of the women had stood in her presence, just exactly as if they were all *ladies*.

"So lovely to see you enjoying yourself, and with all these nice people, also," said Panshilara. "I was seeing and speaking with a Good Brother and on my way back home when I saw His Highness the Tregrefin in a carriage riding to the North Keep here, and now I shall not be interrupting you, because he has a book to show me from our own land, that I am thinking to give to Her Royal Highness the Princess Iamina."

"How kind," Miriuzca murmured.

"There is much talk all over the city," the Archduchess went on, still gripping Miriuzca's hands in her own bony fingers, "about the celebratings, and I know everyone would be glad to know that Your Royal Highness is taking some time for yourself, and for pleasure, also, considering all your duties."

"Just a few friends who've come to join me at lunching," said the Princess, and if there was a gentle emphasis on *friends,* Panshilara didn't hear it—or chose not to.

"Her Grace and I," said the Tregrefin, "have been discussing the sad plight of unbelievers."

"A thing that is concerning Princess Iamina, also," added the Archduchess.

Mieka stared resolutely down at his hands. He ought to have guessed that this self-righteous little ferret would get on with the newly pious Iamina. Add Panshilara, who was from the same country as Ilesko, and married to the highest-ranking nobleman in Albeyn, and one had a charming threesome indeed.

Panshilara was still talking. Mieka wondered how the Archduke ever shut her up, or if he even bothered trying to untangle her sentences that never actually worked themselves into sentences. One thing was for certes: She was rude. All the men were on their feet, unable to sit down again because Panshilara was still standing.

"What has emboldened so many disbelievers and unbelievers is that with the doubling of the cost of everything in the last years and months, putting the celebratings on a path towards so much debt, then Chapel, High Chapel and Low Chapel and all, where so much good is done and lifting spirits towards the Lord and the Lady also, which is the fundamental transformation of Albeyn."

Mieka looked round the table. Everyone wore expressions of polite interest, though a corner of Derien's mouth was twitching towards distaste. Jed and Jez were trying to hide bewilderment; Crisiant suddenly seemed to find her empty plate fascinating. It was perfectly clear that no one had understood a word this woman had said, and frankly didn't care to make the effort.

Cayden had not only not understood, he hadn't even heard. He swayed slightly, and when Mieka looked up at him, he saw that the cloud-gray eyes had gone out of focus. He was in the middle of an Elsewhen. Somehow his knees had locked, and this kept him upright, but there was no conscious mind to steady him. Mieka got his arm around Cade's back and hoped he didn't unbalance them both right onto the grass.

Rafe, directly across from them, had seen it, too, and looked at Mieka with a worried frown. Everyone else was still attending courteously to the Princess, who was murmuring well-bred nothings. Her brother said something in their language, and just as he finished and Miriuzca frowned, Cade gave a start. He was back.

Mieka sent heartfelt praises to whichever deity was watching over them.

A moment later, he was cursing whichever of them had seen fit to abandon them. For Cade spoke, interrupting the Archduchess.

"Don't," he rasped. "Don't do it."

Anger, surprise, confusion—and abrupt frightened comprehension on the faces of those who had seen Cayden return from an Elsewhen before. Rafe opened his mouth to speak, but no words came out. Mieka found himself equally at a loss. It was Jeska, the masquer, who improvised at will, who smiled and wagged an admonishing finger at Derien.

"You heard your brother. Don't steal all the cakes before the rest of us have had a chance at them!" He turned to the Princess. "We most humbly beg Your Royal Highness's pardon. I daresay you'll find out in a few years that boys of Derien's age grow an inch between one dinner and the next, and eat like starving dragons in between!"

"And your pardon, again, Your Royal Highness," said Crisiant, "for we have not yet asked about the Prince and Princess. They are well and strong, yes?"

"Oh, very. And I understand about boys and food," she told Derien kindly. "It isn't so long since this one was eating our father out of house and home!" She freed one of her hands—Panshilara had held on to her this whole time, Mieka noted with amazement—and tapped her brother's nose. He looked as if he would have slapped her hand away if there hadn't been people around. "Ilesko, on your way to see Her Grace to her carriage, could you have them send out another plate of cakes, and more berries? Oh, just more of everything! Beholden. So nice to have seen you today, Your Grace. Please, gentlemen, do sit down, and we'll continue our lunching after we've been resupplied by the kitchens."

The Tregrefin escorted the Archduchess none too gracefully from the garden. The men sat back down—Cayden almost collapsing into his chair—and Crisiant engaged the Princess in chat about little boys. Derien had learned a lot at the King's College, Mieka reflected; he had every right to be miffed at being singled out as the excuse for Cade's words, but the only emotion in his eyes was worry when he looked at his brother.

At last Jed spoke up, saying, "Please forgive me, Princess, but . . . what was the Archduchess talking about?"

Miriuzca laughed rather ruefully. Mieka glanced from her to Megs, who was staring at Cade, not even trying to hide her confusion.

"It's been suggested," Miriuzca said, "that the Good Brothers and Good Sisters hold special services all over Albeyn on the appointed day, High Chapel and Low, so that everyone can have a chance to celebrate King Meredan's rule. But they are wanting to be paid for this. Oh, your pardon—not *paid for* but *donated to*."

Blye snorted inelegantly at the cynical correction and tapped a burn-scarred finger on the table. "They balk at showing their loyalty, and at giving everyone else the chance to do the same?"

Miriuzca waited to reply until the servants had placed more platters and bowls on the table and departed. "They say it's the cost of refreshments—cakes and ale only—they're wanting. I believe that it's the opinion of His Majesty that—how did he put it? Oh yes. 'They can bloody well cough up.' " Laughter danced in her eyes.

"His Majesty is bloody well right," Mieka said. "But let's go back to talking about children, because that's what we came here to tell you." He stuck his fork into a succession of berries—red, black, blue, and yellow. "Well, that and the food, of course." He grinned across the table at her, and she grinned back.

Crisiant rose to her feet. "I think we'll leave you to it, if Your Royal Highness doesn't mind. I hear quite enough about Touchstone as it is, and I've a hankering to see the gardens. Mayhap you'll be our guide, Lady Megueris?" She curtsied, collected everyone else with her gaze, and they set off across the lawn to the river, leaving Mieka, Rafe, Cade, and Jeska to beguile the Princess with their plans.

A scant hour later, she was suitably beguiled and they were in hire-hacks returning home. Mieka rode with Cade and Derien, and was impressed when the boy didn't instantly demand to know why he'd been singled out as a conversational distraction. He really was learning how to be a courtier, Mieka thought. But he'd compliment him later. Right now he had something he wanted to say to Cayden.

"So," he said, leaning back, arms folded. "Lady Megs. She looked rather well, didn't she?"

"Did she? I didn't notice."

"Nice try, Quill! I was watching you both. She watched you not watch her, while at the same time you watched her not watching you, which means you were both watching each other pretend *not* to watch each other. I'm sure it was exhausting, all that effort spent keeping watch on not watching—"

"Enough!" Cade exclaimed.

Derien eyed his crimson-faced brother, then looked at Mieka. "You really will have to teach me how to do that."

Before Mieka could reply, Cade pointed a finger at him. "Don't even consider it."

"You never let me have any fun."

They were at Redpebble Square, and Dery had jumped out to go tell Mistress Mirdley all about the afternoon, when Mieka stopped Cade in the middle of stepping out of the hack.

"You'll tell me about that Elsewhen?" he asked softly.

Cade hesitated, then nodded. "Tomorrow at rehearsal."

Satisfied, Mieka watched him go, then settled back to think during the drive over to Waterknot Street. He didn't get much work done on his thoughts, though. The bluethorn of late this morning had worn off, and all he really wanted was some privacy and his thorn-roll, replenished by Master Bellgloss—complete with glass thorns—until Auntie Brishen could send him his usual.

21

Each night since the abrupt departure of Lord Kearney Fairwalk from Number Eight, Redpebble Square, Cayden had gone upstairs to his room, opened his thorn-roll and stared at it.

There was a certain gloomy fascination in knowing which little twists of paper contained thorn that brought lunatic energy, or painted ordinary objects with bizarre and throbbing colors, or stimulated dreaming, or tossed his thoughts into a steep spiral like a water-whirl in a draining sink, ending in a mind emptied of all but sleep. The precise meanings of the various markings were a mystery to him, but Brishen Staindrop had been supplying him for so long that she knew what worked on him and how—and that very little worked on him the way it did other people. He knew that blue plus green was one thing, and yellow was another, and three purple lines with a white dot was something else, and blockweed—his first foray into thorn and still his favorite, for its dreamless sleep—was in the paper twists with blue edges. It was rather like the colors of their withies, he mused, and as familiar to him by now. Perhaps Brishen had other codes for other people, the way each group coded its withies; he knew only what she sent to him, and only she knew what it was.

Mieka's request for thorn hadn't surprised him. He knew

how much he'd been using, and Mieka's consumption was at least half again as much as his. The difference was that Cade was capable of rationing himself and Mieka was not.

Cade had also remembered, on the way to Frimham, to send a letter to Brishen so that more thorn would be waiting for him in Gallybanks. The package had been sent to his flat, of course. He didn't want to think too much about Mistress Mirdley's reaction when she found it. The fleeting hope that she hadn't known what it was died almost before he hoped it. Mistress Mirdley knew everything.

Yet it had been waiting for him, unopened, in his fifth-floor room at Redpebble Square, ready to be used, and to be shared with Mieka.

Neither did he think too much about what Mieka would be like if completely deprived of thorn.

Now, tonight, after dining with his brother and Mistress Mirdley in the kitchen—Lady Jaspiela had been invited to the Palace, of all places, to dine with her husband, of all people—and helping Derien tell most but not all of what had happened at the North Keep that day, he joined the Trollwife in chivvying Dery up to his room. He would return to the King's College in two days, the fees having been found (with Mieka's help), and there were books waiting to be read so that he could catch the other students up without too much difficulty. When Dery was gone, grumbling, Cade relaxed into the deeply padded chair by the empty hearth with a cup of hot tea. Mistress Mirdley bustled about, cleaning up after the meal, wrapping extra food, saying nothing.

Cade pulled out today's Elsewhen for examination.

{ If they hadn't been outside, strolling through the gardens, they would have died.

He knew this at the very instant the Keep behind him shattered and the sound of it deafened him and the shock of it knocked him down onto the grass. Dust clotted in his lungs, stung his eyes and throat. He could hear nothing but what seemed an endlessly repeating echo of the explosion, timed to his rapid heartbeats. Pushing himself upright, he turned to where the Princess had been. It was difficult to see through the billows of dust, but the butter-yellow of her gown was a bright splash on the green lawn. She sprawled with her baby daughter beside her.

He groped his way towards them, knelt, touched her shoulder. Shook her. She flinched, coughed, raked her hands back through her straggling hair. He pulled the baby free of her mother's arms and lifted her up. Levenie was screaming lustily, but Cayden couldn't hear it.

Sense had come back into Miriuzca's eyes, and she reached for her daughter. Her blond hair straggled about her forehead and neck, and there was a slice on her cheek that bled freely down to her lacy white collar. But she was alive and otherwise unhurt, and with her child clasped to her shoulder, she looked up at Cayden, then at the North Keep. Shock drained from her face. Fury replaced it. He spared a moment's admiration that she didn't succumb to panic, that her immediate reaction was rage that anyone could have done this horrible thing. He wondered how he would ever be able to tell her it had been her own brother.

He hauled her to her feet and pointed to the river. He didn't bother to shout. He knew she wouldn't hear him. His own ears buzzed and hummed as if his head were filled with a million swarming insects, a million times worse than the brief deafness outside Prickspur's inn. And just as had happened then, just as he'd feared, there was smoke in the air now as well as dust. The fire would be contained inside the Keep for a time, until windows burst with the heat. The safest place he could think of was out on the water. So he pushed her towards the river, where the dozens of boats always sailing past would come in and take her and the baby away, safe— unless they were terrified of having the North Keep collapse into the Gally River, the way Mieka's little turret had done at Wistly Hall. No; this was their adored Princess; they would do anything to save her. She paused just long enough to say her son's name—he understood it by the movements of her lips— and he nodded, and she ran with her daughter in her arms.

Cade squinted frantically through the clouds of dust and smoke, stumbling to the place they'd left Megs. She had held back with little Prince Roshlin as they climbed the half-dozen tall steps from the lower garden to the upper. The boy had been frustrated by the stiffly embroidered blue silk longvest he wore, and Cade couldn't blame him. The thing was beautiful, but it came to his toes and he kicked at it, furious when the adults smiled at him. So as Cade and Miriuzca went ahead with Levenie, Megs paused halfway up the steps to help Roshlin out of his longvest, kneeling to undo the score of buttons.

Cade's ears were still throbbing and his vision was smeared. He coughed, wiped his eyes, and finally saw a scrap of blue silk trailing out from beneath a hunched and huddled green gown.

He ran towards her, fearing that Roshlin had been not just protected but smothered. But somehow Megs had managed not to fall atop the child. She looked as if she'd been knocked forwards and then toppled to one side, her back curved over the little boy, trying to protect him. Cayden clawed the swathing green gown aside and picked Roshlin up, and as he did so, Megs slid into a limp heap. Shards of glass, some thick and some needle fine, protruded from her back and her neck. She was dead. He paused a terrible moment, touching her cheek. What he didn't notice until he stood up

with Roshlin in his arms was the blood on the boy's forehead where he'd hit the hard stone step. }

It took him several minutes to recover from seeing it again. He didn't understand why knowing what he would see had made it even worse. Calming himself, he put this Elsewhen together with that other one, the one in which Tregrefin Ilesko had decided on black powder rather than magic. Scant wonder that on recovering from his turn in the garden of the same Keep, he'd said, *"Don't. Don't do it."*

"And so," Mistress Mirdley said, and he looked up. "What was it this time?"

He waited until she had refilled his teacup and settled in the opposite chair with a cup of her own. Then, slowly, finding the words with difficulty, he began.

"I've never seen anything like this before. There were things almost as bad—like when I saw what would happen—what *did* happen—to Briuly and Alaen that Midsummer Day. Things that might happen to Mieka if—" He broke off, shaking his head. "Not that I really remember them anymore. I got rid of them all. I unremembered them. And I refused to see anything more."

She didn't bother to ask why he'd refused the Elsewhens, or why he'd accepted them again. "But you saw this."

"Mieka . . . persuaded me. It wasn't just that I might've seen what happened at the Gallery, how Jez was injured. I'm not sure I would have seen. What could I have done to change it?"

"Any number of things. That's not the issue here, though, is it? You say Mieka persuaded you."

"Yeh. What convinced me . . . he said that without the Elsewhens, I'm not completely myself. And he's right. It'd be the same if I decided I wasn't going to write anything ever again, not even inside my own head. It wouldn't be me walking around, it'd be—just portions of me, nothing that could become what

I'm supposed to become because parts of me would be missing. Like in that reworked play at Seekhaven—oh, I forgot you didn't know about that."

"I know about it. Whose idea was it, to have the man's soul be worthless because it had never grown up?"

"I don't remember." He smiled briefly. "You'd think I would, but I don't. I guess it just seemed the right way to end it. It could've been my idea—telling myself something, like Mieka said. But I honestly can't recall if it was me, or Vered, or Rauel, or Mirko, or maybe one of the others. It doesn't really matter. Because Mieka was right." He paused. "That damned crazy little Elf was *right*."

"How inconvenient of him."

"He said I can't cripple myself. So I started seeing the Elsewhens again. But none of them was ever like this. It's always been small things—not great doings or an event that would affect Albeyn. I'd see people I knew, or people I'd soon meet—I saw Kearney Fairwalk a time or two, did I ever tell you? I didn't know who he was, but I saw him. Not as a warning, nothing awful at all. The strange thing is, I never saw Mieka, not until after he showed up that night in Gowerion."

"His choice, to seek you out."

"And I had nothing to do with it. It wasn't up to me. But this is. I saw it, and when I came back, I said, 'Don't do it,' and Jeska covered for me. But he and Rafe and Mieka and Blye—and Jinsie, too, maybe—she knows that it happens. I'm not sure she recognizes when it does. But that doesn't matter. They knew. I haven't told them yet. Mieka's coming by tomorrow morning, and I have to tell him. But I don't know what I can do about it."

"You haven't yet said what you saw."

He blinked in confusion. "Didn't I? Oh. I was at the North Keep, in the gardens with the Princess and her children and—and Lady Megs. There was an explosion. I pushed Miriuzca and the baby down towards the river. It took a little while to find Megs and Prince Roshlin, when I did . . . Megs was dead. I picked up the Prince and I'm not sure but that he might have been dead, too." He remembered the stark staring deadness of those lovely green eyes, and the sharp straight line of her nose, and—

"And now—" The Trollwife's interruption of his thoughts was more welcome than he could ever have told her. "—you know who's responsible."

"Miriuzca's brother. I saw him—in an Elsewhen, I mean—with a couple of Nominatives. They were helping him, and they'd messed up using magic to explode the new Gallery—I know I'm not being very clear about any of it, but—"

"I'm understanding enough. I'm surprised he'd use magic for anything."

"It was supposed to show how dangerous magic can be. But for the North Keep, he wanted to be absolutely sure, so he decided to use black powder. And he did—I mean, he will, unless I stop him." He shook his head. "His own sister! And her children! And all those people—they're all going to die unless I *do* something." He met her calm, quiet gaze. "But what? How do I prevent it?"

"You're thinking that you haven't the power to stop him."

"I don't."

"You know people who do."

"Not Miriuzca. She'd never believe it. He's her brother, and she loves him."

"Who else?"

"My father? That's a laugh. And not Mother."

"Nor Fairwalk."

That road was forever closed—and it wasn't as if the man had much real influence at Court, anyway. "It has to be somebody who knows about the Elsewhens, and that they're true visions of what might happen."

And the one person who knew, and was powerful . . .

"No," he blurted. "I can't. Not him."

The Trollwife frowned slightly, and he remembered that she couldn't know what he was talking about. So he explained how Mieka, very drunk, had let it slip to his wife about Cade's foreseeings, and how the girl had told her mother, and her mother had told the Archduke.

"For the longest time I convinced myself that he didn't believe her. It's a bit much, isn't it? The notion that somebody can see what might happen in the future. And then I thought, even if he does believe, and wants me to see the Elsewhens for him, if I didn't see them anymore, then there'd be nothing about me that he could use. And that's why I crippled myself, I think. One reason, anyways. It just—it hurts so *much* sometimes, I can't describe how much it hurts."

She was silent for a time. The tea grew cold in the cups, and the clock in Lady Jaspiela's drawing room chimed midnight. At last she spoke again. "You could let it happen."

Cade recoiled in his chair. "No—*no!*"

"You say you saw yourself save the Princess and possibly both her children. That's worth whatever you care to name from a grateful King Meredan. Title, land, income—"

He could see nothing but the dead eyes of Lady Megueris. "Gods, no!"

"Whereas if you tell the Archduke, it would put *him* by way of being the hero. He'd never let you take credit for stopping this—not unless he was prepared either to make up a convoluted story about overhearing things you couldn't possibly have overheard—"

"—or telling what he knows about the Elsewhens," he finished for her. "And he'd never do that. It's a secret he wants to keep to himself, for reasons of his own that we can't yet understand."

"I don't doubt that one day we will. But not yet."

"If I tell him, he'll believe it. You're right, he'd take the credit, and that would make him beholden to me."

"A thing you might need at some point."

"Just in case."

"Just in case," she agreed stolidly.

"So tomorrow I'm off to Great Welkin? Yes, I suppose I am."

"Shall I wake you early, so you can avoid the Elf?"

"Early? Mieka?" He snorted a laugh. "Don't bother. But I ought to get out there as soon as I can."

"You might make it in time for the Archduchess's daily devotions."

"With Princess Iamina attending? She certainly made a show of herself that day at the Gallery."

Mistress Mirdley shrugged her uneven shoulders. "There's a fashion in piety these days."

"Not much fashion, if Iamina is the standard. I've seen her in her gray robes."

"And not much piety, either, unless bruised knees and eyestrain are indicators. Falling onto one's knees in Chapel," she explained, "and reading broadsheets printed in type so small that a fly landing on the page blocks out half a paragraph." She sloshed the teapot, scowled to find it empty, and asked, "Did you want more? Or a tot of something other than blockweed to send you to sleep?"

He felt his cheeks burn with shame. "You don't know what it's like out there on the circuit. The night we get used to the hammocks swaying, that next night we're sleeping at an inn. Or trying to sleep. As for priming the withies and performing—"

"I'm not judging you, boy. You'll all four of you do what you feel you must, and it's a good thing all four of you have somebody to piece you back together again."

"We take care of each other, out on the road," he mused, then amended, "mostly, anyways," thinking of the shouting and the arguments and the practical jokes and the days one or another of them wasn't speaking to anyone else. And he also remembered not being able to breathe, and what Mieka had done—had that insane little Elf really saved his life? He probably had. And what had Cade said to express gratitude? *"Now you know how it feels."*

Gods. What was wrong with him?

Aware that Mistress Mirdley was watching him with a frown, he said, "But I think the hardest thing isn't not getting enough sleep, or working up the energy for a show when it's the fifth in as many days. We love what we do. That's not in question. I'd never want to do anything else. But the hours afterwards, with the applause still ringing in your ears . . . and maybe you're staying another night and maybe you have to get back to the wagon because you're due someplace else in a couple of days, but either way you can't *settle*. You've just been out in front of hundreds and hundreds of people, and now it's just the four of you, and you can sit and stare at each other, or try to get some sleep, or go down to the taproom and drink half the night—and there's the other thing, the drinks keep coming, because there's always somebody there who'll stand a round for the famous players. Sometimes," he finished, embarrassed that he'd rattled on so long, "it's a wonder any of us can stand up, leave alone walk."

She was thoughtfully silent for a time. "Tell me more about being onstage."

"Haven't I ever said?" He smiled. "And all those nights I came back here after a show at the Downstreet or the Keymarker! Surely you noticed!"

"What I noticed was that you came home later and later, and sometimes not at all, once the girls started clustering round the Artists Entry," she said dryly. "And now that girls are actually allowed into theaters—tell me, O Great Tregetour, do you spend part of the time you're onstage picking out which little birdie in the audience will be making cow-eyes at you in private later on?"

"A bird making eyes like a cow." He shook his head sadly, to tease her. "Mistress Mirdley, you would never make a writer."

"Did you understand what I meant? All right, then. I noticed in your recital of things to do after a play, you didn't mention the girls. Oh, I'm not criticizing that, either—though I can only hope you have more discretion and care than that silly little Elf, and don't risk bringing home anything I'd have to cure you of."

"Mieka is quite the lad," he admitted.

"I expect his wife wants more children. That's the only reason I can think of for not gelding him with a rusty pair of garden shears." She paused, then said, "You've been gone all summer. This fashionable piety I spoke of—there are those within Chapel who encourage it, and not just amongst the nobility."

"Though it's the nobility who have money to contribute to Chapel," he put in.

"Don't state the obvious. Along comes the Princess's brother, reminding her of the religion she came from, finding common cause with Iamina and the Archduchess—who also comes from their part of the Continent, married to a descendant of that same region. If Iamina spends so much time in their company, it means she forgives the offenses of the Archduke's father against her own father, so why shouldn't the rest of us? They raised that whelp carefully, I'll give them that. Kept him out of Gallybanks for the most part, gave it out that he's mad for theater and not much else. So inoffensive is he that he's sent to the Continent to bring back the Princess, even standing as proxy bridegroom."

Cade remembered that night very well indeed. "And he's kin to the Royals, don't forget."

"Precisely. Yet consider the Royals themselves. I don't think anybody's heard the Queen say five words together in the last thirty years. Ashgar is a wastrel and a waste of good air. King Meredan does his best, I suppose, but he's not his father and never could be. What's more, he never wanted to be. Who's left?

Iamina has turned religious for reasons nobody can say. Her husband is about to be divorced, did you know? What happens if she marries again? She's not yet forty, still able to have a child."

"The only Royal who matters," Cade said slowly, "is Princess Miriuzca."

"And it will be fifteen years at least before her son is ready for the throne."

"You know, I rather think she might make a decent job of it herself. She's far from stupid, no matter how innocent those big blue eyes might seem. But I gather what you're really saying is that the Archduke is close cousin to the Royals, and wouldn't mind getting all of them out of the way for himself and his children."

"His wife is snaking her way into the best graces of the Chapel. There might be a powerfull ally there."

"Yeh, but—" Suddenly he sat up straight. "That's not it at all! Suppose this happens, suppose the North Keep falls right on top of Miriuzca and both her children—and the Archduke can prove it was her brother and the Nominative Brothers and even Iamina and his own wife—there can't be all that many in the Chapel hierarchy who want to get rid of honoring the Angels and the Old Gods, and stay strictly with the Lord and the Lady—but if that's true, then why did Black Lightning do that play? The one where everybody except Wizards and Elves is unclean? Oh, of course," he said, answering his own question. "*They* must lean towards the idea of only the Lord and the Lady—though Thierin Knottinger never struck me as being particularly spiritual." He paused. "But he doesn't matter. If the Archduke lets this happen, if I warn him and he still lets it happen, he can place the blame on the Tregrefin and Iamina and his own wife, and that shows how wrong this whole new religious line is—he's got a son and a daughter by Panshilara, she's of no more use to him now—he can get rid of her and Iamina *and* win the Chapel traditionalists to his side forever!"

Mistress Mirdley held up both hands, both in jest and in earnest. "Enough! What pathways there must be in that mind of yours, to take you such places!"

He laughed ruefully. "Well, I know now why I never wanted to be in politics or at Court. My head is splitting!"

"Come into the stillroom and I'll give you something for that."

They left the kitchen and on the short walk down the hallway, he draped his arm around her shoulders. "We haven't sat and talked like that in a long time. D'you remember when I was little, and I spent more time in your kitchen than anywhere else but Cindercliff Glassworks?"

She leaned into him, then shook off his arm and opened the stillroom door. "It was so much simpler when you were a child. All I had to worry about was skinned knees and hurt feelings. Now it's Princesses and Archdukes and magic and theater, and I don't know what-all else. You've put years onto me, boy, and no mistake."

Cade disregarded her frown and put both arms around her for a hug. "You know what?" he murmured, resting his chin atop her head. "Whenever anybody at school said that with a face like mine, I must be part Troll, I was secretly proud."

For one of the few times in all the years he'd known her, she hugged back. But only for a moment. Then she wriggled away and got down a blue jar and a silver vial and a white bottle and a copper bowl to mix things in.

"Don't think that all those pretty words will please me into making this taste good," she warned.

"It never crossed my mind."

"Fetch me that green bottle over there. And tell me what it's like, this writing that you do."

The request surprised him so much that the bottle nearly slipped out of his fingers. "How do you mean?"

"You know very well what I mean."

Cayden chewed his lower lip. "It's . . . actually, it's awful when it isn't going well. You get out the paper and sharpen the pen, make sure there's enough ink in the bottle, and then there's *nothing*. It just won't happen. You know you'll never be able to write something that has any relation at all to how you want it to be. You want to kick the furniture and the walls—"

"And yourself."

"Oh, especially yourself! For being such a lackwit as to think you might actually have something to say. You can't get the words to budge. They're all in your head—too many of them, sometimes—and they won't do what you want them to. But you can't stop working at it, because it's the only thing you've ever really wanted to do, it's the only thing that you can do that really matters. And the insane thing is that when it's all jumbled up like that, you know that you must really have something important to say. Important to *you*, at least."

"And when it goes well?"

"You feel like all the Gods and Angels rolled into one."

He heard what that sounded like, and felt himself blush again. But Mistress Mirdley was nodding.

"And the Elsewhens? What do those feel like? All of them, not just the ones that hurt."

"The outer world goes away. What I'm seeing becomes the real world. It's not like dreaming, at least the way I understand most people's dreams. Sometimes I'm there, doing things, like the one about the North Keep. Other times I'm just watching and listening, *I'm* not really there at all, if you see what I mean. Seeing the Tregrefin and the Nominative Brothers was like that. Things happen and I can't affect them, I can't communicate or warn or anything like that." A small, sardonic laugh escaped him. "It *definitely* doesn't feel like being one of the Gods!"

"And so you write." She poured the mixture into a clay cup and swirled it round. "Because of all these things—the Elsewhens and the performing and the writing—the writing is the only thing you can control."

"Sometimes it controls me," he admitted. "Sometimes it's a little like an Elsewhen, and it just sort of happens to me—" And then he remembered that the piece Touchstone had rehearsed but had yet to perform, "The Avowal," had come to him *as* an Elsewhen. He'd mused once or twice on what it might be like to have all his writing come to him like that—and realized that when it was going really well, all his writing really was like that. The difference was that the writing was like a waking trance, not a sleeping dream or an otherworldly Elsewhen, and that Mistress Mirdley was right in that he could control it. More or less. He grinned to himself and quaffed the potion handed to him.

It tasted absolutely foul. But his headache was gone by the time he reached his room upstairs. Tonight he merely glanced at the thorn-roll. No need for it. He would sleep tonight, and tomorrow he'd go to the Archduke's residence just outside of Gallantrybanks, Great Welkin. And somehow he'd convince him to thwart the Tregrefin's plot, not take advantage of it. He shuddered slightly under the sheet as he remembered Miriuzca's furious face and the glass stabbing Megs's back and neck. But he also remembered the swiftness with which the Princess had acted on his order, and her trust in him—and that Megs had shielded little Roshlin, possibly saving his life. He wished the Elsewhen had gone on just a few moments longer, so he could be sure she had not sacrificed herself in vain.

22

Early as Cayden was in his waking and washing and dressing, Mieka was downstairs waiting for him. Mieka, who considered *morning* to be the foulest of curse words, considered that what he heard from Mistress Mirdley that morning went beyond foul. It was fortunate that he arrived so early at Redpebble Square; he had time to recover from the shock. He would have to be in firm possession of all his cleverness if he was to accompany Cade to see the Archduke.

When Cayden showed up, he was ensconced in a chair beside the kitchen hearth, placidly sipping spiced mocah from a big earthenware cup, telling Mistress Mirdley all about the Royal Circuit. He had just reached the tale of the mud baths when the door swung open and Cade stepped through, stopped, stared, and looked as if he wanted to turn right back around and flee the house.

"Oh, good! You're up," Mieka said. "Have something to eat and drink, and then we'll be off."

"Off?" He declined the Trollwife's offer of a plate of sage bacon and raisin muffins.

"Off," Mieka affirmed. "And do eat something, Quill. It won't do to cross verbal swords with the Archduke on an empty stomach."

He gave Mistress Mirdley a frown of betrayal. "You told him?" "I did. And he's right. Sit. Eat."

Cade did as he was bidden. Mieka roused himself from his comfortable chair to pour him a glass of peach nectar, then sat back down with his cup of mocah. Taking a critical survey from neatly combed hair to shiny black boots, he nodded. "You're dressed for it, that's a start. That gray jacket always did look very elegant. But you'll have to go back upstairs for that falcon pin Dery gave you. It would look better in a neck-cloth or a scarf, just for some color, instead of holding your collar together. . . ." When Cade frowned, he shrugged. "As you please. Now, how do you plan to get there?"

"Hire-hack." He picked up and eyed a strip of crisp bacon, and started chewing.

"Absolutely not. You can't show up at Great Welkin in a hack!"

"You're suggesting we ought to hitch up the wagon?"

"Don't be so silly. I have a plan." Mieka grinned again. "Don't ask. Eat."

A short while later Mieka waited in the entry hall of Number Eight while Cayden fetched the silver falcon pin. A little while after that they were both looking into the mirror as he pinned his collar closed. His fingers twitched suddenly, and Mieka saw his eyes widen.

"What?" he asked softly.

"It's—" His gaze flickered to Mieka in the mirror, and it was remarkable, really, how easy it was to watch the decision forming in his eyes as he chose not to lie. "Nothing substantial. Memory of a memory, I think. It's silly, is what it is. I've looked into this mirror a million times."

"And in Elsewhens?"

"That's what it feels like." He hesitated, then reached inside his jacket and pulled out a short length of glass, barely five inches long. "Blye made a few of these for Dery when he was little."

Mieka accepted the toy withie. He sensed the presence of Cade's magic within it. "So that's what took you so long upstairs."

"We might have to get past an obstacle or two."

"Mm. It's a right bright lad, innit?" He slipped it up his sleeve, made sure it was secure, and led the way out the front door, hiding how stunned he was that Cade was actually encouraging him to do such a thing.

"Not the Archduke," Cade warned. "I have to see him alone."

Mieka had been thinking about this since Mistress Mirdley had told him Cade was planning a visit to Great Welkin. Much as it pained him, he had to nod. "I don't trust meself around him, 'specially not with one of these."

"It isn't that you're not wanted," Cade began anxiously.

Mieka interrupted with, "I know that, too. It's that I'm not needed." He saw this register in startled gray eyes and wondered why Cayden never could believe that Mieka had every faith in him. More lightly, he went on, "And I'm not dressed for it, am I? Now, where's the nearest jewelry shop?"

Cade gaped at him. "You want me to bring him a gift?"

"I take back what I said about you being smart. Never mind. Save your wits for your talk with Himself, and don't spend any before you have to. But first we have to get you there. Barely enough money for a hack, I take it? Well, don't worry. Like I said, I have a plan."

"I almost always hate your plans."

"You won't much like this one, either. But that makes no nevermind. Jeweler's?"

Cade led him out of Redpebble Square, one block down and two blocks over, and through the substantial iron-barred door of Spindletwist Fine Gems. The shop's windows were many and narrow, six of them on either side of the door, allowing a glimpse inside at the sparkling wares but no hope of entry. Mieka strolled through the door as if he had just bought not only the shop but the whole block of buildings from street corner to street corner, too. Cade flinched slightly as a little bell rang with the opening of the door. Mieka paused, tilted his head as if listening, then beamed his approval.

"A lovely note," he said to the man who looked at them over a glass-topped case of gold and silver and glistening jewels. "My father is a lute-maker, and that happens to be one of his favorites for testing purity of tone. But I see by this marvelous display that your discriminating taste extends to all things." He laughed, radiating pleasure. "Even to the color of the walls and carpets and chairs! Do you know, I was once in a jeweler's shop—well, he called himself a jeweler, though by the time I left, empty-handed I might add, I very much doubted it—but I tell you with my hand on my heart that all his walls and furnishings were shades of brown. Brown! Every gem he brought out, from sapphires to emeralds to pearls—even the diamonds!—they simply *lay* there, poor things, trying their hardest to shine but doomed from the instant he placed them onto brown velvet. This elegance of blues, however, is perfect."

From a corner of his eye, he saw Cade grimace slightly. Really, he ought to be accustomed by now to Mieka's interminable chattering. The proprietor, who introduced himself as Master Spindletwist, was nodding his approval of Mieka's discernment. Most jewelers—most people who worked with metals—were at least partly Goblin. This man looked Human from his rounded ears to his straight white teeth to his long limbs.

"My wife's choosing," he said. "What may I show you today?"

"Wives!" Mieka sighed dramatically. "One has so much to do to keep them happy, isn't that so? I'm just returned from months away, you see, and damned if I could find anything anywhere that would please her, and worthy of her beauty. Don't you think so, Cayden?"

"Oh, of course."

For a moment, Mieka thought Cade really had fallen out

of the stupid tree this morning and hit every branch on his way down. He had underestimated his tregetour's powerful understanding. Cade smiled at Spindletwist and went on talking.

"Shollop, Dolven Wold, Sidlowe—well, you couldn't really expect to find anything in Scatterseed, could you, Mieka? But New Halt and even Lilyleaf were vastly disappointing, too. And as for Frimham—" He flicked a hand in the air as if to brush away all memory of the town.

Mieka had mentioned a long absence from Gallantrybanks. Cade had named in order most of the stops on the circuits. Master Spindletwist might or might not be devoted to the theater, but Mieka was hoping he wasn't a moron.

"And now, of course," Mieka went on, "with all these festivities coming up, my darling girl will need something new and wondrous to wear." He laughed, looking up at Cade. "While you and I and Rafe and Jeska rehearse day and night for the celebrations, which means I probably won't be seeing much of her at all!"

"It's a pity," Cade said, "that Blye isn't as clever with gold and silver as she is with glass."

All their first names, mention of King Meredan's anniversary and rehearsals for same, with Blye the famous glasscrafter—who was the first to receive the Gift of the Gloves—they were running out of hints. Surely they'd provided enough by now?

They had.

"Of course, Master Windthistle. Delighted to be of use to yourself and Master Silversun."

His part in the proceedings accomplished, Cade had the sense to wander round the shop while Mieka dithered over trays of everything from hair ornaments to toe-rings. At last a brooch was settled on: a spray of gold leaves dripping diamond dew. Mieka expressed his raptures and assured Master Spindletwist that Mistress Windthistle would, too.

Next came the slightly tricky part. Mieka was presented with the bill while the brooch was wrapped. The jewel had been carefully chosen, not for beauty and craftsmanship, but for price. It had to be expensive enough that no man could be expected to carry that much cash on him, but not so expensive that it would not leave the shop without at least a quarter of its value in the proprietor's hands. Mieka signed the bill, hoping he'd guessed correctly.

Master Spindletwist smiled and handed over a little wooden box painted bright blue and tied with a white ribbon.

Mieka smiled back and left the shop vowing in the warmest terms to tell everyone he knew, including Princess Miriuzca, about the exquisite glory of wares to be found here. Once they were outside, he turned to Cade. "Where's the nearest pledge-broker's?"

"Why d'you want a—?" Cade's mouth stayed open, though no more sound came out. Mieka almost laughed as understanding made his jaw drop just a little more before he shut it firmly.

The shop was a dim and dismal place on a side street, selected only because Cade knew of no such places and Mieka knew of several and chose the one closest to an ostler's. The broker knew Mieka, too, and the amount of time they spent haggling back and forth obviously grated on Cade's nerves. Mieka kept one eye on him as he tried to raise the price to cover the cost of a nice little rig to take them to and from Great Welkin with some left over for trimmings for the ostler, which was the mark of a true gentleman. The little things did matter quite a lot, and it was to their advantage to be known as blithely generous with their money when they didn't have any money. They had to keep up the pretense as long as possible, while they worked every night they could so that by the time the fakery was found out, they had enough to pay off at least a few of their bills.

Presented with this concept, Cade would of course object that applying to a pledge-broker for a loan with this jewel as collateral was fatal advertisement of their financial straits. From long experience, Mieka knew what Cade did not: establishments of this type were as silent as death about whose belongings were on display for sale at a goodly fraction of what they were really worth. Any pledge-broker who gossiped about Lord Thus-and-So's silver plate or Mistress Guildmaster's-Wife's amber necklace was soon out of business. Nobody would pawn their possessions to someone who would spread their names and thus their financial troubles all over Gallybanks.

Cade was looking depressed. Granted, the sight of other people's valuables, everything from jewelry to clothing to furniture to the tools of various trades, was saddening. But at least there were no lutes. Mieka had heard from Jinsie only last night that Alaen, thrown out of his latest digs, had pawned one of his lutes. Not that he'd used the money to find a place to live. No, it had gone to dragon tears. Jinsie knew this because she was friends with Deshananda, Chattim's wife, and Deshananda had had it from Chirene, Sakary's wife, with whom he was hopelessly in love, that Alaen had taken to sleeping in a shed in their garden. She'd come across him one morning while playing with her children, and he'd given them the fright of their lives before running away—leaving a thorn-roll behind. Chirene had left it where it was, knowing he'd come back for it. Mieka had no idea how much dragon tears could be had for the pledge-price of a lute, but he didn't want Cade to see any reminder of Alaen and Briuly Blackpath.

Mieka's work was finally done. He scraped the coins off the counter into a leather drawstring purse and left the shop without a word of farewell. Outside in the street, he set off at a brisk pace for the ostler's.

"No reason to linger and be robbed. Most dangerous place in Gallybanks isn't the intersection of Beekbacks and Whittawer, it's outside a pledge-broker's!"

Cade said nothing until they had paused at a corner to wait for an overladen vegetable wagon to pass by. "You seem rather expert at this sort of thing."

"Only when times were *very* hard at Wistly. It's easier to come up with the pledge-broker's money than the original price, at which point, one simply returns the item to the place where it was bought, with some blithering about its not being suitable, or the person it was meant for didn't like it." He took Cade's elbow as they crossed the street. "Come on, let's find you something nice and neat to ride in. I'll play coachman, shall I? Oh, stop looking so horrified! Yazz lets me drive the wagon, and that's four huge horses! How much trouble could one be?"

"Oh, Gods," was Cade's only comment.

The ostler had a pair of two-wheeled rigs for hire. Both seated two on slightly threadbare upholstery; one was larger, and had a raised perch in the back for a driver. It looked hideously uncomfortable. Mieka chose it anyway, for its size and its newer coat of black paint. He let Cade make friends with the bay mare while he haggled down the price, and shortly before noon they were rattling out of Gallybanks on the road to the Archduke's residence, Great Welkin. Cade insisted on driving. Mieka didn't object. It gave Cade something to occupy his mind besides the coming interview with His Grace. Pleased with his gambit, Mieka leaned back, put his feet up, and enjoyed the ride.

Great Welkin was not on the river. It was located down below the Plume on the only solid land in the middle of a marsh. Being so near to Gallantrybanks, Great Welkin needed no fields or pastures to support it. Two raised roads led to it, one from the south and one from the west. Seasonal rain turned it into an island, covering the roads ankle deep if the inhabitants were lucky, and hip deep if they weren't. A mere ten miles from the city, the gray stone pile was close enough to keep an eye on, and to keep a potentially dangerous child—Cyed Henick—isolated for years as he grew to manhood. As the rig bounced up the western road and the marshland spread before him, Mieka shivered inwardly at the thought of what it must have been like to live so remote a life, and in such a silence. It wasn't exactly a prison, but it came damned close.

On attaining his majority, the Archduke had spent large sums to improve the road and his ancestral dwelling. Heavy stones had been cut for the former; for the latter, trees and shrubbery and flowers had been planted, and new curtains, upholstery, carpets, and so on had been ordered. But neither sunny summery day nor flowering vines could soften the stark blocky lines of the house. Four stories high, surmounted by what looked like a crow's nest transferred from a ship, only made of stone, to Mieka it resembled a huge, ugly gray box with a sloping lid of black tiles and a little gray handle on top.

Mieka sat up, scrunched around, and said to Cade, "Time for me to take over. Oh, c'mon, it's only a half mile! And you can't go in there driving yourself!"

Shuddering dramatically, Cade relented. Mieka waited until he was seated in the rig, reins still in his hands, before climbing up to the little perch, which turned out to be just as uncomfortable as it looked. Cade handed him the reins, saying, "If I end up in the ditch—"

"Yeh, I know, you'll kill me. Slowly. Painfully. Whatever. Good Gods, would you look at that horrible house! I wonder why he didn't sell this and buy something more convenient in the city when he came into his money." He clicked his tongue at the horse, flapped the reins once or twice, and the rig started moving again. Mieka kept one eye on the road and one eye on the back of Cade's head.

"P'rhaps he got used to it here, when he was a child."

"Or it's just as useful to him to live here as it was to King Cobin to have him raised here. Nice and private, innit? For keeping him away from the Court, and the Court away from him."

"You may be right. Bet you can see for miles and miles from that thing on top."

"It's called a *cupola*, Quill." When Cade turned round to show him an incredulous face, Mieka told him, "My brothers build things. And I *can* read, y'know. Even architectural plans."

"And stark amazement grew apace."

Mieka instantly finished the couplet with, "Don't be snide—it warps your face."

"Oh, and it's a poet now, is it?"

"I have been hopelessly corrupted by six years in your company. Or is it getting on for seven now?"

"Were we reckoning by the amount of sheer annoyance, it's been half a lifetime."

"Only half? One of us must be mellowing."

Just as well they could share a laugh. They had reached a massive gateway guarded on each side by a huge stone dragon with wings outspread and claws poised to grab anything that got too close. Mieka and Cayden were on the Archduke's land now, invading his home, and with demands that he wouldn't much like at all.

The rig bounced over the rounded cobbles of a wide courtyard. Mieka reined in. "I'll go in with you, shall I? Just inside out of the sun, not all the way to Himself."

Nodding tightly, Cade descended from the rig and tugged his jacket into place. Mieka waited for a groom to take the mare's bridle, then jumped down to join Cade. Two guards in orange-and-gray livery advanced, one of them demanding to know who they were and what business they had with His Grace.

"Our business with His Grace is private." Cade looked down his long nose as only he could do, and Mieka inwardly applauded his assumption of the *My Bloodlines Are Infinitely More Impressive Than Yours* face. "And he won't be grateful if you leave us out here to bake in the sun."

Mieka knew there were two ways this could go: Obedience might be so drilled into them that anybody who gave orders in such a tone with such an expression on his face had better be obeyed and right quick—or they could be immune to any orders but those of the Archduke. If they had glanced at each other, he would have guessed the former. They didn't take their eyes off Cade and Mieka. One of them said, "State your business."

Mieka regretted their attitude, because it would whittle away at Cade's confidence. Once again, he had underestimated the man. With Lady Jaspiela in his tones, Cade said, "Not to anyone but His Grace. You will be so good as to step aside so that we may enter, and while we are being served something cold to drink, you will inform the steward or the chamberlain or whomever you report to that Master Silversun and Master Windthistle have arrived."

"Do you have an appointment?"

Mieka took his turn, saying, "Yes, and if we don't take care of this little matter with the Archduke soon, we'll be late for it. Open the door, there's a good fellow." As he spoke, he let the withie slip into his palm from his sleeve, and concentrated a bit, and two shakes of a dragon's tail later, the guards were escorting them up the four broad stone steps to the front doors of Great Welkin.

A fist pounded—most inelegant, Mieka thought disapprovingly—and the left door opened. Mieka's immediate reaction was that if this hall was a result of the Archduke's expensive redecorating, he had more money than taste. Why was it, he mused as they walked towards the wide, orange-carpeted stairs, that really rich people so seldom had the sense to consult people who actually knew what they were doing with tapestries and paintings? Possession of a fortune was no guarantor of style. It had pleased the Archduke, evidently, to buy as much as could possibly be crammed into every conceivable space—and, as the hall must measure fifty feet by thirty feet, there were a lot of spaces to cram.

Ah well. At least I don't have to live here, Mieka told himself.

Cade paused at the foot of the stairs, waiting for a gray-suited functionary to descend. Orange braid at the neck and cuffs of his jacket, and the quality of the gray material, identified him as an upper servant, but a servant just the same. Persons more important would not be wearing a variation on the Archducal livery. Their servitude would be shown in more subtle ways.

Mieka once more slid the withie into his hand, but it was unnecessary. The servant escorted them up the stairs (Mieka amused himself by leaving fingerprints and palmprints all over the industriously polished brass handrail, and regretted having washed his hands of this morning's bacon grease), turned left, and ushered them through a double doorway into a huge chamber. Then he bowed and vanished.

This was, at a guess, a ballroom. Light spilled in from floor-to-ceiling windows all along one wall. Outside was a spacious balcony bedecked with potted plants. Directly opposite the windows was a mural, but at this angle, Mieka couldn't discern the subject. At the far end of the room, overhanging a collection of dust-sheeted chairs, was a minstrels' gallery made of carved oak. The floor was gray marble, polished to a shiny slickness that made him want to haul off his boots and slide the length of the place in his stockings.

"No mirrors," Cade remarked as they advanced a little ways into the room.

"Huh? What?"

"Mirrors. There aren't any. If there's a wall of windows on one side, there ought to be mirrors facing it. Gives the illusion of symmetry and reflects the sunlight during the day. And by night, ladies like to admire themselves and their gowns and jewels while they're dancing."

"Master Silversun," came a voice from the doors just behind them, "His Grace will see you now."

Mieka met Cayden's nervous gaze. "Miriuzca and the children," he whispered. "Think of them, not anything else. And say what you need to, Quill. Promise whatever will make him put a stop to it."

"The only promises," Cade replied grimly, "will be his."

Mieka felt like applauding. He watched Cade stride briskly out and could almost feel sorry for the Archduke. Almost.

The door shut again, and Mieka was left to his own devices in the ballroom. He meandered over to the windows, peering at the balcony, the gardens beyond, and the gray-green marshlands past the gray stone walls. Except for a few scrawny saplings in the enclosed gardens, there wasn't an honest tree in sight.

Turning, wondering again if he could get away with a long slide in his stocking feet, he approached the mural wall. It seemed familiar somehow.

In the middle of the room he stopped cold. Familiar. Yes. It was.

He'd last seen these scenes in the Kiral Kellari, the mural rejected by Master Warringheath for being repulsive and insulting. The only differences between that painting and this was that the theme of a cellar no longer applied, there was no magic to make the figures move, and the figures themselves were much larger.

For instance, that rural scene of a dirt road curving between green wheat fields and an apple orchard, where a girl slept beneath a tree, was at least four feet wide. The fruit was falling from the branches as a hideous creature in dark clothes and a tall hat laughed, spinning cobwebs between his fingers, trickling the thread down into the girl's ear. Goblin. Or, rather, the nasty despised version of a Goblin, with crooked yellow teeth, single across-the-forehead eyebrow, red-splotched skin. His laughter made the apples plummet from the trees. He wove nightmares to slither into the sleeping girl's mind.

Next was the Piksey on a giant toadstool. All in green, grinning a grin that crinkled the corners of his upslanting eyes as a bewildered farmer coaxed his exhausted horse to the plow— the horse the Piksey had been racing around the fields all night long. A trail of gold and silver footprints led to the toadstool, footprints of Piksey dust.

Mieka walked the length of the mural. A Harpy played cards with a Gorgon who sat with her back turned, and on the large table between them crouched a terrified Human child: the living wager. A Selkie lured a young and handsome knight to his death in the sea. Caladrius, Touchstone's own pure white raven, perched in the window of a sick woman's room, its face turned away— which meant that the woman would die. *Vodabeists* rampaged along a river while their land-dwelling cousins thundered through a village. A wyvern devoured a beautiful young maiden. A Troll hauled a whole family screaming into the river beneath a bridge. Merfolk laughed on a ragged rock as their daughters' singing lured a ship to disaster. One Gnome wearing birch-bark shoes squared off against an arched, spitting cat, while another stood over a firepit, stirring soup that cat would soon flavor. A Fae with a redheaded Human baby in her arms watched through an open window with malicious glee as a Human mother reached into a cradle.

Mieka needed wine, brandy, anything to get this taste out of his mouth. Was there some kind of thorn that would remove these images from his mind? There was neither alcohol nor thorn to hand. There was nothing but himself. He coughed, and the sound echoed from windows to ceiling to polished marble floor.

He wouldn't look at the paintings again. He went to the windows, tried to open them. Locked. Every single one of them. He tried them all. There was a corner door just below the minstrels' gallery, presumably leading up to it. This, too, was locked. He turned and stared the length of the ballroom to the door he and Cade had come in by. Had that been locked by now, too?

And if it had . . . why? Who could think him a danger to anyone? Cade was the one with the brains and the magic. All Mieka had was a glib tongue. And a noteworthy facility for getting into and out of trouble. And now, as of this moment, a new and understandable aversion to locked rooms.

There was no sound except his own breathing, but all at once he knew he was being watched. He could feel it all along his skin. He turned, and again, seeing no one, hearing no one. Yet whatever his other senses told him, his magic shrieked that he was being watched, and by someone unimpressed with his Kingdom-wide fame and prodigious talents and winsome good looks.

There was the faintest rustle of material up in the minstrels gallery. Only Elfen ears would have heard it. He turned, squinting up at the carved and latticed wood. "You up there, I can hear you," he called. "Why not come down?"

No answer.

Nervous apprehension was quickly turning to fear. He knew it was all the thorn he'd been pricking, intensifying his emotions, but he'd never been able to figure out if the sensation was more powerful at the start, in the middle, or while the thorn was fading away. This morning's whitethorn was definitely fading by now, and it took a real effort to keep his voice steady and his hands from shaking—and he could tell himself all he liked that it was anger, but he knew it was sudden unreasoning fear.

"Who are you?" he snarled.

"No one you would know."

Deep voice, highborn accent. A panel of fretwork slid aside up in the minstrels' gallery and Mieka peered up at a very old man. Tall and bald, with eyes so dark they were almost black set in a cadaverous face, he stood in the little window with his clasped hands hidden in the baggy sleeves of his brown robes.

"So you're the Elf," he went on.

Desperately grabbing hold of his composure, Mieka replied, "Beholden for singling me out as special, but while there's only one of me, there's more than one of us, if you see what I mean." He congratulated himself on sounding almost casual.

"Have you any idea, I wonder, how very special you are?"

The congratulations were, it seemed, premature. There was something in the old man's voice that iced Mieka's veins and stopped the breath in his lungs.

"I've heard that your performances on the Royal Circuit this year were outstanding, even for Touchstone."

That wasn't what he'd meant by *special,* and Mieka knew it. He didn't want to be special, not to this man. He took one step back, then another, barely able to restrain himself from turning to run for the main doors.

His body betrayed him with a twitch to one side, and the child-size withie fell out of his sleeve and clattered to the floor. The old man began to laugh.

Mieka snatched up the withie. As he rose, he happened to look at the mural again.

It was alive.

The Gorgon had won the hand of cards and, with a reedy chortle, stroked a talon down the Human child's arm, leaving a line of blood that burst into flame. The wyvern crunched the maiden's leg bones, threw back its head, and shrieked its delight. The Piksey was giggling madly, the Goblin was singing some ghastly off-key song as he wove misted nightmares. Mieka stumbled a step back, to the side, back again—and gagged when the hideous yellow *vodabeists* seemed to be clawing their way out of the mural, coming for him.

Thorn, imagination, or the magic of the old man up there in

the minstrels gallery? Mieka gripped the withie in his hand like a sword and shouted, "Who the fuck *are* you? Stop it! Let me out of here!"

"You're free to go at any time, Elf." The old man was laughing at him. "Free to do exactly as you please—isn't that your primary goal in life? To waste it doing exactly as you please, with no thought to anyone else?"

Had there been the slightest magic left in the withie, Mieka would have blasted him to the northernmost peaks of the Pennynine Mountains.

"Oh, don't think I disapprove. In point of fact, I rather admire your ambition. It's not everyone who can be so single-mindedly selfish without feeling the slightest hint of guilt."

Pride and defiance had kept Mieka where he was until now. When the *vodabeists* lunged for him again, he decided that pride and defiance could go fuck themselves. He turned and ran for the doors.

But his legs moved so slowly. His feet felt so heavy. He gritted his teeth and struggled on, gaze fixed on the doors. If only they could be like the ones in "Doorways," doors he had created with Cade's magic, doors that were not locked. He clutched the withie, but it was a dead thing, hints of Cade and Blye within it, but no useful and usable magic.

Suddenly he needed the sound of his own voice, his Elfen voice. Only Elves and Wizards were blessed by the Lord and the Lady. What about all those other things he was? Some of them were shown in the mural. How could people dance and laugh and flirt and drink gallons of bubbling wine in a room with all that muck on the wall? And quite probably that horrible old man watching from behind the latticework like servants peeking into bedrooms at a whorehouse—

If only this door ahead of him was one of his own doors, his and Quill's. He could open it and walk through it and be safe. "This life, and none other," he heard himself whisper, breath coming short and fast.

And like a talisman constructed only of words, of sounds, the sentence once spoken made the door open. He knew it was only coincidence. He knew that.

But he couldn't help but feel that it was magic, to have said those words and have Quill open that door.

23

Doing this crazy thing—going to Great Welkin, demanding to see the Archduke, saying what he must say to convince, persuade, bully, bribe, plead, whatever it took—it had all seemed impossible when he woke before dawn, shaking and sweating, fighting his way free of a nightmare in which the Archduke was laughing at him, throwing gigantic daisies with the malevolent yellow eyes of the Fae and petals that were fat, writhing white maggots.

He lay there until all the shadows in his bedchamber had been banished by fresh sunlight. Tense and determined, he rose and washed and dressed. By accident (certainly not willingly) he happened to meet his own eyes in the looking glass as he shaved, and it occurred to him that he was nobody and nothing, and that to confront Archduke Cyed Henick was an insanity seldom equaled in his life.

When he saw Mieka in the kitchen, he wanted to run away and hide.

Yet Mieka had, with his blithe acceptance that this was what Cade would do, and he would in fact be able to do it, settled his thoughts and emotions. Mieka didn't believe in much, but he did believe in Cade. And somehow that was enough.

When Mieka magicked the guards into letting them inside Great Welkin, Cade was at last reminded of what he was that the Archduke was not. Cade and Touchstone were famous, admired, celebrated, creative, successful, trusted by the only Royal who really mattered. Henick was famous, too—for being the son of the man who had lost a war. He lived his life as if none of that had ever happened and he was merely one more nobleman— with better bloodlines than most, and more money, once he'd turned twenty-one and invested a small inheritance into a major fortune—content to spend his days in amusing himself, creating nothing, eyed askance by the whole of Albeyn.

Cayden would be giving him his chance to shine.

The servant left him in the open doorway of a library stuffed with books. Three walls of shelves nearly to the ceiling, with rolling ladders for access; a range of waist-high shelves down the middle of the long room; glass display cases here and there for rare and precious volumes; Cayden could quite happily have spent years in this room that was undoubtedly Drevan Wordturner's particular version of Hell. A smile twitched one corner of his mouth as he walked slowly along the wall, glancing at titles, wondering how many of these books had been pinched by Drevan for Vered Goldbraider on the sly and then returned with the Archduke none the wiser. A nice little gambit, that had been, and Cade congratulated himself.

"I am told," said a deep, cold voice, "that you have private business to discuss. Welcome to Great Welkin, Master Silversun. Do sit down."

Cade paced the length of the room and finally saw the Archduke, seated at a broad, cluttered desk. He rose, gestured to a quartet of deep leather chairs, and sat in one of them. Cade chose one angled towards the Archduke, and settled into its softness. Before them was a low table with books stacked at either end, as if space had been cleared for a tea tray.

"It's good of you to see me," he began. Why had he ever thought this man so formidable? He was paunchy and going bald; each inhalation was shallow and there was an unhealthy color in his cheeks. Memory supplied Cade with a scene from his childhood, when Mistress Mirdley had taken him along to one of the other houses on Redpebble Square, up to the servants quarters, where the chief steward lay in bed. Despite the Trollwife's medicines, he was dead of heart trouble before two Winterings had passed. He had looked the way the Archduke looked now.

"Not at all," Cyed Henick replied to Cade's opening pleasantry. "It's not every day one receives a visit from a renowned tregetour. May I be of use to you somehow?"

Cade had the distracting thought that it would be interesting to know how much use Black Lightning was to the Archduke. Schooling his mind to his purpose, he said, "I hope so. I think you're the only one who can help."

Eyebrows twitched upwards, settled back down. "Indeed?"

"At Seekhaven this year, my partners and I were honored by Her Royal Highness Princess Miriuzca with an invitation to lunching at the castle. Her brother the Tregrefin was also in attendance. Your Grace has met him, of course."

A faint grimace that instantly smoothed to blandness. Cade would not have seen his expression change if he hadn't been watching for years the subtle play of emotion over Jeska's face onstage.

"The Tregrefin has been a frequent guest here and at Threne. My wife enjoys talking to someone from her own land."

"Just so." He drew breath for his next sentence—planned out on the way here, when Mieka had kept most uncharacteristically quiet—but the Archduke had something else to say.

"He was not especially pleased with the play you and the Shadowshapers and Crystal Sparks performed at Trials."

Cade couldn't help a grin. Surprisingly enough, the Archduke grinned back. And for that scant moment, they were thinking the same thing.

The point of contact might be useful. Cade went on, "I had heard as much. But what I wanted to tell Your Grace is that at this lunching, the Tregrefin was curious about the Keeps. I found this . . . interesting, as he was staying at the North Keep with his sister, rather than at the Palace."

"He prefers, I'm told, not to mingle with the ministers and officials who are every day at the Palace. The boy is an appalling snob."

"Yes. But I believe that he has been asking more questions of other people about the North Keep."

"To what purpose?"

Bluntly, Cade said, "To use black powder and blow the place sky-high."

He had the satisfaction of seeing the Archduke's color fade to sickly whiteness.

"I'm sure Your Grace remembers the incident at Lord Piercehand's new Gallery. In the rubble was found the crimped end of a withie—precisely where the explosion was centered. This evidence has been lost, unfortunately, but I can assure you that it did exist."

"Whose withie? If it was the crimp end, there would be a hallmark." His eyes narrowed. "Unless it was made by Mistress Windthistle. But I cannot believe that she would be so careless as to lose something of her making—or that those theater groups who use her withies would be so careless, either. Nor would she supply it to someone whose actions would put her husband in danger. I'm told his brother was badly injured."

"He's healed very well, beholden to Your Grace. The hallmark on the withie was that of Master Splithook."

Again his eyebrows tightened, this time drawing together

over his nose. "Which groups does he supply?"

Cade shook his head. "It didn't happen that way. I don't know who primed the withie to do what it did, but I do know that it was stolen from Black Lightning. And that the Tregrefin was angry that it had not worked. Using magic—"

"Using magic to cause such damage would, in his view, emphasize how dangerous magic is. So now, rather than magical means, you say he intends to use more mundane methods. I'm not versed in military lore, but it seems to me that it would take a substantial quantity of black powder to topple the North Keep."

"Whether he will be responsible with his own hands for placing it and lighting the strings that lead to it—I don't think so. I think he will be far from the site when it happens. But he will be behind it, Your Grace. Many people will die, and it will be because of him."

"Why have you come to me with this information?"

Rather than answer directly, Cade said, "You haven't asked me how I know."

The moment came and went in silence. Cade knew that the Archduke knew about the Elsewhens. Now the Archduke had no excuse not to know that Cade knew it. But he would not admit it. His eyes glinted for just an instant before he looked down at his hands and picked idly at a rough spot on a thumbnail.

"I assume that you or your friends and associates have heard things which you assembled into this tale—which, I may say, makes a remarkable amount of sense."

No, he wasn't going to admit it.

The Archduke continued, "The boy is destined for their version of Chapel, you know. He finds much to disgust him in Albeyn. I'm told that even his own sister is counting off the days until he is on a ship back home."

"Princess Iamina is said to be quite taken with him."

"And so is my wife—isn't that what you were thinking?

No, Her Grace is simply homesick for the sound of her own language." All at once, his expression darkened and he said, almost as if against his will, "At least, this is what she tells me. I have no idea what they discuss together, gabbling away in words that would strangle any normal person."

Cade wasn't fooled. Why this man had married Panshilara in the first place was beyond his understanding, but he didn't make the mistake of thinking that the Archduke had ever trusted her. She existed to make children. Thus far, she had made two: a daughter and a son. Cade damned himself once again for slicing the Elsewhens out of his mind, for he had a squirmy feeling that there had been something worth recalling about the birth of the girl, aside from the tidy sum that he and Mieka had collected from a wager with Slips Clinkscales. Still, why would he need an Elsewhen to tell him the obvious? A daughter could be married to Prince Roshlin. A son could inherit the Archduchy. He wondered briefly why Panshilara was still around, now that her husband had had satisfactory use of her. . . .

{ "I'm terribly sorry, Your Grace."

He met the physicker's gaze. "Did she suffer?"

"Not beyond the first instants. She was knocked unconscious, you see. Not like Princess Iamina, may the Lord and the Lady keep her soul."

"And the boy? What of the Tregrefin?"

The man shook his head and stroked the folds of his green robes down his chest. "When he was pulled from the river, Your Grace, he was not breathing. Someone did the usual, pounding on his chest and so forth, and though it was a most inexpert job, he did cough up water and begin to breathe on his own again. But there is a limit on how many minutes may pass without a breath, and the Tregrefin had passed that limit. He breathes, but he is gone."

"What will be done?"

"I had hoped that Your Grace would be able to suggest . . ." He paused delicately.

"Hm. We can't send him back to his family in such a state. They would attribute the condition to magic. Neither can we let it be generally known what happened to him." He paused. "You are to say this to anyone who asks. The Tregrefin, on recovering from his near-drowning, went at once to—what's the nearest Minster? I've forgotten."

"Seemly Swale, Your Grace."

"Too big. Anything smaller?"

"There is a small Minster northeast of there . . . Good Brothers only, and few, who care for the fishing villages scattered along the coast."

"That will do. Find out the name of the place and say that the Tregrefin went there to pray for Iamina and the Archduchess, and to meditate on his own good fortune in surviving, giving praise to the Lord and the Lady for his life, and so on. After a week or so, it will be said that he fell into a reverie—all that fasting and praying, not enough rest or food, a terrible strain for one in his already frail condition—and then give him whatever thorn will stop his breathing so that it will not start again."

The physicker nodded. "A merciful and dignified solution, Your Grace. I will make the arrangements."

"And if his sister demands to see him, tell her he's still in shock. Then get him to that Minster. I'm assuming it's one with a Contemplative Brother or two?"

"Four, in fact. And five Brothers who tend to them as well as the fishing villages."

"Very good. Miriuzca won't be allowed to set foot inside that Minster."

"It will be done as you have said, Your Grace. And again,

please let me say how very grieved all of us are about the Archduchess. A terrible loss."

"You are very kind. I don't know how I'm going to tell the children." }

The Archduke was watching him with pale blue eyes like shards of a sickly winter sky. Cade had just allowed the unthinkable to happen: an Elsewhen in front of an enemy. It hadn't even occurred to him to shove it aside.

"So that's what it looks like. I've spent some time wondering, but it didn't seem polite to ask."

His voice had changed completely. All the urbane smoothness was gone, leaving a slight rasp, a quickness of consonant that lingered just slightly on *s* like a snake.

The Archduke rose and went to a closed cabinet amid the bookshelves. From its bottom shelf he took a pitcher and two silver cups. Setting them on the desk, he poured and said, "Wordturner's. He thinks I don't know about his little weakness. It's likely to become a great weakness, but if we're all fortunate, that won't happen until he's through cataloging all my books and all Piercehand's books, and checked them against what's in the Royal Archives. In any case, he keeps this hidden for himself. But as it's my wine and my silver, I think we can partake without his being any the wiser. In truth, he's nearly at the point where he doesn't exactly recall how much he drinks. Is your Elf there yet? I hear he's quite the enthusiast when it comes to alcohol. And women. And thorn."

Cade sat rigidly in the leather-covered chair. Whatever had happened to Princess Iamina, the Archduchess, and the Tregrefin, it had been no accident. He knew that as surely as he knew that all pretense was over between him and this man. This was his real voice, and these were his real eyes.

"Drink up. You must need it. What happens to you must be

rather exhausting. Or is it stimulating? I really am curious, you know. It's a talent unique in my knowledge of magic. Having no magic of my own, I've made it a point to do my research."

Cade took the silver cup but did not drink.

"Oh, come now. Whatever you're thinking about poison or whatever else your imagination can come up with, you did see me pour into both cups from the same pitcher. Here, I'll have a bit from both, just to prove—"

"That won't be necessary. I'm not thirsty."

"As you wish. But please believe me when I tell you that I am not a stupid man. Besides, your Elf is loitering around here someplace, and I really do have to return you to him in proper working order." Seating himself again, he leaned back and regarded Cayden over the rim of the cup. "Now, tell me. Did you see that ridiculous boy plotting with the Good Brothers? Did you see the North Keep fall? Do you have any warning when these things come upon you? Forgive me, but I find your gift utterly fascinating. You wouldn't be willing to share a glimpse or two of the possible futures with me, would you? I thought not." He drank deeply and set the cup aside on the table. "I'm the only one you could come to with this. You might as well tell me everything."

"As long as Your Grace believes that what I say is true, the details aren't important."

"True enough. But allow me to observe that while you are as unsubtle as your grandmother, you're nowhere near the fool your father is. Now, my own father, he was a man lacking both subtlety and brains. You and I are alike in that we struggle under the burden of outstandingly stupid forebears. And we are alike in other ways, as well."

Cade felt his lips pull into a smile. "Please elaborate, Your Grace."

"I will, because it is so seldom that I meet with anyone

who has the wits to comprehend." He matched fingertip to fingertip, then laced the fingers together and held both hands under his chin. "Only consider. You stand there onstage while your masquer prances about and your glisker waves his withies and your fettler—Gods only know what a fettler does, but let's assume it's necessary. And yet there you stand, doing nothing. Everything you have to contribute is done long before you stand on a stage. Although you stand with them on a stage, it's all done for you.

"And in this, we are indeed much alike. We plan what will happen, set things in motion, and let others do the work for us. The difficulty both of us encounter is doubt. Can we fully trust those we have chosen to carry out our work? You seem to have solved this problem—and yet I venture to guess that even now, after years of working with them, you don't absolutely trust those you work with."

He leaned forward to take the cup from the table. He poured more wine, looked at Cayden with arching brows asking a question. "No? Pity. It's a very good vintage from a rather exclusive Frannitch maker. Wordturner knows wine, as well as books." After an appreciative sip, he went on, "Trust is a problem for us both, and one of the reasons I'm here at all is that I trust no one. My father trusted. Look what it got him. No, it's better to select tools for use that put their own interests first in carrying out a plan. The trick, of course, is to find out each person's wants and needs and ambitions, and present your own plans accordingly—so that it is understood that by advancing my cause, they advance their own."

"And that makes you and me alike?" Cade smiled again. "Not to my way of thinking."

"No? Did you select the Elf for his talents, or because what he wanted and what you wanted were essentially the same thing? In brief, do you use him to get what you want, or does he use you?

Or is it mutual? Ah, of course. It must be. As for the thing you want—I take it that present triumphs and everlasting glory factor into your desires. I don't think either matters much to the Elf. Glisking is the only thing at which he is supremely competent. In all other respects, he's rather a failure, wouldn't you agree? But he serves your purposes onstage, and thus it is in your interests to keep him out of too much trouble offstage."

"You seem improbably interested in Mieka Windthistle."

"Only as he provides insight into yourself. And what I've found out through him is indeed rather interesting. There you are, with your magical shapes and shadows and feelings and sensations, all of it lies, and yet you are content. You might have worked with real people, real emotions, learned the exquisite satisfaction of knowing that you and you alone have caused a particular sensation—for pain or for pleasure—in another person. You are a coward, Cayden Silversun. You settle for the imaginary, the unreal."

"The thoughts and emotions of imagination are just as real as any other." But it was rude to quote oneself, so Cade asked, "While you are ambitious for . . . *what*, exactly? The power your father tried to grasp? Is that your idea of what's real? I've never understood people whose motivation is power. With all the plays I've read, and all those I've performed, and everything I've ever written myself—it just doesn't make sense to me. Mayhap you can enlighten me."

"If, after all that study, you still don't know, then nothing I could say would ever make you understand."

"No, I'm curious, truly I am. What is it that you'd do with power if you got it? Order people to go here or there, to do this or that, buy what you please, live as you like? All anyone has to have in order to do any of those things is enough money. Rather vulgar, don't you think?"

"Power is desirable for its own sake."

"But what does it *get* you? That's what I don't understand. I suppose the Tregrefin would like the power to tell everyone precisely what to believe and how to honor the Lord and the Lady, and never to use magic again. But he could never be absolutely sure that people aren't thinking and believing things he doesn't approve of, and as for not doing magic . . . if it's there, people use it. They do on the Continent, despite their official line."

"Yes, they do."

"I still don't understand what it is that *you* want."

The Archduke laced his fingers beneath his chin again. "What do you think *power* means?"

"Well . . . let's say I want you to do something that you don't want to do, and I have a sword or a knife, and that's a kind of power. But I can't really force you to do whatever that thing is. The most I can do is to make sure, with my blade, that you never do anything again. Where's the power in that? It's just killing. Anybody can do that."

"The power of death," he mused. "Is that not what you have just given me?" The Archduke chuckled softly, ruefully, and shook his head. "It seems that I owe you a debt of gratitude. I do have enough power to stop that silly boy from blowing up the North Keep—with his sister in it, I presume? Yes, if he could manage it, I think he would. How much worse it would be, in what passes for his mind, for her to live her life in religious error than it would be for her to die. And her children with her?"

Cade looked him straight in the eyes. "No. Princess Miriuzca, yes. But not the children. I didn't see the children."

"Ah. Well, then, I shall arrange for him to be caught with black powder, and give him a choice between going home or going to Culch Minster. Will that suit?"

"He has to stay alive," Cade said. "His death would bring questions, no matter how cleverly it was devised. Beyond keeping him alive, I don't care what happens to him."

"Neither do I."

So they were in accord again. Cade felt soiled.

"I'll know if the Tregrefin gets any closer to his goal," he said suddenly. "I'll know if nothing has been done."

It was, of course, a bluff. The Archduke couldn't know that, any more than he could know that Cade had lied about not seeing the children.

"I quite understand," was the reply. "What we were saying about trust—in this, you're relying on my belief that this will be to my advantage. Neither of us cares about the Tregrefin. He is of no use to us."

"If he's arrested," Cade pointed out, "his sister will fight for him, and not believe the evidence if it's brought to her on a golden plate."

"So it must be done with . . . subtlety." Another smile, another brief twitching of his brows. "Call up your visions in, say, two days. No more than that, I think."

Cade got to his feet. "Your Grace may trust that I will." He used the word *trust* deliberately, and saw brief appreciation flicker in the man's eyes.

Pushing himself out of his chair, his cheeks flushing with the effort, the Archduke clapped his hands together once. The library door opened with a distant scratch of wood on stone. Somebody ought to plane down the door, Cade thought, then realized that the sound was not carelessness in construction. It was notice of entry. Glancing the length of the room, he saw the gray-suited man who had led him here—when? It seemed like hours ago.

"Lauxen will show you back to your Elf. I have enjoyed our talk, Master Silversun."

Cade decided to make it absolutely clear one more time. "I would say that I am beholden to Your Grace, but that wouldn't be accurate."

"No, it would not." Irony glittered in the pale eyes. How

crudely amusing it must be, to be reminded that he was now indebted to a common player. "Mayhap you ought to thank me instead? I'm told that's becoming popular. Why is that, do you think?"

Cayden shrugged. "It's all a question of who's indebted to whom, isn't it?"

"Indeed. I'll look forward to seeing Touchstone perform at the Royal celebrations."

Cade nodded but didn't bow, and turned for the door. Then the Archduke spoke again, in a very soft voice that would carry no farther than the place where Cade stood.

"I forgot to compliment you on that exquisite little falcon at your collar. A gift, as I understand it. Tell me, purely as a matter of intellectual curiosity, do you ever see your young brother in any of your visions? Does he inhabit any future you've ever seen?"

He kept his back turned to the Archduke, aware that fear was all over his face. He had never seen Derien in any Elsewhen, ever. The realization terrified him, because he understood very well the implied threat. Controlling his expression with an effort, aware that he could do nothing about the telltale pallor of his face, he turned and said, "I doubt that Your Grace would find my brother very interesting."

"That's very likely true, Master Silversun. Good afternoon."

He was taken back to the room where he'd left Mieka. He opened the door on the Elf's scared and startled face, and saw a thousand questions in those eyes. Shaking his head, he took Mieka's elbow and pulled him along behind Lauxen, down stairs and across the vast entry stuffed with garish ornaments, and finally out into the warm summer sun. The rig waited at the side of the house, and as it was brought to them, Cade whispered, "Not until we get home. I'll tell you everything there."

"Fine. Me, too. One thing, though. Can we stop at a swordsmith's on the way?"

"What do you want with a swordsmith?"

Fiercely, he muttered, "Because the next time I'm in a place like this, I'm coming *armed*."

Cade didn't know whether to laugh or scoff or take him seriously. "You don't know how to use a sword."

"I'll learn."

"You're not joking."

"Once that withie was spent, I was helpless. I didn't like it. Especially not in that ballroom. I'm buying meself a goodly length of sharp steel, I am, and lessons in how to use it. I don't ever want to go helpless into a place like that again."

24

Scarcely a day passed before another Elsewhen showed Cayden what the Archduke was planning. It was nothing so simple and direct as a view of guards catching the Tregrefin with black powder, or the boy's departure from Albeyn on a ship taking him across the Flood. For the first little while after this Elsewhen was over, Cade had no idea what was going on.

{ "...a worthy life, if a brief one." A tall, plump, bewrinkled man in the robes of a Good Brother poured wine for the woman seated opposite him. She wore similar robes, and a white woolen scarf draped across her shoulders.

"Such a shame," she said. "So devout. But I heard he was never quite the same after his return. Of course, the permanent loss of his hearing must have been a trauma, but other things have been said."

"Our friends on the Continent were rather sparing with information," the man admitted. "I'm surprised he recovered as much as he did."

"A terrible thing." She shivered and pulled the scarf more closely around her. "And one did hear rumors at the time."

"A friend of mine was the Brother Physicker who tended him. The loss of his hearing upset him dreadfully, you're right. But something also happened to his mind, for he could not remember a single thing about that night. He went back upstairs to his chambers after dinner and dancing, and a servant was just leaving his room after delivering a flagon and some cakes. He found a copy of the *Consecreations* on a tall lectern such as tregetours and fettlers use, only with a candle on either side. Such a beautiful cover, he said, tooled leather with his family crest in gold."

"Such a thoughtful gift," she said acidly. "Such a cunning method of murder!"

"Yet he lived. Not for very long, and crippled, but he did live."

"He lit the candles, the better to read by, opened the book that was no book at all—"

"But he had no memory of whatever happened next."

"He didn't even recall what livery the servant wore?"

"Even if he could, it would mean nothing. Who would be stupid enough to send that gift by someone wearing telltale colors? If he didn't notice at the time that the livery was different from that worn by his sister's servants, then it probably *was* one of his sister's servants."

"Had the person been truly cunning, the bearer would have worn our robes."

"Which proves, to my way of thinking, that it was not the Archduke, no matter what anyone said after. The Lord and the Lady witness that *he* is clever enough to have thought of that, to cast suspicion on us. And who but those of the True Chapel would gift the Tregrefin with a copy of the *Consecreations*?" He scowled and tucked his many chins into his collar like a disgruntled turtle. "No, it could not have been the Archduke. Probably, as was judged at the time, it was an enemy from his homeland."

"Well, it couldn't have been any of those close to the Princess who feared his influence on her. After all, his rooms were very close to hers, and when people came to rescue him, the ceiling fell down and made Lady Eastkeeping a widow. Although that might have been an accident, something unforeseen—"}

He came back to himself to find that his partners were all watching him. Jeska thoughtfully refilled Cade's glass with ale, and he drank gratefully before saying, "I'm not sure what was going on. Give me a minute, all right?"

They went back to discussing Rafe's play. Cade heard snatches of their conversation, but most of his mind was engaged in sorting out that Elsewhen. It took some effort: the shock of learning that Lady Vrennerie could become a widow kept demanding that he rush to the North Keep right now and warn her.

The Tregrefin had been injured, had lost his hearing—which must mean black powder. Cade knew well enough what it was like to be deafened for long minutes after an explosion. But something loud enough to deprive someone permanently of his hearing, and violent enough to cripple him somehow, and bring down the ceiling . . . a copy of the *Consecrations*, a gift from someone unknown. The Tregrefin unable to recall anything. And not being the same after his return to his home . . . could an explosion have damaged his mind?

Cade worried at it awhile longer, then decided abruptly that sorting it all out didn't matter. Vrennerie's husband mattered. He would have to contact the Archduke and tell him that whatever he was planning, his plans would have to change. About the Tregrefin, Cade cared not at all, so long as he wasn't killed. But Kelinn Eastkeeping . . . Cade had guested at his castle and played with his children and considered him a friend, and of course he still had a warm place in his heart for Vrennerie. She was *not* going to be a widow at twenty-three.

"Hand me a sheet of paper, would you?" he asked Rafe, who obliged and gave him pen and ink as well. Cade thought for a minute, then wrote three words and his family name on the page. Mieka came over to stand at his shoulder and read aloud.

"'Change your plan.' That's it?"

Rafe scratched at his beard. "Somewhat . . . um . . . is *peremptory* the word I'm looking for? Or just plain *rude*?"

"That works," Cade replied. He folded the page twice and wrote *His Grace the Archduke—urgent and private.* Then he glanced round the undercroft of Number Eight, Redpebble Square, where Touchstone was rehearsing, and saw one footman he recognized and two he was fairly sure didn't work for his mother, pretending to scrub the stairs. Touchstone had used the undercroft so seldom in the last years that it was impossible for anyone who worked here—or, evidently, his friends—to pass up the chance to see as much as they could of the famous First Flight on the Royal Circuit.

"Here, you!" he called, suddenly ashamed that he didn't even know the boy's name. "Come here, please!"

"How will he get past the layer upon layer of servants?" Jeska wanted to know. "Not to mention the guards."

Cade had no ideas. He'd been too busy being grateful that the Archduke was accessible, no longer at Great Welkin. He and his wife and children had moved into the apartments kept for them at the Palace, two days in advance of the colossal celebrations for King Meredan and Queen Roshien.

Mieka was eyeing the boy. "That's not your livery."

"No, Y'r Honor, this is me work clothes."

Cade began to see what Mieka was after. He assumed what he hoped was a kindly smile. "You have a formal jacket—gray with silver braid, right? For when you serve tea, or go with Her

Ladyship to the shops, and carry her purchases, and all that?"

"Yes, Y'r Honor, but not for nothin' else, not never, not unless Her Ladyship says it so."

"Well, you're about to go on an errand for me, so go put that jacket on." When brown eyes widened with alarm, Cade went on, "There's half a royal in it for you. I want you to go to the Palace and give a note to the Archduke."

Alarm became panic.

"If you're there and back in good time, my mother will still be out paying calls."

"Wait half a tick." Mieka came round to Cade's chair and bent down, fingers busily working at his collar to unhook the falcon pin. "He noticed this at Great Welkin. Use this as identification to the Archduke—no, don't wear it, just keep it in your pocket! And remember to come back with it!"

It would have to do. The boy listened in tense silence to Cade's instructions, which now included not just the half royal but also a promise to see to it that he lost his job if he didn't return the pin and if this note did not go from his hand to the Archduke's, without anyone else having touched it in between. Cruel but effective.

"As for you two," he said to the other boys, still at the steps with pails and brushes, "take that lot back to Mistress Mirdley and scoot on home. You've seen enough for one day!"

When all three of the boys were gone, Mieka asked, "So what was in the Elsewhen?"

"Does it matter?" Jeska asked with a shrug. "Cade didn't like it. The Archduke will have to think up something else." Turning to Cade, he said, "Unless you want to present him with your own plan?"

"Well . . . no. And not just because I don't have one. Even if I thought something up, how could I get it to happen?"

"So what *did* happen?" Mieka asked.

"He sends the Tregrefin a lectern and a copy of the *Consecreations* that seems to be filled with black powder. Or maybe it's hidden in the lectern—that's more likely. There are two candles attached to it, and I suppose that had something to do with it. But you're right, it doesn't matter. I only hope that whatever he comes up with next, I get to see it in advance."

"If it's something you can change, then you will," Mieka reminded him. "Now, can we get back to putting the last touches on this thing?"

"If by that you mean we really have to think up a name for it," Rafe said dryly, "then, yeh, let's. Any ideas?"

The word came out of Cade's mouth before he knew he'd thought it. " 'Bewilderland.' "

Rafe snorted. Jeska looked confused. But Mieka frowned and searched Cade's eyes, and finally said, "That sounds familiar somehow. But it fits."

He didn't ask Mieka just why it sounded familiar—had he mentioned it as part of an Elsewhen? Had it *been* part of an Elsewhen? He couldn't quite recall.

Neither had he asked Mieka to elaborate much on his encounter with the old man in the minstrels gallery. From the description, he had a fairly good idea of who the man might be—but that was insane. Why would Sagemaster Emmot associate himself with the Archduke? Whatever he'd done in the war for the Archduke's father had landed him in Culch Minster with iron rings on his thumbs, and at the end of his sentence those thumbs had been lopped off as a warning to others. True, a few years after Cayden had left the Academy, Emmot had left it as well, but Cade's understanding was that he had retired. How could it possibly be that he was in the service of the Archduke? And how old was he now, anyways—ninety? Wizardly blood usually meant a fairly long life span, though not so long as Elves and nowhere near that of Trolls. No, Cade told himself, it couldn't have been Master Emmot. It made no sense.

But in spite of how little help he suspected such a thing might be when it came right down to it, he began to agree with Mieka's determination to acquire and learn how to use a sword. However convenient and even instinctive the use of magic might be—such as that time on the continent when he'd put up a wall of Wizardfire against some rather unfriendly people—the use of magic in that way, without a withie to focus it, was exhausting and, truth be told, much less permanent than the pointy end of a sword in someone's guts.

Not that he thought Mieka capable of killing anybody that way. Or any way. Not even by accident—and the Lord and the Lady and all the Angels and Old Gods knew full well that the Elf was careless at best and reckless at worst.

All the same, he reminded himself to ask Derien if the King's College taught fencing, and if so, whether the master could recommend a good teacher.

Derien. Why had he never seen his little brother in any Elsewhen? He told himself it was because Derien made his own choices and decisions. After all, Mieka hadn't shown up, either, because following them to Gowerion had been his own idea. Nothing to do with Cade at all. But Derien . . . damn the Archduke for his maliciousness, and damn him again for knowing precisely what would worry Cade the most.

The other three had kept talking while he was ruminating. "Bewilderland" it was. Rafe said it to himself, several times, as if tasting and feeling the silly word on his lips and tongue, a slow smile beginning somewhere beneath the thick black beard.

"So," Cade said, "remembering all the while that we're playing to children, how do we introduce ourselves?"

Jeska worried at a hangnail on his ring finger, then shook his head. "Hadn't realized that they'll have no idea who we are or what we do. I should've brought Airilie along today, or Tavier and Jorie. Certainly they all ought to be at the performance. We could borrow Chat's tribe as well—and what about Tobalt's daughter?"

It might have been the scant thornful of earlier this morning, or what he'd had for breakfast, or a special alertness for the quiver of a warning Elsewhen at the edges of his mind. Just before it coalesced, he wished rather forlornly that he could learn how to call them up at will. The Archduke seemed to think he could.

{ The curtain parted to rather tepid applause, led by the parents in the crowd. The little ones had no idea what to do or how to behave in this intimidating adult situation. Cade shared a smile with his partners and stepped forward.

"My name is Cayden Silversun. I stand over here, at this wooden thing called a lectern. I'm the Tregetour, the one who tells everybody else what to do."

Mieka, behind the glass baskets, exclaimed, "Doesn't he wish!"

Ignoring him, Cade went on, "That man over there with the beard, his name is Rafe Threadchaser. He's the Fettler. That means he's in charge of the magic."

"A likely story!" Mieka grumped.

"Rafe stands opposite me, at his own lectern. By the way, it was a gift from his lovely wife, Crisiant, who's here today with their son."

Touchstone bowed to Crisiant, and Bram wriggled in his seat with delight, especially when his father grinned at him. He was almost ten, which meant he wasn't yet old enough to think that his parents and their friends were hopelessly old-fashioned and even a bit ninnyish. *Wait a couple of years,* Cade thought with an inward chuckle.

"This is Jeska Bowbender," he went on, "and he's the Masquer. That means he's the person who plays all the parts.

The way he can do that is by his voice, and his gestures, and the expressions on his face—"

"And the magic!" yelled Mieka.

"And the magic," Cade conceded. And then he was quiet.

"Well?" Mieka prompted.

"Well, what?"

"What about me, then?" he demanded.

"What *about* you?"

"I'm Mieka Windthistle!"

Rafe said, in a loud aside to the audience, "And praise be to the Lord and the Lady and the Angels and Old Gods that there's only one of him!"

"I heard that!"

"He's Mieka Windthistle," Cade told the audience, hooking a thumb in Mieka's direction.

More silence.

The Elf stamped a foot. "Mieka Windthistle, of Touchstone!" When there was no reaction, he added, "The Glisker!"

Still nothing.

He picked up a pair of withies and began to juggle them. Right on cue, Tobalt Fluter—somewhere in the audience with his daughter, who was older than most of the offspring here but adored theater in general and Touchstone in particular— called out, "Is that all he can do?"

A smattering of laughter. Mieka caught both withies in his fists and planted those fists on his hips and declared, "I'm Mieka Windthistle, the Glisker for Touchstone!" After a few moments, while he stood there looking as if expecting something—anything—by way of reaction, he stamped the other foot. "The one at the back!"

Jeska laughed at him. Mieka twirled a withie between his fingers, then pointed it at Jeska.

The Masquer disappeared. In his place was a very large potted plant.

"Oy! Stop that!"

The potted plant was replaced by a very large squirrel.

"Mieka!" he wailed.

By now the children were laughing. The squirrel became a lamppost and then a lady wearing a too-short purple ball gown and workman's hobnailed boots. At last Jeska himself reappeared, glaring at Mieka.

"Have you finished?"

"I've only just got started!" Addressing the audience: "Because we've a story to tell you today, and what d'you say we get on with it?"

Cheers, applause, laughter—it happened every time. Cade grinned at Princess Miriuzca, who sat in the front row with her daughter—it was Levenie's very first time at a play—and called out, "All right, then! Let's begin!" }

"Well," he heard Rafe say, "it wasn't about the Archduke, anyways."

"Just because he's smiling?" Mieka scoffed. "Maybe he saw the Archduke getting caught up in his own plot. That'd make *me* smile!"

"It's a lovely thought," Cade admitted. "But I doubt the boy's got past the first guards at the Palace yet. Much too soon to see any changes."

"Hells," Mieka said glumly, then brightened. "What d'you think, another half hour or so?"

"Perhaps. But for now—Rafe, write this down. I've got the perfect beginning for 'Bewilderland.'"

And what a perfect relief it was, he thought as he told them what he'd seen, to escape into their work. If he had to sit about all day and half the night waiting to see (or not see) how the

Archduke planned to thwart the Tregrefin, he'd end with his nerves scraped raw and bleeding.

Two hours later, they'd run through the delightful silliness of a befuddled young farmer trying to find his pig's lost *oink* in a journey that took him all over the countryside and featured a dog that cackled like a chicken, a chicken that *moo*ed like a cow, a cow that chittered like a squirrel, a squirrel that *baa*ed like a lamb, and any other absurd thing they could think of. As the farmer came upon them and they heard their own voices, which startled them at least as much as it did the farmer, they followed him and his pig (Mieka was very happy to have another pig to play with) until he finally came upon a cat that *oink*ed. It was Rafe's plan to have the audience help sort everything out by applauding when an animal got its own voice right again.

Cade was just saying to Mieka, "I think you ought to work on that horse," when the boy in Silversun livery raced back into the undercroft, red-faced and panting, with a large folded letter in one hand and the silver falcon pin in the other.

Jeska kindly gave him a glass of Mistress Mirdley's lemonade while Cayden broke the seal and read. His face must have shown his emotions all too clearly, for he was only halfway through the letter when Mieka told the boy to go on upstairs and change back to his work clothes before Lady Jaspiela got home and caught him. By the time the undercroft door slammed behind him, Cade had finished the letter. He cleared his throat, wished for some whiskey, and read aloud:

I am grateful for your advice. Upon further consideration, it seems to me that the most efficient course is to prevent anything from reaching certain hands while at the same time providing proof that those hands were in fact reaching. I will inform you of developments.

I have undertaken to repay my debt to you by paying

Touchstone's debts. If you would do me the favor of listing those establishments currently holding outstanding bills, these will be taken care of—quietly, and with no names mentioned, which I am sure you will appreciate. Once this is accomplished, I will consider my debt to be settled.

I trust that you will communicate any further necessary information, which will reach me more surely and swiftly if your name appears on the outside of the letter.

Cyed Henick, Archduke

Rafe broke the horrified silence. "We'll refuse, of course."

"Of course," echoed Jeska.

"Of course?" Mieka exclaimed. "Have you run mad? He's offering—"

"—to buy us," Rafe said flatly. "Just like he did before."

"How is it *buying* us when it's to pay back the debt he owes Cade?"

"How is it that you're so stupid that you think he won't hold this over our heads? Don't you understand that we'll be beholden to him?"

"Better just him than all the people we owe money to right now! Fairwalk ruined us, we're skint, all of us—well, mayhap not *you*," Mieka sneered at Rafe, "with the bakery to live over free of charge—but what about Jeska and Kazie and their new baby that's coming? What about Cade, and Derien's school fees? What about *me*?"

Cade listened to the argument but took no part in it. He was thinking sourly how much it helped to have friends in high places. Fairwalk's clerks had fiddled with the books of Blye's glassworks for years; the Princess's Gift of the Gloves had saved Blye from being investigated and taxed; now the Archduke was prepared to solve all Touchstone's money problems. Yes, friends in high places . . . except that the Archduke was no friend, and—

Rafe was right—if they accepted his offer, they would owe him and possibly even be owned by him.

"—just the same as if he'd paid for the information, don't you see?" Mieka was saying. "I'm sure he has a thousand spies all over the place doing the same thing—"

Spies such as your mother-in-law, Cade didn't say.

"—somebody not even in his employ who came to him with a valuable piece of information, and gets rewarded for it! We'd be at evens with him, not beholden to him!"

Cade raised his head from the letter. "And what makes you think," he asked quietly, "that what we owe all over Gallybanks is worth all those lives? He's getting nothing out of this. I have nothing to threaten him with, except knowledge of possible futures—and I can't call those up at will, or be specific with them, which is what he'd want of me."

Mieka shrugged angrily. "You can tell him whatever he wants to hear. What would be better would be to tell him that whatever he's after, he might as well stop trying, because you haven't seen it happen."

"We've discussed this before," Cade pointed out, reminding him of a conversation in the kitchen of Wistly Hall before setting off for Trials. "If I say that I've seen Prince Roshlin as King, what would you wager that he'll do everything he can to make sure that doesn't happen? He could plot and plan for years, or he could be more direct and—what did he say in the letter? Ah yes. *Efficient.* How long before the Prince has an 'accident' and dies?"

Mieka squirmed slightly in his chair, then got up to pace the brick floor. "If he doesn't do anything about the Tregrefin, he knows that you'll know it. That's threat enough."

"Really? And whom would I tell? Miriuzca? The King? Unless the Archduke works this so that he gets the credit for stopping that stupid boy, he gains nothing. That's why the lectern and the black powder and the *Consecreations* were unexpected. It doesn't get him anything. The next thing I see will be a lot more subtle and a lot more obvious, both of them together. Subtle, because nobody will die—and obvious, so he can be hailed as a hero."

"*If* you see it," Mieka snapped. "None of this gets us any closer to paying our bills!"

"Why don't you buy a carriage or something really big and expensive and then take it to a pledge-broker?" Cade returned nastily.

"I'd get less than half its worth," Mieka shot back. "Why won't you listen to reason?"

"Why won't you admit that if we accept his money, he's *bought* us?"

"Enough," Rafe ordered. "We're not taking his offer. And there's an end to it."

"But—"

"End to it!"

Cade pushed himself to his feet and crossed to where Rafe sat at a wobbly old table with paper and pen and ink to make notes. Selecting a fresh sheet, he leaned down and wrote, *Further information will be forthcoming. And though we appreciate your offer, we cannot accept it.* He signed his own name, then held the pen out to Rafe, who scrawled his signature below Cade's. Jeska appended his name. They all looked at Mieka.

"Oh, all right," he grumbled. "But it's a good job that Auntie Brishen doesn't charge us full price. We're going to need all the thorn we can get, to make it through a solid autumn and winter of giggings." He scribbled his name and tossed the pen down. "Even so, we won't make enough to pay off everybody. So it's the same constant working into the spring, and anything we can find during the Royal next year. That's what we've set ourselves up for—you realize that, don't you?"

They did. But it was the only choice they could make.

25

With only a day left until the celebrations—a parade through most of Gallantrybanks ending at the Palace; free food and drink throughout the Kingdom (High Chapel and Low Chapel had finally coughed up); speeches by Court ministers (but only two; His Majesty was easily bored); performances at Court by the Crystal Sparks and Hawk's Claw tonight, and the Shadowshapers, Touchstone, and Black Lightning on the night itself; musicians, dancing, bonfires, and fireworks—Mieka wondered if it was entirely wise, putting on this afternoon show for the Princess, her ladies, and whatever children of an appropriate age they could round up. And for free, too. He suspected that Miriuzca would have a nice jingly purse ready for them, so at least they'd be paid something. Cade said they ought to look on it as an investment in the future. Mieka saw it as something to tire them the day before they had to be at their very best, and after working for Master Warringheath at the Kiral Kellari in the morning, too. Word had it that not only would the Crystal Sparks do their wondrous version of "The Glass Glove," but Hawk's Claw had worked all the hitches out of Trenal Longbranch's popular piece, "Mistress Ghost," so that now it was as deliciously scary as it was sardonic. To complete with them, and get the most giggings this autumn and winter and spring, Touchstone had to be great, and better than great. Which would have knackered them all senseless, if not for bluethorn.

Ah well. Perhaps Cade was right, and this performance would pay off in ways other than money. Miriuzca was as excited as the children—and there was quite a crowd, some of them page boys dressed in the various liveries of the Royal family, some of them the sons and daughters of various nobles and ladies-in-waiting. The Princess had returned to the Palace from the North Keep about a week earlier, still minutely involved in preparations for tomorrow's festivities. Mieka thought she looked tired, and though her gaiety in front of the children was not an act, there was something strained about her eyes that worried him. She had set up a space for Touchstone's appearance in the very back of the gardens, with a twelve-foot stone wall as a backdrop between a pair of apple trees, and a stage made of planks that rose about a foot from the ground. Chairs were scattered about for the adults, but the children would sit on the grass (which was why, he supposed, some of the mothers and fathers had brought along blankets so their offspring's clothes wouldn't be ruined by grass stains). Tobalt was there with his wife and five-year-old daughter, sitting in a large group that included Chat and Deshananda and their children, Kazie, Jeska's daughter Airilie, Crisiant, Jinsie, Tavier and Jorie, Blye and Jed, Jez, and Mieka's wife. Mieka regretted that neither Jindra not Bram were old enough to come to this, their fathers' first performance of "Bewilderland"—and he still had no idea why that word sounded so familiar. Had he thought it up himself, or had Cade mentioned it at some point?

The day was warm, but with just a breath of autumn in the breeze to keep things pleasant. Miriuzca herself, lithe and lovely in her own forget-me-never blue, approached the stage to greet them, then turned and clapped her hands together twice for silence—and introduced them herself. It was an honor they hadn't expected.

And then it was time for that wonderfully silly Introduction to Theater that Cade had literally dreamed up. His instincts had been correct. The patter was eagerly received, Tobalt played his part, and Mieka had a lovely time throwing magic at Jeska that included a horse, a sheep, and a four-foot-tall baby dragon (for Tavier, of course). And then they got down to the first performance of "Bewilderland."

They had all agreed that play would include sights and sounds only. No need to confuse or scare the little ones with tastes on their tongues or sensations on their skin, though Mieka had been voted down on doing a scent here and there. *"Horses and cows and sheep? Smelly!"* Jeska had said, his perfect nose wrinkling. Especially were there no emotions evoked. At fourteen or so, a child would understand that it was magic at work; at seven, it would be weird at best and frightening at worst.

The laughter as Jeska wandered about, plaintively trying to find his pig's *oink,* drew people from other parts of the garden and the Palace itself. Gardeners and grooms, maids and cooks, secretaries and minor nobles—and at last Queen Roshien herself, tiptoeing to the outskirts of the crowd, giggling and clapping her hands as enthusiastically as the children all around her.

At last all the animals had lined up onstage, with Jeska and his pig in the middle, and as he pointed to the goat and the horse and the squirrel and the lamb and so on, the children roared out whatever sound was appropriate and Mieka echoed it in the animal's voice. When that was done, Jeska took a step forward.

"I am so very much beholden to all of you for helping me! Now, just one more time, just to make sure—I want all of you to call out the sound made by your favorite animal. Take a moment to think about it. Are you ready? One—two—*three!*"

The noise was deafening and hilarious, like a gigantic barnyard gone utterly mad. Mieka, who was contributing absolutely nothing to it, knew that Tavier would be trying to sound like a dragon—which was not one of the animals included in the search, having been judged too scary even in miniature form. Jeska began to applaud the uproar, took another step forward, tripped, and purposely fell off the stage, did a somersault, and landed on his bum. While everyone was laughing at him, all the magical animals ran off behind the apple trees and vanished. They'd had a time figuring out how to clear the stage without upsetting the children, and it would have been easier with curtains for the animals to disappear behind, but it was managed here without causing alarm.

Miriuzca was on her feet, clapping her hands crimson. All the rest of the audience—quite the crowd by now—joined in.

Triumph. Another triumph to add to Touchstone's already impressive list. Not much money to be had from this perfor-mance, but Mieka felt much better, certain that Cade had been right about this investment in the future.

Afterwards there were refreshments for the children in another section of the gardens while Touchstone packed up lecterns and glass baskets and frames and withies. Miriuzca stepped up onstage as they worked, and Mieka grinned to himself as she turned as if to look out on an imaginary audience.

Turning back, she approached them and said, "Oh, I'm having not one word to tell you how wonderful! Beholden, beholden!"

"Our pleasure," Cade replied with a smile.

"Were you seeing the Queen? I had no idea she would come! And to be loving every instant of it, too!"

Evidently she lost her grip on Albeyni when she was excited. Mieka finished fastening the glass baskets into their padded nests—the same ones Cade had made for Blye's work years ago, respelled every now and then by Mieka for protection against bumps—and said, "I'll be glad when the Prince and Princess are old enough. And my own little girl, of course."

"I have something for you—a surprising—I mean, a *surprise*. Come! Someone will take all that back to the Palace, don't worry. Please come! I want for you to see my present for the King!"

They went. The grounds were extensive, and that twelve-foot wall went all around them. Trees, shrubs, elaborate knot-beds of flowers and herbs, little rock grottoes tinkling with waterfalls, vast swaths of grass—everything, in fact, except the hedge sculptures for which Cilka and Petrinka were becoming famous. Mieka reminded himself to remedy that—after all, it was in Miriuzca's father's own gardens that he'd first seen them, and brought the idea back to his sisters. Miriuzca chattered gaily with Cayden the whole while they were walking. But again Mieka was concerned, for her merriment seemed a trifle feverish.

At last they entered a back wing of the Palace, down a rather dark hallway to a pair of double glass doors. Mieka inhaled deeply the smell of newly sawn wood, familiar from his brothers' work. His jaw simply dropped open when the doors slid aside into the walls and Miriuzca proudly flung out a hand to show them what she'd had made as a present for the King.

A theater. Not a very big one—it would hold perhaps one hundred—but a real theater all the same. Brown carpets on the floor, sea-green velvet seats, rich tapestry curtains drawn back on either side of the gorgeously planked and polished stage. A huge candle-branch hung from the ceiling, with crystal drops and brass fittings. When Cade, obviously feeling impish, waved a hand and set the candles alight with soft blue Wizardfire, Miriuzca clapped her hands together and looked as if she'd throw her arms around him and kiss him.

"Well? What do you think?"

"I think," Rafe said in his slow, deep voice, "that this is a sight as close to perfect as I've ever seen in all my days—except, of course, for the sight of my wife emerging from her bath."

Miriuzca laughed. "Lady Megs helped me with it, the planning and designing and things. She's been to so many theaters, and she took the best of all of them for this."

Cade asked, "Is this where we'll be performing tomorrow night?"

"It is! And many, many times in the future, I am hoping—I hope," she corrected herself. "No longer must any of us wait for Trials to come round each year to see theater—"

"Or show up disguised in young men's clothes someplace in Gallybanks?" Cade said softly, gray eyes twinkling down at her.

"I'm sure I don't know what you mean," she said at once, then giggled. "Come along, I'm sure you're thirsty and hungry. I cannot be joining you, for there is so much to do still—but I had to show you this!"

Mieka knew that Rafe and Jeska and Cade were memorizing the dimensions of the theater, judging the possible ways the magic could bounce, possible slapback, all the things that needed to be understood about a new place. To give them some more time, he engaged the Princess in conversation—how long it had taken to build the theater, whether she'd chosen the seats after testing them herself—

"Of course! Master Glintlark had several chairs to choose from for me, but none were right for a theater. I didn't know that until I sat in them and imagined myself looking up at the stage, and when I couldn't imagine it, I said he would have to design something new."

"He did very well," Mieka said. He chose a seat in the last row and plopped himself down into it. "Oh, yes, very nice indeed," he went on after bouncing a few times. "Comfortable without being sleepy. Would it be wrong of me to guess that the Gift of the Gloves is in Master Glintlark's future?"

"It is possible," she admitted. "Do you like the lights, with all the crystals shining? Can you guess who made them?"

"Not Blye! Blye? She never said a word!"

"And all the wood for the floors and walls, that was your brothers!"

No wonder the smell had been familiar.

And the loathsome thought occurred to him that since they had all been paid a pretty sum for their work, they might lend Touchstone some money.

"The crystal drops, she made them from an idea of Master Silversun's," the Princess was saying. "See how they spark rainbows?" She wagged a finger at him. "And you're *not* to break them, Master Windthistle! Not a single one!"

Pretending to pout, he said, "*Nobody* lets me have any fun anymore!"

"But the play this afternoon—you didn't have fun?" She looked anxious.

"Of course I did!" He smiled. "I hope we do 'Bewilderland' again and again and again!"

"I so much wanted my brother to come see it," she said, abruptly sad. "But something happened—perhaps I'd better not say."

"He's all right, isn't he? Not ill or anything?"

"I suppose not. I don't know. He—he left for the Continent this morning."

Mieka stood up. "He didn't stay for the celebrations? I thought he'd be here another week or two at least."

Her beautiful blue eyes darkened and the sweet curves of her lips thinned. "He was not allowed."

He knew he shouldn't be asking questions, but he couldn't help it. He hoped she would take it for concern and not a rampaging curiosity about what the Archduke had done. "But he's your brother."

She looked ready to burst with the explanation. He begged the Old Gods to occupy Cade and Rafe and Jeska for just a few moments more.

"He—" Her voice lowered to a whisper. "They say they found him late last night, waiting by a garden gate with one of his servants—and opened the gate to another of his servants and someone dressed as a Good Brother but wasn't, and they had a huge crate they were carrying and it—it was black powder, like that which is putting into cannons to fire them and make explosions."

He regretted the sudden tears in her eyes, but not that he'd got the information out of her. "Who told you this?"

"My husband, the Prince. The guards who caught Ilesko came to him, not wishing to be bothering the King, and—and my brother was not denying it! That is what they told me. I don't believe it. I can't believe it. What would he want with black powder?"

"No idea," Mieka lied. "What happened then?"

"I saw him, and asked him, and he would tell me nothing. He only said he would leave this morning and gladly so, he was sick of Albeyn and hated everything and everyone here, and especially me because—because I have been straying from the true religion—" She choked, near to sobbing now.

"Sweetest lady," he said softly, putting a hand on her shoulder, "my dear Miriuzca, your brother is very young and very proud, and proud young men do and say some very reckless things sometimes. I say this because it's not so long since I was his age, and do you know what I did? I went all the way to Gowerion one night, just to see Cayden and Rafe and Jeska with their old glisker, who was *very* bad at his job, and I took the crazy chance of telling them I was so much better than this glisker, and they—because they weren't that much older than me, and just as crazy, I think!—they gave me the chance to work with them, and now here I am! I was silly and arrogant and a complete quoob—"

The bizarre word—one of Uncle Breedbate's—distracted her more than his babbled tale had done. The tears dried up and her brows arched, and he gave a rueful little shrug.

"A *quoob* is an eccentric fool, and that we most certainly were!"

"What a ridiculous word!" A tiny smile played around her mouth, and in her eyes he saw that she knew he had diverted her attention on purpose, and was grateful for it. "Where did you learn it? From Master Silversun?"

"Oh, no. I have an uncle who spends his life being more Elf than the first Elf ever, and that includes using words that are about a thousand years old that nobody knows anymore or cares to, just to prove he's keeping up old traditions—like his clothes, a dagged-hem tunic and trousers bloused at the knee over pointy-toed boots, usually yellow, and I can't even begin to describe how silly he looks!"

"A right quoob!" she said, and laughed.

At this opportune moment Cayden came up to them and said something about not taking up any more of her time. A footman escorted them to a small chamber overlooking the main courtyard, where food and ale and a lovely fat purse were waiting for them. Mieka didn't dare share his new knowledge with the others where they could be overheard, and told himself to wait until they were back at Wistly. Yet when he and Cade and their glass baskets were safely loaded into a hire-hack, and Jeska and Rafe with the lecterns and withies and wooden braces were in another, he turned to his partner and the whole of it tumbled out in no particular order but, to judge by Cade's expression, comprehensibly enough.

When Mieka had finished, Cade asked, "Did they stitch him up, d'you think? Lure him into it? Probably not, not if it was his own servant who went out for the black powder. So I guess they caught him fair and square. I wonder if they found the Good Sister's cousin in the Firemaster's unit. Where do you get yours?"

The blunt question startled him. "Quill! I haven't bought any black powder in—well, not years, exactly, but months, certainly."

"Where did you get it?" Cade persisted, frowning.

"A cannonneer in the King's Guard who went to littleschool with me," he admitted. "He's Wizard enough to light the stuff with your sort of fire. But he was promoted and now he's responsible for every grain instead of putting a bit to one side for me in exchange for something Auntie Brishen makes that nobody else does—"

Horrified, Cade gripped his arm. "*Please* tell me that he doesn't prick thorn when he's in charge of the cannon!"

"We prick thorn when we work," Mieka pointed out, annoyed.

"That's different!"

"Is it? The magic in the withies, spreading out across an audience—how is that less dangerous than some black powder and a big round cannonball? And what does it matter, anyways? The Tregrefin is still in one piece, and gone, and everybody's safe. D'you realize what that means?"

He looked confused. Mieka reflected that despite that big, complicated brain, and all the thoughts roiling around inside it, and all that reading and studying, he really could be hopelessly dense sometimes.

"It means," Mieka said as the hire-hack pulled onto Waterknot Street, "that the Archduke did exactly what *you* told him to."

A corner of Cade's mouth quirked wryly. "And you think that means I'm powerful?"

"I think it means that he still owes us a favor. Let's let that hang over his head for a long, long time, shall we? And when we finally do collect, let's make it a really *big* one!"

At Wistly Hall, site of all Touchstone's celebrations, Mishia had taken advantage of the warm summery weather to serve dinner out on the river lawn. Once everyone loaded their plates inside, they went outside to sit on blankets and quilts. Mieka sat with his own little family—his wife, her mother, and Jindra—thinking that his choice bit of gossip about the Tregrefin would have to wait to be told, and toned down a lot when he told it. That the boy was gone under mysterious circumstances was all he would say, and not unless someone else brought up the subject.

"She greeted me, you know," his wife was saying for the third time to her mother. "She was so kind, and so lovely in her blue dress! And she asked about *you*, my moppet," she told Jindra, tapping the child on the nose. "You're not that much older than her daughter, and perhaps someday you'll be asked to go play with Princess Levenie at the Palace or the North Keep!"

All at once his imagination called up the scene Cayden had described of explosion and flying glass. He wanted to scoop Jindra up in his arms and take her away to Hilldrop Crescent and keep her safe. He knew, of course, that he couldn't wrap her in silk and stash her away from all harm. He knew that. But he couldn't help wishing that it were possible.

"Well, Jindra, when you do," Mistress Caitiffer said, "remember to let the Princess win."

Mieka laughed at his daughter's stubborn scowl and jutting chin. "Every so often, anyways," he told her. "If she's half as smart as her mother, she'll know it if you let her win all the time."

"Is her brother that smart as well?" his mother-in-law asked.

He met her innocent gaze. "You'd have to ask Cayden. He's closer to the Princess than I am."

"Ah." She smiled with a contentment that set his teeth on edge. "Mayhap I will."

Jindra was only about a year older than Prince Roshlin. The woman couldn't possibly think—no, not even she was that ambitious. Besides, to hear Quill tell it—before he'd stopped seeing the Elsewhens—Roshlin was destined for the Archduke's daughter, Belsethine. It might be funny, though, to watch this woman scheme and plot to get her granddaughter wed to Royalty. As long as Jindra didn't suffer for it, and kept her sense of humor about it all. Mieka refused to see her hurt or humiliated. Perhaps Mistress Caitiffer's connivings wouldn't be so amusing after all.

Why had he never asked Cayden whether or not he'd seen Jindra in any of the Elsewhens? Such a simple, obvious question, and he'd never asked it. Years of Elsewhens were lost to Cade's stubborn desire to live like an ordinary person, though Mieka flattered himself that he had talked him out of that silly notion for good and all. But—Gods and Angels, why had he never asked?

"C'mon, sweeting," he said, gathering up his daughter and lifting her to ride on his shoulders. "Let's go see what Auntie Threadchaser has brought us for cakes and pies!"

Cade was over by the drinks table, and standing beside him was someone whose name Mieka was sure had not been on the guest list: Lady Megueris Mindrising. Cade was describing to her the various wines, beers, cordials, brandies, and Brishen Staindrop's whiskey—the only whiskey ever served at a Windthistle party.

"You seem terribly well informed about liquor," Megs said mildly.

"I worked for a while at a wine shop."

"And," Mieka said at his shoulder, "has been devotedly adding to his knowledge ever since. Welcome, my Lady!"

"Beholden to you, and especially to your mother for so kindly allowing me to intrude," she replied smoothly.

"Is there news from the Palace?" He reckoned it was just as well to be direct about things.

"Nothing we haven't already heard," Cade said. He reached up to brush a lock of black hair from Jindra's cheek. "How are you today, Jinnie?"

"Who is her?"

"This is Lady Megs. And this is Mistress Jindra Windthistle." Megs gave the child a short curtsy, which made her giggle.

"Honored to meet you. Do you like the party?"

"Mine is better. Granfa says a pony next time!"

"He does, does he?" Mieka craned his neck around, trying to look into his daughter's face. She was smiling sunnily—an expression he immediately found suspect, knowing what it meant when he wore it.

"Don't tell me," Cade said, amused, "that she's going to throw family tradition to the winds and learn how to ride?" To Megs: "There's not a Windthistle born, as far as I can tell, who can keep his hind end in a saddle for more than two minutes."

Mieka gave an elaborate shudder, which caused Jindra to yelp and grasp his hair for balance. He yelped in his turn. "Off, you pesky pest! Let go of me!"

Cade lifted her off Mieka's shoulders and settled her on one hip. "I want an ice," he announced. "How about you? What sort shall we have? Lemon or cherry? How about both together?" They departed, merrily debating the merits of each.

"I really didn't mean to invade your party," Megs told Mieka. "The Princess asked me to come by and tell you, first, that she's very grateful for this afternoon, and second, she hopes it didn't tire you too much for tomorrow evening."

"Not a thing to be worrying about," Mieka assured her.

"Not when there's enough thorn?" she asked pointedly.

He shrugged and smiled.

"Third," Megs went on, "except it's really first, I suppose, because it's my personal reason for coming here—" Her green eyes looked anywhere but at him. "—I've only just heard that you're . . . embarrassed for funds. Cade already told me no. But I do wish you'd persuade him otherwise, and let me help. My father always says what's the use of money if you don't use it to help your friends? I like to think we're friends. Won't you let me—?"

"Cade speaks for us all," Mieka said with no small regret.

Indebtedness to the Archduke was one thing; Megs really was a friend.

"Well, if you change his mind . . ." She sighed. "There is a third from Princess Miriuzca. Before her brother left—" A raised brow asked; he answered with a slight grimace to tell her that, yes, they knew all about the Tregrefin. "Anyway, he said that she ought to have a care, because not everyone in the Kingdom was so adoring as she would like to think. When pressed, he told her he'd heard that disruption of the celebrations was possible. He wouldn't say by whom, only that he'd heard rumors. But I think we can all guess where he heard such things, considering some of the company he kept whilst he was here."

"Rotten little cullion, wasn't he?" Mieka remarked. "I don't think she has anything to worry about. Princess Iamina and the Archduchess will be in the procession, and they're both known to sympathize with . . . certain people. Nobody'd dare harm them."

"That's what I told her. But she wanted to warn you, all the same. They especially detest theater, you know."

"Oh, I know." He made his voice a high-pitched whine. "One of those filthy, disgusting plays will fill a theater faster than the *Consecrations* can fill High Chapel! Shocking! Simply shocking!"

The smile didn't reach her worried eyes. "Do you know there are people demanding that all the theaters, new and old, and any tavern that presents plays should be closed?"

He waved that away negligently. "There've always been people like that. Plays are disgusting, people who go to see plays are even more disgusting, and as for the players—! Misfits! Vagrants! Corruptors of public morals! Bores me witless, frankly, especially when you consider that theater got its start acting out stories from the *Consecrations*."

"Did Cayden tell you that?" She smiled again, and this time it was genuine.

Why was it that people always assumed that anything he

knew, he'd learned from Cayden? It really was quite annoying. "My glisking master. Couldn't lace up his own boots without tying knots in his fingers, but he was fantastic if he had a withie in his hand. He droned on about theater history so much that I couldn't help but remember some of it."

"Why," she wanted to know, "would anyone think that 'Bewilderland' could corrupt anybody? I thought it was charming. The children all loved it. And it's something that parents can enjoy *with* their children, and surely that's to be encouraged."

"His Noble Tregrefin-ness would probably say that the reason the animals got their voices all switched around was because of the magic of an evil Wizard."

Megs nodded slowly. "But, you know, there's something going on inside that play—something other than the obvious of having fun, I mean. What you're saying to these children is that everybody has a particular thing to say and a voice to say it in. Further, that no one's unique voice ought to be silenced."

Now she sounded like Cade. *Meant for each other,* he told himself with an interior grin. The magic-wielding tregetour and the girl with the fettling skills who wanted to be a Steward—and didn't Stewards rein in any extremes of magic? Cade was an idiot not to see it.

What he said aloud was, "I think Himself would've objected to that, too."

"Enjoyment of diversity isn't one of his accomplishments," Megs agreed. "But why does he have to hate us for it? And his superstitions—Mieka, you have no idea! It started when he got up in the morning, or so the servants said. Not just daily devotions to the Lord and the Lady, but all sorts of nonsensical things. Protection in this nasty land of magic." Her nose wrinkled rather attractively. "For instance, he had to make sure he was wearing a bit of steel someplace—anything from a button on his trousers to the eyes for the shoelaces on his boots!"

"Against Fae, yeh?" He kept his face blandly pleasant, thinking about a certain old iron coin. "It worked, didn't it?" he teased.

"Oh, very funny. All of us live together without wearing talismans to protect us from each other, or—or—spouting off little rhymes to scare off Pikseys or making gestures with our hands under the table to ward off a spell from an Elf."

"What's the point of all that?" he asked. "I mean, we're all here, aren't we—Elves and Wizards and Goblins, and people with Fae ancestry, and Giants, and all the rest—what's to be done except live with it?"

"That's what worries me," she replied, her voice low and earnest. "What might be done. Albeyni folk aren't superstitious, not just because it's silly and wouldn't have much effect anyway, but because we all know each other. We all live together. It's people like the Tregrefin, who don't know and can't understand that we're all the same when it gets right down to it—they think they have to make everybody the same in all things by having them believe exactly what everyone else believes, and—and guard themselves because they're afraid of what's unfamiliar, when if they'd only take a little time to understand, they wouldn't have to be afraid!"

There was more to her somewhat incoherent passion than mere disgust at senseless superstitions. Mieka eyed her, noting that the flash of her eyes and the color in her cheeks made her quite appealing.

As for those gestures and rhymes and so forth—there really were things that worked as protection against the Fae, and nobody knew that better than he, so it was only logical that there had to be things just as potent against every other sort of magical folk, or where had the superstitions come from?—as he became aware that he was getting rather incoherent himself and it was making his head ache and his nerves wriggle inside his skin, he put a smile onto his face and refused to think about any of it at all.

And because it wasn't his job to investigate other people's passions—except when caused by and directed at him, in a bedroom far away from his wife—he said, "He could've done without all the iron and steel for the Fae, y'know. All it takes is a daisy."

Megs stared back at him for a moment herself, then laughed. "Oh, of course it does."

"No, really."

"Oh, I believe you."

She didn't, but that didn't matter.

"To return to something we both know about," she said, "I heard or read that the latest objection has to do with indecent attractions. The theater being a moral middens in the first place—" She laughed at his expression of outrage. "Well, look at all the naughty puns that the Mother Loosebuckle and Master Fondlewife plays depend on! And all the cross-dressing!"

"But it's all for a laugh!"

"You know, I think that's what I object to more than anything else. This new piety has a horrid effect on the sense of humor. To hear them tell it, if the girl onstage is really a man—"

"—then a man attracted to the girl might really be attracted to the man playing her," he finished. "Yeh, heard that one before."

"What's worse, a spectator might be attracted both to the female character *and* the man beneath the magic, which is a double corruption. And now with women in the audience, is it the man playing the girl they're attracted to, or the girl the man is playing? I wonder which they think more scandalous!"

Mieka rolled his eyes. "Is there any limit to this? Personally, I think there's something squirmy-slimy about people who're so interested in other people's bedroom lives. As for onstage, with all these attractions straying about, confusing everybody, the poor masquer is fu—the masquer can't win for losing," he amended hastily.

She grinned. "Oh, I think you were right the first time. Girl or man, there's always *somebody* in the audience who wants to fuck the masquer."

A sharply indrawn breath behind him made him turn. His wife stood there, wide-eyed with shock. "Uh," Mieka said intelligently, "Lady Megs, this is my wife."

"Her Ladyship and I have met. I hope Your Ladyship is well?"

They exchanged pleasantries. Iris-blue eyes met bottle-green eyes, and Mieka wanted to giggle when his wife linked her arm with his and leaned against his shoulder. In her sweetly smiling face was wariness that her husband was having such a good time with another girl, but also disbelief that this rather plain and badly-dressed woman (who used such dreadful words) could be any sort of competition whatever. Moreover, in Megs's face—just as sweet and just as smiling—was full knowledge of this reassertion of possession *and* full knowledge that she was being condescended to because of the way she looked. Mieka scarcely knew which of them to look at; he had rarely seen anything so funny.

"Mieka, dearest, Rafe and Crisiant are taking Bram home. Something about half a bowl of buttercream icing," she confided to Megs, "meant to go fresh onto the cakes that ended up in *him,* the clever little imp!"

Both women laughed. They were so friendly, so delighted with each other, so insincerely sincere—Mieka wished Jeska were around to make notes on some really good acting.

26

Happily for Touchstone, they were not part of the parade through Gallantrybanks. Neither would they be part of the cheering populace, not in the streets and certainly not at any of the three services of gratitude the Royals and nobles were due to take part in at three different Minsters. Touchstone had in fact been hired by Master Warringheath, owner of the Kiral Kellari, to craft a display that took up the whole exterior of his building on Amberwall Square. When the Royals and ministers and officials drove past, the magical scene was to animate itself into a spectacle worthy of Warringheath's loyalty (and the money he was paying Touchstone). Other groups were putting up similar presentations all over the city, the most anticipated being the one that the Shadowshapers were doing that stretched from one bank of the Gally to the other across the main bridge, which this year had been named the Meredan Bridge in His Majesty's honor. Cade was a little disappointed that he wouldn't be able to see it, and perfectly thrilled that he wouldn't have to go through even one of the long ceremonies before the Flame and the Fountain. Religion was leaving a bad taste in his mouth these days.

He was just as glad to occupy himself with their display. He'd eventually been able to talk Master Warringheath (and Mieka) out of a dragon. Prince Roshlin and Princess Levenie would be riding in their parents' carriage, and the day would be stressful enough for such young children without the sudden appearance of a fifty-foot-high dragon erupting from the wall of a building. This was not even considering the children who would be in the crowd, brought along so they could say in their dotage that they had waved to the King. No dragon, Cade kept saying, and eventually Master Warringheath (and Mieka) sighed and agreed.

It was easy enough, after talking of children, for Jeska to suggest, with the finest appearance of spontaneity Cade had ever seen off a stage, that it would be fun for the little ones in the crowd to show all the animals from "Bewilderland" bowing to His Majesty. Mieka took up this idea with enthusiasm, for of course it meant he could include a pig. Rafe, pretending mild interest, remarked that nobody else would think of this sort of tribute: that every living thing in Albeyn was grateful for King Meredan's rule. Master Warringheath thought that over and liked it, and thus here they were on the great day, withies primed to embellish the pastoral scene of grass and flowers, trees and river, broad sky and distant mountains, with a parade of animals to begin when the first carriage entered Amberwall Square.

That this would be splendid advertisement for themselves was only a secondary consideration, of course.

Despite what they were being paid, Cayden would much rather be doing this for the Downstreet, where Touchstone had got their start. But the procession would go nowhere near there. And Master Warringheath was paying *very* well for this salute to the King. Mayhap things would be so successful that he'd stop blaming Mieka (half seriously, half in jest) for the expense of having to repaint his walls yet again; women coming to performances really didn't want to be greeted with a mural of other women stark naked. "All your fault!" he'd accused the Elf more than once, until Mieka had finally given an unanswerable reply: that the next time he saw Princess Miriuzca, he'd be sure to tell her so.

There had been a slight hint of autumn in the air early this morning, warmed away by brilliant sunshine. On his way to the Kiral Kellari, Cade was amazed by the sight of Gallybanks dressed in every color of the rainbow. Hanging from windows on every street, even those where the King would not be passing, were printed congratulatory banners, bolts of bright cloth, luxurious carpets. Other windows were decorated with pasteboard shields of every size and description, glowingly painted with the symbols and devices of every noble family and every guild and every city and town in Albeyn. When the King drove by, the windows would be filled with people waving and cheering. Even now, standing in a second-floor window opposite the empty Kiral Kellari, with the basics of Touchstone's magical mural already established on the wall across the square, he could hear the distant trumpets and drums of the procession. Soon the crowd would start making their own noise, and Touchstone would add to it, and the golden stones of Amberwall Square would tremble with jubilant uproar.

Mieka tugged at his sleeve. "I've had an idea."

"You know how I feel about your ideas."

"No, really. Listen, Quill. Why don't we include people along with the animals?"

Cade sighed. "I assume you're not talking about fishermen, farmers, and farriers."

"Of course not. Wizards and Goblins and Elves and Trolls— it would be wonderful!"

"It would be provocative. Princess Iamina and the Archduchess are riding in this procession, you know. And who can say, of all the Good Brothers and Good Sisters trailing along, which of them aren't—?"

"Do you really care?"

"For myself? Not at all. But we said we'd do the animals from 'Bewilderland,' and that's what we're going to do. And don't be thinking I'll give you enough stray bits of magic to work the thing yourself," he warned. "In fact, we'd best get ready. Hand me those withies."

Mieka sulked, then did as told. He was flushed with more than excitement; whitethorn or bluethorn, Cade couldn't tell which and it didn't matter anyway. Still, it was rather early in the day for Mieka, and they had a performance tonight at the new theater at the Palace. Cade wondered briefly if the Elf would require a second or mayhap a third pricking of thorn, and if he did, whether Cade himself would have to adjust the magic in the withies to account for all that surplus energy—and then the worry fled his mind as a bellowing noise announced the arrival of the procession.

Mieka and Rafe were doing the work of this, once Cade had supplied magic in the withies. He looked across to the Kiral Kellari's window, smiling to recall that once he'd stood there and wondered why all those girls were down in the square, eager to see the players even though, or perhaps because, they weren't allowed to see a play. Today people were hanging off the streetlamps and packed ten and twelve deep along the streets and in the central square behind stiffly watchful King's Guards. A score of trumpeters in tabards of sea green over brown trousers stepped smartly from the side street into the square, blasting away. Their instruments were no less bright than the gilding on the open carriages that followed. King Meredan and Queen Roshien, wearing golden crowns studded with twinkling gems, smiled and waved. Behind them rode the city dignitaries of Gallantrybanks: the Lord Mayor and his wife, the Lord Director of All Guilds and his wife. Next came Miriuzca and Ashgar, holding their children. Beside each carriage were boys dressed in the colors of every guild, connected by chains of flowers.

"Just another tick," Rafe murmured to Mieka, and Cade turned to look at his fettler and glisker. "Not yet . . . they're not quite there . . . ready . . . now!"

Everyone in the square gasped and cheered to see the wall of the Kiral Kellari come alive with dancing animals and soaring birds and leaping fish. A minute or two of this rioting movement and noise—Mieka was gripping each successive withie tightly, and there was a sheen of sweat on his forehead—and then, just as the King came round the corner of the central square and was on the street right in front of the building, all the creatures would stop and bow. Just exactly how Mieka planned to make a fish bow was something Cade had wisely not asked.

A further gasp and a few startled shrieks told him the moment had come. Perfect timing; he saw the King down below, half-rising from his seat in the carriage to gape at the display. The Queen, tiny beneath a towering crown of diamonds and sea green beryls, was madly clapping her plump little hands. Two carriages behind them, Miriuzca was pointing out the wonder to her son, laughing. Ashgar seemed not to notice what was going on at all.

And then the procession passed, and it was all over. Mieka tossed the last withie aside and ran both hands over his face, then looked up at Cade with a grin. Rafe, carefully letting the magic fade, turned at last from the window and gave a tired, satisfied sigh.

Master Warringheath was first up the stairs. He burst in, wreathed in smiles and calling for drinks all round—until he realized that this was a lawyer's office, not a bar, at which point he abandoned the idea of refreshment in favor of expressing his ecstasies.

"Brilliant!" he cried. "Gorgeous! No one else will have anything like it! Not even the Shadowshapers will do so well!"

Jeska was close behind him, a more professional assessment evident in his broadsmile. "Absolutely perfect. Nary a hitch nor a twitch all the way to the roof."

Behind Jeska were the lawyer, his family, everybody who

worked in his office and their families, a random selection of admiring citizenry—all in their go-to-Chapel best—and, interestingly enough, Pirro Spangler and Thierin Knottinger of Black Lightning.

"It was wonderful, Miek," said one glisker to the other. "I brought all my little brothers. However did you manage it?"

Cade watched a brief interior battle play out on Mieka's expressive face. Pirro was a friend from student days, but he was also a member of much-loathed Black Lightning *and* he had once given Mieka some thorn that had had frightening effects. Triumph, however, had put Mieka in an expansive and forgiving mood. He smiled at Pirro and they discussed the execution of the display.

Cade turned his attention to Thierin. He expected some snide observation accompanied by one of Knottinger's snaky smiles. But the man was all admiration that looked and sounded sincere. Cade accepted the praise with a nod and a few pleasantries, then asked if Black Lightning was ready for tonight—and before Thierin could reply, said, "You'll have seen the new theater, of course."

A blank expression was followed by a flash of anger, quickly smothered by a look of startled interest. "New theater?"

"At the Palace. The Princess's surprise gift to His Majesty. Though I'm hoping there's a page or a footman to show us where it is, because I'm not at all sure I could find it again!"

"A well-kept secret," Thierin remarked. "Anything to notice about the construction?"

"Well, Mieka's brothers did the building of it, so it's structurally and acoustically excellent. Please excuse me, I ought to be helping pack up."

It annoyed him that Knottinger followed him to where two glass baskets rested on chairs. Mieka was holding the velvet bag of withies, fingers toying with the tassled ties as he talked to Pirro.

Cade noted that however much bluethorn Pirro was pricking, it certainly wasn't doing anything for his figure. How he ever could have aspired to the kind of quick, limber dance that was Mieka's way of glisking, Cade couldn't imagine. He didn't have the build for it to begin with, and quite frankly he looked as if he'd eaten his way through every town on the circuit.

"Well?" Thierin asked his glisker. "Did you get him to spill his secrets?"

Mieka crowed with laughter. "It'd take more than a few compliments! Are we ready to leave, Cade? Things to do before we head over to the Palace."

Cade was pleased to note that whereas Pirro might have been forgiven, more or less, Mieka wasn't falling on his neck and swearing undying friendship. He smiled down at his glisker and opened his mouth to reply.

"Oy!" Mieka exclaimed suddenly. "We'll take care of those."

Cade felt a snarl come to his lips as he saw Thierin run a finger round the lip of a glass basket. He damned near slapped the man's hand away.

"Sorry. Such beautiful work. Blye Cindercliff, yeh? From before she married whichever of you Windthistles?" He looked up, dark eyes shining oddly. "Or did her father make them?"

"His hallmark is on them," Cade lied. He picked up the basket and cradled it in his arms, the way he used to before he'd made the cushioning crates for them. Rafe was holding the other one as if it were his second child.

"Oh, of course. Of course. Well, see you over at the Palace!" Collecting Pirro with a glance, Thierin waved gaily and departed.

Master Warringheath's raptures were marred by a slight frown as he watched them descend the stairs. "I *cannot* like that boy," he muttered.

"You don't mean to say that you actually *tried*?" asked Mieka, withies wrapped protectively to his chest.

"Huh! Very good, Master Windthistle, very good! No, I've had them at my place naught but the one night, and some of my customers complain of it, for it seems they're very popular—but even though they were warned off, they performed that poisonous piece of theirs about the Lord and the Lady and their children."

"We've seen it," Cade said tersely. "And *poisonous* is exactly the word."

"You don't suppose they'll do it at the Palace, do you? Plenty of folk there with other than *pure* blood in them." His broad, amiable face screwed up with disgust.

Rafe shrugged a shoulder. "Who can say?"

"They really wouldn't, would they?" Jeska asked on the way downstairs. "I mean, if it's a splash they're looking to make at Court, that play that could end up drowning them."

"They performed it at Seekhaven," Cade reminded him.

"But not tonight. Not before all the officials that will be there. The people who run the country and haven't time or leisure to attend Trials." He paused, frowning. "I know for a fact that the Lord High Magistrate is partly Gnome with Piksey and Elf in him as well. His wife must be the same sort of mix, because they had two sets of twins—that's the Piksey—and one set had Elfen ears." To Cade's silent question, he replied, "Mum used to work for him, back before he was on the High Bench. He asked her one morning for the name of the man who'd kagged my ears, and she set down her polishing cloths, closed the door tight, and gave him a lecture on how dreadful it was, to do that to a tiny baby. She hadn't any say in the matter, you see, when my grandsir was alive."

"So the Lord High Magistrate's children were spared a kagging?"

"Mum always said it didn't compensate for not standing up to my grandsir when it was done to me, but at least there were two children in the world who'd grow up looking exactly as the Lord and the Lady intended, ears and all."

"One official out of dozens won't keep Black fucking Lightning from doing that play," Mieka remarked glumly. "I wish we could muck about with them the way they did with us!"

"That was never really proved," Cade reminded him. "But I know what you mean. And talking of that, if Thierin had kept his finger on that basket one more instant, I'd've mucked his face to a bloody pulp!"

"We'd best check it, and the withies," Rafe said.

"Of course," Mieka agreed. "You know the saying about not trusting anybody as far as you can see 'em? Well, I was looking right at Pirro the whole time, and I *still* don't trust him!"

As it turned out, Mieka had good cause. Cade found the rogue withie while he was priming magic into the lot for the night's performance. Had Pirro thought that Cade wouldn't be able to tell the feel of Blye's work from this thing? It was a childish and ridiculous attempt to interfere with Touchstone, and it set Cade to wondering what had made Black Lightning so desperate as to try once again to mess with them.

He had the greatest satisfaction at the Palace that evening, in the antechamber being used as a tiring room before the performances, of handing the glass twig to Knottinger with a viciously sweet smile and the words, "Lost one of your withies, I think."

"Oh, did we?" Thierin glanced at the withie, then snagged a glass of wine from a passing footman.

"You still use Splithook, don't you? It's his hallmark on the crimp. Take more care of your equipment, there's a good lad." He walked off to the corner where Vered and Rauel were holding their customary argument, and Romuald Needler was, as usual, trying to calm them down.

"Vered," Cade said, interrupting Rauel without a by-your-leave, "I have to talk to you. Now." To make sure of it, he took the man's elbow and almost bodily hauled him off.

"Oy! Have a care to the jacket, mate!"

"Shut up and listen." The room was small, which was bad, and packed with people, which was good: the chatter of so many players in stage clothes and servants in various liveries crushed into a confined space meant that nobody was really hearing anybody else. Cade leaned close to Vered's face and said, "Drevan Wordturner works in Lord Piercehand's library—you know him? Good. He told me to tell you two things. First, there's a book in translation at the Archives that will tell you everything you need to know about a certain subject." When black eyes lit with excitement, Cade shook his arm. "I said *listen*! Don't go for it yourself. Find somebody you trust, who's not directly connected to you, and have him look into it. The Archduke knows what you've been researching. The archivists keep him informed. You're a tregetour, write yourself a plot where you can get the information in a roundabout way without anyone being suspicious."

Vered nodded, white-blond hair gleaming in the light of a candle-branch overhead. "And the other thing?"

He hated having to say it. The words went against everything he believed about Art and the artist's right to create what needed creating. And just look at the trouble he'd caused by writing what he'd felt he had to write: Briuly Blackpath, wandering aimlessly about the Brightlands, nothing to him now but pointless songs. . . . "What you're writing is too dangerous to write at all. It shouldn't be finished, leave alone performed."

As Cade had known it would, this caution served only to increase Vered's desire to complete his second play about the Balaur Tsepesh. He'd promised Drevan that he'd deliver both messages, and he'd done so. But now he felt compelled to add something of his own, something Drevan had told him and had perhaps forgotten to warn him to keep secret.

"Vered . . . there's one more thing."

"That's three."

"This one's from me." He lowered his voice and leaned in closer. "One of the Knights was a Henick. The Archduke's own family."

Vered flinched like a startled horse. "For certes?"

"It's why he doesn't want anybody looking into—the subject."

A look of gleeful cunning appeared on the dark face. "Much beholden for the information, Cade. Especially as now I know whose features to put on Rauel when he plays the Knight!"

Not a wary bone in his body, had Vered Goldbraider. Not a single instinct of self-preservation. They had much in common, the pair of them. But at least Vered would be forewarned—and that, too, was something they had in common, Cade reflected sourly, even if his own forewarnings came as Elsewhens. "He doesn't look like a Knight of anything. He's too fat, and he's got heart trouble."

Rather than laugh, Vered looked down, bit his lip, then said, "That's something else about them, y'know. They have no heartbeat—because they have no hearts."

Little as he knew of even basic anatomy, Cade was aware that this was impossible. "Anything living has to have a heart to pump blood."

"Who said they were *alive*?" Vered stepped back and bumped into a wall. "Beholden, mate. Now it's time to go let Rauel win, like I intended all along." With a wink, he added, "He'd be *so* disappointed if I didn't fight!"

Cade watched him thread his way through the crowd to his partner. Yes, Vered would fight. But against the Archduke, how could he win?

Cade had won. He had told Cyed Henick what to do, and what *not* to do, and been . . . *obeyed* wasn't the word for it, and it didn't really feel like winning, but he reckoned that it was probably as close as he'd ever get.

And anyway, he told himself, what was the risk to the Shadowshapers if Vered finished his play and the Archduke didn't like it? Drevan Wordturner, whose life was under the man's direct control, was a coward, a quailer, and a quakebuttock. Pleased with the alliteration, he grinned and sipped a glass of bubbly white wine.

Romuald Needler was coming towards Cade, looking both grateful and worried. "Beholden to you for separating them. It's been a nervous few weeks, I can tell you."

"Things not going well out on their own?"

"Oh, no, not that. It's been most gratifying. And I've been there to keep them from each other's throats." He shook his head. "Ludicrous, that two people who care for each other that much can fight like wyvern and dragon over a sheep carcass. One day, one or the other of them will say something unforgivable, though, and I won't be there to settle them down, and I don't know what will happen after."

"They work together too well to let things get that far," Cade soothed. "I've been hearing all afternoon and evening about the show on the bridge. Through a bower of trees, was it? All of them dripping jewels and filled with songbirds?"

"And bells. Tuned precisely by Alaen Blackpath—and I don't like to think about what a time Sakary had keeping him sober long enough to do it." Needler looked more depressed than ever. After a moment, though, he seemed to rouse himself to a cheerier reply. "While everyone applauded, the King was heard to say to the Queen that he hadn't known people liked him so much." He looked up as a single warning note sounded from a horn. "That's the start. You'll be following Black Lightning, and the Shadowshapers will follow you." A smile tried to work free of his gloom. "It's not a position they relish, having come so very close to it at the last Trials."

"What?"

"You didn't know? A few scant points separated you. Next year I feel it might well have been a tie, or perhaps you would have won outright. I'm not saying that simply because there won't be any more Trials performances for them, and my surmise can't be tested. It's the truth."

"Beholden," Cade managed.

Needler glanced out over the packed tiring room—easy enough for him, topping every man there, even Cade, by a head. "There's Chattim waving at me. I'd best go. Luck to Touchstone."

"And to the Shadowshapers."

Black Lightning performed their "Open Things" or whatever it was called, with the naughty bits excised. No opening a virgin girl's legs, for instance. Cade hadn't really thought they'd have the balls to do "The Lost Ones." He'd heard they were working on something new, something to do with a staircase, with every step an advancement towards knowledge and righteousness. He presumed it involved kicking Gnomes and Trolls and Pikseys and Goblins out of the way during the climb.

Touchstone worked free of the tiring room and into a side hall, dodging a sudden influx of servants bearing fresh food and drinks, then stepped onto the stage behind the curtains to set up while Black Lightning was still packing their gear. Cade helped Mieka with the glass baskets and frames, then lugged his lectern to its proper place onstage. They would do the good old "Dragon" tonight because the flunky who'd brought the formal command, sealed and beribboned like a Trials invitation, had said flat-out that the King wanted to see it. By now they could have done it in their sleep.

It went well. Mieka's dragon wasn't the biggest he'd ever done, but it was big enough in the high-ceilinged theater, snarling and growling and breathing fire. Rafe was the master of subtlety, as ever. Jeska's Prince, wearing the Royal colors tonight, was elegantly weary as he said, "Let them sing not that I was mindlessly brave, but that I was frightened and overcame my fear. *That* is the legacy I leave them, the same, I see now, that my fathers left to me. The overcoming is what fashions a man into a prince, and a prince into a king." And because he was playing to a king, he paused at this point and bowed deeply to the man in the center of the front row.

When it was over, and the magic had faded, Mieka and Rafe shattered a couple of withies (well out of range of the audience). Touchstone met center stage to bow. Evidently it *was* the King's favorite play; he actually got to his feet to applaud. Cade wondered idly what fears Meredan had had to overcome—a renewal of the war, perhaps, that his father had fought? Or maybe, he thought, maybe the peace after a brutal war presented difficulties all its own. A war was, after all, fairly direct, and with a sure ending: You won or you lost. But what to do after, even if you won? Politics and governance bored Cayden witless, but he began to think that there was something courageous that he'd never before considered in the management and preservation of something so delicate and complex as peace.

He was still thinking about it as he carried nested glass baskets into the crowded little hallway leading to the tiring room. He smiled at the Shadowshapers as they went past, a bit tardy in setting up their own equipment. Mieka was just ahead of him, counting withies because he hadn't had time when gathering them up onstage. All at once he stopped, and Cade bumped into him.

"What the fuck is this?" Mieka exclaimed, pulling a withie from the velvet pouch. "This isn't one of ours, Quill—"

Cade set the crate on a side table, pushing aside a huge ceramic bowl of roses, and took the withie in his hand. No, not one of theirs—it was of a pale apple-green color Blye didn't use. He squinted at the crimp end, but it was blank.

"It was Pirro, it had to be," Mieka spat. "We were all together out there, them gathering their things and us setting up—stupid git! Can't even keep track of his own withies! And twice with the same fucking trick!"

"This isn't one of theirs, Mieka. No hallmark. They use Splithook."

He looked at Mieka, and Mieka looked at him, and in that instant, they both knew the danger they were in.

Cade's eye lit on the bowl of roses. Still holding the withie in one hand, he dumped the bowl over, spilling flowers and water. He was about to put the withie on the table and cover it with the bowl—it was all he could think of to contain a nasty spell, realizing the stupidity of it all along—when the sound of breaking glass made him flinch. Mieka had upended a crate. The largest of Blye's beautiful glass baskets had cracked onto the floor.

"In here!" Mieka cried.

He almost made it. The withie was inside the magically cushioned crate and his hand was almost clear when the glass twig shattered to splinters.

27

"... only if he wakes and there's pain," someone said. The low, masculine voice had a ring of authority. "The salve on his hand should take care of most of it, but a little more of this won't hurt him."

"I understand."

What was Miriuzca doing here?

Where was *here*?

"Are you quite, quite certain there's no other damage?"

And—Megs?

"His hand is still attached to the rest of him," the physicker said. "I'll know more in a few days. But mostly it's cuts and burns, nothing very deep. All the splinters have been removed. No, I'd say he'll be just fine, Your Ladyship."

"But it was done with magic."

Well, of course it had been done with magic. He could have told her that. Pirro's magic, Thierin's magic—they'd finally got him, the grimy bastards—pretending admiration, pretending to be Mieka's friend—

"Mieka!"

"Hush now, Cayden, it's all right." Miriuzca again, a rustle of silk and a scent of lilies. She'd changed her perfume. "Mieka is just fine. No glass touched him at all."

He managed to get his eyes open. To his right were two elegantly gowned women—the Princess and Lady Megs—and down at the foot of the bed was a green-robed physicker packing up his case. The bedchamber had blue forget-me-nevers painted on the white windowframes, and for a single shocked moment he thought he was lying on Princess Miriuzca's own bed. But then he saw the hangings, turquoise silk decorated with quiverfuls of black arrows, and realized he was in the bedchamber and the bed belonging to Lady Megs.

"Now, don't you dare try to get up, you silly man."

This woman's voice came from his left, and he turned his head to find Lady Vrennerie standing there, and her husband right beside her.

Lord Eastkeeping smiled at him. "I had a singularly hellish time getting you up here—whoever gave you permission to grow your legs so long?—so do us all a favor and stay here a while, won't you?"

"Sorry," Cade mumbled.

"Well, you were in shock, I should think. But I really do wish you hadn't fought me quite so hard." He rubbed his chin.

"Don't be such a baby," his wife chided. "You should learn to duck faster, like Rafe did. Now, Cade, I know you're full of thorn right now, but do try to listen and understand. Everyone else is just fine. The physicker says that your hand is scratched and scraped, but none of the cuts were deep enough to damage the muscles or anything. You'll be all wrapped up for a fortnight or so, but you'll heal very nicely."

"Jeska," said Kellin Eastkeeping, "commanded a carriage from the Royal stables. He should be back soon with your Mistress Mirdley. She'll tell you exactly what Vren just told you, so don't worry."

He nodded because it seemed the thing to do. Whatever

thorn he was full of, it wasn't the few drops of bluethorn he'd used before the performance. This was something floaty and misty that made his eyes want to cross. But there was no pain, and considering the state his hand must be in, he was very grateful.

"Hells," he muttered. "That's two Shabbyshappers—I mean, Shadowshapies—shows I've missed in one day."

Megs laughed and patted his good hand. "I'll tell them you said so."

"Are you sure he'll be all right?" Miriuzca asked the physicker.

"Perfectly sure, and perfectly all right. Some scarring. But nothing that will impede the use of his hand."

His right hand. The one he wrote with. Should it be damaged after all . . . should the physicker be wrong, or lying to make him feel better before somebody broke the bad news in a day or two . . . He turned his face away and closed his eyes, wishing that this thorn, whatever it was, would have the decency to do something about his fear. The others present in the room had the decency to withdraw a little and leave him to what they must be assuming was sleep. Only Megs was still beside him. He could smell her perfume, something that made him picture a forest glen full of flowers and berry bushes.

When Mistress Mirdley arrived, she reassured him that the physicker had been right. With her came Mieka, Rafe, and Jeska, none of them reassured about his condition until they saw him for themselves. Cade wondered idly how they'd been kept out of the room thus far, then reflected that command of the Palace Guard might be useful. Rafe searched his eyes, then nodded curtly before his expression settled into seething rage; Jeska's worry became simple relief. But Mieka came in looking both angry and guilty, and stayed that way, and Cade knew why.

"Wasn't your fault," he managed to say. The thorn was well and truly in his veins by now, and it was difficult to stay awake. "Don't even think it."

"I shoulda known, Quill."

"Me, too." Rousing himself once more, he said, "Who knew they'd try the same thing twice on the same day?"

"Who tried what?" Miriuzca asked.

"Nothing. Nobody," Mieka said, and from what Cade could see of her face as his eyes tried to cross again, she knew the Elf was lying.

"All right, then," Mistress Mirdley said as she rewrapped Cade's hand after applying a salve of her own. "That's enough. Out, all of you." Spoken as peremptorily as if they were all in her kitchen at Redpebble. "It's time for this clumsy idiot to get some sleep."

The physicker was already gone, ushered out earlier by Lady Megs. Clever girl; he would only have bristled at Mistress Mirdley's presence, and she would have bristled right back, and they would have argued over him just for the sake of asserting authority. Jeska left, and then Rafe, with Lord and Lady Eastkeeping. Mistress Mirdley inspected the paper twist of thorn left by the physicker, grunted reluctant agreement with the choice, and ended by saying, "A fine lot of trouble you'll go to, only to skive off helping with the dishes."

Miriuzca stared and giggled. Lady Megs grinned. Cade was rather put out. Wasn't there a single woman in the world who cared about him enough to keep on worrying even when worry was deemed unnecessary?

When the Trollwife had gone, escorted by Mieka, Miriuzca stayed a few minutes longer before trading glances with Megs and saying, "I'd best return to the banquet. You're in excellent care here, Cayden. Sleep well."

"But—" He squinted up at Megs. "You don't have to stay." This struck him as silly; it was her room. "I mean, you stay, I can go home—"

"Not a bit of it," she said briskly. "Lie back, close your eyes, and sleep."

He did.

The next thing he knew, someone was groaning softly. Him. His head hurt and his hand felt as if it were on fire.

"Hush," she said.

She had lit a candle, and by its light was very competently preparing a glass thorn.

"Works funny . . . on me," he slurred. "Auntie Brishen says so."

"Whoever she is, she's not here. And this will work just fine. Both the physicker and your Mistress Mirdley said so."

She set the glass aside. She pulled back the counterpane but didn't roll up his sleeve. Instead, she unbuttoned his collar and then his shirt and slid it off his shoulders. He had no strength to protest or to push her away, and he blushed, but she was so matter-of-fact about it that he was ashamed of himself for thinking what he wasn't even really certain he'd been thinking. He was naught but a player on a stage, despite some noble names in his ancestry, and she was rich and important, and Mindrising was a *very* old name, one of the oldest, like Eastkeeping, indicating someone trusted to hold secure the borders of the Kingdom, and she was undoubtedly destined for some rich and handsome and wellborn man, not the likes of him—naught but a skint, scrawny-chested, big-nosed, thorn-pricking tregetour—

As he felt the little sting of thorn on his neck, he heard himself ask, "D'you still wanna be Steward?"

She smiled and rubbed some sort of cream into his neck, and then into the marks on his arms. "Of course. I've been working at it. Not lessons, exactly, but advice and a tip here and there from the ones who're so old that they're grateful for any attention from a young woman, pretty or not."

"You're pretty," he said dreamily. This was truly excellent thorn. He'd have to find out exactly what it was. "It'd help if you'd stop wearing turquoise. Not your color."

"No? Mayhap not." She sat back, looking him over. "You're feeling that, I take it."

"Mmm. Good thorn." He wriggled luxuriously into the pillows. "Glad you're not dead. You an' Rosish . . . Roshlish . . ."

"Oh, yes, it's good thorn, all right." There was laughter in her voice. "And I'm glad I'm not dead, too. Whatever you're talking about. Go back to sleep."

"Mmm . . . not yet."

Auntie Brishen was right. Thorn didn't do to him what it did for other people. All at once he was wide awake. Neither his hand nor his head hurt. He was very glad she was alive, and very glad he was alive, too.

Yes, alive in a pretty girl's bed, and the girl herself was sitting next to him on that bed, and it was late at night in the soft glow of a candle that put flashes of gold into her deep green eyes, and he wouldn't have been mortal if he hadn't coaxed her into his arms and kissed her.

Oh yes, very much alive, and very grateful that one hand was still in perfect working order. Within a very few minutes, she was grateful, too.

"What joy you must feel, to have kept Cayden Silversun happy!"

"Am I to understand that you don't approve?"

"Your Grace will, or perhaps will not, forgive me for saying that this was an opportunity that was . . . how shall I phrase it? *Bungled*."

"You appear to be drunk."

"I have been toasting His Majesty's twenty-five years on the throne. It's the duty of everyone in Albeyn over the age of twelve to get at least a little drunk tonight. How could you have allowed Cayden to—?"

"To what? Tell me, great Sagemaster! Should I have said I didn't believe him? We know what he is—"

"Yes, and now that's out in the open. We know, and it is acknowledged that we know—and he will be a thousand times more alert to any hint of interference. Speaking of which, those imbecilic young men await us at Great Welkin."

"Let them wait."

"Of all the monumental stupidities—slipping that charged withie into Touchstone's—may I ask why Your Grace is laughing?"

"There were two withies. One at their display for the King, and one tonight. Neither had anything to do with Black Lightning."

"And this amuses you?"

"You don't honestly think they'd disobey my orders about interfering with Touchstone again? They have too much to gain tonight to indulge in such foolishness. Knottinger and Seamark are far from being fools. Oh, they're greedy, and very young, but Spangler is a thorn-thrall who does what they tell him, and the fettler—I can never recall his name—"

"Crowkeeper."

"He knows where his advantage lies. No, it wasn't Black Lightning."

"Then who?"

"My dear Master Emmot, I cannot describe how gratifying it is to know something that you do not. Great crushes of people in both locations, yes? No telling who might be there, sliding a withie into an unguarded velvet pouch. The first was of the sort that garbles magic. Had it gone undetected, the other withies would have produced effects that were not exactly intended."

"Which would be blamed on the Elf and his drink and his thorn. Yes, I see. But there was never any chance that Cayden wouldn't recognize something not of Blye Windthistle's making."

"And that ought to tell you something about the intellectual powers of the person who arranged it."

"What of the second withie? The one that shattered in Cayden's hand tonight?"

"Ah. Now we get to the amusing part. Deeply as she now despises magic, or purports to, my cousin the Princess Iamina is not above using it. And—"

"Iamina?"

"She really *is* quite monumentally stupid, you know. Never notices the faces around her unless they belong to handsome young men. A boy dressed in her livery could be anyone in Albeyn, employed by anyone in Albeyn."

"I know that you have her watched, but I never thought—I mean, her connection with Tregrefin Ilesko was obvious, but—"

"Who do you think told him about the Good Brother who bespelled the withie tossed into Piercehand's Gallery? I don't know why she chose Touchstone for another little demonstration of how dangerous magic is. Perhaps there's a private grievance. It was a puny spell, the Good Brother having little talent to begin with and, it seems, no desire to slaughter everyone in the King's Playhouse."

"So it harmed nothing but Cayden's hand."

"The Brother lacks the true spirit of the thing—which reminds me it might be that Iamina targeted Touchstone because it was Silversun's grandmother who first proposed using withies in that way. Now, *there* was a woman who understood magic."

"How did you know that neither withie would be any real danger?"

"I counted on them to discover it as they discovered the first. But, as I say—little talent, and undoubtedly a rather shaky command of what he does know. But all that is beside the point. I want to know what you think I ought to have done about Silversun's vision. Allowed things to go forward to the deaths of Miriuzca and her children? He lied to me about the children.

When a man looks you straight in the eyes, it is because he is confident that he can control the expression in his eyes and doesn't want you to notice the rest of his face."

"A lesson of mine that you learned and he evidently did not."

"And what lesson of yours would have taught me how to take the best advantage of what he told me that was true? For one thing, it offends me greatly that this strutting little Tregrefin sought to bring his notions of proper religious devotion to Albeyn in the first place. Let him preach in his own country. This one is mine."

"Not yet. Your Grace will forgive me for pointing that out."

"You're lucky I'm in a forgiving mood. No, I could do nothing but what I did. We both know what it must have cost Silversun to conclude that I was the only person he could go to. The only person with access and power who would believe what he had to say. He no more wanted to admit that he knows that I know than I wanted to admit it to him myself. I tested him, you know. Setting up a plan, commissioning the lectern—and damned if he didn't know within a day!"

"It happens like that sometimes. Where's that wine bottle? Ah. He was probably surprised that you didn't think up something that would devolve all credit onto yourself."

"Probably."

"Did you cause things to happen as they did to earn credit with *him*? If so, you will be disappointed."

"In gathering power, it is best to persuade others that those who are their enemies are also your enemies, for the simple fact that they are *other*. Killing these enemies is not murder but merely ridding the world of vermin. If your enemies are seen as not quite Human, then they may be slaughtered in the way men slaughter deer or elk or any other prey."

"That much I understand, beholden to Your Grace. The Tregrefin was Cayden's enemy because he was a threat to the

Princess and her children. He was your enemy because—why? His religion offended you?"

"He would have overset some very important plans, as you well know, had he succeeded. By not killing him, I have shown Silversun what he will believe is mercy—"

"He will see it for what it is: self-interest."

"Yet he will also see that whereas he had no power to retaliate against me if I *had* ordered the Tregrefin's death, I honored our agreement. It is vital to convince the people you will rule that you yourself are a cut above the merely Human. That you have qualities of wisdom and strength, of cunning and leadership, beyond those of the ordinary man."

"Don't refer to him as *ordinary*. He's not. He never could be."

"That's one of his weaknesses. He *wants* to be, in many ways, and knows he is not, and the pull of those against each other is a constant torment to him. As for his other weaknesses . . . you never did tell me how your conversation with the Elf went."

"Not much of a conversation. I had a little fun with him, that's all. He was thorned, of course. I gather he is thorned from almost the moment he wakes up until he pricks the red variety so that he can sleep at night. He's a pretty thing, certainly, with those eyes and that face. But that won't last."

"Another far-from-ordinary man. Still, consider all those thousands who *are* ordinary. They have no wish to be ruled by one such as themselves. Every man knows his fellows to be stupid and venal, selfish and vain, lacking intelligence—while at the same time he considers *himself* to be unlike his neighbors, and congratulates himself on how smart he is to recognize their flaws and not share them. Secretly, though, he knows he hasn't the education, the noble bloodlines, the money—whatever he believes to be necessary in a ruler. His real desire is to look up to a man smarter, braver, stronger, shrewder than he. A superior man."

"A word of caution, Your Grace. Should anyone present

himself as that man, these ordinary men will seek to kill him."

"But present yourself as *unwillingly* being that man—convince those you wish to rule that you are just like them but for this accident of nature, this random gift of gifts beyond their own that you must use, having seen the suffering all around you—present yourself as better but not superior to these ordinary men, and they will smile and cheer and follow you."

"And then, because you are indeed superior, you may treat all other men, both your enemies and those you rule, as inferiors. In short, as prey."

"Exactly."

"Which doesn't do anything to negate the fact that now you owe Silversun a debt."

"Which I will honor. I did try, you know. Touchstone is in financial difficulties. They refused."

"You should have just paid everything off without telling them. You could have found out to whom they owe what sums, and—"

"Young men have their pride, Emmot. Besides, this way is better. Can you imagine how hard they'll have to work for the next year? Can you imagine that they will be able to do that work without thorn?"

"Hmm. A good point. Pun intended."

"So you're in better humor now?"

"Enough wine, and the prospect of watching the Elf destroy himself, seems to have had a salutary effect. I gather, by the way, that you have utterly given up on bringing Cayden into the fold."

"Unless someone he cares for is threatened, he will never tell me the truth of his visions. And even when that threat exists, he will *still* attempt to lie. I could never trust him. Not the slightest word he said could be trusted."

"Forgive my laughter, Your Grace, but do you seriously think you can trust Black Lightning?"

"Of course not. Or, rather, I can trust them to do what benefits them and advances their various adolescent ambitions. Much more reliable, really, and easier to discern than trying to keep track of who Silversun loves and what he's willing to do for them—and that isn't even to mention his morality and his scruples."

"Ah well. He would have been useful."

"Since he cannot be that, he must be rendered useless."

"In favor of other, less potent but more reliable tools. Speaking of which, shall we remove to Great Welkin for further festivities? I told them midnight, which annoyed Spangler. He wanted to stay at the celebrations and get as drunk as he possibly could."

"It's at least an hour past midnight."

"The timing was only a sop to their imaginations. It can be done at any hour of the day. But these little details mean so much to the ignorant."

"True. The ballroom, then."

"The Archduchess is remaining at the Palace tonight?"

"Yes. Ah, if only she knew the uses to which we'll put her pretty painted ballroom tonight!"

"If only she knew what is in her own bloodlines, that we have reclaimed for your children."

"And won't it be interesting to see how those bloodlines play out! Do you need a hand, or can you stand up on your own?"

"Your Grace, I have never been so drunk that I could not preside over a ceremony of any kind—especially of *this* kind."

THE PLAYERS

(most of them, anyway)

Bellgloss, Master purveyor of thorn
Blackpath
  Alaen lutenist
  Briuly Alaen's cousin; lutenist
Bowbender
  Airilie Jeska's daughter
  Jeschenar masquer, Touchstone
Challender, Mirko tregetour, Crystal Sparks
Coldkettle, Lord Prince Ashgar's private secretary
Crowkeeper, Herris fettler, Black Lightning
Czillag
  Chattim glisker, the Shadowshapers
  Deshenanda his wife
Daggering, Lederris masquer, Crystal Sparks
Eastkeeping
  Lord Kelinn Vrennerie's husband
  Lady Vrennerie lady-in-waiting to Princess Miriuzca
Emmot Sagemaster; Cade's teacher, now retired
Fairwalk, Lord Kearney Touchstone's manager
Fluter, Tobalt reporter, *The Nayword*
Goldbraider, Vered tregetour and masquer, the Shadowshapers
Grainer
  Chirene Sakary's wife
  Sakary fettler, the Shadowshapers
Henick, Cyed Archduke
  Panshilara his wife, the Archduchess

Highcollar
  Lord Isshak Lady Jaspiela's father
  Lady Kiritin Lady Jaspiela's mother; born Blackswan
Kevelock, Rauel tregetour and masquer, the Shadowshapers
Knottinger, Thierin tregetour, Black Lightning
Longbranch, Trenal tregetour, Hawk's Claw
Mistress Caitiffer Mieka's mother-in-law
Mistress Gesha Trollwife at Shellery House
Mistress Luta Trollwife in Seekhaven
Mistress Mirdley Trollwife at Redpebble Square
Mistress Tola Trollwife; friend of Mistress Mirdley's
Mistress Wingdove innkeeper in Lilyleaf; "Croodle"
Needler, Romuald the Shadowshapers' manager
Oakapple, Lord distant cousin of the Blackpaths
Piercehand, Lord Rolon owner of Castle Eyot; compulsive collector
Robel Yazz's wife; part Giant
Seamark, Kaj masquer, Black Lightning
Silversun
  Cadriel Zekien's father; Master Fettler
  Cayden tregetour, Touchstone
  Derien Cade's younger brother
  Lady Jaspiela Cade and Dery's mother; born Highcollar

Zekien their father
Spangler, Pirro glisker, Black Lightning
Staindrop, Brishen Mishia's sister
Tawnymoor, Lord Princess Iamina's husband
Threadchaser
  Crisiant Rafe's wife; born Bramblecotte
  Rafcadion fettler, Touchstone
  Mistress Rafe's mother
  Master Rafe's father; baker
Warringheath, Master owner of the Kiral Kellari
Windthistle
  Barsabias Hadden's great-uncle; "Uncle Breedbate"
  Blye Jed's wife; born Cindercliff; glasscrafter
  Cilka Mieka's sister
  Hadden Mieka's father
  Jedris Jez's twin brother
  Jezael Mieka's brother

Jinsie Mieka's twin sister
Jindra Mieka's daughter
Jorie Tavier's twin sister
Mieka glisker, Touchstone
Mishia Mieka's mother; born Staindrop
Mistress Windthistle Mieka's wife; born Caitiffer
Petrinka Cilka's twin sister
Sharadel Hadden's great-grandmother; born Snowminder
Tavier Mieka's youngest brother
Yazz Touchstone's coachman; part Giant

THE ROYALS

Ashgar Prince; heir to the throne
Iamina Princess; King Meredan's younger sister
Meredan King of Albeyn
Miriuzca Princess; Ashgar's wife
Roshien Queen of Albeyn

GLOSSARY

aflunters in a state of disorder; discombobulated

agroof flat on your face

backspang a tricky evasion

blodder to flow with a gurgling sound

bonce head

brach a hound bitch

breedbate someone who likes to start arguments or stir up quarrels

bully-rook a bragging cheater

caitiff witch

carkanet necklace

chavish the sound of many birds chirping or singing at once; the sound of many people chattering at once

clinquant glittering

clumperton clownish, clumsy lout

cogger false flatterer; charming trickster

Consecreations, the *consecrate* collided with *creation;* the local holy book

crambazzle worn-out, dissipated old man

cullion rude, disagreeable, mean-spirited person

fliting an exchange of invective, abuse, or mockery, especially one in verse set forth between two poets

frustle to shake out and exhibit plumage

giddiot "giddy" and "idiot"

ginnel a narrow passage between buildings

glunsh to devour food in hasty, noisy gulps; by extension, a glutton

grinagog person with a stupid, gaping grin

grouk become gradually enlivened after waking up

hindering a warding put on an individual's magic so it cannot be used

kagged mutilated Elfen ears

naffter stupid person

pantomancer person who sees omens in all events

pillicock idiot

poofter silly, effeminate man

quakebuttock (aw, come on—isn't it obvious?)

quat a pimple; used in contempt of a person

quod jail

quoob eccentric fool

stitch up frame

tiring room from *retire;* a private chamber

yark vomit

ABOUT THE AUTHOR

Melanie Rawn is the author of the bestselling Dragon Prince trilogy and of the Dragon Star trilogy. She graduated from Scripps College with a BA in history, and has worked as a teacher and editor. Rawn lives in Flagstaff, Arizona.

MEMOIRS OF LADY TRENT
MARIE BRENNAN

Everyone knows Isabella, Lady Trent, to be the world's preeminent dragon naturalist. Here at last, in her own words, is the true story of a pioneering spirit who risked her reputation, prospects, and her life to satisfy scientific curiosity; of how she sought true love despite her lamentable eccentricities; and of her thrilling expedition to the mountains of Vystrana, where she made discoveries that would change the world...

A Natural History of Dragons
The Tropic of Serpents
Voyage of the Basilisk

"Her Ladyship is a determined and canny woman in search of dragons—I wholeheartedly approve!" Melanie Rawn

"Fans of fantasy, science, and history will adore this rich and absorbing tale of discovery." *Publishers Weekly* (starred review)

TITANBOOKS.COM

THE COLLEGIUM CHRONICLES
MERCEDES LACKEY

Follow Magpie, Bear, Lena and friends as they face their
demons and find their true strength on the road to becoming
full Heralds, Bards and Healers of Valdemar.

Book One: Foundation
Book Two: Intrigues
Book Three: Changes
Book Four: Redoubt
Book Five: Bastion

"Lackey makes a real page-turner out of Mags' and the collegia's
development... this book's outstanding characters, especially
Mags, will greatly please Valdemar fans."
Booklist

"The tone, characterization, and rampant angst recall
Lackey's earliest Valdemar books... this is a worthy entry
in the overall saga." *Publishers Weekly*

"Lackey's Valdermar series is already a fantasy classic,
and these newest adventures will generate even more
acclaim for this fantasy superstar."
Romantic Times

TITANBOOKS.COM

THE VALDEMAR OMNIBUSES
MERCEDES LACKEY

In these classic coming-of-age fantasy omnibuses, spellbinding storyteller Mercedes Lackey chronicles the history of the magical kingdom of Valdemar.

The Heralds of Valdemar
Arrows of the Queen, Arrow's Flight & Arrow's Fall

The Mage Winds
Winds of Fate, Winds of Change & Winds of Fury

The Mage Storms
Storm Warning, Storm Rising & Storm Breaking

"She'll keep you up long past your bedtime." Stephen King

"Lackey's storytelling is impossible to resist." The British Fantasy Society

"Lackey is a spellbinding storyteller who keeps your heart in your mouth as she spins her intricate webs of magical adventure."
Rave Reviews

THE SILVERED
TANYA HUFF

The Empire has declared war on the were-ruled kingdom of Aydori, capturing five women of the Mage-Pack, including the wife of the Pack-leader. With the Pack off defending the border, it falls to Mirian Maylin and Tomas Hagen—she a low-level mage, he younger brother to the Pack-leader—to save them. But with every step into enemy territory, the odds against their survival grow steeper...

"Huff delves into an overwhelming yet improbably seamless mix of steampunk, epic fantasy, and paranormal romance... Huff fans who prefer her second-world fantasy tales (e.g., the Quarters series) will be pleased by this return to the form."
Publishers Weekly

"This is an exciting romantic quest fantasy... Fans will enjoy the trek of the werewolf and the mage into the heart of the enemy."
Midwest Book Review

For more fantastic fiction, author events, exclusive excerpts,
competitions, limited editions and more

VISIT OUR WEBSITE
titanbooks.com

LIKE US ON FACEBOOK
facebook.com/titanbooks

FOLLOW US ON TWITTER
@TitanBooks

EMAIL US
readerfeedback@titanemail.com